MOSCOW EMBASSY

THE *Angara Club*

THOMAS J. MITCHELL

outskirts press

Moscow Embassy
The Angara Club

v5.0

Outskirts Press, Inc.
http://www.outskirtspress.com

Paperback ISBN: 978-1-9772-1493-5
Hardback ISBN: 978-1-9772-2095-0

Library of Congress Control Number: 2019909751

PRINTED IN THE UNITED STATES OF AMERICA

FOREWORD

The United States first established diplomatic relations with the Russian Empire in 1780. Diplomatic relations were broken off in 1917 when the Bolsheviks seized power, and they were not re-established until 1933. The idea of having a US Embassy complex in Moscow began in 1934. Joseph Stalin promised the Americans land in Lenin Hills with views of the Moscow River. As terms and conditions were worked out, the US embassy personnel would use quarters near Red Square. The negotiations took nineteen years, and then the Russians finally granted an existing office building to the Americans for their use. The building was cramped, and it was far away from the Kremlin where the action was.

In 1969, the Russians and Americans brokered a deal which was known as the "Agreement for the Exchange of Sites." This meant the Americans would agree to a suitable embassy site for Russia in DC, and the Russians would do likewise for the Americans in Moscow. The USG accepted a 10-acre site which would also include the 1.8 acres on which sat Spaso House—the US Ambassador's residence since 1933—and with it, an 85-year free lease. On December 4, 1972, the Conditions of Construction Agreement was bilaterally signed governing the construction of both the American and Soviet Embassies, with a requirement of simultaneous occupancy. After years of horse-trading between the two countries, the American embassy in Moscow celebrated the laying of the cornerstone of the New Office Building (NOB) in September 1979.

In August of 1985, work was suspended on the partially completed NOB due to a security compromise of such consequence that there was serious doubt the building, if completed, could be used for the purpose intended. The top floors of the NOB stayed empty for seven years while Congress decided its fate. In 1993 Congress appropriated $240 million for the deconstruction and rehabilitation of the building. In January 1995, Hellmuth, Obata & Kassebaum, P.C. (HOK) was contractually notified to proceed with the design. On May 2, 1996, a fixed-price award fee competitive contract was awarded to the American joint venture Zackary, Parsons, & Sundt (ZPS) for the partial deconstruction of the NOB, rehabilitation of remaining portions of the building, the addition of four new floors plus a penthouse, and completion of all the electrical, mechanical, and security systems of the building. (From Wikipedia and US Embassy website.)

In the following pages is a story inspired by true events. This novel takes place during a real-life event, the construction of the US Embassy in Moscow between 1996-2000. Real places that existed in Moscow at the time are used, mostly historical facts; celebrities are mentioned along with musical selections with the composers or artists listed as well. It is a story of American construction workers that get recruited as assets by the Russian KGB to plant listening devices and engage in other espionage activities while the embassy building is under construction. It is also a story that involves our intelligence agencies working together with MI6 and to what lengths they will go to accomplish their directives. And lastly, it is a story of the men and women in the public and private sectors whose job it is building these embassies. These interesting, colorful nomads that go from one country to the next, building these beautiful facilities for the US government. They work long hours and do what it takes to get these projects built within budget and on schedule.

"Angara: A river in southeastern Siberia that flows northwest from Lake Baikal to become a tributary of the Yenisei River."

CHAPTER ONE

WELCOME TO MOSCOW

(NOVEMBER 1996)

JT Miller leaned back in his seat and looked out the window. Clouds were covering the wing, making a portion seem invisible. He let his mind wander to the new opportunity ahead. Previously, Miller had owned a small surveying and civil engineering consulting firm in Tucson, Arizona. After a year-long process of investigations and acceptability reviews, he received a Top-Secret security clearance and accepted a position as project engineer on the American Embassy NOB (New Office Building) in Moscow, Russia. The government contractor awarded the contract was a joint venture effort involving three international construction/engineering firms: one out of Texas, another out of California, and the last out of Arizona. At peak, it would employ more than 300 cleared American workers, or CAW's. The conglomerate was called TRIAD. The award date was July 1996 and the notice to proceed came in November 1996.

In 1985, this same Moscow NOB had been 70% completed when it was discovered the building was compromised by Russian listening devices embedded inside of concrete precast panels used for floor and wall construction. These devices were made from material that was undetectable to initial security probes. Obviously, the security protocols set in place by the US government, at that time, were not effective against this particular security threat. The Moscow NOB upper floors stayed vacant and unused for seven years while Congress reviewed these protocols and tried to figure out how to salvage and secure the compromised building for its intended use. In 1995, Congress appropriated funds and decided to demolish the building completely, from the roof down to the 5th level floor slabs. From the 5th level down, the only building elements that remained from the original building would be the concrete beams, columns, and floor slabs. Any listening devices left in this lower part of the building would be of no consequence because no secret or secure activities would take place there. The building would then be refurbished, and four new floors would be added.

Miller was forty years old and currently unmarried. He had been married by a Navajo Hat aalii or shaman in the mid-eighties, but that relationship had since soured, and sometimes he still felt the sting. He decided to focus on his career, save a pile of dough, and participate in more short-term romantic pursuits. Known as a knowledgeable and hardworking civil engineer who loved his job, the profession suited Miller to a tee; 70% of the time in the office or meetings, and the rest in the field. Miller had just finished a re-surveying and mapping project of a portion of the Gadsden Purchase in southern Arizona and New Mexico. The Gadsden Purchase, finalized in 1854, was the transaction in which the United States agreed to pay Mexico $10 million for a 29,670 square mile portion of Mexico that later became part of Arizona and New Mexico. The Gadsden Purchase provided the land necessary for a southern transcontinental railroad. Miller loved getting up early, having his coffee, slipping on his boots and going to work. He worked hard, and on occasion played hard. Now he decided to shuffle the deck and get into embassy construction, and Moscow was the big kahuna of embassy projects.

Delta Airlines flight 1767 started its descent, headed for Moscow's Sheremetyevo International Airport. Miller smiled at the Russian girl sitting across the aisle trying to catch his eye. He thought to himself, *JT, I think you're going to like this assignment.*

Miller measured in at six feet tall and 165 pounds. He had a muscular build and brownish-blond hair with a few greys. He liked working out and enjoyed staying fit. The plane landed, and JT retrieved his bags and went through customs. On the outside, he saw a man holding a cardboard sign with his name on it. He was met by Kurt Scanlen, TRIAD HR (Human Resource) manager, and was dropped off at the Belgrade Hotel near the Old Arbat district and about six blocks from the American Embassy. Kurt said he would be back at 7:00 to collect Miller and have dinner with the other members of the construction management team. Miller checked in and went to his room on the 16th floor. At 6:45, Miller took the elevator down to the hotel lobby to wait for his ride. Kurt showed up just before seven and the two got into the rented Land Cruiser and headed out.

"Where are we going to have dinner? I could eat a horse," Miller interjected.

"We are trying a new place called the Angara Club. The rest of the team will meet us there. We are only a few blocks away."

Miller asked," What kind of place is it?"

"It's a nightclub and restaurant that serves pretty good food, so I am told. Very popular with the embassy staff."

The Angara Club was owned by two brothers from Siberia, Zakhar and Georgy. They worked in the Siberian gold fields in the Olekma-Vitim region of the Lena Valley in south central Siberia. Over the course of five years, every day the brothers were able to sneak out and hide small amounts of gold dust. They continued this until one day they had amassed a small fortune. When the time was right, just after nightfall, they crept out of the gold camp and travelled the old trade route down the Lena and Angara rivers, then over land to Moscow.

As Kurt and Miller walked into the club, they observed a lower lobby where you had to pass through two big Russian goons scanning the customers with metal detector wands. Once allowed to enter, the patrons would then walk upstairs to where the club and restaurant were located. As they entered the nightclub, the pair noticed a young Russian girl talking in the corner with an older Western man. The place was loaded with beautiful women. The two men were amazed. Never had they seen so many drop-dead gorgeous women in one place before. There were short ones, tall ones, skinny ones, medium ones, blondes, brunettes, black-haired, etc. The place was unbelievable. Kurt motioned JT to a table down in front of the stage where three men were sitting with drinks. The stage was empty, but a band was to begin playing at 9 p.m.

Kurt introduced everyone. "JT Miller, I would like you to meet the project manager Harry Clark; Charlie Manes, the construction manager; and Bo Beecher, the Quality Control manager."

"Hello, gentlemen. Nice to be in Moscow," Miller offered.

"We are glad to have you here, Mr. Miller," answered Harry.

"Same here," said Manes.

"How y'all doin," replied Bo.

"Well, I see you guys brought out the first-string talent on the ladies front this evening. I appreciate it," Miller said.

The men laughed and Harry answered, "Sorry, this is all we could do at the last minute. You ain't seen nothing yet. Wait until 1 or 2 in the morning. That is when the real first string shows up. Hungry for love, and of course, your wallet."

They all laughed. Harry Clark was sixty-two years old, divorced, and was a building construction master. If you were paying the bills, Harry was the guy you wanted. This project would be Harry's last hurrah after a 40+ year career. He was tough as nails and would not put up with any nonsense from his staff. He was fair and respected by both the US government and the joint venture partners.

Charlie Manes was fifty years old and married to his high school sweetheart. He was equally tough and a pure construction professional. If he told you something, you could take it to the bank.

Bo Beecher was forty-seven years old, ferret-faced, and divorced for the third time. A Texas boy, he was good at his job but had a different world view than most. He fancied himself a devout evangelical Christian and believed God worked in mysterious ways. He was also known to quote scripture on occasion when the mood struck him.

And lastly there was Kurt Scanlen, the HR guy that everyone liked. He was sixty-three and nearing retirement. He expected this to be his last job. He and his wife Nadine had a retirement place picked out in North Carolina, and she could hardly wait. Just two more years. Pleasant and funny, he got along with most—another consummate professional.

Like most construction guys, they all liked to bend the elbow on a Saturday night, and this one was no different. The vodka flowed as they got to know each other. They ordered pork chops and ribs with baked potatoes and salad.

At another table, a middle-aged Russian man and younger Russian woman were surreptitiously gazing at the table. They were interested in the new construction staff assigned to the embassy project. *Perhaps one of them could be useful*, the man thought. The man was 49-year-old Dimitry Karlov, or Major Karlov. The major had worked for the KGB's Second Chief Directorate Security Unit for over twenty-five years. The Second Directorate's main function was to compromise embassies and the foreigners who worked for them. As a small boy, Karlov had loved to pull the wings off flies to see them squirm. Now he loved to see people squirm. His attractive companion was 24-year-old Irena Anarbekova, a schoolteacher who taught embassy employee kids Russian at the embassy school on Tuesdays and Fridays. She was very thankful for the job, because many Russian people in Moscow were living on the streets or starving in their own homes. The ruble was collapsing, and there were no jobs. Sometimes on Saturday night Irena would make it down to the Angara Club in hopes of attracting a Western man. Was she successful? Sometimes yes, sometimes no. She longed to fall in love with a rich Western man and leave Russia forever. Unfortunately, many young women in Moscow had the same idea, and the competition could be stiff. Some psychologists refer to this as the "Cinderella Syndrome."

Major Karlov looked at Irena. He had recruited her very easily. She was hired for the embassy teaching position through a branch of the foreign ministry called the UPDK. The Americans were under the impression the UPDK was merely a state-run labor broker required to hire Soviets as embassy employees. Later it was learned the UPDK was run by the KGB. The KGB, through the UPDK, could staff the American embassy with Russian agents or informants. The informants could eventually be turned into Russian agents if the circumstances warranted it. Karlov thought it was time to turn Irena into one of these agents. She would become what was known as a KGB swallow. A KGB swallow was the term for an agent who was an attractive young Russian woman who could be used to entrap a foreign embassy employee into a compromising position. This was a KGB specialty in recruiting new foreign assets. He simply told Irena if she did not play ball, he would place her and her family in the gulag for twenty years for the crime of treason, but not before a nice rubber-hose beating to say "bon voyage."

In 1996 The Angara Club was located on the new Arbat in the location which as of 2019 is known as The Penthouse Club.

The next morning was Sunday, and Miller woke up in his room on the 16th floor of the Belgrade Hotel. His head ached from the previous night's merriment. He took two aspirin, got dressed, and headed out for a walk around town. He stopped at a McDonald's on the old Arbat that had just opened a few months before. Even at 7 a.m. the lines were long. He ordered two egg McMuffins and a large coffee. He found an empty small table and sat down. On a rack next to him was a newspaper called the *Moscow Times*. It was written in English and slanted toward the Western way of thinking. Miller read the paper, finished his breakfast, and headed straight up the Arbat to the Kremlin. He had always wanted to see St. Basil's, and now was his chance. He stopped in at the GUM, The State Department Store, used as a propaganda weapon during the Cold War to show the West how efficient the communist system was. This was the only mall in Russia at the time and served mostly the communist elites. The common Russian had to contend with small neighborhood grocery stores or kiosks to secure the few items they offered. As he continued to walk, he passed the Kremlin skating rink. He watched the skaters and listened to Tchaikovsky's *Swan Lake* blasting from the outdoor speakers.

Major Karlov was on his second cup of coffee. He lit another Kent cigarette and inhaled deeply. He was going over the dossiers that had been compiled on the new American Embassy construction staff along with their visa requests. He was trying to decide which one he could target to advance his purposes and be easiest to recruit. The Russians were aware of a room deep in the embassy building's bowels nicknamed the "Vault." This was a Communications Program Unit or CPU. Inside it had thick metal alloy walls, floor, and ceiling. It also housed a secured air infiltration system. The room was used for meetings which were considered sensitive and was the only completely secure space on the embassy grounds. Top diplomats used this room, along with embassy employees and government contractors, for site security and CIA briefings. When the president or secretary of state visited, this is where they would meet with the ambassador to Russia.

The CPU was to remain untouched during construction and would be incorporated into the new design. The only things that would be changed were the entrance door and frame. Karlov believed this entrance door could be compromised during construction with a listening device and a doomsday gas canister filled with 3-methylfentanyl. It was really an aerosol and not a gas but could be dispensed using a small CO2 cartridge built into the door next to the upper hinge. The gas or aerosol was powerful enough to imperceptibly kill everyone in the room in a matter of seconds. The gas would be used only for a high-level strike on American leaders or defecting Soviets if circumstances warranted it and the opportunity presented itself. Until then, they would receive top-secret information via the listening device. This information could prove priceless to the security of the Russian state and disastrous to the United States. The Russians could replicate the door and frame to look like the approved American-manufactured door and frame plus incorporate the added goodies in such a way they would not be detected even with the use of X-rays. The challenge would be to switch the approved American door with the tainted one under the noses of the USG's site security team and 24-hour camera surveillance. Karlov needed one or maybe two Americans working on the inside.

Miller followed a trail that led away from the Kremlin and down to the Moscow River. There was a walkway on both sides of the river that followed the bank. Several other pedestrians were also making use of the walkway. It was a reasonably nice day compared to Moscow standards for that time of year, about 27 degrees and partly cloudy, with no wind or snow on the ground. Miller decided that a bit of a workout in the crisp air was just what he needed. He started a fast walk south along the walkway.

Major Karlov looked at the dossiers prepared on the Americans. Kurt Scanlen, HR Manager, sixty-three years old. Too old and would not be allowed in the secured work areas. "Nyet," he muttered to himself. Next, he looked at Harry Clark, Project Manager, sixty-two years old. Too risky to compromise. Then Charlie Manes, Construction Manager, married and fifty years old. *Perhaps*, Karlov thought. Bo Beecher, QC Manager, forty-seven years old, divorced three times. *Yes, possible*, he thought. He picked up the last dossier. James Miller, Project Engineer, forty years old, unmarried and liked the women. "Yes, I think I can work with this one," he said out loud, smiling.

The night before, Irena left the Angara Club at 1 a.m. She walked around before going home thinking of what Major Karlov had proposed. He wanted her to make one of the Americans fall in love with her. She asked him which one. He said he would let her know. Irena worried about Major Karlov. If he wasn't pleased, he would send her to the gulag. She thought about the Americans at the table in the club. Could she actually do it? Irena liked the younger one with his horseshoe moustache. He reminded her of a cowboy without the hat. She walked down Novy Arbot, turned right at Novinsky and left down a side street that bordered the south side of the American embassy compound. She passed the south gate, which was being used as the construction entrance for the new building. She continued walking, turning left down the alley to her apartment. The apartment was small, and she lived there with her mother and younger brother. She slipped in quietly and went to bed.

The next morning, Irena's mother was up at 7:00, making coffee and breakfast. Her brother Alexei was stirring. When the buckwheat porridge was ready, Irena got up and joined them. Later they would walk together to St. Andrew's Orthodox Church for Sunday service. After, they would walk to the Arbat McDonald's and wait in line for a delicious cheeseburger or perhaps a Big Mac with French fries, then maybe some ice cream for dessert. They loved McDonald's and the three of them looked forward to this time together all week.

Irena's mother's name was Svetlana, or Sveta for short. She was forty-five years old. Irena's father, Egor, had been killed ten years before in an explosion at the Smolenskya metro station. Egor was a low-level party official and had been travelling with other party officials. Four men were killed, and Egor was one of them. A party opposition group was blamed. Sveta and Irena were devastated. Alexei was only about four or five at the time, so he really didn't understand what had happened. One day his father was there and the next he wasn't. The apartment in which they lived had been given to Egor's grandfather by the Communist party sometime in the 1920s, and the family had lived there ever since. The apartment could be taken away only by special action by the Russian government. This type of action rarely occurred, but it still worried Sveta.

☭

As JT Miller walked along the river, he thought about the new job and the team members he had just met. He liked Kurt and Harry. Charlie was okay, but he had some reservations about a guy who would marry his high school sweetheart. He knew he would have problems with Bo. Miller did not get along well with religious types. He thought they all had a case of the "I am never wrong because I believe Jesus guides me" syndrome. Miller had worked with worse and for the most part felt lucky with the hand he was dealt. Miller's thoughts then drifted to all the beautiful Russian girls at the Angara Club. If it were up to him, this was what heaven would be like. He thought about the girl sitting at the table near his with the older man--he thought perhaps it was her father. Occasionally he would catch her looking at him, and she would then smile and look down. He thought of making her acquaintance, but with his new boss at the table, he thought better of it. *Don't want to give him the wrong impression*, he thought. The wind had picked up and Miller hurried back to the Belgrade Hotel.

☭

The next morning, Miller got up and went down to the lobby for coffee. His boss Harry had planned for Kurt to meet him at the south gate of the embassy. They would be escorted through Post 1 at 7:00 a.m. From there, he would be escorted by the SSM (Site Security Manager) for processing, security briefing, and badging. Miller had two espressos and felt like he could run a marathon. *Nothing like a caffeine buzz in the morning*, he thought. Rather than wait for a driver, Miller had told Harry earlier he would walk to the embassy in the morning. Miller left the lobby and made his way the few blocks to the embassy.

South entrance of NOB with CAC building and Russian militiamen guard booth in front. The contractor's construction offices just left of CAC. Jan 1997

Kurt was waiting at the south gate. He was smoking a Marlboro and talking to one of the CAG's (Cleared American Guards) on duty. He was wearing his parka with the hood zippered all the way up, exposing a small porthole in front of his face to see and breathe out of. He was also occasionally stamping his feet against the cold. As Miller walked up, he could see Kurt.

"Morning, Kurt. A bit cool this morning," Miller said.

"You bet your ass it is. I hope you brought warm clothes," Kurt replied.

"You can bet I did. I brought the big guns and bigger guns. I would be warm as toast on Mars with the stuff I brought. I just haven't dug it out of my suitcases yet. I could use one of those Russian fur hats, though. I always wanted one," Miller said.

"I know the perfect place to get one of those. The place is called Izmailovo," Kurt offered.

"Can you repeat that again?" Miller asked.

"Okay, listen. IZ-MOLL-AH-VA. Got it? It's an open-air market. Over 300 vendors, a hundred of which will probably be selling Russian fur hats. We can go some Sunday if you want."

"Sounds good, let's do it," Miller responded.

They walked through the CAC (Command and Control) building and signed in.

"This is as far as I go, JT. The SSM will be waiting for you on the other side of Post 1. Good luck. See you later," Kurt said and walked off.

A CAG escorted Miller the rest of the way to Post 1. Post 1 was the last line of defence for embassy access. Once you were past it you were in. It was always occupied by at least one marine guard. The guard took Miller's passport and issued a temporary access badge. The barred door was buzzed open and Miller walked through. The SSM was waiting for him on the other side. She was holding some files and looked a bit frazzled. Her long grey hair looked like she forgot to brush it that morning. She had been working long hours getting people and suppliers cleared and processed for embassy compound access. It appeared to be wearing her down a bit. Her name was Vera Collins; she was in her mid-fifties and a bit plump.

"Good morning. You must be Mr Miller," she said.

"Yes, I am. How are you this morning?" he answered.

"I will be fine once I clear some of this work off my plate. We will stop by my office first to pick up some forms for you to fill out; then we will head to the vault for the briefings," she said.

"Sounds good," he replied. They chatted as they walked. Vera was on a two-year assignment and had a year to go. She would be the one enforcing the new security protocols. Vera worked for a section of the state department called the FBO, or Foreign Building Operations. It was in the middle of a name change to OBO, or Overseas Building Operations. Miller surmised the state department decided the word "overseas" had a better neutral ring to it than "foreign." He really didn't see much of a difference. Miller told her he lived in Tucson, Arizona and that this was his first overseas assignment. They walked the back way to the Spode building where her office was. This building was separate from the NOB but connected by a concrete walkway or sidewalk. There was also a secret tunnel that connected the two buildings, but access was reserved only to the government staff. The rest of the OBO team resided in the Spode building as well: the project director, construction manager, and an electrical, mechanical, and civil engineer. The team was employed in a quality assurance capacity along with settling any contract disputes that might arise with the contractor during construction. The USG wanted to make sure they were getting their money's worth.

Vera and JT arrived at her office, where she fiddled with the push-button combination lock at the door. They entered. "Please sit down and I will bring the forms you need to fill out," Vera said. She then went to the file cabinet and selected some forms. She laid them down on the back side of her desk where Miller was sitting in a chair. She added, "Please fill out what you can now. I have a few things to take care of before we go to the vault. When we leave, take the forms with you, and I will answer any questions you might have in the secure area. You will then sign the forms and the originals get sent to DC. I keep a hard copy here, along with the electronic file that will be uploaded into a secure database."

While Vera checked emails, Miller filled out and read the forms. Most of the information was already filled in; he just had to fill in the blank spaces, read, and sign. When it appeared, he had completed the forms, Vera closed her computer and said, "If you are ready, Mr. Miller, we can walk downstairs."

They used the stairwell and walked two flights down then out to a long hallway. At the end of the hallway was a security checkpoint where two CAG's were on duty. The CAG's were part of Vera's team. This checkpoint was called Post 2 and was the entrance to the CAA space where the vault and other secure rooms were located. CAA stood for Controlled Access Area. To enter this area, Miller had to surrender his temporary embassy green badge for a red CAA access badge. His name was also entered in a log. Vera and JT walked through the metal detector into the CAA space. As they walked down the hallway, he noticed a big vault door about halfway down on the left side. As they got closer, Vera told him this was the place. A new security feature they were trying out was a retina scanner. The state department wanted feedback on how efficiently this technology performed. Iris recognition would come along later. Vera swiped her badge and placed her eyes in the scanner's visor. When she did, a green light flashed, and the door locks popped open. They entered the room.

Major Karlov sat at his desk at a KGB annex office that was located on the fifth floor in a residential apartment building across the street from the south gate of the US embassy. At each embassy gate, the Russian government placed guards called militiamen in little guard booths out on the sidewalk. The Russians told the Americans the guards were for their protection. They were actually there to report the comings and goings at the gates. There was a direct phone line from the south gate Russian guard booth to this KGB office. This was no secret to the Americans, because you could physically see this line running from the guard booth to a power pole across the street to a fifth-floor apartment window. Old technology, but it worked fine for Karlov's purposes. He was informed that Miller was in the embassy and knew he was probably getting processed and receiving his access badge. JT Miller and Bo Beecher were his first choices to compromise. One the project engineer and the other the QC manager—between the two of them, they would have access to all the secured areas and the vault. No one would question their reasons for being there.

In the past, Karlov would rather turn married men with a family. They were easier because they had more to lose, but Karlov had been involved in the successful recruiting of an unmarried marine security guard, Sgt. Clayton Lonetree, in 1985 by using a sexy KGB swallow named Violetta Seina, whom the marine guard fell in love with. Allegedly, after the marine was compromised, the operation led to KGB agents' free rein inside the building, planting bugs and taking photos when Lonetree was on duty. Later Lonetree would serve nine years in prison for the crime of espionage. Karlov thought he could use the same tactic on Miller and/or Beecher, but instead of using Russian agents to plant listening devices, the Americans would do this work themselves. Karlov smiled at the thought.

Irena sat at her kitchen table with her mother Sveta. Alexei was at school. At first Irena did not want to tell her mother about Major Karlov but decided it would be better if she did. She told her mother how Major Karlov had recruited her at the Angara Club. She was sitting at the bar when the major introduced himself. He said he wanted to talk with her and invited her to his table for dinner and drinks. She accepted and listened to what he had to say. He told her he wanted to use her as a special agent and would be on the KGB payroll, starting at $500 US a week paid in rubles. She preferred US dollars, but he told her that was not possible. When the major detected her reluctance, he played hard ball. He told her if she refused, he would consider having her and her family sent to the gulag for the crime of treason where the minimum sentence for such a crime would be 20 years.

"That is a lot of money. What does he want you to do as a special agent?" her mother asked.

"He wants me to get one of the American construction men to fall in love with me," she answered.

Her mother was frightened for her. She was also frightened for herself and Alexei. She thought about taking her family to the Ukraine where her sister lived and running away. If she did that, they would find her eventually, and she probably would lose her apartment and be sent to the gulag. She knew if her daughter did not do what the major asked, their lives could get most difficult. She did not know a way out of the trap.

Her mother said, "Irena, you must do what the major asks. We can use the money. Just think of it as our patriotic duty for Mother Russia."

As her mother said the words, she herself was not convinced. But there was no other choice.

☭

When Vera and JT were in the vault, she closed and locked the door. Automatically, the security system was activated, and the air filtration system began to hum. The interior of the vault or CPU looked like any other conference room--20'X40' with a long conference table in the middle with about twenty chairs gathered around. Miller asked, "Vera, I assume they call this place the vault because it has a vault door? We can speak freely now, correct?"

Vera answered, "Yes, we are now safe from prying ears. Well, the vault door is partly right. This room is actually a giant safe with a metal alloy composite half an inch thick, welded together installed on the walls, floor, and ceiling. Russian microwaves or radio signals cannot penetrate it."

Miller asked a few questions about the forms, added something, finished reading, then signed them. The security briefing started a few minutes later. Vera explained the reason for the high security protocols. She told him that in 1985 when the NOB was nearing completion, bugs or listening devises were found throughout the building. The building was sealed off and DC tried to come up with the best way to fix the problem going forward. This took seven years. The USG had egg on their face and had to clean it off.

She told him about marine guard Sergeant Clayton Lonetree. She told him about a CAW (cleared American worker) from Alabama who was staying at the Belgrade Hotel. This gentleman was a farm boy and the Russians found out he had an affection for farm animals, particularly sheep. One Saturday night he went out drinking and when he got back to his room, he was quite drunk. He opened his door and inside were two sheep, one male and one female. They were dressed in pink and blue panties with garter belt stockings, wearing lipstick and eye rouge. To his detriment, the CAW decided to get frisky and the Russians videotaped the encounter. When the Russians threatened to use this video against him, the CAW reported the incident to the SSM. The CAW was terminated from the project and was on a plane heading back to the States within 24 hours. Vera loved telling this story. She loved seeing the reaction it got. Miller wished she wouldn't go into such detail. She went on and on in hopes that the recipient, when the briefing was completed and they went out onto the street, would think everybody they saw was a Russian operative.

"Mr. Miller let me reiterate. Every contact you have, or any member of your team has with a Russian national must be reported within 24 hours of the contact. I am not talking about casual contact such as a bus driver, bartender, or clerk. We are talking about any Russian that seems to take a particular interest in you, who wants to exchange cell phone numbers or wants you to visit their home. Any sexual contacts must be reported."

As Vera said this sentence, she was staring into Miller's eyes. Miller thought she wanted to see his reaction, or she wanted the words emphasized, or she was coming on to him. He thought about this and dismissed it. He was like most men, who thought most women were coming on to them.

"Mr. Miller, besides what we have discussed, please review the security protocols in the project specifications. Do you have any questions?" she asked.

"No, Vera. I think you covered everything very well. And I assure you if I find any sheep in my hotel room, you will be the first one I contact," he smiled as he replied.

She continued, "Just remember, Mr. Miller, I am available 24/7 if you have any questions or run into any problems out on the street."

"Thank you. I will keep that in mind," he responded.

"Okay, I think we're finished here. Let's go get your embassy access badge and you can get to work," she said ending the briefing. They walked out of the vault room and down the hall.

South face of NOB. Trash shoot installed at each floor to remove demolition construction debris. Jan 1997

Harry Clark, the TRIAD project manager, was walking through the building checking on the work progress. The interior demolition was going well. Presently just ten CAW's with jackhammers were working. Another ten were working in another area on the housing units for management and the workers. More workers were expected in the coming weeks. They had started on the northwest end of the building. Harry still needed to use space in the building for a few months, for temporary construction offices until the permanent ones were built. These rooms were being framed and partitioned in the southeast portion of the building that wasn't scheduled for demolition for another three months. These rooms would be complete the following morning, and the staff could move in. As Harry continued his walk, he was forming an attack plan on how to finish the work as efficiently as possible. He paused to look at a concrete column that was scheduled for demolition. As he was doing so, Miller walked up.

"Morning, Harry. I just got finished with Vera's briefing. What would you like me to do to help?" he asked.

Harry looked at him. "Done so fast? When Vera had me in there, I swear it was like three hours. She just went on and on."

"Did she tell you the sheep story?" Miller asked, laughing.

"Hell, yes, she did. I thought I was gonna wet my britches trying to keep a straight face when she mentioned the panties. That woman is something else," Harry answered, smiling.

There was silence for a moment, and then the two looked at each other and cracked up. They laughed hard for a minute or two until they couldn't breathe.

"I'm getting too old to laugh like this," Harry interjected, and changing the subject, he added, "JT, follow me. I want to show you something."

Harry led him up to the 6th floor that would eventually be demolished. Inside several rooms, Miller noticed small red X's all over the walls, ceiling, and floor. There seemed to be hundreds of them. "What are the X's for, Harry?" Miller asked.

"They are Russian bug locations. The Russians gave the US ambassador a partially completed map showing their locations. The CIA has been here for years, mapping the locations and trying to find them. They could never be sure if they got them all, so that is why we are tearing everything down to the 5th level slab and building up from there," Harry answered.

Miller walked around the room and other rooms looking at the red X's.

At one location, a portion of a bug assembly was visible. Miller tried to pull it out and then thought better of it.

Harry strolled up. “JT, there is really not much to do until our temporary offices are ready tomorrow. They may still be finishing hooking up computers or phones, but we can move in and have a place to roost. I will need you to start doing the daily construction reports in the morning. I don’t want to get behind on those. In the meantime, take the rest of the day off. I gave the other guys the day off as well. I will be here with Kurt, and that is more than enough supervision for what we’ve got going on today. I would suggest going to a grocery store and picking up anything you may need. Snacks, toothpaste, that type of thing. Starting tomorrow, you won’t have time to do much of anything. The stores aren’t well stocked, but they have a few items.”

Miller nodded and left out of the south gate. He headed toward the Arbat, where he thought he saw a grocery store.

It was Monday, Irena’s day to clean the apartment, wash the clothes, and go to the market. Sveta, Irena’s mother, worked at a cigarette kiosk on Mondays and hardly anyone used the building’s washing machine on that day, so Irena chose this time do her chores. The machine was in the basement, and Irena had already done two loads. She did not like going down to the basement. She always heard strange noises down there. She was afraid the noises were mice, or worse, rats, or even worse, raccoons. She grabbed the clean clothes quickly, climbed the stairs back to the apartment and hung them on a clothesline in the bathroom. She got dressed and put on her coat. She was headed to the Seventh Continent market right on the corner of Stary Arbot and Smolenskya Ulitsa, about a fifteen-minute walk from her apartment. She needed eggs, beets, buckwheat groats, and milk. She was hoping they were not out of eggs, which was common.

As Miller walked to the grocery store, he laughed thinking about Harry and the exchange they had just had about Vera. He felt lucky to be working with him. Harry was a good guy. It was approximately 11 a.m. when Miller thought he would stop at McDonald's before going to the store, which was next door. He thought a Big Mac and cheeseburger with fries would hit the spot. As he was passing the grocery store, he saw a familiar figure walking into the store. He knew he had seen her before but wasn't sure where. He kept walking toward McDonald's then suddenly stopped. He remembered. It was the girl he had seen at the Angara Club with the older Russian gentleman. He walked back to the grocery store and went in. He saw her fingering some beets and walked closer to her, all the while thinking of something to say. He knew three phrases in Russian: no, yes, and good morning. He chose the last.

"Dobre utra," he said.

She looked up, startled, and then looked more startled when she recognized him. "Dobre utra," she replied and then added, "I speak English."

Miller smiled and said, "Good thing, because the only other Russian I know is da and nyet." She laughed and he continued. "I believe I saw you at the Angara Club the other night."

She pretended not to recognize him and then with a show of faint recollection she replied, "Oh yes, I remember you now. You were at a table with some other men."

"Yes, some guys I work with. I just got to Moscow that day and they were showing me some of the sights. I guess you were one of them."

She smiled and asked, "Did you like the Angara Club?"

"Yes, very much," he said, then asked, "How about you? Do you go there much?"

"I go there occasionally, usually on Saturday night," she answered.

"Who was that man you were with?" he asked.

This caught her off guard. She thought and then answered, "I just met you and I don't even know your name, and you're acting jealous already?" She laughed and then added, "That was my uncle."

Miller smiled and replied, "Good thing, because I did not want to have to challenge him to a duel." They both laughed. "My name is JT Miller; what is yours?"

"I am Irena Anarbekova," she answered.

"An-ar what?" he asked, confused.

"It is very simple, Americanski. An-ar-bek-ova. What is wrong with you? Are you simple?" she laughed.

"Sometimes," Miller responded. He liked it when she called him Americanski and the way she pretended to be giving him a hard time. He waited for her while she paid for her items. They were out of eggs, so she would have to come at another time. As they walked out of the door, he asked if she wanted to go to McDonald's with him for some coffee or something. She said okay, but not for long because she had an appointment. She did not tell him the appointment consisted of ironing the clothes she had recently washed.

They walked up to the counter and JT grabbed the English menu. The girl came over and he pointed to the photos of a Big Mac, cheeseburger, fries, and a coffee. Irena ordered a cheeseburger, hot fudge sundae, and coffee. Miller paid, and they chose a corner booth. They took off their coats and sat down. Irena was wearing a knitted sweater with a colourful Caucus mountains display. The snow-capped peaks design on the sweater gave a particular erotic emphasis to Irena's figure. She really was a classic Russian beauty. Tall, 5'-11," about 135 to 140 pounds with long, wavy blonde hair. She wore it naturally like a '60s hippie chick, and Miller thought she had a rear end to die for.

Over lunch they talked about Moscow, about JT's job at the embassy and Irena's English classes there. She was Russian, but her family originally came from the Ukraine. Miller told her that his old country roots were Slovenian and Austrian on his mother's side and English/Scottish on his dad's.

"So, you are part Slavic. Ukrainians are Slavic. See, we are related," she laughed.

Miller loved the way she laughed. Her whole face seemed to light up when she did. When lunch was finished, she apologized and said she really needed to get going. She said, "You can walk me home if you would like." When she saw Miller was looking a little too pleased with himself, she added, "I need somebody to carry my groceries." She laughed. They walked together, speaking only occasionally. They were both lost in their own thoughts. When they were outside her apartment building, she took the groceries from him and thanked him. He asked if he could call her sometime.

"I guess that would be okay, Slav; just don't get drunk and lonely and call me at 3 in the morning someday," she replied, warning him with a smile. She ripped off a small piece of brown paper from her grocery bag, wrote down her digits, and gave them to Miller. They stood there for a few moments; then she quickly gave him a peck on the lips and hurried off to her apartment. Miller looked a bit startled. He wasn't expecting a kiss. As she disappeared into her building, Miller slowly turned and walked away.

Arbat McDonalds as of 2017.

Major Karlov was at the annex office eating a roast beef sandwich at his desk. He ate lunch at his desk most days, except when he had a meeting at the Kremlin. On those days he would eat at one of the restaurants inside the GUM. As he took a big bite of the sandwich, the phone rang. He waited until he was through chewing at about the fourth ring and answered, "Major Karlov." It was Irena, and she told the major of her contact with the American. "Good work, Irena. Keep him on the hook. Let me know how the relationship progresses. Do not move too fast or he may get suspicious.

Do not move too slow or you may lose him." Irena said she understood and would keep him informed.

☭

Miller floated back to his hotel. He was feeling good. When he wasn't thinking about Irena, he was congratulating himself about what a man he was. When he walked into the Belgrade he went over to the bar and ordered a gin and tonic. He then went to the counter where they sold cigarettes and cigars and picked up a five-pack of Cohibas, then went back to retrieve his drink. The Cuban cigars had been reasonably priced, and he thought it made sense since Russia was Cuba's number one trading partner. Miller liked a good cigar and smoked them often. He lit a Cohiba and drank his drink. Then the reality hit him. *How in the hell can I contemplate a relationship when I will be working six-day weeks, twelve hours a day? I need a Saturday night/Sunday girl, not a relationship. I am here to work, make some dough, and not get distracted.* As he thought this, a kind of relief went through him. A relief and contentment, but short of the excitement Irena could provide.

☭

After Irena got off the phone with Karlov, she ironed the clothes and put them away. She sat on the sofa. She was thinking about this American. Who was he really? She loved his blue eyes. She thought that when he laughed, his eyes appeared to twinkle. She liked the way he did not get upset when she gave him a hard time. He was different from Russian men. She got up and on the way to her room she dusted her mother's matryoshka dolls that rested on a living room shelf. They were a gift to her mother from her father one Christmas. She continued to her room and from a drawer, she retrieved a bent pack of Marlboros with about five smokes left. The pack had been there for over a month. She picked out one of the smokes and walked back to the sofa. She lit her Marlboro and inhaled. She let her thoughts wash over her. Then in an instant she knew it was not in her best interests to have those kinds of thoughts for the American. He was a mark, a pawn, someone to be used for the greater good of Mother Russia, not to mention to keep her and her family out of the gulag.

☭

Bo Beecher, TRIADS Quality Control manager, was heading up to the 19th floor of the Belgrade Hotel. When he first got to Moscow about a month previously, he met a German guy at the hotel bar. This guy told him about this Russian masseuse that gave a great one-hour deep tissue massage for $50. After, if the client wanted—to relieve any additional stress, you understand—she would perform the act of fellatio for an extra hundred bucks. She accepted only American dollars. This would be Bo's second massage since he had been at the hotel. He didn't feel he had the excess stress built up on the first visit to take advantage of her offer. He thought that he might let the Russian touch his golden staff today, though.

He got off at the 19th floor, turned left from the elevator, and walked down to suite 1907. He knocked on the door. A few moments later there was a fumbling of a lock and the door opened.

"Hello, Mr. Bo. Please come in." Natasha was a knockout. She was maybe twenty-two years old, about 6'3", and maybe 150 to 155 pounds. Her face was erotically beautiful, like a Hungarian Magyar woman. She had long, thick, dark hair tied in a ponytail to keep it out of the way as she worked. She wore a blue Japanese kimono and the room smelled like jasmine and musk. The massage table was set up with clean sheets, waiting for the next victim.

"Mr. Bo, please take off your clothes and hang them in the closet. I will be back with warm coconut oil for your massage," Natasha instructed.

When she left, Bo shed the clothes and lay down on the table with the top sheet over his privates. When Natasha came back, she adjusted the sheet and told him to lie on his stomach. When he did, she draped the sheet over his rear. Natasha dripped some of the warm coconut oil on Bo's back and began to rub it in.

☭

The first gin and tonic Miller had tasted so good he had two more. He was getting a pretty good buzz and was watching the barmaid behind the bar. She was from Odessa, Ukraine and had been in Moscow for a year working at the bar. She had long very blonde hair, almost white-looking. Her name was Snezhinka (Shne-zin-ka) which meant "snowflake" in Russian. She was in her mid-twenties, Miller thought, but sometimes it was hard to tell. In Moscow, the hotel bartenders usually worked a 24-hour shift, took 24 or 48 hours off, then did it again. Miller ordered another drink and Snezhinka, in Miller's mind, just kept getting more and more attractive.

☭

Natasha was an expert at using her elbow and thumbs to get deep into the hard muscle tissue. At first it had been uncomfortable for the American, but now she was almost through and he felt like a well-relaxed noodle. All of his muscles were kneaded to perfection, except one. As she finished, she wiped away any excess oil from his body. "Time is up, Mr. Bo. My next appointment is not for another hour. Is there anything else you desire?" she asked with a smile.

Bo asked, "What do you propose, Natasha?"

"I can take my hand and stroke your penis for $50 or use my mouth for $100," she answered in a business-like tone.

Beecher thought it over and feeling he was a little short of cash, decided on the hand job. Beecher was getting bled dry by two of his three ex-wives. Even though he was making a six-figure income, he couldn't save a dime. He was hoping this project he could do better. Natasha led him to a chair and laid a towel on the seat. She sat him down and took another towel and laid it on his thigh. She took warm coconut oil and rubbed it over his manhood. She added some to her hand as well and began stroking him gently until he was hard. Just before his release, Natasha picked up the towel from his thigh and expertly caught the passion fluid. Bo slowly got up from the chair and went to the closet to retrieve his clothes. He thanked and paid Natasha.

She guided him to the door, and before Bo walked out into the hallway Natasha said, "Welcome to Moscow, Mr. Bo," and smiled. Beecher nodded, then took the elevator down to his room.

☭

As Miller sat at the bar giving Snezhinka his undivided attention, Kurt and Nadine walked into the lobby from outside. All the American staff stayed at the Belgrade on the 16th floor. They would be there until their housing units were completed on the embassy grounds. They had just been out to dinner and were going back to their room. They greeted Miller, and Kurt introduced his wife Nadine. As they said good night and headed to their room, a dark, heavyset gentleman walked up to the register and waited for Snezhinka. She saw he was there to pay his bill, but she took her time to make him wait. When she finally sauntered to the register, the man said something. Snezhinka was on him like a cat on a mouse. She laid into him, shouting in Russian relentlessly. Miller couldn't understand it.

When the man finally paid and hurried out of the bar, Miller asked Snezhinka, "What was that all about?"

"I do not like that man," she replied.

"That's obvious, but why?" he asked.

Looking defiant, she said, "He is Italian."

"What are you talking about, Snezhinka? Don't you like Italians?" he asked.

With her nostrils flaring, she replied, "I do not like Italians, Negroes, Latins, Arabic people, Jews, or Chinese."

Miller was dumbfounded. Suddenly Snezhinka was looking a lot less appealing to him. On that note, Miller paid his bill and went up to his room to bed.

☭

Natasha gathered up the oil-stained sheets from the massage table and threw them into the hamper. She got fresh linen from the cabinet. As she started putting the clean sheets on the table, she started laughing to herself. She was thinking of some of the things this Bo man was saying during their encounter. Things like "Stroke my golden staff, you dirty whore," and "You are doing God's work by pleasuring my cock."

She chuckled again. She wondered just how far he would be willing to go. "Maybe we shall see," she said, thinking out loud.

Chapter Two

SPASO HOUSE

The next morning, Miller and the rest of the construction management staff rode the van in to work. Today they would move into the temporary offices. They would have access to desktop computers, the 60% completed design drawings and project specifications. The 60% set would be reviewed and commented on. The comments that were worthwhile would be implemented into the 100% set and reviewed again. When the USG and TRIAD were satisfied, the Issued for Construction drawings and specifications would be certified, then distributed, and the project would be built accordingly. Harry held a staff meeting after everyone was settled. He first spoke to Charlie Manes, the construction manager.

"Charlie, I need you to go over the structural part of the drawings and specs. I need your comments by the end of the week. Bo, that leaves you to review the MEP (Mechanical, Electrical, Plumbing) portion. I will give you ten days. JT, I want you to review the civil part and look for any material submittal items we can get in early for USG review. Remember, everybody, the USG has fourteen days for review and comments, and they are never early. I do not want to hold up work progress because we are waiting on OBO review approvals. Also, JT, please do the Daily Construction Reports starting today. Bo, QC Daily reports will not be required until we begin doing permanent construction work. Any questions on the design review?"

No one spoke up. Harry continued, "Kurt, how many carpenters do we have in the loop?" Kurt was responsible for all the craft personnel.

Kurt answered, "We have four coming in on Friday and another five on Monday. There are ten others awaiting their deployment dates."

Harry replied, "I do not want any more coming in until we have the workers and staff housing units finished. Charlie, make sure the nine that are coming in this week and next will be working on the units. I am hoping we can get those completed by the end of this month. That gives us three weeks to finish. Charlie, push them every chance you get."

With that, the team got to work.

Major Karlov was concerned that Irena had not been in contact with Miller for over a week. He was afraid she had lost him. Irena was surprised the American did not call her after she gave him her digits. She did try to run into him at the embassy and around the Arbat, but to no avail. On Sunday afternoon, she went to the Belgrade and had coffee at the bar in hopes of seeing him. She did not. Miller was up to his ears in work and put in long hours. On the third floor of the old building they were demolishing, TRIAD set up a temporary mess hall. The mess hall was catered by a Filipino outfit called Universal Suppliers. Later, Harry would use this same company to cater the permanent mess hall and the laundry service located in the housing unit building.

Miller liked the food at the mess hall and had been eating there after work. He would then walk back to his room, take a shower, lie in his bed, and read until he got tired. He would go to sleep, get up, and do it all again. This became the routine. He borrowed the book *King Rat* by James Clavell from Kurt, and that offered a nice escape for an hour or two in the evenings. All the guys were readers and shared books with each other. All except Bo. He preferred to read a few passages from the Good Book in the evenings and had no notion of reading anything else unless it was work related. JT had thought about Irena from time to time over the past week. He thought maybe after things slowed down a bit, he would pursue that. He laughed at the thought. He knew in this business things never slowed down a bit, but still, he would like to see her.

☭

The following Saturday night, JT went out to dinner at the Angara Club with Kurt and Nadine. They sat at their usual table, and a few minutes later Harry showed up with Charlie and his wife Kathy. Kurt saw them first and called out jokingly, "I see they let anybody in this joint!"

Harry called back and asked, "What are you horse thieves doing here?"

Kurt replied, "Waiting for you, boss. Please sit down. Hi Charlie, Kathy. How are you guys?"

Charlie answered, "Well, Kurt, it's Saturday night, we get to sleep in tomorrow, and we are not due back to work until Monday. If things were any better, I couldn't stand it."

They all laughed and ordered food and drinks. It was close to 9 p.m. and the band was about to start. They kicked off with "Bambalaro," a favorite of the disco and bar scene. It always seemed to get people dancing. The band played Russian and American hits or standards with a few international tunes thrown in. They had a female singer who played piano with men playing bass, drums, and guitar. When they did Russian folk songs, the woman played the balalaika (a Russian stringed instrument).

The group finished eating and ordered more drinks. Kurt and Nadine got up and danced; soon, so did Charlie and Kathy. Even Harry got up and danced. Miller needed another drink, so he went to the bar to get one. He ordered a gin and tonic and was waiting. He felt a tap on his shoulder. When he turned, he saw Irena. She asked, "What are you doing here, Slav?"

Miller liked it when she called him Slav. Miller was feeling no pain, so he hugged and kissed her. "Irena, it is so good to see you," he said.

"It is, huh? Why have you not rung me up? You have my digits," she asked.

"I know, I know," he replied. "I was just so busy I never got around to it. Please don't be angry with me."

"Come dance with me, Slav," she said.

Miller grabbed her hand and held it as they walked to the dance floor. The band was between songs and then they kicked into the Eagles tune "Lying Eyes." *Not a bad version*, Miller thought. Just a slight Russian accent with some of the words, but the music was flawless.

Major Karlov was at a table watching them. He mumbled to himself, "Now is your chance, my little sparrow. That's right; pull the noose a little tighter."

☭

Miller and Irena stayed on the dance floor. They danced song after song until they were worn out and perspiring. Irena suggested they go to another popular bar called The Hungry Duck by the Kusnetsky Most metro station. They took a taxi and Irena negotiated the fare. The Hungry Duck was a bohemian bar and icon for Moscow hedonism. It was famous for encouraging young girls to get up and dance on top of the long horseshoe-shaped bar, wearing a dress and no panties. For the inebriated young girls, very little encouragement was necessary.

JT and Irena had a few drinks and watched the carryings-on. They left in time to catch the last metro train to Smolenskya station. When they got out on to the street, Miller volunteered to walk her home. As they walked, she reached down and grabbed his hand and held it. As she did, Miller took her into his arms and kissed her, looked into her eyes, then kissed her again. As they continued the walk, Irena stopped abruptly and said, "Let's go to your room, Slav."

"My sentiments exactly," he replied with a mischievous smile. The couple did an about-face heading in the direction of the Belgrade.

☭

The next morning, Miller slept in until almost 10. Irena left at 5 a.m. because she wanted to be home before her mother got up. She knew her mother would be angry if she did not attend church and McDonald's with her and her brother, Alexei. Miller went down to the lobby bar and ordered an espresso. Then another. He felt better. He pulled out his cell phone and called Vera.

"Good morning, Vera. This is JT Miller. How are you this morning?"

She answered, "Good morning, Mr. Miller. What can I do for you?"

Miller thought for a moment and said, "Vera, I have to fill out a contact report. You mentioned it had to be done within 24 hours of the contact, so that is why I am calling."

She asked, "Is there any problem, Mr. Miller?"

He answered, "No, Vera. I just didn't want to break any rules this early in the project," he said half-jokingly.

"In that case, Mr. Miller, the contact report can wait until Monday. If 9 a.m. works for you, come to my office and we will get it done," she replied.

Miller said, "Sounds good, Vera. Thank you. I will see you then."

Miller thought, *Okay, great, I got that done*. He finished his espresso and left the hotel. He felt like walking.

After McDonald's with her family, Irena told her mother she wanted to shop for a hat, and she would be back to the apartment later. She said goodbye to her mother with a kiss on the cheek, in Russian fashion. She walked west down the Arbat and her mother and Alexei walked east. She pulled out her phone and dialed. A voice answered, "Major Karlov." Irena informed the major what had transpired the previous night. The major replied, "Excellent, Irena, excellent. Now that he has taken a bite, we must sink the hook. Irena, take the next month and get him eating out of your hand. I want him to believe he cannot live without you. After our meat is well tenderized, we will put it on the grill."

Irena continued walking. She felt a strange emotional conflict. All these feelings and emotions were going crazy in her head. She really liked the American, but she could not like the American. She wanted to be true to him, but she had to be true to Karlov and protect herself and her family. Well, she decided she had a month before anything would happen. She said to herself, "I will worry about it when the time comes. Better to pass a danger once than to live in fear." Suddenly a big smile could be seen on her face. She started running. She ran faster and faster. Irena weaved in and out of people walking.

She ran across the street against the light. A traffic cop on a beat started to go after her, then decided against it. She ran and ran and ran until she was in front of the Belgrade Hotel.

☭

Miller really didn't walk anywhere in particular. He walked up by the embassy then back toward the Arbat, just walking and thinking about Irena. They had made love twice—once when they got to his room and once before she left in the morning. He felt tired but exhilarated. She had felt so warm beside him. He loved it when she lay on her back and snored like a wildebeest. He smiled at the thought. He had just gently turned her over on her side and she stopped. She did not even come close to waking. Irena had a sliver of a scar on her abdomen and explained she had her appendix out when she was a small girl. Besides that, she had perfect, beautiful white skin. Her body was slim and long. Her breasts were shaped to perfection. As he walked, he saw her laughing and smiling in his mind. Then his thoughts did an about-face. *This is bullshit. JT, you've got to stop this crap. This could get to be a problem. You won't be able to do your job effectively, thinking about her all the time. The last thing you need is to fall for a Russian girl.*

☭

Irena walked into the lobby and up to Miller's room. She knocked and then knocked again. He was not home. She wondered where the Slav had gone. She walked back to the lobby and went to the bar and ordered an American coffee. Snezhinka brought her coffee and smiled. Irena disliked her immediately. Snezhinka was too attractive. She did not want the Slav to get any ideas. As she sipped her coffee, she imagined the Slav and Snezhinka were already having an affair. He was with her the whole week she did not hear from him, that lousy svenina (pig), she thought. She finished her coffee and walked out of the lobby and descended the stairs to the sidewalk. At the bottom of the stairs, she saw Miller coming back from his walk. He smiled and waved, but she did not return the smile or wave. She had a stern look on her face. He could not understand it and when he got close to her, he asked, "What's wrong with you?"

She answered, "You are such a svenina."

"What the hell are you talking about? What is a sve.....svegeeza or whatever you said?"

"Snezhinka is a very attractive woman," she said.

Miller answered, "I suppose so. What does that have to do with anything?"

"You have been having an affair with her, Slav," she said as tears started to well up in her eyes.

Miller saw this and hugged her tightly. She started to cry. He said, "My dear, silly, beautiful Irena. Please stop crying. I am not having an affair with Snezhinka. She has a pretty face but a damaged heart."

She asked, "Are you sure, Slav?"

"Yes, Irena," he said.

All of a sudden, her eyes lit up. She smiled and almost hugged him to death. She warned, "You better not be lying to me, Slav."

"Irena, believe me. I am not."

"I do believe you, Slav. You are not really a svenina," she said.

Miller asked, "What the hell is a sve-nee-na?"

Irena smiled as she hugged him tighter and said, "I will tell you later. Can we go up to your room now?"

Miller took her hand and led her up the stairs, through the lobby, and up to his room. They made love for two hours until Irena left and went home. Irena was afraid her mother would worry about her. She was just going to buy a hat and had already been gone over four hours.

☭

The next morning, Miller rode in with the rest of the guys instead of walking. He started thinking about Irena on the way in. He thought to himself, *I've got to stop this.* They pulled up to the south gate, the work week started, and the days passed. During the next few weeks, Miller would see Irena on the weekends and one night a week, usually Wednesday or Thursday. During the week they would have dinner at the Belgrade restaurant. After, they would go for a short walk and Miller would smoke a cigar. Irena did not like cigars, but she did not say anything. They would then go to his room and lie in bed, talking about everything. Before she left, they would always make love. The rendezvous would usually end by midnight

On one of these nights after Irena went home, Miller could not get to sleep. After tossing and turning for an hour, he decided to walk back down to the bar for a drink to help him sleep. As he walked in, he saw about seven Russian hookers lounging around the bar and restaurant area. Two of them were speaking to what looked like potential clients. Miller sat down at the bar and ordered a Baltika dark. As he was waiting for the beer, he heard a man's voice yell, "Hey, Americanski."

As Miller looked up, he saw a big heavyset Russian guy smiling and walking toward him. The guy was wearing a black leather jacket, had a shaved head which resembled a light bulb, and his fingers were adorned with heavy rings. "Hey holmes, what's up? My name is Moshi."

Miller replied, "Hello, Moshi, I'm JT."

Moshi put out his hand and Miller shook it. Moshi asked, "Mr. JT, is there anything I can get for you?"

"No thanks, bud. I'm just going to finish this beer and go to bed. Got to work in the morning," Miller replied.

Moshi thought for a moment and asked, "How about one or maybe two of my girls to help you sleep?"

Miller wanted Moshi to think he was hep with the jive and replied, "Dude, if they were in my room, I wouldn't be doing much sleeping."

Moshi laughed and said, "I like you, Mr. JT. I would not make this offer to just anybody, but because I like you, how about some Thai stick to help you sleep? Hey, Americanski? Just $200 US a stick."

Miller responded, "No thanks, Moshi, maybe later."

Moshi made another attempt, "How about cocaine, opium or codeine?" Miller said no. "What about a gun, knife, or bazooka?" Miller said no. "Do you have anyone you wish to disappear? Another one of my services."

Miller replied, "Moshi, you are the man. I'm good for now, but if I ever need someone to disappear or a bazooka, you're my guy."

Moshi smiled and added, "Mr. JT, are you sure you don't want to take Tatyana to your room? Half price." Miller just shook his head, finished his beer, and went back up to his room.

At work the next day, Harry announced the staff had been invited to Spaso House, the ambassador's residence, for the annual Thanksgiving Ball celebration. The OBO staff would be there as well, along with other embassy people. This was a tradition for Spaso House. This and previous ambassadors thought it was a nice gesture to bring people together during the holidays. The shindig would be on Wednesday night because the ambassador would celebrate on Thursday with his family and just a few top diplomats. No work activities were allowed on Thanksgiving per contract, so the diplomats would not be inconvenienced or disturbed during the holiday. All American holidays were treated this way, and some Russian. The contractor could request to work on a holiday or late work hours, but the request would have to be approved by the embassy's DCM (Deputy Chief of Mission) then finally the OBO. Usually if the request was accepted by the DCM, it would be accepted by the OBO. The additional staff required by the government to support the extra work hours would be billed to the contractor or negotiated for any extra work items the contractor performed not included in the contract.

It was to be a formal affair and would be catered by Sergey Rominoff, a descendant of the last czar of Russia. He was famous throughout Moscow. There would be a choice of two entrees. First the traditional America feast with all the trimmings; the second one, with more of a Russian flair, included black Russian caviar, a borscht, salmon with mushrooms, potatoes, buckwheat groats, and a salad consisting of diced onion, cucumber, and beets tossed in olive oil and white vinegar. The Russian National Orchestra would provide a thirty-piece ensemble playing the music of Tchaikovsky and other selections. The Russian National Orchestra (RNO) was organized in 1990 and had become very popular.

There would be formal seating arrangements set up with name plates showing where the guests would be seated. The seating placements were given much thought. The dance floor would be set up in front of the orchestra. Two walk-up bars would be provided with waiters serving the guests hors d'oeuvres and drinks on silver trays. As Harry finished explaining the get-together, he added, "I hope you guys brought suits. If not, go out and buy or borrow one.

This is a formal affair. You will not be allowed entry without a suit."

Harry checked, and only Bo had not brought a suit. Kurt said he had an extra and Bo could wear that. They were about the same size.

The party would be in two days. Miller thought they could have given more notice, but he was good with it. He thought it would be fun to bring Irena. He doubted she had ever been to such an elegant affair. After Harry finished the announcement, Miller went to see Vera. Miller walked to her office. The door was open, as she was busy reading reports. He knocked on her door. When she looked up, he asked, "Hi, Vera. Do you have a minute?"

She took a pen and marked the page where she ended reading and put the report down on her desk. "Yes, Mr. Miller. What can I do for you?"

JT thought, then answered, "Vera, remember the woman I have been filling contact reports on?" She nodded, and he continued, "I would like to bring her as my date to the Thanksgiving Ball at Spaso House."

Vera replied, "Well, nothing negative has come up on her background check. She has been teaching school at the embassy for over a year. Being a Russian national could be a problem, though."

Miller countered, "There will be other Russian nationals there, Vera. The waiters, bartenders, and the like."

She answered, "Well, Mr. Miller, you have a point. I can ask the DCM if he has a problem with it. I cannot promise anything, but I will ask."

"Vera, could you possibly ask him today? I don't know if Irena has a dress, and she may need time to put something together."

Vera thought he was being a bit pushy, but she understood and said, "Mr. Miller, the DCM may be in meetings all day and won't answer my calls. Come back here at 5 p.m. and I will inform you if I have been successful."

"Thank you, Vera. You are the best," Miller replied, thinking the compliment would not hurt his case. Miller left the Spode building and went back to work. At 4:45 p.m. he walked back to Vera's office. She had a habit of leaving at the stroke of five o'clock and he did not want to miss her. Vera's office was open. She saw him and motioned him in. Vera was on the phone talking to the DCM. She put down the phone and Miller waited.

"Mr. Miller, your request has been accepted," she said, trying not to smile.

"Thank you, Vera, and thank the DCM," he replied as he headed out the door.

Miller left work a little early that day. He wanted to get over to Irena's apartment to tell her the news. As he told her, and she translated for her mother Sveta, the two of them got excited, held hands, and started jumping up and down. Irena told him that her mother had the perfect gown for her to wear, but a few modifications had to be made so it would fit properly. Before she had finished telling him, Sveta was already hauling the sewing machine out of the closet. Irena gave Miller a kiss and shooed him away, so she and her mother could get to work. Miller left and walked home to the Belgrade.

When Miller got back to the Belgrade, Nadine and Kathy were sitting at the lobby bar. They had drinks in front of them and were chatting excitedly about the event at Spaso House. That day at work, Kurt and Mike had been complaining about how much their wives' gowns would cost. They were using a Russian seamstress recommended by the DCM's wife. They did the fittings that afternoon and had to pay extra for the 24-hour service so they could pick them up the next day.

"God damn, Harry. You're gonna have to give me a raise so I can afford this shindig," Kurt said jokingly."

Harry answered, "Fat chance that happening. You are just going to have to tighten the belt a bit, Kurt. FYI...your belt could use a bit of tightening."

Kurt frowned. He knew he was putting on a few pounds in the midsection, and Harry loved to keep reminding him. Miller said hello to his coworkers' wives, and they informed him of the new gowns they were having made. Miller got an earful, then excused himself and went up to his room. He did not eat at the mess hall that evening because he went to see Irena. He took a shower, put on some clean clothes, and headed to the Angara Club. He had a yen for pork chops.

View of Spaso House, US Ambassador's residence in Moscow as it appeared in 2016.

☭

The night of the ambassador's event had come. Irena and her mother had finished her gown. She was looking in the mirror, and her mother was helping with the last finishing touches. The time was 7 p.m. and Miller would be over at 8 p.m. to retrieve his date, then the couple would walk over to Spaso House. Irena's mother looked at her daughter and smiled. She thought she looked beautiful.

☭

Nadine and Kathy were almost ready, and Kurt and Charlie were putting on their suits. The day before, Harry made the staff bring their suits into the office and he paid to have them cleaned and pressed. Harry said, "I don't want any of you guys showing up at Spaso with crumpled suits. When you are there, you are representing TRIAD, so act accordingly. I don't want the ambassador to think he has a bunch of guys working on his embassy that look or act like they just got off a tuna boat."

Kurt and Charlie were shining like new pennies. Nadine and Kathy were finally ready, and the foursome headed out.

☭

Miller put on his dark-blue suit. He was glad Harry cleaned and pressed all the suits. He always brought one with him when he worked on a project, just in case he needed one. He was finishing giving his shoes a quick Insta-Shine with one of those sponge pad gizmos. He phoned Irena and told her he was on the way and would be there in about twenty minutes. He put on a long black Russian overcoat he had picked up a few weeks earlier. It worked fine as a dress or topcoat. He made sure he had his room key and walked out into the hall to the elevator. In twenty minutes, he was standing in front of Irena's apartment building. In the lobby, he pushed her button and was buzzed in. He walked up the stairs to her apartment on the third floor. He knocked, and Sveta opened the door. She gave him a kiss on the cheek and jabbered something in Russian and motioned him to a chair.

A minute later, Irena walked into the room. She looked so beautiful. She was wearing a long burnt-yellow strapless evening gown with white shoes and white fur topcoat. Her hair was done in ringlets, and her long nails were manicured and painted with clear nail varnish. Her mother's white pearl necklace, which had been given to her by her mother, was around Irena's neck. She was a picture. He moved over to hug her, when she pulled away and said, "Do not wrinkle my dress, Slav." She then laughed and hugged him gently.

☭

As they walked arm in arm and approached Spaso House Irena asked, "Do I look beautiful, Slav?"

Miller stopped and looked at her. He knew she was nervous meeting all these new people, especially the Americans. These people were high on the food chain, and she was not. He kissed her and said, "Irena, tonight you are the most beautiful girl in all of Russia."

As they continued to walk, she snuggled closer. She stopped and kissed him on the cheek before they reached the entrance of Spaso House. At the gate were two marine guards checking names off the invitation list. As they walked up, the marine asked, "Names?"

Miller answered, "James Thomas Miller and Irena Anarbekova."

The marine checked off the names, handed them their name tags, and said, "Thank you, sir. Please enjoy your stay at Spaso House."

Miller and Irena walked through the gate and up to the house with other guests. Everybody was dressed to the nines. As they entered the house, there was a receiving line before you entered the main ballroom. The ambassador wanted to meet each of his guests. In the line was the ambassador, DCM, the OBO Project director John London, and their wives. As Miller and Irena entered the gauntlet, the ambassador read JT's name tag and said, "Hello Mr. Miller. You are with TRIAD if I am not mistaken, is that correct?"

"Yes, ambassador. Thank you. This is Irena Anarbekova. She teaches school here at the embassy."

The ambassador looked her up and down and replied, "So very nice to meet you, Irena. I think that perhaps you are the most beautiful woman here tonight." He continued, after his wife gave him the hairy eyeball, "That is, of course, except for my wonderful wife Nancy."

Nancy was a good sport and said, "Good cover, darling. I would hate to think of you sleeping tonight on that hard, lumpy sofa in the library."

Miller and Irena laughed, and so did the ambassador and his wife. They moved down the line to the DCM. Miller thanked him again for the invitation. The DCM introduced his wife Margo, and after a few more pleasantries, they moved on to the OBO Project Director. Miller would be working very closely with this man. John London was OBO's golden boy, the best they had. His wife was Filipino; he had met her at the US Embassy in Beijing at his last post. He fell head over heels and left his wife and two small children for her.

Miller said, "Hello, John. Nice shindig."

Miller had met London a few times for meetings at the Spode building. They would also meet occasionally where the demo was taking place in preparation for the new embassy construction. John responded, "Hello, JT. I don't believe you've met my wife. This is Foo."

Miller replied, "Hello, Foo. Nice to meet you. I want you two to meet my friend Irena." Irena smiled and shook their hands. John said he hoped to talk with them later, and the couple walked into the ballroom.

Across the street, Major Karlov watched Miller and Irena enter Spaso House. He had a tail on both and had been informed of the ball. The only concern the major had was that Irena had not told him about it. *I will question her about this*, he thought. *Not a big complication, but I now know I must tighten the leash.*

Nadine and Kathy looked great in their gowns. The Russian seamstress was expensive but worth it. Nadine's long lime-green affair with low neckline, paired with white shoes with a turquoise and jade necklace, was a good combination. Kathy wore a fire-engine red gown with black shoes and a black gemstone necklace. The husbands were looking equally dapper. Kurt was wearing his blue pinstripe and Charlie his black suit with red tie. Kathy thought it would be cool if her husband's tie was the same color as her gown. They were standing by the punch bowl, watching the other guests enter.

Nadine said to her husband, "Look, Kurt. There's JT and his Russian girlfriend. She's beautiful. I love the fur jacket. I just hope there are not any PETA advocates here tonight."

Kurt smiled, "Just don't say anything, honey."

"Mum's the word," she answered. Nadine thought they made a nice couple. Just then the RNO (Russian National Orchestra) began to play, not too loud nor too soft—perfect background music. They started with Tchaikovsky's "Romeo and Juliet Fantasy Overture after Shakespeare."

☭

Miller took Irena's hand and led her to the bar. He ordered a gin and tonic and she a glass of champagne. He saw the group at the punch bowl, waved, and walked over. He introduced Irena and they all complimented each other on the way they looked. Just then, Harry arrived with none other than Vera. They all looked. JT commented to Charlie, "That sly old dog."

"You don't think anything is going on, do you?" Charlie asked.

"You never know on these projects. Anything can happen," Miller answered and smiled.

When Harry and Vera entered, Vera went over to talk to the DCM's wife. Harry grabbed a scotch and water from the bar and joined his colleagues. The first thing Harry said as he approached the group was, "Don't anybody say anything, or I will cut your lunch hour at work to fifteen minutes."

Kurt spoke up. "Harry, old boy. Wouldn't think of it."

"Yeah Harry, that would be baaaahd," Miller offered in his best sheep impersonation, trying to keep a straight face.

Charlie and Kurt could not help themselves and started laughing. Even Harry was laughing. The girls just looked at them and didn't see what was so funny. Harry said, "John called me after lunch today and asked if I would escort Vera to this affair. What was I gonna say? Fuck you, John, Vera drives me nuts? Hell no. I said that I would be delighted. I thought I could take one for the team."

Miller replied, "All kidding aside, Harry, Vera looks nice and you guys make a good couple."

Harry answered, "Let me reiterate. I am doing this strictly for public relations initiatives by agreeing to a direct request by the project director and the US Government." After, he pulled Charlie, Kurt and JT out of the others' earshot, Harry continued, "That is, unless she wants to fool around; then all bets are off."

They all chuckled, and Harry asked, "Has anyone seen Bo? Vera said he requested a Russian national as his date."

Everyone looked surprised, and Nadine interjected, "I didn't know he was seeing anyone." Just then, Bo showed up at the door with a tall, beautiful Russian girl. She was wearing a sheer sleeveless black gown, red lipstick, black shoes with heels, and a necklace that looked like she was the queen of bling—something like Catherine the Great might wear. She was also wearing a white fox shoulder wrap. Bo and his date passed through the receiving line, and like the others had before him, headed to the bar. He ordered a Jack and Coke and she a painfully dry vodka martini. Bo was 5'-9" and his date, with heels, was 6'5." They made an interesting pair. The couple stayed to themselves and sat down at one of the tables where they found their names on place cards. The RNO slipped into Tchaikovsky's "Capriccio Italien, Opus 45."

Miller and Irena mingled. They were talking to Joe Amato, OBO's electrical engineer, and his wife. Joe was a good guy. Originally from the Bronx, Joe was a street kid made good. He enlisted in the navy when he was sixteen. Somehow, he swindled his way into ROTC classes and became a 1st lieutenant at twenty-four. He then continued with electrical engineering and passed the PE (Professional Engineer) examinations for the state of New York when he was thirty-six. After twenty-five years with the navy, he took his pension and went to work for the OBO doing electrical QA (Quality Assurance) on embassy projects. He married Rosa when he was thirty-five and had been married twenty-two years to date. They also talked with John London again, and he informed them that Spaso House had been the US Ambassador to Russia's residence since 1933.

Miller introduced Irena to Vera. He then spoke with the OBO civil guy. His name was Hameed Hussain, an Iranian American who seemed to know his onions when it came to the civil side of things. The OBO mechanical guy was a Russian national named Andre Petrov. Andre had worked for MEBCO (Moscow Embassy Building Control Office) since 1986, keeping the embassy's mechanical systems running. Because the new office building would have to tie into older piping systems, John London thought Andre's knowledge would come in handy and he would be a good candidate for the OBO position. Andre jumped at the chance. Last but not least was Lou Bost, OBO's construction manager. An architect by trade born in New Orleans rounded out their team.

The ambassador announced that dinner was served, and everybody should adjourn to the tables. As people were milling to their seats the RNO played Tchaikovsky's "Serenade for Strings." Two tables were set aside for the TRIAD and OBO staff. John believed in partnering, and he wanted the tables to be split between the TRIAD and OBO teams. At one table you had Miller and Irena, Harry and Vera, John and Foo, Joe and Rosa, Andre and his wife Tanya. The second table held Kurt and Nadine, Charlie and Kathy, Hameed and his wife Adara, Lou and his wife Ethel, Bo and Natasha. Bo had continued seeing Natasha at the Belgrade for his massage and stress relief treatments. He could not keep himself away from Natasha. He did not mind spending his money for her, and she was glad to take it. Occasionally, he had taken her out on the town. This was one of those occasions.

The waiters came around to the tables and took orders as to which dinner they had preferred. Irena ordered the salmon and Miller ordered the turkey. All the dinners were passed out and the guests were chowing down like buzzards on the Serengeti. The time was 9:30 p.m., and they were ravenous. Miller shared some of his turkey with Irena, and she her salmon with him.

After dinner, the RNO changed things up and started playing Strauss waltzes for the guests that wanted to dance. They started with "The Blue Danube" and the ambassador and his wife moved to the dance floor; this was the cue, and several couples got up. Miller and Irena and Kurt and Nadine were among them. "The Vienna Blood Waltz" was next, and then came an assortment of other numbers from the Strauss collection. Most of the guests stayed on the dance floor. Everyone seemed to be having a great time. Finally, the orchestra took a break and people began moving back to their seats.

At that point the ambassador got up again to make an announcement. "Ladies and gentlemen. This year, my wife talked me into doing something a little different. She and two others have been going around and judging, in their opinion, which ladies are wearing the best gowns. They have chosen five ladies. We will name the ladies later tonight and if they will be so kind, each lady will come to the dance floor when her name is called. We will then go to each lady and ask the audience to show their appreciation by applauding. The lady who receives the loudest audience applause response will be the winner. The lady who gets the second-loudest response will win second prize and so on. The applause level will be measured with a decibel-level meter borrowed from the TRIAD safety department. All five will win a prize of some sort which will be announced after the selections. Of course, my wife Nancy is disqualified from the competition because she is one of the judges. The other two judges are male and wish to remain anonymous for fear of reprisals after the competition."

Chuckles were heard in the audience. The ambassador paused, then continued, "Nancy, will you come up here, please?"

Nancy walked up to her husband then faced the crowd and spoke into the microphone, "Distinguished guests, the time now is approximately eleven o'clock. The winners will be announced at midnight. Until then, the RNO will play for your dancing pleasure—and most importantly the bar will remain open. Enjoy."

With that, Nancy and the ambassador retired to their table. The room was abuzz. Every woman was chatting about who was wearing the best gown, secretly hoping she herself would win. The men were smart enough to know to keep their traps shut. Speculation abounded about who the other judges were. They definitely weren't talking. The RNO started up again with a Bach suite.

Miller turned to Irena and said, “I know you will win, Irena.”

She answered, “Do not try to make me feel good, Slav.”

He countered, “You have the best dress here—I mean, gown.”

“I do not know, Slav. Natasha and Nadine’s are quite spectacular, and Natasha is sexier than me.”

Miller took a moment too long to answer. “Are you kidding? You got them hands down.”

She looked at him and frowned. “You had to think about it, did you not, Slav?”

He was quick on the draw this time. “Of course not, Irena. You will see. Let’s dance.” They moved to the dance floor.

Natasha and Bo had just got another drink and had sat down. Natasha was a bit buzzed and took off her shoes. As Bo was enjoying his drink and munching on some fruit that was set on the table, he felt something rubbing the inside of his thigh; then the angle changed, and it moved to rubbing his manhood. He looked at Natasha. She laughed, then winked and erotically licked her lips with her tongue. His manhood stood at attention.

Bo warned, “Natasha, behave yourself. Someone might see.”

Natasha leaned over close to him and whispered in his ear, “I want your golden staff inside me, you lousy good-for-nothing sick fuck.”

At that moment, Bo’s body spasmed. He looked around to see if anyone had noticed. It didn’t appear so. He looked at Natasha. She was laughing at him, then stopped abruptly and said, “You must be better trained, Americanski. You are a weak, pathetic pig.” As she said this, Bo could feel his loins begin to stir a second time.

Harry had been an excellent escort. He listened to Vera’s stories and laughed at her jokes. He brought her drinks and was attentive. He was thinking all night that he should ask her to dance. He wasn’t exactly hep on dancing to

Bach, unfortunately. Even with music he could dance to, he had two left feet. He leaned over and asked John to meet him at the bar. They both got up and headed that way. At the bar, Harry asked, "John, I was wondering if it would be appropriate for RNO to play a more contemporary selection?"

John replied, "They do have a list of contemporary tunes they play, Harry. Let me confirm with the ambassador. Maybe for the last selection after the gown contest. On the chair by the cellist on the right is a binder that has their music list. It is in English. Pick which one you would like them to play, and I will run it by the ambassador."

Harry answered, "Great, John. Give me five minutes."

He then started for the cellist and the chair. He walked behind the orchestra and over to the binder on the chair. Harry put on his glasses and thumbed through the binder. When he seemed satisfied, he set the binder back on the chair and made his way back to the bar where John was waiting. Harry whispered something in John's ear. John nodded his head and walked to the ambassador's table. Harry watched as they spoke. After a minute, John was on his way back to Harry. About halfway back, John gave Harry the thumbs-up sign.

☭

It was almost midnight. RNO had just finished Bach's "Orchestral Suite No. 2 - Minuet & Badinerie." Nancy and the DCM's wife moved up to the podium. The ambassador's wife started, "Ladies and gentlemen, distinguished guests. Before I call out the names of the five finalists, I want to inform you this has been a very difficult decision. Ladies, you all look so wonderful; I wish we had a prize for each of you. Margo, if you please."

Margo handed her an envelope and Nancy opened it then announced, "The five names on this list are equal at this point. As mentioned, the winner and runners-up will be chosen by the audience." Nancy looked down at the list and said, "Natasha Stasevich."

Irena squeezed Miller's knee and said, "I told you, Slav."

Natasha made her way to the dance floor. She was smiling, and the crowd went wild. Nancy continued, "Foo London."

Again, as Foo made her way the crowd was very enthusiastic.

"Irena Anarbekova." Miller jumped up and cheered with excitement. He helped Irena up to the front.

"Nadine Scanlen."

Kurt was as bad as Miller. He was visibly excited as he helped Nadine up from her chair. As she got up and started to move to the front, a waiter bringing a full tray of glasses of champagne to one of the tables, slipped on a wet drink someone had spilled and stumbled right into Nadine. The champagne spilled all over Nadine's gown and shoes. As she tried to move away from the hazard, she slipped as well and fell to the floor. The crowd gasped. Kurt and Harry were closest and helped her up. Another waiter brought towels and dried her off the best he could. Nadine was so embarrassed. She thought about just leaving and having Kurt take her home. Instead, she had another thought. She straightened and tried to smooth out some of the damage. After she was through, she stood up straight, put on a smile, and walked up to where the other finalists were waiting, as if she were the queen of England. Everyone applauded, then stood up and gave her a standing ovation. At that moment, Kurt was very proud of his wife.

After everyone settled down, Nancy continued, "And the fifth finalist is Rosa Amato."

Joe was excited, just like the other husbands had been. The guests were in their seats, and the five finalists were standing together on the dance floor. Nancy walked up and put her hand above Rosa's head. The crowd roared with applause. Rosa was wearing a light-blue chiffon gown and looked stunning. Nancy looked at Andre Petrov, OBO's mechanical guy, who was measuring the decibel levels. John London was there as well, as a witness. Andre nodded to Nancy, and Nancy moved on to the next finalist, Foo London. The crowd went wild. Some inebriated guest yelled "Fix," because Foo's husband was at the decibel meter. Andre nodded again, and they moved on to Natasha. Again, the crowd went wild, then to Irena. Miller whistled as loud as he could. Miller thought for sure Irena had the contest.

Nancy then walked to Nadine. Nadine was standing there with wet splotches on her gown and stains on her white shoes. Her makeup was smeared, and she appeared to have dried champagne in her hair, but there was a big smile on her face. Nancy placed her hand above Nadine's head, and the biggest roar of the night went through the ballroom. Even the waiters joined in on the clapping. It was obvious that Nadine had won. The decibel results would just be a formality.

Andre nodded, and Nancy motioned for the crowd to quiet down.

When they did, Nancy announced, "Okay, ladies and gentlemen, give us a few moments to tally the results. The RNO will play the last song of the evening. A more contemporary piece for the last dance of the night."

Harry was with the orchestra leader and slipped him $40 to play his song. Harry tried to slip him $20, but the orchestra leader gave him the hairy eyeball, so Harry added another $20, and the orchestra leader was satisfied. The orchestra stood at attention as Harry made his way back to his table and walked up to Vera, who was chatting with Kathy, Charlie's wife.

She turned to face Harry as Harry bowed and asked, "Vera, may I have this dance?"

Vera smiled and said, "Well, of course, Mr. Clark; the pleasure is all mine." She got up and took Harry's arm. Harry nodded to the conductor and the RNO kicked into an instrumental version of Glenn Campbell's classic "By the Time I Get to Phoenix." Harry held Vera close, but not too close, and the two shared a moment.

John London smiled and muttered to himself, "Harry, you are one class act." Miller grabbed Irena's hand and walked to the dance floor as well, along with many other guests. The floor was packed, and the attendees were enjoying the last dance of the evening, but not as much as Harry and Vera.

After the dance, Nancy walked back up to the podium and announced, "We have the results of the contest. The winner is Nadine Scanlen, as if anyone had any doubt." The crowd cheered. "Nadine will receive a $300 gift certificate at the commissary store, and a 20-pound turkey." The crowd applauded. "First runner-up, Irena Anarbekova." The crowd cheered. Miller was squeezing her shoulder and rubbing her back. "Irena will receive a $150 gift certificate at the commissary store and a 20-pound turkey. The second runner-up is Natasha Stasevich. She will receive $50 in cash and of course a 20-pound turkey. Rosa Amato is third and will receive $25 in cash and a turkey--and Foo London, sorry my dear, no cash, just a turkey. Please let's have a big round of applause for the finalists." The crowd again roared.

☭

Miller and Irena left Spaso House and walked toward the Belgrade. Irena was walking on air. Miller looked like he was walking a tightrope but was steadied by Irena.

"You drink too much tonight Slav?"

He answered, "Maybe a little. This was a fun night, huh?"

"Oh yes, Slav. It was wonderful," she said and continued jokingly, "I would have won if that clumsy Nadine would not have fallen down. How about that woman?"

Miller laughed and pulled her closer. "How about when Harry brought Vera up to dance? I thought I would die," he said.

"Yes, that was nice. I did not think he liked Vera," she replied.

"He doesn't, I don't think. You never can tell, though. I think he was just being chivalrous," he answered.

She asked, "What is chivalrous?"

"Charming, my Russian beauty. You know, like me," he answered, laughing.

She replied, "You are charming, my Slav." Then she held him tighter as they walked.

☭

Vera had an apartment in the diplomats' housing area on the embassy compound. Harry walked her home and then met Kurt and Charlie and their wives at the south gate, where the van was waiting to take them to the Belgrade. They climbed into the van and the driver pulled away.

Harry asked, "Isn't Bo coming with us?"

"No, Harry. Bo said he and Natasha would take a taxi," Kurt answered.

They continued in silence, each thinking about the night's festivities. They arrived at the Belgrade and took the elevator up to the 16th floor. They said their good nights and went off to their rooms.

On the 19th floor, outside room 1907, Bo and Natasha were saying their goodbyes. Natasha was holding him close and nibbling on his earlobe. She then said in a voice like a mother scolding a child, softly and seductively into his ear, "You perverted little bastard," at the same time squeezing his groin hard. "You have been bad, and Mommy has to punish you. That is want you want, is it not? To play with yourself while Mommy punishes you."

She could feel Bo's tool of indulgence growing in her hand. Without letting go, with her other hand she reached for the key to her apartment in the pocket of her fur wrap and opened the door. She kicked the door open, still holding on to Bo like a vise, and led him into the room. When she kicked the door closed, the sound reverberated through the hall.

Major Karlov was happy with the night. The operative that had been following Miller and Irena had reported. *That is good, my little pigeon. The closer he becomes to you, the closer it is for our mission to be implemented.*

On the embassy work site, the construction activities were going well. Demolition was coming along, and the worker/staff housing units would be ready to move into on December 5th. Harry wanted to get everyone out of the hotel as quickly as possible. Not only were the rooms costing the project a fortune, Harry could now staff up additional needed personnel and have a place for them to stay. The housing unit rooms were like small dorm rooms for one. Nobody had to share a room. Harry was adamant this be the case. Harry had worked on a project in Saudi Arabia where they had to share rooms. His roommate had been a snorer, and Harry could never get any sleep. After a twelve-hour day, the last place you want to go relax is to a room shared with a co-worker. Harry thought this was cruel and unusual punishment and made sure it would not happen with this project.

The CAW rooms were 12'X12'. All these rooms were single status. The management single status rooms were 12'X15'. The extra three feet really seemed to make a difference. The rooms had single beds in them, equipped with a small TV and VCR at the foot of the bed. There was a small desk and chair, and the room had a small refrigerator. There was also a window in each of the rooms with a combination AC/heater unit. There was also a small bathroom with a commode, small sink and shower installed. No frills, just efficient housing. There were also double rooms and some apartments set up for the married status folks, such as Kurt and Charlie.

Besides the rooms, the housing units also included a mess hall, laundry facility, a commissary, a recreation room that included a pool and ping-pong table, an exercise room that had free weights, a few treadmills, and finally a full functioning bar and lounge stocked with American beer and spirits. Harry had ordered a large oak horseshoe-shaped bar with stools to accommodate about twenty, with additional tables and chairs set up in the lounge area. There was a big-screen TV and a dart board, along with a juke box which would play three selections for a quarter--all the comforts of a bar in Boston or Chicago. The bar and lounge was christened "The Gulag." Unfortunately, the establishment would be a Mecca only for inebriated construction workers, because Russian women would not be allowed inside. All Russian nationals were verboten.

Contractor housing units on embassy compound.
Russian militiamen guard booth in front of entrance. Jan 1997.

By mid-December, all the Americans were checked out of the Belgrade and installed in their new housing unit apartments. The mess hall and laundry facilities were up and running. Good hot meals were at the ready, and all an employee had to do was to drop off their dirty clothes in the morning in a provided fish net laundry bag and pick up the clean ironed clothes that evening. The facility could house 300-plus people. Harry, Miller, Kurt, and Mike met most mornings in the mess for coffee and breakfast. Bo would show up occasionally. One of the things on the menu was biscuits and gravy. Charlie usually had this with his eggs every morning. As Miller, Kurt, and Harry were sitting at their usual table, Charlie joined them with his breakfast tray. He greeted them and started on his coffee. Kurt noticed that the gravy covering the biscuits had a slick new-car shine to it. Kurt surmised this was either because of additional lard thrown in or they added super plasticizer, a concrete add mixture. He didn't suspect the latter.

Kurt said, "Charlie, your gravy has a nice sheen to it this morning."

Charlie answered, "Yes, it does. I like it when it's like this. Seems to have more flavor and slips out easier on the commode."

Yeah, extra lard would do that, Kurt thought. Kurt got up and walked back to the chow line to get seconds. He skipped the biscuits and gravy.

During the last three weeks of December up to about the 6th of January, the embassy always ran on short staff. Most Russians took this time off for the holidays, and the embassy people took this time to visit their families back in the States. Most businesses were closed as well, except for restaurants, grocery stores, and the like. This time around, the embassy's short staff would not hinder the construction progress. Harry's main activities were demolition and erecting a scaffold around the building, which would eventually hold a shroud. The whole building being demolished would be enclosed in a green netted nylon shroud so dust and debris would not go outside the work area. Harry was reasonably happy with the progress. The cold weather was a factor. The guys were bundled up like mummies and had limited flexibility doing their work.

Miller was in his office getting ready to head outside to the west side of the building. This was to be the location of a tower crane that would be used to move around materials during construction and to remove interior demo debris. Harry asked Miller to layout the concrete pad it would sit on. Harry wanted to make sure there would be no conflicts with the location. Miller was slipping on his Refrigiwear overalls. Most of the guys wore Carhartt, but Miller wasn't a big fan because they could be stiff as cardboard until they were worked in. Miller wore Refrigiwear for the extreme cold and blue Walls for the lesser cold. When Miller had completed the layout, he called Harry and they both looked over the location. It would work. Harry called Charlie to get the guys started on the excavation.

NOB during interior demolition before exterior shroud is installed. Jan. 1997.

It was Sunday afternoon when Miller and Irena found themselves on the metro train. They were taking the brown line train from Krasnopresnenskaya heading to Dobryninskaya station. The couple was looking for an apartment they could use on the weekends. They were looking outside the city center, where the rents were more reasonable. Irena found one for $320 a month and was taking Miller to look at it. Miller thought he would be money ahead, because a one-night stay at a cheap hotel in Moscow was about $125 a night. They pulled into Dobryninskaya and the train lurched to a stop. They got out and walked up the stairs and out on to the street. From there it was a six-block walk to the apartment. The apartment was not far away from the Starlite Diner. The Starlite Diner was made to look like an American diner from the 1950s. There was Elvis and Marilyn memorabilia all over the place, and it served those great artery-clogging American breakfasts that both Miller and Irena enjoyed.

The pair walked west down Ulitsa Koroviy Val until Irena said, "This is the building, Slav."

Miller thought the building was old but not too bad. The owner left a key in a hiding place for Irena. She retrieved the key and she and Miller entered. They walked up to the third floor to apartment 303. Irena opened the door and they walked in. The apartment was small. It was a three-room studio with a larger room that would serve as a living room and bedroom space, a kitchen, and a water closet or bathroom. It also had a small balcony that Miller could utilize to burn a cigar or two on occasion. Miller liked the location but thought the apartment was a little dingy but would do. The apartment was partially furnished with a double bed, kitchen table, and stove. There was no refrigerator. Miller thought Harry would lend him one of the small refrigerators they had left after furnishing the housing units.

Miller looked at Irena and said, "Let's do it."

Irena hugged him and told him they would have to sign a six-month lease. Miller was good with it, and he and Irena went downstairs to where the owner lived in another apartment in the same building. They signed the papers, and Miller paid the first and last month's rent, along with a $200 security deposit. He paid in American dollars. Before going back, they stopped at the Starlite Diner for a bite.

Major Karlov was at home when his phone rang. On the other end was the operative he had tailing Miller. The operative informed him that Miller and Irena had just rented an apartment on Ulitsa Koroviy Val and he had just finished installing two listening devices; one in the big room and one in the kitchen after the couple had left.

Major Korlov said into the phone, "Good, Sergey. Make sure you or Anotoly stay with them and keep me informed. Remember, a bird will not fly into our mouths already roasted."

Sergey answered, "Yes, sir."

The major put on his coat and stepped out onto his balcony. He pulled out a Kent cigarette and lit it with a Bic lighter. He stared at the dark lighted sky and remembered a saying or proverb from boyhood: "A dog gnaws the bone because he cannot swallow it whole." He thought, *Now is the time to meet this Mr. Miller.*

Chapter Three

CHRISTMAS STORY

It was Christmas Eve in Moscow. It was cold and windy, with snow on the ground. On the sides of the streets the snow piles were a mixture of snow, dirt, and mud with a slushy frozen texture at the base. Harry had arranged to take the staff out to the Angara Club for dinner. Rodney Carusso from the Arizona company's corporate office was there as well. A full-blooded Italian American from the south, Rodney was Vice President of the Overseas Division. He was sixty-three years old, married, with three kids and five grandchildren. His profile reminded Harry of Julius Caesar. Rodney would make occasional site visits just to make sure there were no project hiccups and ensure the client or USG was happy. He made Harry nervous. Harry liked Rodney but knew his easygoing persona was just camouflage. He was a smart corporate manager and could be ruthless when the bottom line was at stake.

Another few new faces at dinner were Tom Scaraponi and his wife Terry. Tom was the new safety manager, and his wife was the site nurse. Miller thought he had a good thing going with the dual incomes. Tom knew he did. Tom and Terry were in their mid-forties from NYC. They also had a seven-year-old daughter, named Tricia. Tom had lobbied to get some Sinatra on the jukebox at The Gulag. Occasionally you could hear "Fly Me to the Moon" seeping through the walls of Tom and Terry's apartment. Tom got one of the few two-bedroom apartments available in the housing units. This stipulation was set up in their contract before Tom and Terry would sign.

Dinner was over, and everyone was getting ready to leave. Miller told Harry he was going to stay and wait for Irena. She said she would meet him at 10:30 p.m., and it was almost that time. Miller said good night and Merry Christmas to everyone, then took a seat at the bar. He thought about getting a micro brewed beer. The club brewed this themselves. Miller liked the taste of the beer, but it was a little on the green side, and it gave him the worst hangover in the history of hangovers. He chose a vodka and tonic instead. They were out of gin.

As he sat there, he felt someone start to rub his back. He turned around quickly to give Irena a hug, but it wasn't Irena--it was Natasha.

"Oh, hi Natasha. I thought you were Irena. Bo just left. All of us were having dinner earlier," he said.

"I know, Americanski," she replied. She was wearing a very low-cut red dress with high black boots. She looked like she was on the prowl. She leaned over and kissed him on the cheek and said, "Hello, Miller. Nice to see you."

Just then, Irena came into the bar area and saw the kiss. She walked fast to where the others were at the bar. As she walked up, she said, "Hello, Natasha," with a look like a dog protecting a bone. Natasha nodded, and Irena continued, "Let's go, Slav. My uncle wants to meet you."

She led Miller by the hand past Natasha like she was not there. They walked to the dining area. There, sitting at a table, was Major Karlov. "Slav, this is my uncle Ivan."

The major spoke first. "Hello, Mr. Miller. So nice to finally meet you. Irena always talks about you. I think perhaps she is smitten."

Miller smiled. "Nice to meet you, Ivan. Are you Sveta's brother?" Miller asked.

"No, Mr. Miller. I am Irena's father's older brother. Poor Egor. He went into politics and I went into business. I guess I made the better choice," Karlov answered.

"What business are you in, Ivan?" Miller asked.

Karlov answered, "I work for an oil and gas company. Irena tells me you are a building engineer working on your new embassy. How exciting."

Miller replied, "I wouldn't go that far, but I can't complain. What is the name of the company you work for?"

Karlov answered, "Zhazprom. Perhaps you have heard of it. I have been with them since the company started in 1989. I have been lucky. It provides me a good living. Please, may I order drinks for everyone? Mr. Miller, Irena?"

JT ordered the usual, and Irena a Coke. They chatted for a few more minutes, then Ivan said, "I am sorry, Irena. I really must go. I just wanted to meet your Mr. Miller and say hello. I am sure you young people have things to do."

Miller was the first to reply, "Nice meeting you, Ivan. I hope we meet again."

Ivan answered, "I am sure of it. Good night, Mr. Miller. Good night, Irena."

She replied, "Good night, Uncle."

He leaned over and kissed her goodbye. When the major left, Miller noticed a kind of relief on Irena's face. She seemed to be more at ease after he had gone. Miller just figured it was a family thing. They finished their drinks and left.

Major Karlov felt good about the meeting. His driver was waiting for him in a blue Lada Riva, and they drove off. Karlov wanted the first meeting to be brief. He wanted to start slow. *Just a drop or two at a time will fill the bucket*, he thought.

Miller and Irena walked to the Krasnopresnenskaya metro station. They were heading to their new apartment. This would be their first time spending the night there. They were both looking forward to the adventure. Harry not only gave Miller a small refrigerator but also one of the extra double beds. Harry had the logistics guys deliver them early in the week. Irena had met them at the apartment and had them place the items where she wanted them.

She put sheets on the bed and bottled water in the refrigerator. There were already pots, pans, silverware, and glasses in the apartment. She cleaned and straightened until she was satisfied. *Yes*, she thought, *the Slav will like this.*

They got off at their stop and walked toward the apartment. As they walked holding hands, she asked Miller, "How did you like my uncle?"

Miller replied, "Okay, as far as uncles go, I guess. His English was good." Because of Irena's reaction around her uncle, Miller thought he'd better just go with the lukewarm review. He changed the subject. "I brought three great movies for us to watch while we are here." Miller had picked them up at one of the many bootleg VCR movie kiosks in Moscow.

She laughed before she spoke. "I hope you brought some erotica, Slav," she said as she squeezed his butt playfully.

"You bet I did, my Russian beauty," he replied. Irena liked it when he called her his Russian beauty. He continued, "I also brought *Doctor Zhivago*."

She interrupted, "I have heard of that one. I have not seen, though."

He continued, "Also *A Christmas Story*."

She interrupted again. "Is that the one where the stupid kid gets his tongue stuck to the frozen flagpole?"

"Yes," he answered.

"Good. I like that one. And the last?" she asked.

"*The Adventures of Robin Hood*. This one stars Errol Flynn, not the one with Kevin Costner. I think you will like it," he said, knowing she liked adventure and love stories.

Irena asked, "Who is this Errol Flynn? I have not heard of him, Slav."

Miller became animated and replied, "He was the greatest swashbuckler of the 1930s, '40s, and '50s to ever hit the silver screen. When I was a boy growing up, I would have gladly traded my Schwinn Typhoon bicycle, my Ron Santo autograph baseball mitt, and my hockey skates if I could be Robin Hood like Errol Flynn."

Irena laughed. She pulled out her Russian/English dictionary and looked at it for a moment and said, "I do not find this swashbuckler word, Slav. What does it mean?"

Miller answered," Do you know what adventurer means?"

"Of course, I do," she replied.

"Great, because I do not want a bonehead for a girlfriend," he laughed.

Irena looked at her dictionary, fumbled through the pages and stopped, then read out loud, "Bonehead meaning: fool...halfwit...dunce."

She pretended to be angry with him, and he blocked a playful hit over his head and a punch to the stomach. A few minutes later, they found themselves in front of the apartment. Miller and Irena walked up the stairs and into their flat.

Natasha was still at the Angara Club, sitting at the bar talking with a young Russian punk rock girl. She was eighteen and had tattoos, pink spiked hair, and a gold nose ring. Natasha thought she was sexy and invited her to dance. This was not unusual for straight women to do in Russia. Her name was Zhanna. She was wearing a white tank top with a plunging neckline and no bra. Her breasts had a nice wiggle when she walked. Natasha could see her nipples were pierced and wondered what else might be. After about three dances, Natasha asked Zhanna if she wanted to go to the Irish bar down the street. Zhanna agreed. As they walked out onto the street, Natasha grabbed Zhanna's hand, pulled her close, and kissed her.

Zhanna kissed her back and asked, "Do you have a place we can go?"

Natasha smiled. "Yes, I do, my little cherry. I think you need to be popped."

Zhanna laughed as she replied, "You bet I do, you old slut."

Natasha laughed with her, then grabbed her hand, leading her to the Belgrade.

After dinner, Bo ended up at The Gulag. He was there sucking up Jack and Cokes like a sponge. He stumbled up to the juke box and pushed F-7. A few seconds later, Merle Haggard's "Tonight the Bottle Let Me Down" started blasting out of the speakers, and Beecher started to sing along. He got back to his roost at the bar, and as he did, his phone rang. He pulled it out and answered, "Hello."

A flirty voice on the other end said, "Hello, Mr. Bo. How is your cock? Does it need some extra attention?" She laughed.

"Natasha, it's late," he slurred.

"You get over here now, sissy boy. I have a surprise for you," she demanded.

Bo tried to protest, but he was no match for her. He called a taxi and made his way to the Belgrade. As he got to Natasha's room, the door was slightly ajar. He pushed it open and he saw some pink-haired young girl lying on her back with her legs up and spread apart. He squinted then he recognized the back of Natasha's head between them. When Bo closed the door with a thud, Natasha looked up and said, "It's about time you got here, sissy boy. Now take out your golden staff and get over here. You better know what to do with it, or Mommy will have to punish you." The vision and message gave Bo a second wind as he moved toward the girls.

☭

After Bo got back to his room, he took a shower. It was 4:00 in the morning, and he planned to sleep until noon. Just before he went to bed, he got down on his knees at the foot of it and said, "Please God, have mercy on me and heal me of my perverted desires." He said this several times, and then more times, until it became a mantra. At the same time, he slapped his face, alternating between the left and right hands. He started out slow until he worked himself up into a frenzy and continued for a minute or two, then slowed until he finally stopped. His face was red and blotchy as he got up from his knees, crawled into bed, and went to sleep.

A sermon one Sunday at Bo's church was titled "The Mortification of the Flesh." The minister explained the term comes from the Book of Romans: "For if you live according to the flesh you will die, but if by the Spirit you put to death the deeds of the body you will live. Put to death what is earthly in you: fornication, impurity, passion, evil desire, and covetousness." Support for such behavior was found in the Old Testament as well: "Blows that wound, cleanse away evil; strokes make clean the inner most parts." As far as Bo was concerned, sexual activities that were for desire or enjoyment and not only for procreation were evil. To deal with the guilt feelings or sins within his heart, the religious purgation had become the ritual after an unorthodox tryst with

Natasha. The purging had been his penance, but with few results. He could not control his impulses with her. On the other hand, Natasha believed there were no sins of the flesh. If the appetite was there, it was to be enjoyed by the right of being a human being.

Miller and Irena planned to go to the Arbat and walk around to enjoy the goings-on. The Arbat, as it was called, was a one-kilometer pedestrian street in the historical district, near the city center and Kremlin. It is one of the oldest streets in Moscow, dating back to the 15th century. Both poet Alexander Pushkin and novelist Leo Tolstoy owned houses there in the 1800s. Now, the Arbat was a favorite place for Muscovites to stroll, soak up the atmosphere, and enjoy the entertainment. There were jugglers, artists of all types, restaurants, and shops. Just walking around and observing was very entertaining.

As they walked out of their apartment and down the stairs, about halfway down Miller said, "Irena, I forgot my wallet. I will be right back."

"I will wait for you outside, Slav," she answered. Miller ran up the stairs, located his wallet, and ran back down the stairs and outside to where Irena was waiting. Her back was facing him, and she was standing funny. As he walked on up to the front of her, he could see her tongue was stuck on a frozen metal fence post. Miller laughed and laughed. He ran back to their apartment and retrieved a glass of warm water and freed his sore-tongued companion.

Irena spoke first. "Don't say anything, Slav."

He replied, "My lips are sealed, my Russian beauty."

Miller knew he got a lot of mileage out of the "Russian beauty" phrase and used it often in touchy situations. This was one of those.

Today, Karlov was relaxing. He had slept in until 8:00 a.m. and was sitting down at his kitchen table, having coffee. He was looking at the view of Moscow from his 19th-floor apartment's kitchen window. He could see the Moscow River and the Russian White House. The major remembered the failed coup attempt in '91 which he had been part of. He got up and walked to the door of his apartment. He opened the door and picked up the newspaper lying on the floor in the hallway. Karlov retreated back to the kitchen table, sat, sipped his coffee, and began reading the paper. When he finished his coffee, he got up for another cup. As he did, his phone rang.

"Major Karlov," he answered.

On the line he heard, "Dimitry, you old Bolshevik. How are you?"

Karlov replied, "Yuri, you old hardliner. Are you calling me from one of your torture rooms? Who is your guest this morning, Comrade?"

Yuri responded, smiling, "It will be you if you continue with this insolence, Bolshevik." They both laughed together, and Yuri spoke again. "How is your beautiful wife Tanya, Dimitry?"

Karlov answered, "She is fine. She has been in Kiev, visiting her mother. Yuri, I heard you were coming to Moscow. When will you be here?"

Yuri replied, "I am here now, and I need to see you. Can we meet for lunch?"

Karlov was delighted. "Of course, old friend."

Yuri Belevich was the major's oldest friend. They both studied law at Saint Petersburg State University and graduated in 1971. After graduation, both joined the KGB and trained at the 401st KGB school in Okhta, Leningrad. After training, they were both assigned to the Second Chief Directorate (counterintelligence unit). The main objective of the Second Chief Directorate was compromising embassies and the foreigners that worked for them. The major had been a part of this unit for twenty-five years. Yuri was transferred after ten years to the First Chief Directorate. The First Chief Directorate conducted intelligence operations overseas. Yuri was assigned to the Saint Petersburg district and Karlov was assigned to the Moscow district. Yuri actually dated Tanya before Karlov. Karlov either stole her heart, or Yuri broke it off with her. There seemed to be some disagreement regarding the actual events between the two. Yuri married another woman not long after the break-up.

In 1991, Yuri resigned from the KGB with the rank of lieutenant colonel to get involved with politics. Now, five years later, he was the current president's senior aide and one of the more powerful under-the-radar leaders in Russia. Yuri intimidated most, but not Dimitry Karlov. He was the closest thing to a brother the major had. They chose the Café Pushkin, named after the Russian poet, for lunch and would meet at one. Yuri liked the borsht there.

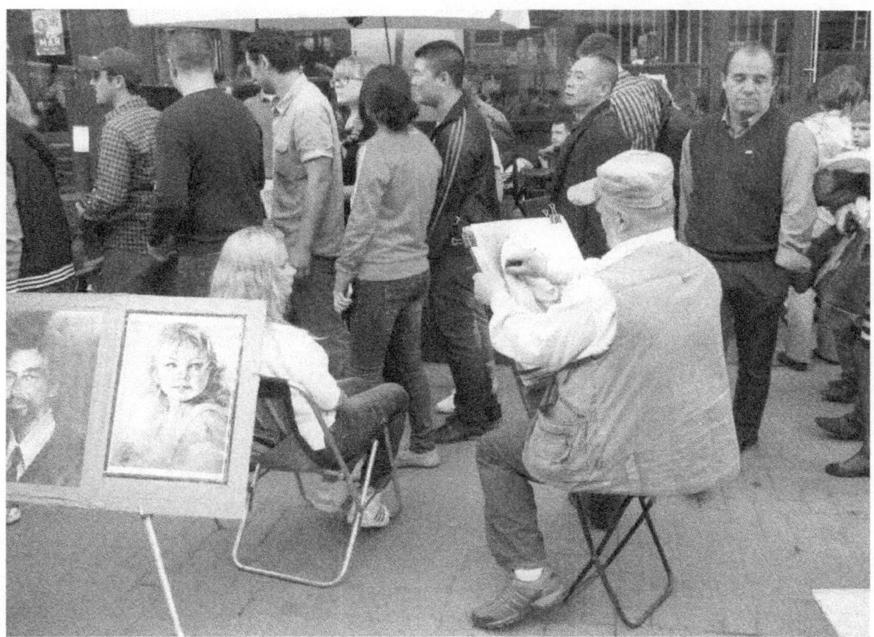

Artist on Arbat Street 2014.

Miller and Irena were slowly walking down the Arbat, taking in the sights. They stopped by a group of artists who were doing portraits for people on the street. Miller saw one of the artists had just finished a little girl and thought the portrait was very good. He pointed this out to Irena and suggested she have her portrait done.

She replied, "No, Slav. He will make me look fat."

Miller answered, laughing, "No problem. We will just tell him to make you look skinny."

"Only if we do it together," she said. The artist was willing, so they sat together on a small bench and he got to work. When he was through, Miller thought it looked good. Irena thought the artist made her nose look too big. He touched it up to her satisfaction and sprayed the portrait with a clear acrylic. Miller paid him the $5 he was asking, and the artist rolled it up and put a rubber band around it. He suggested they buy a frame for it down the street. When they found the frame guy, he looked suspiciously like the artist's brother. Miller paid for a frame, and the two of them continued on.

As they walked, Miller saw a sign written in Japanese along with English letters spelling "Evrasia Restaurant." Miller said, "Look, Irena, a Japanese restaurant. Do you like Japanese food?"

She replied, "I do not like raw fish, Slav."

He answered, "They have other things."

She reluctantly agreed to give it a try. They went in and sat down. The waitress brought green tea and the menus. Miller thought she was Mongolian or from Kazakhstan. Miller and Irena ordered box lunches that consisted of shrimp tempura, mixed sea vegetables, baked salmon, a small lettuce and tomato salad, rice, and three California rolls.

"I like this, Slav," Irena said. "It's a nice change from meat and potatoes all the time."

Miller answered, "I understand there is also a Thai restaurant around here somewhere. We will have to try that sometime."

When the waitress came back, Miller ordered a small carafe of sake. When the sake came, it was warmed to perfection. Irena took a large sip. She liked the way it warmed her body all the way to her toes.

Major Karlov was just sitting down in the atrium at Café Pushkin. He ordered a bottle of Tsarskaya (pronounced Czar-Sky-Ah) vodka iced in a champagne bucket. This is the way he and Yuri had ordered there Tsarskaya in Saint Petersburg over twenty years earlier. Sergeant Dudnik, who had been their counter-intelligence instructor at the KGB training school, had showed them this little exercise. He would tell his students, "When you are courting a fly at a restaurant who is a target, it is best to have some honey, fly paper, and perhaps even a fly swatter, depending on the occasion." He explained that an ice bucket at the table was common and usually would not cause suspicion. With it, you had a place to hide something you might need close at a meeting. A waiter could be instructed beforehand on what to insert, such as a small bomb made to look like a cube of ice, an ice pick, a pen gun, or an ampoule of polonium-210. He explained the Tsarskaya was the honey, the ice pick or pen gun was the fly paper, the bomb or polonium-210 the fly swatters.

The Kostka Ledu Bombe, or Ice Cube Bomb, was developed by Czech Professor Bolek Bozik for the Russians in 1970. The KGB had found this device quite useful in counter-intelligence operations. Once Yuri had the assignment to eliminate a high party official if he refused to negotiate. The official was making waves and planned to expose others who were taking bribes in a Saint Petersburg district. When the pair were having lunch to discuss the matter, Yuri simply ordered the iced Tsarskaya. Beforehand, the waiter installed what looked like a plastic ice cube at the bottom of the bucket. When in place, these bombs were virtually undetectable.

They each had a glass of Tsarskaya and ordered dinner. When the official refused hush money, Yuri told him, "Thank you, Comrade. We had to make sure you were incorruptible. You are a patriot to Mother Russia. A toast to you, sir."

They finished lunch and had several more glasses. Yuri excused himself to use the toilet. Once inside the water closet, Yuri used the urinal and washed his hands. After he had finished, he pulled a remote-control device from his vest pocket and casually pushed the red button. Yuri felt the shudder of the blast, smiled, and said to himself, "Give my regards to Leon Trotsky, Comrade."

Yuri simply walked out the back door of the restaurant and back to his office. The official account of the incident was a mafia hit on a corrupt and misguided party official. His wife and daughter were sent to the gulag, where they would later die from inadequate nourishment and exposure. Yuri received a promotion after the incident.

As the waiter set up the ice bucket and vodka, Major Karlov smiled. After the waiter finished, Yuri arrived and greeted the major. "Hello, Dimitry. I see you have ordered the honey. I hope there is no fly swatter in the bucket this afternoon, my old friend." They both laughed.

☭

After the Japanese lunch, Miller and Irena continued their walk. Miller pulled out a Cohiba and lit up.

"Do you have to smoke those stinky things, Slav?" Irena asked.

"My Russian beauty, is it your intent to deprive me of this simple pleasure?" he asked, smiling.

She compromised and said, "Okay, Slav. Just outside, and never in the apartment except on the balcony."

"Agreed," he replied. As Irena turned, two Russian teens came out of nowhere and grabbed her handbag. Miller blinked, then went after them. The teen boys split up, and JT followed after the one with the bag. When Miller started gaining, the youth tossed the bag. Miller retrieved it and brought the bag back to Irena. She checked, and nothing seemed to be missing.

"Spasibo—er, thank you, Slav. I did not know you could run so fast. Stupid kids," Irena said, a little shaken.

Miller replied, "Well, no harm done, my Russian princess. Let's just enjoy the rest of the day." Irena liked it when he called her his Russian princess. She could not decide what she liked better, to be called Russian beauty or Russian princess. *Either one*, she thought. As they walked, the couple decided that it would be nice to go to Gorky Park and watch the skaters. They made their way to the Arbatskya metro station and boarded the train.

☭

Karlov and Yuri were enjoying each other's company as they sipped their vodka and reminisced. As they ate lunch, Karlov wondered what Yuri wanted to discuss with him. He would not have long to wonder, as Yuri asked, "Major, how are you coming with your assignment on recruiting the American fish?"

Karlov was surprised by the question. A person as high as Yuri was in the government would not normally be informed of or involved with this routine KGB mission. Karlov answered, "Things are going according to plan, Yuri. Why do you ask?"

Yuri fingered his vodka glass and said, "Dimitry, this operation has been given high priority. We must accomplish this mission and our tainted vault door must be installed. We must not fail. We need to accomplish this by the beginning of August. Will this be a problem, my friend?"

Karlov thought a moment before he answered, "I believe it is possible, Yuri. The only miscalculation that could occur in the equation is the time frame the Americans intend to install the door."

Yuri took a sip of vodka and swallowed before he replied, "We have intelligence that the Americans are planning high-level meetings sometime in September. It is our assumption the Americans will want this new door in place before the meetings."

Karlov replied, "Well then, we will have to get the new door specifications, so it can be fabricated. We will have to move a little faster on the American fish than I would have liked, but not impossible."

Yuri looked into the eyes of his old friend and said, "The Americans will purchase the vault door from one of two companies, Rex Technology or North Plains Industries. In either case both companies will sell these same vault doors to banks, usually for rooms that house safety deposit boxes. Now the National Bank of Moscow, of which I am on the board of directors, is planning a remodel of several of these rooms. If we can get the specifications of the door the Americans plan to use, we can order this same door through one of our American shell companies and have it legally shipped to Moscow with no one being the wiser. We can then do the needed modifications. There would be less chance of detection during inspection and installation if we used the exact door the Americans are using instead of having a Russian manufacturer try to duplicate one. How to switch the untainted door with the tainted one will still have to be worked out."

Dimitry thought before answering, "Yes, Yuri. That would work. What are your ideas on how to get this information from the American fish?"

Yuri did not hesitate and replied, "You set up a casual meeting at a restaurant or bar with the fish. I just happen to be there as well; you invite me to sit down. When you introduce the fish to me, you say he is a building engineer working on the embassy, I bring up the vault doors for our bank remodel and ask for his help on choosing the correct door for our purposes. I then ask him nonchalantly about the door he will be using and if this door would fit our purposes as well. If it does, I ask for the model number. This is when I tell him Russian vault doors are of inferior quality and so on and so forth. I will also hint the bank is willing to pay a finder's fee. If we can get the fish to provide us the information and take the money, we will have him. He can either cooperate all the way or he can spend the rest of his years in a US prison for the crime of treason."

The major smiled and asked, "And after we are finished with our fish?" Yuri poured another glass from the iced bottle and said, "Just like with a fly that has become a nuisance, the fly swatter is the only choice, my friend."

They both laughed, held up their glasses, then drained the last of the Tsarskaya.

☭

Miller and Irena got off at the Oktyabrskya metro station and walked the rest of the way to the park. As they approached the skating rink, just like the one at the Kremlin, it had loudspeakers playing classical music for the skaters' enjoyment. As the music floated through the air, Miller listened and knew he had heard this particular selection before but could not place it. As he listened, his thoughts spread out to his growing up in Evanston, Illinois and Saint Mary's School, where he went to grade school. Every year, the nuns would hire Dr. Zipper's Orchestra to play for all the students in the auditorium. This was always looked on as a great treat. There was one particular selection that was very popular with the students and the nuns, as well. Miller could not remember the name, but it was playing over the speakers at that moment.

He turned and asked Irena, while pointing to the speakers, "Do you know the name of this music, Irena?"

She answered, "Slav, you do not know the name of this? This music is very famous."

Miller stopped her and replied, "Just give me a hint."

Irena smiled and said, "Okay, the first word has five letters."

Miller started laughing, "Great clue, Irena. Come on, give me a better clue than that."

Irena thought. She put down her bag and put up her hands like she was clawing something. Then she started to growl pathetically.

Miller watched her and scratched his head, then asked, "What the hell are you doing, Irena?"

She answered, "This is a very good clue, Slav. Quit being so dense. I am pretending to be an animal. The animal's name is in the title of this music."

He replied, "Nice. Go on." She continued her wimpy growl and clawing. He said, "I know...I know--a dog."

She yelled, "Slav, how can you be so dumb? I am not a dog!"

As she continued to protest, it came to him and he said, "I am only teasing, my Russian beauty. As an actress, you are without compare. A better interpretation of a wolf I have never seen." She started to smile, and he continued, "The name of the piece is 'Peter and the Wolf.'"

She replied, "You got it, Slav. It was written by Russian composer Sergei Prokofiev. You are not as dumb as you look."

They both laughed, and he gave her a hug.

CHAPTER FOUR

THE FISH FRY

New Year's Eve was a very important event in Moscow. The city would be abuzz with revelers at the stroke of midnight and beyond. Most of the construction team would be celebrating at the Angara Club. Miller and Irena planned to be there, as well. Miller invited Sveta, Irena's mother, out with them. Everyone was looking forward to another night of merriment followed up with a day off—much better than the alternative of a night of merriment with no day off. Irena had been keeping Karlov informed. Irena did not feel good about this. She was really starting to like this Miller, and she felt she was betraying him. She tried to rationalize it and thought, *There has been no harm in informing the major. He just wants to know what's going on. He will not hurt Miller. If I do not inform him, it may put my family in danger*. Irena felt trapped. She hated Karlov for making her do this. She hated herself for not having a choice.

Karlov was at his desk in his office. He picked up the phone, dialed, and listened to the ringing on the other end. On the fourth ring, he heard a click, and then a voice. "Yuri Belevich."

The major spoke into the phone. "Dobre utra, Yuri."

Yuri smiled and answered, "Ah, dobre utra, my friend. What can I do for you, Dimitry? Do you have something for me?"

The major responded, "Yes, Yuri. It is about the American fish. The fish fry will be on New Year's Eve at the Angara Club."

Yuri replied, "Very good, Dimitry. This will be an excellent time to have the fish in the pan."

Yuri and Karlov went over the details. They would both bring their wives, not only because it was New Year's and the wives would expect it, but also to keep the fish off the scent.

Irena had been teaching her mother English. Sveta was a fast study and was making progress. Knowing English was quite popular in Russia, and learning it made Sveta feel she was hep with the jive. Miller was on his way over to Sveta's apartment and the three of them would walk to the night club. Irena warned her mother that Major Karlov would be there posing as her uncle on her dad's side. Sveta understood and would play along. In her mind, she was damning Karlov and the hold he had on them.

Harry was having a drink at The Gulag. He was waiting for Kurt and Charlie and the wives. Their driver was already outside waiting, as well. When the couples appeared, Harry finished his drink and the five of them walked out to the van and drove away. As Miller walked out of the housing units and out onto the sidewalk, he saw the van leave with his colleagues. He crossed the street and down the alley to Irena's apartment. He rang the bell and was buzzed in. As he walked the stairs to the apartment, Irena and Sveta met him. He kissed them both and told them how nice they looked. He walked with Irena on his right arm and Sveta on his left. Miller walked this way, not just being chivalrous, but because there were ice patches all over and it could be quite slippery when walking. They arrived at the Angara Club and passed through the metal detector and the Russian goon squad. He took their coats and checked them at the cloak room and received the stubs. He put them in his pocket and escorted the women in.

He saw Harry and the others at a table. He led the women over and made the introductions for Sveta. Harry pulled a chair out for her next to his own and she plopped down. Miller and Irena sat opposite them, across the table. Nadine sat next to Sveta and Kurt next to her. Kathy sat next to Miller and Charlie beside her. Charlie already looked three sheets to the wind. He was drinking straight vodka on the rocks. Kathy had asked him to slow down a bit. The night was still young, and she knew that at his present pace, he would be passed out before midnight. Telling a construction guy to slow down was like telling a Republican to vote yes on gun control or the scorpion not to sting the frog. It ain't gonna happen, because it is not in their nature. Sveta looked around the table at all the strange faces. She was a bit nervous, but a few vodkas would take care of that, she thought.

Harry ordered another round of drinks. Sveta and the others thanked Harry, and she sipped her drink. Sveta looked nice. She had on a short green skirt with nylons and stylish black winter boots that came up to just below the knee. The nylons were to keep her legs somewhat warmer during the Moscow winter. Short skirts were the style for Russian women of all ages. Sveta and Irena had similar features. They wore their hair the same and had the same eyes. Sveta was four inches shorter and maybe looked just a bit heavier than Irena. At forty-five years old, she still had a nice shape and retained a certain amount of youthful exuberance.

Irena excused herself to go to the ladies' room. As she did, Nadine and Kathy went with her. Kurt wondered why women always went to the toilet together, almost like it was their duty. If one of them went, they all had to. Kurt figured Sveta wasn't tapped into the ladies' room thing, because she just sat there next to Harry, sipping her vodka. When her glass was empty, Harry noticed and ordered her another. After the drinks, Sveta felt more relaxed. She thought she would practice her English on Harry.

She smiled at Harry and asked, "Mr. Harry, how do you like living here in Moscow? Is it so much different than living in America?"

Harry thought a minute and answered, "I think the metro in Moscow is great. It covers the city very well. I also like the historical aspects of Moscow. Places like the Kremlin, Saint Basil's, the Arbat, and the old churches. I have also observed something interesting. When I take the metro, I have noticed about 80% of the people on the train are reading books. In America, you might see about 2% reading books. The others are gazing at magazines, comic books, listening to music on headphones, just looking ahead, or staring out the window."

Sveta understood most of what Harry said but not all. She asked, "Have you ever read Tolstoy, Mr. Harry?"

Harry said, "Yes, in high school. *War and Peace* was required reading for English class."

Sveta answered, "Oh yes, that is his most famous book. My favorite is *Anna Karenina*."

Harry smiled, thinking back when he had to read *War and Peace*. He had to rely mostly on Cliff's Notes to pass the exam. For Harry, the book was not exactly a page-turner.

The ladies returned from their pit stop. Irena had been looking for Karlov but had not as yet seen him. She hoped he would not show up, but she knew that was unlikely. Harry asked the waiter for menus. He passed them around and when the waiter returned, the group ordered. The band had started playing, and a few couples were on the dance floor.

After dinner, the group ordered more drinks. Then Irena's stomach turned sour the instant she saw him. Karlov was walking in with another man and two women. Yuri and Karlov looked quite dapper. Tanya, the major's wife, had put on a few pounds over the years. She was about the same age as her husband and had bottle-blonde hair cut short. She was wearing a black dress topped off with a brown fox stole. The animal's feet draped down on one side and the head on the other. It looked as if it was still alive. Yuri's wife Vladlina was just the opposite. She was very thin, maybe five years younger than Tanya, and was a redhead. She chose a burgundy dress and not to be outdone, she donned a white fox stole with the same feet and head configurations.

As they entered, Irena's heart stopped. She had not met any of the others but had a good guess as to who they might be. She thought it best to present herself to Karlov and his companions before Miller was aware. After, she would invite the Slav to their table. Irena leaned over and asked Miller for her coat check ticket. She used the excuse that she left her ID in her coat and was worried it might get lost. Miller reached into his pocket and gave her the ticket. Irena started to walk to the cloak room and just before she got there veered off and went to Karlov's table.

"Hello, my dear. So nice to see you," the major greeted her.

"Hello, Uncle," she replied.

The major continued, "Irena, I do not believe you have met my wife. This is Tanya—everybody, this is my niece Irena."

Irena greeted everyone; then Yuri replied, "Nice to meet you, Irena. I am Yuri, and this is my wife Vladlina. Dimitry speaks very highly of you."

Tanya knew the drill. She understood the word "niece" was a code word for operative, more commonly known, as one of her husband's sparrows. She had met several other "nieces" over the years.

Karlov asked, "Irena, please invite your friend Mr. Miller to join us. We would so enjoy the pleasure of your company."

Irena knew this request was in fact an order. She excused herself from the table and walked back to Miller. He was talking to Harry and sipping a fresh gin and tonic when Irena walked up and sat down. She waited until she could talk to him and said, "Slav, Uncle Ivan is here with his wife and some friends. They would like us to join them for a while."

Miller answered, "Sure, Irena. Harry, we will be back in a few minutes."

Harry nodded. Miller grabbed his drink and left hand in hand with Irena. When they arrived at Karlov's table, Miller spoke first. "Hello, Ivan. Nice to see you again."

"The feeling is mutual, Mr. Miller. I would like to introduce you to my wife Tanya, my friend Yuri Belevich, and his wife Vladlina."

After the pleasantries, Karlov whispered something to his wife in Russian, and a few minutes later she and Vladlina excused themselves for the water closet. After they left, Yuri asked, "Well, Mr. Miller, what brings you to Moscow?"

Miller replied, "I am a construction engineer working on a new building. And yourself, Mr. Belevich?"

Yuri answered, "I studied law in my youth but got into business. I have been involved in several ventures over the years in the oil and gas industry. This is where I first met Ivan. Now I am on the board of directors at the Bank of Moscow."

Miller asked, "Have you and Ivan known each other long?"

Yuri replied, "Well, let me think. Ivan, how long has it been?"

Karlov responded, "We met at the Zhanazhol field in Kazakhstan in 1975. Isn't that right, Yuri? We worked for Kazpac Oil and Gas. I as a petroleum engineer and Yuri as a contracts specialist. We were both young and hungry, so Yuri had this crazy idea that we go in together and pick up land lease options around this field from the local landowners. This was done with a modest up-front fee, but in the future the owner would receive a 10% royalty of any oil or gas revenue harvested from their land. Yuri and I would receive 20% and the oil company the remainder. As the Zhanazhol field expanded, as we knew it would, so did our success."

Miller replied, "What a great story. What happened after that?"

Karlov continued, "I continued working with Kazpac and then other oil and gas companies. For a short time, I worked for a small American company called American International Petroleum, also in Kazakhstan. After Perestroika and a freer market ensued, Yuri got into Moscow real estate. Did I leave anything out, Yuri?"

Yuri answered, "I think you got the basics, my friend."

Irena stayed quiet, and Miller started to like these guys. Yuri could sense that the made-up story broke the ice. He and Karlov calculated this and knew an American could not resist a rags-to-riches story.

Yuri began the probe. "Mr. Miller, you said you were a building engineer?"

JT thought building engineer was close enough for horseshoes and replied, "Yes, Yuri, but please call me JT."

Yuri took the plunge. "JT, I have a question that you may be able to help me with."

Miller replied, "I will try."

Yuri continued, "As I have mentioned, I am on the board of directors for The Bank of Moscow. At about half of our branches, we will be constructing new rooms that will house lockers for depositor valuables. In

English, I believe they are referred to as safety deposit boxes. These safety deposit boxes will be state of the art, built with blast-proof materials, and the room will be protected with a vault door. The Russian vault doors available are good, but they are only available in manual operation. We need vault doors that have electronic locking mechanisms. Is this something you are familiar with?"

Miller answered, "I am sorry, Yuri. I am not. There is one vault door we will be installing in the building I am working on, but I really do not know much about them as a whole."

Yuri tried to close the deal. "JT, I wonder if it would be possible to get the information on the door and manufacturer your company will be using. I could relay this information to our designers and see if it would be a good fit for our banks."

Miller answered, "I don't know offhand, Yuri, but I could check for you."

Yuri finished, "Thank you, JT. If our designers approve, there may be a consultant fee in it for you."

With that, Tanya and Vladlina came back to the table. Irena pinched Miller's leg but did not make eye contact. He took the hint. He stood up and took Irena's hand and said, "Very nice meeting all of you. We really must get back to our friends now."

Karlov responded, "Thank you for visiting with us. Happy New Year to you both."

Irena replied, "Goodbye, Uncle, and Happy New Year to you."

JT and Irena returned to Harry and the others. "Harry, you gonna eat those onion rings?" Miller asked.

"Hell no. That stuff plugs up my pipes. Go ahead," Harry answered.

Miller grabbed a ring and so did Irena. Miller checked the time and saw it was about twenty minutes to midnight.

Bo and Natasha finally showed up and walked to the bar. Earlier they were at another popular nightclub in Moscow called Night Flight on Tverskaya Street, spending Bo's money. Bo ordered two bottles of champagne and extra champagne glasses. The bartender put the order on a tray and carried it, following Bo, to his colleagues' table.

Bo and Natasha greeted everyone, and Natasha said, "We thought it would be fun to open these at midnight."

Harry answered, "Nice gesture, Natasha. Bo, I hope you sprang for the good stuff."

Bo replied, "I got the only brand they had."

Miller picked up a bottle and looked at it and read the label, "So-vet-sko-ye Sham-pan-sko-ye. How bad could it be, with a photo of Vladmir Lenin on the label?"

Natasha laughed a little bit too loud, and Irena noted it. "You are quite right, Mr. Miller. The English name is Soviet Champagne. Perhaps you will help me open one of these bottles at midnight?" Natasha asked.

"I would be glad to," JT replied. Just then, the countdown began. Thirty, twenty-nine, twenty-eight . . . . Miller picked up one of the bottles and handed it to Irena. Ten, nine, eight . . . . Natasha started to jockey her position closer to JT, Irena noticed. Three, two, one.... "HAPPY NEW YEAR!" everyone roared.

Natasha popped open her champagne bottle and a stream of foamy champagne went all over the place while Irena was still fingering hers. Everybody began kissing and hugging each other, as was the custom. Sveta kissed Harry, Kurt and Charlie their wives. No one was feeling any pain. Natasha moved into position and grabbed hold of Miller. As she kissed him, she let her hands slip down to his rear end and gave it a subtle squeeze. Irena saw this, and red obstructed her vision. She aimed her champagne cork at the back of Natasha's head and with her thumbs, popped the cork. At this close range the projectile created a thud at impact, and Natasha went down.

Miller caught her and sat her in one of the chairs. He took a cloth napkin from the table and wrapped some ice in it that he retrieved from someone's finished drink glass. He motioned to Bo to hold the ice pack on the back of Natasha's head. Because of the ruckus celebration, no one saw Irena's deed transpire, except for Miller.

He grabbed her hand and led her away from the table and asked, "Irena, why did you do that?"

She answered, "She put her hands on your bottom, Slav. I did not like that. She is a slut, and I do not like her."

Instead of scolding her, he took her in his arms and said, "Happy New Year, my love," and kissed her. Miller thought it best to beat it, and with everyone preoccupied, he snuck out with Irena. When out on the street, they walked to Arbatskaya metro station and headed to their apartment.

☭

Karlov and Yuri watched Miller and Irena leave. They congratulated each other on their performance. Karlov asked, "Well, Yuri, do you think we spiders will catch the fly?"

Yuri answered, "We shall see, Dimitry. Sometimes a subject is like an ant following its path. Most ants follow the path, but a few veer off. We shall see what type of ant our fly is, my old friend."

With that, both men escorted their wives out of the club.

☭

As Irena and Miller got off the metro at their stop and out onto the street, they could feel the temperature dropping. They walked fast to their apartment. When they got inside, Irena said, "It is cold in here, Slav."

Miller already had the cue and was opening the valve on the radiator, letting more steam in for extra heat. There was no thermostat. They washed their faces, brushed their teeth, and went to bed. As Miller lay there, he thought about the reaction at work from the champagne cork incident. He thought Irena was in the clear but was not sure. He thought about Irena's uncle and his friend from the Moscow bank. He made a note that he would speak with Vera, the SSM, about this. He thought Sveta and Harry were getting a bit friendly and smiled to himself. He knew Harry would see her home. *That sly old dog*, he thought, then started to drift asleep. Just before he dropped off, he was suddenly awoken by what sounded like a motorcycle in the apartment. He thought he was dreaming. He opened his eyes and saw Irena lying flat on her back, snoring like a chainsaw. He got up and gently laid her on her side. She stopped immediately, and Miller went to sleep.

☭

Harry and the others were getting ready to leave the Angara Club. Harry realized Miller and Irena were missing in action, and he had become responsible for getting Sveta home. As Sveta stood up, Harry asked, "Sveta, may we see you home? I have not seen Irena or JT around for a while. I think they may have left."

Sveta smiled and replied, "Thank you, Mr. Harry, but I will walk. Thank you for a lovely evening."

Harry protested, "Sveta, it is not safe for you to walk alone, and it is very cold tonight."

Sveta laughed and said, "Mr. Harry, it is okay. I will be fun...fine...I will be fine."

Harry thought a moment, then told Kurt and the others to go along without him. He walked up to Sveta and offered her his arm. She looked at him and asked, "Are you sure, Mr. Harry?"

Harry put on his most chivalrous tone and replied, "Madam, I would not have it any other way."

Arm in arm, the couple walked down the stairs and out onto the street. As they walked, Sveta asked Harry if he was married. Harry told her no. He said he tried marriage a couple of times before, but neither of them worked out.

She asked, "Why is that, Mr. Harry?"

Harry thought a moment and answered, "I think it has something to do with me not being at home much. I was always working on some project in another country somewhere. But to be fair, most of the time when I would come home, I could hardly wait to leave again. I guess maybe I was not cut out for marriage."

Sveta replied, "Mr. Harry, you just need to stay home more and find a good girl."

Harry said, "No argument there, Sveta. What about you and Irena's father? What happened to him?"

Sveta told him the whole sordid tale. The metro, the opposition party, and the bomb. Harry wasn't sure how to respond, so he kept walking, then finally replied, "Well, it is what it is. It's all in the past. Our job now is to live the best we can with the time we have left."

Sveta smiled and took Harry's hand. They found themselves in front of Sveta's apartment building. Sveta informed Harry of that fact. Harry said, "Well, good night, Sveta. Thank you for celebrating New Year's with us."

Sveta replied, "Thank you for walking me home, Mr. Harry. Would you like to come up for coffee?"

Harry thought a moment and answered, "On one condition."

She asked, "And what is that, Mr. Harry?"

Mr. Harry replied, "Stop calling me Mr. Harry. Just Harry will be fine."

Sveta laughed and said, "It is a deal, Mr.—um, Harry."

Harry smiled, and the couple walked up for some coffee.

Bo had hailed a taxi, and he and Natasha climbed inside. They were heading to the Belgrade. Natasha rubbed the back of her head and asked angrily, "Mr. Bo! You did not see who hit me with the cork? What are you, blind? I know you are protecting Irena. I know she was the one."

Bo answered, "No one saw where the cork came from, Natasha. Harry thinks it came from the table behind us. They had about four bottles of champagne and were popping corks left and right. It was an accident."

Natasha was not buying it and replied, "That is manure. Irena tried to hit me on purpose."

Bo looked annoyed and said, "Natasha, that is ridiculous. Why would she do that?"

Natasha rubbed her head again and looked angry. "Because she is jealous. She thinks I want her Miller."

Bo had noticed Natasha getting kind of close to Miller and saw her kiss him and the probing hands near his backside. He took it in stride and just blamed it on the booze and New Year's antics. It was possible, he thought, but right now there was no proof.

"It was just an accident. Forget about it," he said.

They pulled up to the Belgrade and Bo started to get out. Natasha was angry and gave him a look like he was a black guy sitting down at some southern whites- only lunch counter in the 1950s.

"Don't get out, you bastard. I do not want you near me tonight."

Bo slithered back into the taxi, and Natasha got out and slammed the door. Bo ordered the driver back to the embassy. The driver shook his head and asked, "What is wrong with you, Americanski? Have you not learned how to handle Russian women?"

Bo looked confused and replied asking, "What do you mean?"

The driver started to laugh and then got serious and said, "A Russian woman needs to be treated rough. The man is always the king. Occasionally, to keep them in line, they need to be beaten or at least slapped around. You must teach them to take a slap and like it. If you do not do this, a Russian woman will not respect you."

Bo thought about this, and when they were in front of the embassy, Bo told the driver, "Take me back to the Belgrade." The driver smiled and turned the taxi around.

☭

Kurt and Nadine were getting ready for bed. Nadine gargled and spat in the sink. She finished brushing her hair and lay down in bed. Kurt was already in bed reading an old copy of the *Moscow Times*.

Nadine asked, "What do you think about Harry and Sveta?"

Kurt finished a sentence he was reading, looked at her, and replied, "What do you mean, honey? She wanted to walk, and Harry graciously offered to walk with her. I think that is all there is to it."

Nadine asked slightly annoyed, "Didn't you notice how they looked at each other? You men can be so oblivious to these things. Women always notice."

Kurt had been married long enough to know not to argue the point. He put down the paper and moved close to his wife. "Good night, darling," he said and gave her a quick peck on the lips. He rolled over, pulled the covers up close, and went to sleep. Nadine was not far behind, and in a few minutes, both were in dreamland.

☭

The taxi pulled up to the front of the Belgrade. As Bo got out, the driver gave him a few words of encouragement. "Remember, Americanski, treat her rough and make her like it."

With the driver's last words ringing in his head, he walked with purpose into the Belgrade. He passed the lobby to the elevators and up to the 19th floor to 1907. Bo beat on the door with his fists. Natasha did not answer. He kicked the door for at least a minute; then he heard the fumbling of the inside lock.

Natasha opened the door and he could see the fury in her eyes. "Why, you BASTARD! Get the hell out of here, sissy boy, before I call security and--" Before she finished her last sentence, Bo took his right hand and slapped her left jaw, leaving her stunned. She started another flurry of insults. "Why, you SON OF A--" In mid-sentence Bo took his right hand and backhanded her hard on the right side of her face. She whimpered slightly, and her eyes began to water. She started to say something else, but before a word was uttered, he raised his hand again, and she stopped abruptly. He pushed his way in and closed the apartment door behind him. She stood there in front of him. Natasha was stunned and stared at him with trauma tears running down her cheeks. She saw a demonic look on Bo's face; he looked fiercely energized and fiendish.

Natasha was frightened as she looked at him. She did the only thing she knew to calm the situation and slowly removed her nightgown, revealing her almost flawless body. She then knelt down, unfastened his belt, and unzipped his trousers. Bo held her head in both hands and guided her to make his experience as pleasurable as possible. When he finished, he pulled up his trousers, tucked in his shirt, and left the apartment like a thief in the night.

Natasha lay on the floor in a somewhat fetal position and began to cry. Her body shook as she was trying to make sense of what had just happened. As she thought about the encounter and what Bo had just done, she felt violated and exhilarated at the same time. As her brain played back the events in her mind, she found her right hand as if moving by itself, on a mission, traveling to a rendezvous point between her thighs to pleasure herself. She became wet, and with a bit more coaxing her body shuddered like it had never before. After she climaxed, she stayed on the floor and went to sleep. Before she drifted off, Natasha felt as though every carnal impulse in her body had been satisfied, and she felt content.

Bo ran past the elevator on the 19th floor to the stairwell. He pushed open the door and began to run down the stairs. He had this nervous energy that had to be quenched. As he ran, he felt like he had broken some kind of law. Like he was running away from the scene of a crime. This felt exhilarating. Bo's elation grew with each floor level he descended. He started to settle down and he opened the stairwell door to the 10th floor. Bo was breathing heavily as he made it to the elevator. He took it the rest of the way down to the lobby. As the elevator doors opened, Bo emerged with a new confidence. Maybe confidence was not the right word. More of a power he never knew was in him. It was the transformation to evil or to the dark side that lives in all men that was unleashed. Like Doctor Jekyll to Mr. Hyde, or Caligula who went from moderate emperor to insane tyrant. He stopped at the bar and ordered a shot of Tsarskaya, slammed it back and ordered another. When he finished, he paid and walked calmly, with no internal conflict, back to the embassy and his apartment. This internal conflict would come later.

It was four in the morning, and Harry was walking back to the construction camp. He had spent the time with Sveta drinking coffee and talking about everything under the sun. He had thoroughly enjoyed his time with this Russian woman. She was funny, smart, and laughed a lot. As he walked, he found himself thinking about the little things. Things like how he loved the way she sipped her coffee and the way her eyes would sparkle when she laughed, the smell of her perfume, the way she gave him her undivided attention when he talked.

As he was getting up to leave and was at her door, she gave him a hug and kissed him on the cheek and said, "Good night, Harry. It was so nice making your acquaintance."

He knew she meant it. As he walked, his heart felt warmed like God was within, and Harry was no religious man. He thought how funny it was, that just 24 hours before, he did not know she even existed. He started to laugh, and as he walked up the stairs to the housing units, he found himself humming a song that was originally written in Spanish by Mexican song writer Maria Grever called, "Cuando vuelva a tu lado." The English title was popularized by Dinah Washington: "What a Difference a Day Makes."

CHAPTER FIVE

HELLO, COMRADES

The next morning, everyone slept in to recover from the night's merriment. At 11:00, Miller and Irena went to the Starlite for breakfast. The first thing they ordered were double espressos. After breakfast Miller and Irena would be going to the skating rink at the Kremlin. The rink had skate rentals, and Miller would try to find some skates that would fit. Irena had her own pair of ice skates.

At 11:15, Harry walked over to the contractors' mess hall and got some coffee. He sat down at a table in the corner and sipped his coffee. He looked at the motley crew of construction personnel, all looking bleary-eyed from the previous night's festivities. He knew most of them would stay laid up in their rooms all day. At least he hoped they would, so they would be ready for work the following morning. Harry did not mind the workers drinking, if they could handle it and it did not affect their job performance. If it did, he gave them a chance to clean up their act. If they did not, they were gone. As Harry sat there, his thoughts drifted to the night before and then to Sveta. What a great time he'd had. Harry really liked her but was not sure he should pursue it. Harry went over the cons first in his head. She was much younger

than he, she was Russian--how would a relationship with her be perceived by the USG? Would it put his job in jeopardy? Harry thought if he reported her right away and they did a background check on her and she came up clean, he would be all right. If he tried to hide the relationship, not so much. He knew if he decided to pursue it, the first thing he would do would be to report the encounter. He decided he would report it to Vera the next day then wait a few days to think about whether to pursue or not to pursue. That was Harry's question.

When Bo awoke, it was with a heavy heart. The elation he felt when he went to bed was no longer there. It was replaced by guilt and disgust. He could not believe that guy last night was really him. It completely shattered the image he had of himself. He would ask God's forgiveness like he had in the past. But then he questioned why God would allow him to behave this way. He thought, *Maybe I am evil. Maybe God has forsaken me.* Bo began to weep. He felt an agonizing pain in his gut, like there was no redemption for his soul. He started to blame her. *Why does she make me do those things?* he thought. The flesh was weak. He would have to terminate his relationship with Natasha or terminate his relationship with God.

He knew that when he did his penance this time, he would have to follow a more painful regimen. He got out of bed and looked around his apartment. He saw his pants slung over a chair and eyed the leather belt. He slid it out of the loops and wrapped the belt around his hand with the buckle floating free, with about 18 inches of slack. He then assumed his usual position and knelt down in front of his bed. With his right hand, he swung the belt and buckle around and struck hard the left side of his back. He called out in pain, "Please God, forgive me my sins and make me clean." A nice welt had formed where he struck. He struck again and uttered the same words. Then again . . . and again . . . and again.

Kremlin ice skating rink with Gum department store on right. 2016

Miller and Irena arrived at the rink. This time, a popular Russian folk singer was coming out over the speakers. They made their way to the skate rental room. Miller was looking for size 10. Irena explained to the woman in charge they were looking for size 43 or 44 hockey skates. The actual conversion to size ten was 43/44 or 43 1/2. No one ever carried that size. Either 43 or 44. The woman pointed to where the skates were placed in little wooden cubby holes attached to a wall. Miller looked at a few pairs and tried them on. There were vintage Russian hockey skates, either a little loose or fit too snug. Then he saw them--a pair of Bauer Black Panthers with a size ten stamped into the inside sole. He wondered how the Canadian hockey skates made it to Moscow. They were used but solid, and he took those. He paid the rental for the day, then went to the skate-sharpening guy and paid a buck to have the skates sharpened. The man clamped the first skate in place and expertly guided it toward the stone sharpening disk that was spinning on a wheel. He finished Miller's, then Irena's.

The couple put on their skates and joined the crowd. They skated counter- clockwise around the rink. Miller thought he would be a bit rusty, but it was like riding a bicycle. Just came naturally. He and Irena skated in and out. Occasionally Irena would go to the middle of the rink and show Miller her prowess at doing figure-skating spins. Miller was impressed. Miller also hammed it up, doing hockey moves, to Irena's glee. The couple had a great time.

"Slav, I did not know you could skate so good," she exclaimed.

He answered, "There are many things you do not know about me, my fine figure-skating beauty." She smiled. She liked it when he called her his figure-skating beauty.

"What kind of things?" she asked.

"I don't know, Irena. You know, things."

"I would not ask, if I knew, Slav. What things do I not know about?" she asked.

Miller thought, then had a eureka moment to get out of the conversation with dignity. He replied, "I am being mysterious, my darling. It is best that you discover these things over time."

"What things?" she asked.

"If I told you, sweetie, they would not be a surprise," he replied.

Irena thought, then answered, "I do not like surprises, Slav. Tell me now."

He said, "Irena, my love, you are being difficult. Let me try and explain this. Stupid things, you know, like sometimes I forget to put the cap on the toothpaste, or forget to put the toilet seat down, or sometimes I fall asleep on the couch watching TV. Nothing noteworthy, Irena, just stupid things."

"Oh, I see, Slav," she responded, and he continued, "Just things that you will discover about me and I will discover about you. Most of the time, it is a fun process getting to know another person. Like when I discovered you snore or that you love chocolate."

Irena frowned and looked at him, then asked, "What do you mean, Slav? I do not snore."

Miller was sorry he had opened his trap. He decided he was tired of going down this road with her and interjected, "Irena, let's go to Baskin-Robbins and get some ice cream."

She answered and asked, "Can I get a banana split?"

He replied, "Of course you can, my soon to be a little plump Russian beauty. Your wish is my command."

They walked over to return Miller's skates, then continued in the direction of the Arbat, where the ice cream shop was located.

Major Karlov was having coffee with his wife. She was going on and on about remodeling their apartment. She wanted it more modern. She wanted a new kitchen. She wanted new furniture. Karlov sat and listened. It went in one ear and out the other. He was thinking about Miller and whether his and Yuri's ploy would work. He thought, *Americanskis are stupid. Of course, it will work.* Then he thought, *Well, maybe not all Americanskis. Time will tell, Mr. Miller, if you are one of the smart or stupid ones.* Karlov smiled as his wife continued with her sales pitch.

Sveta and her son Alexei were walking out of Saint Andrew's church. They had just attended service and were walking toward the Arbat. As they walked, Sveta's thoughts turned to Harry. She thought what a nice man he was. It had been years since she spent an evening with a man in that way—just talking the night away and feeling completely comfortable in the other's presence. Even with her limited grasp of English, she thought they communicated perfectly. She loved Harry's piercing blue eyes. They seemed to look right through her. Yes, he was much older than she, but not that much. He would be a good provider for her and Alexei. Then she stopped herself. She knew she was jumping the gun. *We will see what the future holds,* she thought.

She snapped out of it and said to Alexei, "Come on, Alexei, let's hurry to McDonald's. I think I would like a Big Mac and a chocolate sundae today. How about you?"

"I want two double cheeseburgers and french fries," he answered as they picked up the pace to the restaurant.

The next morning, Miller was in his office sitting at his desk. He had made an appointment to see Vera at 10:00 a.m. He was working on submittals for the floor tile they would be installing on the 3rd floor. He was making sure the product they were submitting met the specifications. He was satisfied it did and completed the formal submittal. It was just before ten, so Miller shut down his computer and made his way to Vera's office. She was on the phone when he arrived, and she motioned him in and to sit down.

She finished a few minutes later and said, "Good morning, Mr. Miller. What can I help you with?"

Miller was not sure where to begin, so he thought it best to start at the beginning. He told her that when he first met Irena, she was with her uncle. His name was Ivan Anarbekova. He worked for Zhazprom, an oil and gas company. They had met briefly one evening a few weeks ago and Miller did not think anything of it. Then on New Year's Eve he met Ivan again at the Angara Club. This time he was with a friend of his and their wives. His friend's name was Yuri Belevich, and he was on the board of directors of The Bank of Moscow. He then told her the conversation about the vault doors.

She thought to herself that this was too much of a coincidence, but responded, "Most likely, Mr. Miller, there is nothing to this, but the first thing we will do is take the information on these two gentlemen and do a background check. Do not contact them but let me know if they make contact with you. I will inform you once we can determine the status of these two individuals."

"Thank you, Vera," Miller replied and walked out of her office back to his own. After he left, she picked up the phone.

When Miller went back to his office, he decided to go out and see how the demolition was coming. As he walked the areas, he noticed that the guys were making moderate progress. The scaffold was almost completed and they had already began putting up the shroud. Once the shroud was in place around the building, they could begin taking down the exterior bricks. This would speed up the demolition process. As he walked, he saw Harry up ahead. He had not really talked to him since New Year's.

"Hey, Harry, I see you survived New Year's Eve. Thanks for seeing Sveta home. Irena and I had to leave suddenly; something to do with one of her friends."

Harry smiled and replied, "Oh, I see. Are you sure it wasn't something more like leaving the scene of a crime?"

Miller looked dumbfounded. "What do you mean, Harry?"

Harry had a smile on his face like a cat who had just swallowed the canary and said, "My dear Mr. Miller. You know very well your acquaintance or partner in crime deliberately popped that cork at the Russian woman's head. Would you say that is a fair assessment?"

Miller thought, then replied, "Well, yes and no."

Harry laughed and answered, "I think mostly yes."

Miller knew there was no way out and said, "Okay, Harry, I'll come clean." Miller told Harry the whole story and had Harry in stitches of laughter. Miller asked Harry, "How did you know?"

Harry answered, "I saw Irena point and pull the trigger. Now that you explained it, I can see why--from a woman's perspective, that is. Anyway, mum's the word from me. I think most people believe it was an accident, and officially I believe that too. Just a New Year's Eve bash that got a little rowdy. Nothing more."

Miller felt relieved. "How did you get Sveta home? Did she take the van with everybody?" Miller asked, already knowing the answer. Irena had informed him.

Harry replied, "No, JT, she wanted to walk so I thought it best to walk with her."

Miller smiled. "Oh, I see. And did you also think it best to go up to Sveta's apartment and stay to all hours of the morning doing who knows what?"

"Okay, stop there," Harry said and continued, "Sveta and I had a very nice walk from the Angara Club to her apartment. When we arrived, she asked me in for coffee. We just sat up all night talking. It was a wonderful experience. There is nothing more to it."

Miller asked, "So you like her?"

Harry said, "Yeah, I like her. I haven't had so much fun in years. I would like it to continue but have some reservations."

Miller understood what Harry meant and knew he didn't need any advice from him. Miller responded, "You'll figure it out, Harry. I'll see you back in the office." And Miller walked off.

Vera was on the phone with her section chief in DC, Phil Mitchell. Phil agreed the first thing to do was a background check on these people. Phil continued, "Yes, Vera, that's what I said. The Russians have a way of being able to alter some of the information from a background check on any given Russian. There are signs this is being done, but we don't always see the signs. I agree these need to be thorough investigations. If what you described is true, Mr. Miller may have stumbled onto some of the top dogs. Keep me informed."

Vera replied, "Thanks, Phil, I will." Vera hung up the phone.

After Phil hung up, his phone rang a few moments later. It was his wife Mollie, who asked him to pick up a quart of milk on his way home. Phil agreed once again.

Joe Kelly was the RSO (Reginal Security Officer) in charge of coordinating the background checks. Joe was an undercover CIA agent under the guise of RSO assigned to Moscow. Joe was good at his job and had worked at the agency for thirteen years. Joe knew his onions when it came to security protocols. If anyone could sniff out a phony report on a Russian, this was the guy. Vera had provided Mr. Kelly with the information on the two Russian individuals about an hour previously. Joe was already working on it. He was looking at the information provided and began thinking out loud.

"Okay, let's see who we got. One Ivan Anarbekova and one Yuri Belevich. Hello, comrades, what the hell is your story?"

A week later, everything on site involved with completing the demolition was in place. The scaffold was up around the building, and the shroud was installed. The permanent construction offices were complete, and TRIAD was moved in and functioning. The walls in the NOB for the temporary construction offices were removed and the guys had started demo in that area a little ahead of schedule. The concrete tower crane pad was completed, and the tower crane was being assembled. The CAW workforce had increased to fifty-seven and was increasing weekly. Harry was pleased. As he walked and observed, he was happy with the progress.

He saw Charlie and said, "Things are looking good, Charlie. Keep it up. Oh, before I forget, send a couple of guys with snow shovels and have them clean up the mud out in the street by the south gate. Our trucks going in and out are responsible. Have these same two guys check it daily. It is one of the ambassador's pet peeves."

"I will get right on it, Harry," Charlie answered. Harry liked Charlie and was glad he was on his team.

As Harry walked, he could not help thinking about Sveta. It had been over a week since he spoke with her. Harry had still not made up his mind to pursue or not to pursue--that was still the question. He thought he might ask her to dinner on Saturday night but had not made definite plans. With a personal problem, Harry liked to take his time. With construction decisions after he did his research and was satisfied, he made up his mind quickly. Harry had read the Dwight D. Eisenhower autobiography. There was a part in there that said when Eisenhower and his staff had a tough decision to make, and if in Ike's opinion the staff came up with premature solutions based on conjecture, he would say, "Gentlemen, let's not make our mistakes too fast."

Harry had always remembered this and made sure during his career he did not stand behind any half-baked ideas. If he did his homework and was wrong, that was fine. At least he knew he gave it his best shot, but this decision did not fall into that category. This was a decision of the heart, and Harry knew that most irrational decisions fell into this category. Harry wanted to make sure he made his choice based on facts and not some emotional response. Harry was close to choosing but not quite there yet.

☭

Vera was in her office working on access requests when the phone rang. "Hello, this is Vera Collins."

"Hello, Vera, this is Joe Kelly. I have a preliminary report on the two Russian nationals you submitted for background checks. I would like to meet in the vault at 1400 hours to discuss, if that time suits your schedule."

Vera answered, "Thank you, Joe. That will be fine; see you then." When the call was completed, Vera went back to her access requests.

☭

At 1400 hours, or 2:00 p.m., Vera was at Post 2, entering the CAA area. She walked down the hall and entered the vault room. Joe was already inside, sitting at the table with two folders in front of him.

"Hello, Vera," he greeted.

She replied, "Hello, Joe. What do you have for me?"

Joe opened the first folder and said, "Ivan Anarbekova. On paper, his story checks out. Works for Zhazprom and has been there since 1989."

Vera answered, "Okay, Joe. I'll bite. You say on paper."

Joe responded, "There are two things that bother me. One, I have not been able to verify actual income he has received from Khazprom; and two, there is no record that Ivan has a family. The rest of his dossier is clean. Too clean. I will need to get his photograph to try and get a positive ID. This has the potential earmarks of a KGB cover-up." Joe then reached for the second folder and said, "One Yuri Belevich. Yes, he is on the board of directors at The Bank of Moscow. I have found several income statements of monies he has received for this position. In my opinion, the compensation is far too generous for Mr. Belevich's contributions, leaving me to believe there is something irregular going on here as well. In addition, The Bank of Moscow has alleged ties to the Kremlin. I will need his photograph as well, to complete this investigation."

Vera asked, "How do we proceed from here, Joe?"

Joe began, "I am afraid we will have to get Mr. Miller involved. Let's set up a meeting with him, and I will discuss my plan. These guys may still turn out to be harmless, but I smell a rat."

Vera left the vault and went back to her office. Joe stayed a bit longer. He thought once he had the photographs, he could run them through the FBI and CIA databases and hope for a hit. Even better if he could get fingerprints, but how?

☭

Vera did not like the idea of getting Miller involved. If things went south, there would be a shit storm if harm came to an innocent civilian. She called her section chief to get his opinion.

"Hello, Phil Mitchell."

Vera answered, "Hi, Phil. This is Vera. I need to get your take on something."

Phil replied, "Okay, Vera. I will do my best. What do you have?"

"Well, Phil, you know the background checks we were discussing?"

He acknowledged that he did. She continued, "The RSO in charge of the investigations wants to recruit JT Miller to get further information on the subjects. JT Miller is a civilian."

Phil replied, "I see your dilemma, Vera. The Central Intelligence Agency (CIA) could recruit him as a special agent, but there would have to be some compensation involved, and of course Mr. Miller would have to agree. This way the state department would be off the hook. Do you believe using Miller is the best way to proceed to get this additional information?"

Vera thought a moment, then answered, "I hate to say this, Phil, but I think it is the only way."

The section chief replied, "Vera, this is your call, and I will stand behind it. You are the one with your feet on the ground and know better than some guy like me sitting in a DC office. I trust your judgment."

"Okay—thanks, Phil. I will let you know how we proceed."

"Thank you, Vera, and good luck."

Phil hung up the phone. Vera sat and thought about the conversation. She noted the smooth way Phil put the responsibility back on her. She thought Phil Mitchell would not be the first SOB in Washington to get amnesia if push came to shove. To protect herself, she recorded the conversation in her diary, so she would have a record. This kind of documentation usually held up in court, if it came to that. Vera set up a meeting with Joe the following afternoon at 1400 hours in the vault. She next set up a meeting with Miller at the same location for 1500 hours. She needed time to hash out and agree on the details before she involved Miller. She thought an hour should be enough time.

The next afternoon, at about ten minutes to 3:00, Miller got up from his desk. He stretched, did a few squats and about fifty pushups. He had not left his desk since after lunch and needed to get the blood flowing. He grabbed his coat and hard hat, then made his way to the vault. He did not think too much about it, because Vera had made a benign request that they meet. When he arrived, the vault door was closed and locked. He figured Vera must be inside, so he knocked. A few moments later, the locks opened, and Vera appeared then said, "Please come in, Mr. Miller."

When JT entered, he saw another man sitting at the table whom he had not seen before. Vera continued, "Mr. Miller, I would like you to meet Joe Kelly. He is the RSO and is assigned to do the background check on our friends. The routine background check uncovered some inconsistencies. To be sure your Russian contacts are clean, we need to collect some additional information. Joe?"

"That is correct, Mr. Miller. We need to get their photographs and fingerprints. If they are agents, they will be smart, but we must be smarter. We would like to offer you the chance to help us."

Miller was trying to let what he had just heard sink in. He wasn't expecting this. He had seen the movies. Things never turn out well for the helper guy. Miller asked, "Why do you guys need me? What would I have to do?"

Joe answered, "Not much, really."

Miller thought, *Famous last words.*

Vera took over. "JT, we would like you to contact Irena and ask her to set up a dinner meeting with her uncle and his friend. You give them the information on the vault door they had asked about. Also take the finder's fee they offered. If this is a ruse, they will think they have you by the short hairs, and over time they will ask more and more of you.

"If they are on the level, no harm done. Joe will be using five Russian operatives that work for us. Two of them will be disguised as waiters whose sole responsibility will be to collect items at the table they have touched. Salt and pepper shakers, plates, silverware, and the like. The third operative will be disguised as a customer and will take their photographs. The fourth and fifth are none of your concern. You arrive at the restaurant early and choose the table that has been wiped clean. The only fingerprints that should show up on the collected items from the table will be from the four of you. Irena must not know any of this."

The two noticed that Miller had that deer in the headlights look. He was mulling it over. Miller kind of thought the prospect was intriguing, but the one minus to the equation was that Miller always intended to live to a ripe old age.

Vera looked at Joe and said, "Joe, tell Mr. Miller about the compensation package."

Joe began, "Well, JT, it's like this. Occasionally the company (CIA) will use a civilian operative. A civilian operative is someone who is not trained in combat or security protocols but is assigned to a case, usually as a way in to meet the targets, as in your case. For your help, the company will pay you compensation as a security consultant. There is a set hourly fee that the government allows you to bill. You invoice us once a month."

JT thought it over. Being a capitalist, he considered the compensation package to be the deciding factor. He didn't mind putting his life somewhat in danger if there was a little sweet cabbage at the end of the line.

Vera broke through the pause and said, "JT, I know this is a lot to consider. Take a day to think about it and let me know if you are in. Okay?"

Miller looked into Vera's eyes and replied, "No need, Vera. I'm in."

Miller walked back to his room in the housing units, or man camp, as it was called. He stopped at the video rental store in the commissary. He felt like a movie for a little escape from the events of the day. He probably made the worst choice possible to obtain his desired goal. He chose the James Bond classic *From Russia with Love*. Miller then stopped by the mess hall. He was in luck. It was taco night. He scarfed down about ten tacos and went back to his room. He propped himself up in his bed and slapped in the video. He lay back, watching, thinking to himself, and said out loud, "The name is Miller…James Miller. Yes, give me a gin and tonic—shaken, not stirred."

It was Saturday night, and Miller would be staying with Irena at their apartment. They would meet at the Angara Club beforehand for dinner. He would broach the subject of the meeting with her uncle and his friend sometime over the weekend. Miller was just getting out of the shower singing Johnny River's "Secret Agent Man." He was getting ready to meet Irena at her mother's apartment. Irena said her mother Sveta wanted to talk to him about something. He was hoping the something didn't have anything to do with Harry.

Miller dressed, put on his coat, and walked out the door. He crossed the street then down the alley to Sveta's apartment. He walked up and pushed the button to ring the apartment and was buzzed in. Just before he got to the apartment door, Sveta opened it.

"Hello, Sveta. Nice to see you," Miller said and gave her a kiss on both cheeks in Russian style. He walked in but did not see Irena. Sveta noted this and informed him, "JT, Irena called and said she will be late. She should be here soon." JT nodded, and Sveta continued, "I wanted to ask you about Harry. Is he alright? I have not heard from him for almost two weeks."

Miller answered, "Sveta, Harry is fine. I know he likes you a lot. He told me so. But Sveta, Harry is a very busy man. I am sure he just got caught up in work and you will be hearing from him soon."

Just then, the door buzzer went off and Sveta buzzed Irena in. When Irena walked into the apartment, she looked at Miller and said, "Sorry I am late, Slav," and gave him a kiss. "I am hungry, Slav. I hope you brought a lot of money. I might order the whole menu," she joked.

Miller thought he would ham it up and replied, "My soon to be fat, beautiful Russian princess. How can I deny the vision of loveliness that stands before me now?"

Irena answered, "Sheesh, Slav, you are full of it."

He responded, "I am only full of an undying love that can only be realized in my servitude to you."

"Come on, Slav. Let's go eat before I get sick to my stomach," she laughed.

"Sveta, would you like to join us?" JT asked.

"Thank you, no. You go ahead."

Irena and Miller said goodbye and left for the Angara Club.

Sveta walked into the kitchen to make some tea. She sat at the kitchen table and as she sipped her tea she was thinking about Harry. She was starting to think he was a big sveninia (pig) and was coming to the realization that Harry did not feel the same way about her as she did about him. She would finish her tea and go to bed early. Alexei was staying at a friend's on the floor above. As she sat there feeling sorry for herself, the door buzzer went off. Just out of reflex, she buzzed the person in. *What did Irena forget this time?* she wondered.

She heard a knock on the door and moved over to open it. When she opened the door, a man was standing there. He was dressed in a suit with a heavy topcoat and was holding a dozen red roses. The man stood there with a bit of a sheepish grin on his face. The man was Harry. When Sveta saw him, her eyes brimmed with tears. She wiped them and composed herself. She wanted to jump into his arms, but she could not. The pair just stared at each other.

Finally, Harry tried to explain, "Sveta, I brought you some flowers. I know I should have called on you sooner, but I was not sure and um. Well, you...know...I may have been foolish, and um--"

Before he could mumble another word, she kissed him. Then kissed him again. She took the flowers out of his hand and set them down on the table. She smiled, then slowly took one of Harry's hands and put it into her own. She took her time and led Harry across the apartment floor to her room like she was following some kind of Viking mating ritual. As far as Harry was concerned, she was, because he could feel his procreation gene starting to stir.

After his second gin and tonic, Miller thought he would broach the subject of the meeting with Ivan and Yuri. Irena was just finishing up her pork ribs and had sauce all over her chin. When she had completed the last rib, Miller reached over and wiped the sauce from her chin.

Irena said, "Thank you, Slav. I can be such a svenina (pig)."

The Slav knew what svenina meant and replied, "Yes, you can, my love, but there is no greater svenina in all of Russia."

She rolled her eyes and began to laugh. She then started making little pig noises. They both laughed, and Miller said, "Remember that when we are alone in our apartment tonight, my little svenina."

The Angara Club was not very busy, and Irena and JT got more drinks. Irena had acquired a taste for gin and tonics and was having one now. As they sipped, Miller asked, "Irena, do you think we could see your uncle and his friend Yuri sometime this week?"

Irena was on edge when she answered, "What do you want to see them for, Slav?"

He continued, "They were asking me about vault doors, and I have an answer for them. They wanted to know what kind would be best for the bank's purpose. I promised I would check into it, and I did. You remember."

"Yes, I remember, but I forgot about it," she answered.

Miller thought and replied, "Irena, if you prefer that I forget about it as well, I'm good with that. I was just trying to help your uncle and his friend if I could."

"Nyet...er…no. No, that's fine. Do you want to talk with them here, at the Angara Club?"

"Yes, that will work. How about next Saturday night, if they are free?" he answered.

"I will ask Uncle Ivan. Now forget about this, Slav, and dance with me," she said. Miller smiled, took her hand, and led her to the dance floor.

Now that Harry had consummated his relationship with Sveta, he was on the hook. He spoke with Vera about it, and the contact report Harry submitted to Vera on Sveta came up clean. As far as the USG was concerned, Harry was good to go to pursue the relationship. Harry still had reservations up to the time Sveta led him to her room. Now all bets were off. Harry and Sveta were lying together in Sveta's bed. She was asleep next to him. He just lay there and watched her sleep. He wondered if he could make it work. He still had not yet met her son Alexei. Harry didn't know, but he knew one thing--at this moment in time, there was no other place he would rather be.

Bo had been a good boy and had not contacted Natasha for two weeks. He was starting to go crazy just hanging out at the camp. It took Bo several religious purging's to control his impulses. He could not control them any longer. He had to see her. Natasha would think about Bo occasionally, usually when she was masturbating. Their lovemaking, if you could call it that, was intense. Never had she felt so satisfied sexually. In her mind, she played that scene again and again. The forcefulness of it, her complete submission, a slave to his sexual intentions. Yes, that did it for Natasha. She was usually dominant, but she had really enjoyed the submissive side of things of late.

Her cell phone rang. It was Bo. He decided to go with the unapologetic approach and said, "I am coming over at ten, and you better be there," then hung up.

Natasha could feel her juices flowing. She would be ready for him.

When Irena and Miller got back to their apartment, Irena called Karlov and asked about the meeting with Miller. He told her to tell Miller that it was okay with him, but he would check with Yuri. Irena relayed this to Miller, and he said fine. Miller would meet with Vera in the vault Monday morning to discuss. *They will want to know I made the first contact,* he thought.

Miller and Irena got into bed. She commanded, "Play it, Slav."

He answered, "You won't like it, and it will give you nightmares."

"Good. I like movies I do not like and give me nightmares. So, play it, Slav."

Reluctantly, Miller got up and grabbed one of the VHS tapes from the shelf. It was *The Exorcist.* Irena heard from a friend about the scene where Linda Blair's head turns all the way around and now, she had to see it.

"Are you sure, Irena? It will just scare you," Miller said trying to dissuade her.

"It will not scare me. Anyway, I like to be scared," she answered.

"Okay," he replied and popped in the tape. He then went into the kitchen to read. He read for a while until he heard the famous scene taking place. He walked into the bedroom and Irena was hiding under the covers. He called out, "Nice, Irena" and began to mimic her. "I never get scared. I love to have nightmares. I like movies I do not like."

Irena responded, "Shut up, Slav, and come to bed. I have a present for you." Miller thought about this and it occurred to him that this present might have a slight cod fragrance, so he hurried back to bed and got under the covers. He was right.

On Sunday afternoon, Miller and Irena were having a late breakfast at the Starlite Diner. Irena's cell phone rang, and it was Karlov. When she finished talking with him, she told Miller that Uncle Ivan and Yuri were good with Saturday for now but might have to move it up to Thursday or Friday because of a business deal Yuri was working on. Irena said she told her uncle that would be fine. Miller thought, *Good, the trap is set.*

Monday morning, Miller had briefed Vera in the vault. Miller had left, but Vera had stayed. About five minutes later, the vault door locks popped open and in walked Joe Kelly. Vera looked up and said, "Good morning, Joe. Let me get right to it. Miller has set up a tentative meeting with our subjects at the Angara Club on Saturday night at 8:00. Tentative because they told him they may have to move the meeting up to Thursday or Friday night on short notice because of some business deal one of them was working on."

Joe smiled, and Vera took note and asked, "What's that smile for, Joe?"

Joe responded, "The changing the day of the meeting at the last minute is a standard security precaution. These guys behave like agents. We will have to be on our toes. Our undercover Russian national waiters have been in place and working at the Angara Club for the last three months. We have used them on a few surveillance and information-gathering programs while they have been there. They are smart, and we have leverage on them to keep them honest. One of them is actually the brother-in-law of one of the owners. What that means is even if we only get an hour's set-up time, we should be able to pull it off with no one being the wiser. That will take care of the prints. Now for the photographs, I recruited a new guy. He goes by the name of Moshi. He is known as a small-time hood trying to make it to the big time. No one would ever suspect he is working for us. All we need to know now is the precise day and time of the meeting and I will take care of the rest."

Vera let that sink in. It sounded like they had a plan in place.

On Thursday, just before Miller was off work, his phone rang. "Hello, JT Miller."

"Hi, Slav," Irena answered.

"What's up, sweetie pie?" he replied.

"Well, my uncle just called and asked if we could meet him and Yuri at 7:00 tonight."

Miller looked at his watch, which said 5:16. Miller thought and said, "Let me call you back in five minutes. I think Harry wanted me to work late, and I will see if I can get out of it." He hung up and went to his speed dial and rang Vera.

"Vera Collins."

"Vera, this is JT. It is set for tonight at 7. Will this work?"

Vera looked at her watch and thought, *An hour and forty minutes.* She answered, "Yes, JT, make it happen." Miller called Irena and informed her. He would meet her at the Angara Club at 6:45. Vera informed Joe and he informed his operatives that the mission was on.

Joe hung up the phone and said to himself, "One Ivan Anarbekova and one Yuri Belevich. Who are you really?"

☭

JT was in front of the Angara Club at 6:40. Vera had just called and informed him to choose the table with the dark-blue vase on it. It would be one of the tables in the back by the cloak room. He saw Irena coming. He waited for her and gave her a kiss on the cheek. She asked, “Can I get the svenina ribs again, Slav? I am hungry.”

“Sure, my little carnivore,” he replied. They made their way in and Irena started to go to their usual table. The Slav grabbed her hand and said, “Let’s try a table over here.” He led her to the tables by the cloak room and saw the dark-blue vase. “Let’s sit here tonight for a change, my love.” They sat down, and a waiter came over. Miller ordered a gin and tonic and Irena the same.

Their drinks had just been served when Karlov walked up. “Hello, Mr. Miller. Hello, Irena. Nice of you to be able to make it on such short notice. I have to apologize for Yuri. He is so busy these days.”

Miller replied, “No need to apologize. I understand. Can I order you a drink?”

Karlov said, “Yuri and I have reserved a table on the other side of the room and my drink is there. Would it be too much trouble if you two joined us there?”

Miller thought, *A snafu right off the bat.* Miller knew he could not refuse, to avoid suspicion, and replied, “Sure, Ivan,” and he and Irena picked up their drinks and headed to the other table.

Yuri was on his cell phone but hung up just as Miller got to the table. “Hello, Mr. Miller. Good to see you again. Hello, Irena; looking as beautiful as I remember.” She thanked him. Yuri continued, “Please order something to eat, you two. It is on me.”

Miller thanked him, and he and Irena looked at the menus. Irena ordered the pork ribs and he ordered the roasted chicken. Yuri and Ivan had already ordered the borsht with steak and potatoes. Miller noticed an iced bottle of Tsarskaya on a small cart not far from the table, with four glasses. They made small talk while they waited for their dinners. The CIA operatives posing as waiters noticed the table switch. This was not a table they were assigned to, and if they spent too much time around it, their cover could be blown.

Nonetheless, they had to figure out a way to get the prints. This crossed Miller's mind as well. He would play it by ear until an opportunity showed itself.

Yuri was most talkative during dinner, telling stories of some of his and Ivan's escapades in the oil fields. When they finished dinner, Yuri asked, "You have some information for me, Mr. Miller?"

JT replied, "Oh, yes. You asked about vault doors, and I have an answer for you. I did some checking, and the vault door we are using meets the specifications you were interested in. Do you have something to write with?"

Yuri reached into his shirt pocket, pulled out a notepad and pen, and said, "Continue, Mr. Miller."

JT began again. "The vault door number is XD2-309. It is manufactured by Rex Technology. Let your designers take a look at it. I hope this helps."

"Yes, thank you, Mr. Miller. We will do just that. And as I said, if they decide to use your suggestion, you may receive a finder's fee. That is good, is it not?" Miller nodded and Yuri continued, "You have been very helpful, Mr. Miller. Now that business is done, my friend--" Yuri stood up and walked over to the ice bucket with the iced Tsarskaya. He took one of the four glasses filled it and handed to Miller. The second was for Ivan, the third for Irena, and the fourth for himself.

Yuri then held up his glass and said, "To my new friends. It has been so rewarding to make your acquaintance."

Miller and Irena nodded and sipped the vodka. Just then, Miller heard a loud voice calling out. "Americanski...Americanski, how are you?" Miller looked up and Moshi, Miller's old friend from the Belgrade Hotel, was smiling from ear to ear. Miller remembered that if you ever needed a woman or a bazooka, Moshi was your guy.

Miller asked, "Hello, Moshi. How are you doing?"

Moshi turned and faced Miller's companions. He apologized and said, "Sorry, Americanski. I did not mean to interrupt. Come see me at the Belgrade sometime. Tatyana has been asking about you. Ciao."

Then Moshi was gone. Irena pinched Miller and would be asking about this Tatyana later. They all had another glass of Tsarskaya, when Yuri and Ivan made their apologies and said they had to leave. Yuri insisted they all walk out together. When they reached the street, Yuri and Ivan said goodbye and got into a dark-colored Lada sedan and the driver pulled away. Miller and Irena started walking in the direction of Irena's mother's apartment.

One of the CIA operatives posing as a waiter walked to the table Miller just left, carrying an empty ice bucket with four vodka glasses inside it. Without missing a beat, he casually went to the table, put down the four clean vodka glasses next to the tainted ones, took the tainted ones and put them into the bucket. He then walked to the other side of the room and set them down on a table next to some woman. The woman slid them into separate plastic bags and put them into her purse. She casually got up and left. Outside the club on the street, she bumped into another woman and they both dropped their purses. The two women pretended to be angry with each other and when they picked up their handbags, they made the exchange. The woman without the glasses would head to the embassy to see if she was followed. If she was not, the other woman with the glasses would double back and go to the embassy, where Joe Kelly would be waiting.

Moshi walked back to the Belgrade to his room. He took off his coat and removed the small buttonhole camera. He had gotten the photos. He took the microfilm out of the camera, then picked up a ballpoint pen. He unscrewed it and placed the film inside. He put that in an envelope addressed to Joe Kelly.

He then went down to the lobby and told one of his guys, "Nikolai, I need you to go see a woman whose contact name is 'Medusa.' She will be at the Irish Bar just down from the Angara Club. Medusa will make contact with you inside the bar. She will introduce herself and you will give her this package. The woman is expecting you. Is that clear?"

Nikolai nodded his head, took the package, and headed for the door.

There were no hiccups with the vodka glasses. Joe had them in his possession and was working on the prints. He heard a knock at the lab door. He walked over and answered it. It was one of the CAG's.

"Excuse me, sir. This package just arived for you. It was dropped off at the south gate and marked 'Urgent,'" the CAG said.

Joe accepted the package and thanked the CAG. Joe then went into the darkroom to develop the photos. They were on microfilm and he would have to be careful not to distort the images when he enlarged them—the smallest deformation and the identity scanner could come up with a false positive. He would use the fingerprints to verify. Joe cautiously developed the photos. He thought one of the images looked familiar.

Karlov's cell phone rang. "Major Karlov," he answered. He listened to the voice on the other end for a minute or so. Karlov replied, "No, need to stay with them tonight, Anatoly. Pick it up in the morning." Karlov put the phone away and informed his friend, "Yuri, my friend. It seems our little ploy went unsuspected. Miller and Irena went home after we had left them, and no one came close to our table, unless it was a waiter. My operatives removed the listening device, and we have Miller on tape selling out his country--and he does not even realize what has happened, silly boy."

Yuri said, "Listen, Bolshevik," which drew faint smiles from both men. "We must not let our guard down. There might be more to Miller than meets the eye, or maybe not. We must be careful, Comrade."

Karlov replied, "Agreed, Yuri. We must be sure our fly flies the straight and narrow before he collides into our brick wall."

Yuri smiled and responded, "Well said, my old friend."

Joe Kelly had just made some coffee. He knew it would be a long night. He poured himself some, then scanned the fingerprints and photos directly to DC using the US Marisat communication satellites, which would run directly through to the FBI and CIA databases. DC would be in touch as soon as they uncovered anything. He took his coffee and went down the hall to an empty office where the guys would go sometimes to smoke. He slid a Newport from his pack and tapped the end. He opened the window, lit it, and took a drag. The decreased oxygen to his brain seemed to have a calming effect.

He took another drag when he heard his phone ring. He answered, "Joe Kelly."

"Joe, this is Phil Mitchell. We have some information for you and will send via secure fax back through the Marisat network."

"Yes, Phil, I understand," Joe answered. He walked back down the hall to the vault room. Joe entered and closed the door behind him. He heard the fax machine kick in and waited.

Chapter Six

DOUBLE AGENT

The next morning, Vera walked into her office. She knew the meeting went well the night before and Joe had the information to get positive ID's. She checked her emails and opened one from Joe Kelly. Joe wanted to meet Miller and herself in the vault at 10:00 a.m. Vera went into the break room and grabbed a cup of coffee. It was still reasonably fresh. She walked back to her office and continued with her emails. She then worked on a report until almost 10:00. She got up and headed to the vault for her appointment. Miller was already there waiting for her at Post 2. They walked into the secure area together then entered the vault. Joe Kelly was not there yet.

Vera locked the door and took a seat at the table, then asked, "How did it go last night, Mr. Miller?"

He answered, "I am not sure, Vera. They switched tables on us at the last minute. I am not sure if we got the fingerprints or photographs."

"I mean on your end?", Vera inquired.

"I think it went well. I do not think they smelled a rat," he replied.

She smiled and wondered if he had been watching too many 1950s gangster flicks on the tube lately. Just then, the locks popped open on the door and in walked Joe Kelly. He looked haggard, like he had been up all night. He smiled, took a seat at the table, and said, "Good morning, Vera; good morning, Mr. Miller. Before I get started, I would just like to thank you, JT, for a job well done." Miller just nodded, waiting for the meat and potatoes. Kelly continued, "Our mission was a success, and we now have complete profiles on our subjects. The first subject, one Ivan Anarbekova. There is no Ivan Anarbekova but a made-up identity. The KGB invented him and put false information out in his file. Our subject's real name is Dimitry Karlov or Major Karlov. He is a high-up in the KGB Moscow division, and it appears he is assigned to the Second Chief Directorate. This is the agency that targets foreigners and embassies. He has been involved in many important operations for the KGB and is a trained assassin. He and our other suspect, Yuri Belevich, went to KGB school together in the 1970s in Saint Petersburg. They have been close friends ever since."

Miller was dumbfounded. He could not believe it. Ivan, Irena's uncle, was Major Karlov, big shot for the KGB.

Kelly continued, "The other subject, Yuri Belevich, is also tied into the KGB but for the last five or six years has been in Russian politics. There is talk that he may be considered for a presidential run in the next election. Yes, Vera, Mr. Miller, we have indeed hooked some big fish."

Vera asked, "Do we know what they are up to, Joe?"

"Well, not exactly, but you can be sure it has something to do with the new vault door that will be installed in this very room. It could be a diversion, but I don't think so. I think the vault door is the mission and if these two guys are on this, it is important to them."

"Joe?" Miller asked. "Do you think it is possible for Irena to be in on this?"

Joe replied, "Unfortunately, Mr. Miller, I would say yes. Maybe only for the introduction, but now she knows about the vault door. I would say that after this mission is complete, whether successful or not, she will become a casualty of war. That is usually how it works with their one-time civilian operatives. It does not appear she is a career operative for the KGB. If they have another use for her on another mission then she might be okay, for a time."

Miller let that sink in. Joe explained, "They probably picked her for this mission because she already had a job teaching English at the embassy and a US government background check had already been done. I would not be critical of her, JT, because if she was approached, she must comply. If not, she and her family could end up in the gulag, or worse."

Miller let that sink in as well.... He felt sick. How could Irena do this to him? He had no idea. Was she really a KGB swallow playing him for a fool? Or was it she just did not have another choice?

Joe read JT's mind and continued, "Mr. Miller, the only way this is to work is for you not to let on that you suspect Irena. We will carry on as before. We will let them contact you, and we will see this through."

Vera added, "JT, I will inform Harry that Svetlana may also be involved, whether cooperative or not. He must be made aware and report anything suspicious."

When the meeting was over, Miller walked back to his office, his head spinning with what he had just heard.

Harry had just left Vera's office, and the two of them headed out. She told him she wanted to speak with him, and he invited her to lunch. They walked to The Hard Rock Café on the Arbat. They ordered hamburgers and iced tea. Vera sipped her iced tea and said, not beating around the bush, "Harry, I have to inform you that your friend Svetlana may be a Russian agent." This hit Harry like a ton of bricks. Maybe that was her intention. He waited. Vera continued, "It is not confirmed, but you must be aware of the possibility and inform us if you uncover anything suspicious. Do not let on what you know about her, however. She may be part of a bigger plot. Just go along as before and keep us informed."

Harry said he understood. The understanding was the easy part. The hard part would be continuing the relationship. He had to try.

A month went by. It was early March, and it felt like spring was just around the corner. It rained now more than snowed. The day before was International Woman's Day, a very popular holiday in Russia. It was a day where Russian men bought their wives or girlfriends flowers and took them out to dinner. It was also required for American men who had Russian girlfriends to comply as well. Harry and Miller followed suit. The work on the building was going well. All of the non-load-bearing interior walls had been razed. The workers now were on the 7th floor taking down the roof and wall slabs as well as the brick skin. They would continue down two more levels to the 5th level floor slab. From there, they would build back up, pouring into existing columns and securing with structural steel and earthquake-proof steel column wraps. These columns would go from floor to floor, and a web of structural-grade beams would be poured into them. The structural steel would be attached using anchor bolts. On the structural-grade beams, precast concrete floor and wall panels would be placed.

Harry was as happy as a project manager could be with the progress, but Harry's job was to do it faster. Harry wanted more CAW's, but the top-secret clearance reviews were killing him. Only one out of four CAW's submitted would be approved, and this was hampering production. Harry had put in a claim for more time to be added to the contract because of it. Harry had a good case. Miller and the rest of the management team were in project mode. This meant long hours, six days a week, with every thought focused on the job and not much else. That is, except for Saturday night and Sunday. That part of the week was like an oasis in the desert—a night and a day to get out of the work routine and have a little fun or take a much-needed rest.

There had been nothing for Harry to report to Vera about Sveta. Harry did not think she was a spy but still kept one eye on her. Harry would see her at least once a week, usually for dinner on Saturday night and a tryst at either Sveta's apartment or the Ukraine Hotel. The hotel was popular and was located a short walk from Sveta's apartment or an even shorter metro ride. They usually walked. The hotel was located in one of Stalin's seven sisters, a group of seven skyscrapers built by the former Premier of the Soviet Union in Moscow between 1947 and 1953. Stalinist architecture was associated with the socialist realism school of art and architecture. In other words, nothing too flashy but built to last. Harry loved the hotel. It reminded him of what it must have been like to live in Moscow during Soviet times.

When Sveta was a little girl, her father had taken her and her mother there for a weekend one summer. That weekend, her father chartered a boat and they took a sightseeing trip up the Moscow River. Sveta thought it would be nice to do the same with Harry once the weather got warmer. Miller and Irena still spent their weekends together at the apartment. At first, Miller had a problem thinking that most likely Irena had worked with the KGB to recruit him. Now he found it intriguing that he was dating a KGB agent.

Major Karlov reached for his phone and dialed. "Good morning, Yuri. Are you awake or still sleeping like some misguided capitalist, my friend?"

"Good morning, Dimitry. No, I have been up for hours reading the best torture techniques when using an ice pick. The book gives great emphasis on techniques to strictly maim and not kill. A very informative read. To what do I owe this pleasure on this beautiful morning, Major? Something to report, perhaps?" Yuri replied.

Karlov continued, "You are quite right. Our package has arrived and is ready for the modifications."

Yuri answered, "Excellent. Please proceed as planned."

After Miller had given Yuri and Major Karlov the vault door information, Yuri immediately went to his Russian-American business contacts and had them order two doors from Rex Technology. The doors were purchased by a building supply company and freighted to The Bank of Moscow but were confiscated going through customs. From there, they were sent directly to the KGB lab, where the modifications would be completed. First the technicians would disassemble the doors. A determination would be made as to the best way to install the spy hardware. Then one door would be equipped with the new hardware. Rigorous testing would ensue to ensure the door would function as planned. Once the tests were complete and every detail worked out, the second door would be installed with the spy apparatus. Now the only problem would be how the exchange would be made. This would be up to Miller. That is, of course, if Miller played ball. Yuri was confident he could get the Americanski to do just that.

It was just before lunch, and Miller was at his desk, thinking about lunch. His phone rang, and he answered, "JT Miller."

On the other end, he heard Irena's voice. "What are you doing for lunch, Slav?"

"I was just getting ready to go to the mess hall. Why, what's up?"

She answered, "It is such a beautiful day today; let's have lunch outside at the Irish pub. They opened the beer garden and they have the best hamburgers."

Miller thought she was nuts and informed her, "Irena, it is only 50 degrees outside."

She replied, "It feels almost hot in the sun. Anyway, I have an envelope for you from Yuri."

This was what Miller had been waiting for. He said, "Okay, I am leaving now. I will be there in ten minutes."

"I will be there in five and will get a table in the sun. I do not want my poor devochka (baby) to get cold," she joked.

Miller arrived at the pub and made his way to the back and entered the beer garden. Irena was at a table in the middle with full sun. Her coat was off, and she was drinking an iced tea. She informed him, "I already ordered for you, Slav. I ordered two mushroom and olive hamburgers with onion rings and iced tea."

Miller replied, "Nice! That should hit the spot, my Russian beauty."

Miller waited, and Irena said, "Here is the envelope from Yuri," and she handed it to him. Miller set it on the table and took a sip of tea. It was actually a little warm in the sun, so Miller took off his jacket. He sipped his tea again and then opened the envelope. He read a little note from Yuri that said, "Mr. Miller, the designers felt you deserved a finder's fee for the vault door. Please see enclosed check. Signed, Yuri."

"Well, what is it, Slav?" she asked.

JT answered, "Yuri's people sent me a finder's fee check for the vault door."

Irena laughed. "Great, now lunch is on you. How much is it for? $100 or $200? I need to know how much I can spend," she joked.

He looked at her and replied with a concerned look on his face, "It is for $5000."

Irena sat there with her mouth open, then asked, "Why so much, Slav?"

Miller answered, "Not sure, Irena. It may be a mistake."

Irena grabbed the check and looked at it. She became uneasy and said, "I will verify with Uncle Ivan, Slav. He can confirm with Yuri."

The next morning Miller had made arrangements to meet with Vera and Joe Kelly. Miller informed them that he received the check from Yuri. They were both delighted and told him he must deposit the check as soon as possible.

"As soon as you deposit the check, Yuri will think he's got you. He will then show his hand," said Joe.

Vera told Miller she would send it in a special mail pouch that would be in the States the next morning. He pulled out his checkbook and pulled a deposit slip from the back. He filled it out and signed it, then passed it along with the check. Vera took these then put them in another envelope and addressed it to Miller's bank.

Vera said, "JT, the Russians will have verification by the end of the week that you are in the game."

Miller smiled nervously.

Chapter Seven

VICTORY DAY

The next few weeks were uneventful. Major Karlov had told Irena the Bank of Moscow would be purchasing thirty vault doors, and Miller received $166.66 for each door they would purchase—a 1% finder's fee. This seemed to make more sense but was still extravagant. Miller had put all that out of his mind and was focused on the embassy construction work. The job was coming along well, and Harry was pleased. Soon they would be able to start structural steel. The steel was due on site shortly. As Harry walked the building, he watched the plumbers removing old water piping from the level-eight ceiling. The west wall had been deconstructed, and as soon as the old piping was removed, they would finish razing the roof slab and the remaining walls.

Tom Maloney was an apprentice pipe fitter removing the piping on the West side. He was working closer than the 6-foot setback safety requirement to work from a leading edge, so he was wearing fall protection. His lanyard was hooked into a safety cable that ran the length of the ceiling on the west side near the leading edge and the other end of the lanyard was hooked into his harness. This was Tom's first overseas assignment. His wife was at home in Florida with their two young children, Tom Junior, six, and Abigail, four. In Florida, Tom had a good job with a union contractor until he got laid off. Tom had heard about the Moscow project and with the overseas pay uplift, the contract completion bonus, and the federal tax break, he could save enough money in a year to put a nice down payment on a house. He and his wife Nancy decided one year would go by fast and she would spend her time looking for the perfect house in the perfect neighborhood.

Tom had been on the project for two months. It was cold that morning, so Tom was bundled up. It was just about lunch time and Tom was finishing dismantling a section of piping from the ceiling. He let it fall to the floor below. He then unhooked the lanyard from his harness and descended the ladder. When he got to the floor, he stopped and tried to step out of his safety harness. When he did, he stumbled and fell next to the leading edge of the 8th-level floor slabs. As he stood up, he did not realize he was close to the leading edge, lost his balance, and fell eight stories between the scaffold platform and building face. He was killed instantly.

Tom Scaraponi, the safety manager, was on the scene in a heartbeat. He taped off the impact area 25 feet in every direction. He called his wife Terry, the site nurse. She confirmed what he already knew. Mr. Thomas William Mahoney had given up the ghost. She explained the body would have to go to the hospital for the death certificate. Scaraponi called the safety engineer and said, "Kenny, I need the stretcher and transport cocoon over here on the west side."

Kenny answered, "Uh…sure Tom, I will get right on it. Just clarify the transport cocoon."

Tom replied, "A body bag."

That was when it hit Kenny. He knew there had been an accident but did not know it resulted in a fatality. He retrieved the items and met Tom where Mr. Mahoney had fallen. Kenny laid down the stretcher and opened the body bag. Inside was an 8' x 5' nylon tarp for covering the body before it was placed in the bag. Tom and Kenny wrapped the mangled body in the nylon, then gently picked up Mr. Mahoney, placed him in the bag, then zipped it closed. Terry had already called the hospital and was waiting with Harry for the ambulance at the CAC. When the ambulance arrived, it stayed in the sally port. Tom and Kenny carried the corpse on the stretcher to the sally port and into the vehicle. Terry signed a form and the ambulance was on its way back to the hospital morgue. Harry pulled out his Motorola and called Charlie.

"Charlie, this is Harry. Do you have a copy?"

"Yes, this is Charlie. Go ahead, Harry," he answered.

Harry continued, "Charlie, I want you to shut it down for the rest of the day. I want everyone to think about what had just happened here today. Tomorrow night at 7:00, there will be a service at the chapel for Tom Mahoney. I strongly suggest everyone attend."

Charlie replied, "I will take care of it, Harry." Harry turned to Scaraponi and said, "Tom, first thing in the morning I want you to do 'Fall Protection Training' for all the CAW's and staff. I know this is a given but wanted to reiterate. Right now, get statements from anybody that saw anything, and review the security camera footage. Maybe we will get lucky."

"Sure, Harry. Anything else?"

"Yes, I want you to walk with John London and myself after you get the statements and review the footage. We will look this over and see if we can come up with some conclusion as to what exactly happened and ensure it doesn't happen again. I need to have information for the home office when I inform them. I am not looking forward to it. Did Tom Mahoney have a family?"

Scaraponi replied, "I don't know, Harry, but I will find out."

As Harry walked away, he muttered almost to himself, "When a man loses his life just trying to make a living, it's a tough break and hard to swallow--so much more when the man has a family."

Bo had been seeing Natasha regularly. Their sexual passion was growing, and they experimented in many realms of sexuality. Bo was on the 19th floor of the Belgrade Hotel, standing in front of the door to room 1907. He knocked, and in less than a minute, Natasha was opening the door. He asked angrily, "What took you so long, bitch? Don't ever make me wait again."

Natasha just stood there and did not say a word. She was wearing a full nun's habit, with black veil and sensible shoes. A large crucifix hung down across her chest. Bo walked in and Natasha closed and locked the door behind him. She took Bo's hand and led him to a small room in her apartment. She usually kept this room locked, but it was now open. The room contained a 4 x 4-inch-thick wooden post, eight feet high, held up with a heavy stand. On the top of the post were two holes drilled through the wood, where two lengths of chain hung down. On the ends of the chains were leather handcuffs. Natasha helped Bo out of his clothes, folded them, and set them on the floor. She took one of Bo's hands and slid the cuff around it. Then the other. She turned a crank that took up the slack in the chains. She kept turning until the handcuffs were taut above his head. She then went to a table and selected a two-foot-long, 4 inch wide, ½ inch thick wooden paddle.

She stood behind Bo and asked, "Are you ready to be purged of your sins, Mr. Bo?" Bo nodded. She continued, "May God be pleased with the purging, and cleanse you of your sins."

When she finished the speech, she whacked him hard across his buttocks. He yelled out. Natasha got a warm feeling of pleasure. She swung the paddle again, then again and again until the red swollen splotches began to run. As the couple continued the ritual, they had not been aware that this little tryst was being captured on video tape. Karlov had all the rooms set up with cameras and listening devices. These had been in place since before Christmas. Karlov had assumed he might have a use for this Mr. Beecher. Karlov knew he had him in his hip pocket if he needed him. *All in good time*, he thought. But now the time had come. Only about three months to the meeting, and the tainted door must be in place. Karlov thought, *It is time to add this other fish to the fire. I believe there is enough room inside the pan.* He reasoned that he had to recruit Miller first to get the door information. Miller could also push to get the door installed before the target date. Karlov would use Mr. Beecher to sign off on the door inspection, which was part of his job, and also confirm that the tainted door was in place. Karlov lived by the Russian proverb "Trust but verify."

2014 May Day Parade in front of US Embassy consular section.

It was May 9 and the whole embassy had a holiday. No work would be scheduled. It was the Russian holiday "Victory Day." Victory Day commemorates the victory of the Soviet Union over Nazi Germany in 1945. The German Instrument of Surrender was signed late in the evening on May 8 and announced on May 9. Miller was looking forward to the May Day parade, as most people called it. This was where the Russians liked to show off their military force. Miller was especially keen on seeing the rockets. They had always looked so ominous in the film clips he had seen.

Miller and Irena had stayed in their apartment the night before. They were sipping coffee at the kitchen table that morning. The parade would start at the Kremlin and continue down a path of closed streets until it would pass in front of the US Embassy. Irena told Miller a good place to watch is in front of the embassy's consular area on Deviatinsky Street. The consular area serviced hopeful immigrants trying to get a visa to the United States.

JT asked, "What time should we get there?"

Irena took another sip of coffee, then replied, "The parade leaves the Kremlin at one. The parade will probably not make it to Deviatinsky for at least an hour after that. I think if we get there at two, we will be fine."

He countered, "Are you sure? I don't want to miss the rockets."

Irena gave Miller her annoyed look and said, "Slav, do not be so dense. Your rockets are not until the last part of the parade. Two will be most appropriate."

He answered, "Okay...okay. Just checking, sweetie."

Irena was not as excited as Miller to see the parade. When Irena was a little girl it had been a grand affair, but since Perestroika, the Russian government was almost bankrupt, and the parade was not as elegant as it once had been--and besides, she had been to at least fifteen May Day parades.

They decided on a late breakfast at the Starlite and made their way to the city center. They got off at the Smolenskya metro station and walked to the embassy. They approached the pedestrian underpass on Novy Arbot. There were several of these underpasses in the city center where citizens could walk under the busy roads to cross to the other side safely. The Russian government built them for two purposes: first, to get pedestrians from one side of the road to the other; and second, they could be used for air raid shelters as well.

As Miller and Irena walked down the stairs of the underpass, they could hear a street musician playing his violin down below. As they passed the musician, Miller put a few rubles into his open violin case. These underpasses were meccas for street musicians of all types. As they walked up the stairs to the other side of the road, they saw the streets and sidewalks covered with paradegoers. Miller was worried they would not get a good view. As they walked farther down Deviatinsky to the consular area of the embassy, the crowds thinned, and Irena and Miller found a good spot and waited. Almost as if on cue, after they got settled, they saw the parade just starting to turn right off of Novy Arbat on to Deviatinsky.

The first part of the parade consisted of about two hundred of Russia's elite forces, goose-stepping in time. Miller thought their uniforms were just a tad shabby. After that came the Jeeps, about twenty of them, with some pulling Howitzers. Next came the tanks. There were several different varieties, some with big guns and some with bigger guns. Miller thought these were cool. He did notice that one of the main battle tanks had thick black smoke coming out of the exhaust, obviously needing more than a tune-up. Then came the rocket launchers, the personnel carriers, special military vehicles, and finally the rocket transport vehicles. The rockets they carried were the guided surface-to-air missiles, called the V-300 rockets. These were the rockets Miller wanted to see.

The parade ended just as the Russian air force flew over in formation with multi-colored jet streams trailing behind, signaling the show's finale. This was just before 4:00, and Irena was hungry. Miller and Irena decided to stop at the Hard Rock for a late lunch/early dinner. The fireworks would begin at 9:00 over the Moscow River. Miller and Irena weren't sure they wanted to hang out and wait that long. Miller was already thinking a power nap would be good right about now. The beer garden was open, and it was a nice May day, so the couple sat there. The place was packed with parade-goers just like Miller and Irena who had similar cuisine ideas.

The couple had to wait a few minutes for a table. After they were seated, Miller ordered the usual and Irena some Chardonnay. She had been on a wine kick of late. Irena asked, "How did you like the parade, Slav?"

Miller replied, "I thought it was good. You were right about the place to watch it."

She said, "I used to go the Kremlin to watch it with my father. It would be decorated with very nice colored banners. Very exciting, but too many peoples."

Miller corrected her, "You mean people."

She replied, "No, I don't. I mean too many peoples. More than one... peoples."

Miller decided to be diplomatic and explain it to her in a neutral way, "Irena, people is already plural and means more than one. You don't say one people. You say one person. If you have two persons, then you have people. The only time you use peoples is if you are speaking of many different cultures or ethnic groups. A good sentence to demonstrate this, my love, would be 'God looked over the land and smiled at the peoples of the world.'"

Irena had that annoyed look on her face again and replied, "Slav, you think you are so smart. I knew that all the time. I just wanted to see if you knew. You big svenina."

Miller took a large gulp of his gin and tonic and started to reply, but his cell phone rang. He didn't recognize the number. He answered, "JT Miller."

On the other end, he heard a familiar voice. "Ah, Mr. Miller. This is Yuri Belevich. Please forgive me, JT, but I wonder if I could trouble you to stop by my flat tonight. I would like to speak with you."

Miller replied, "Hello, Yuri. This is a surprise. How did you get my number?"

Yuri answered, "I hope you will excuse the intrusion, but I took the liberty of asking Ivan for it. I suppose he acquired it from Irena. Anyway, my flat is at the Ukraine Hotel, room 3402. Say around 8:00. My wife is with me, so bring Irena if you wish."

Miller relayed the message to Irena. She did not like the sound of it but tried to hide her anxiety. Miller noticed but did not let on. He excused himself and walked to the water closet. He paid the attendant, an old woman, one ruble to use the facilities. He took the paper she offered and chose a stall. He called Vera.

☭

Miller and Irena walked down Novy Arbat to the river and then continued along the river on the bank path to the Hotel Ukraine. He had left Irena at the Hard Rock for about thirty minutes while he went back to his room at the man camp. He told Irena he needed to replenish his supply of rubles and would be right back. As he walked into his room, Vera was waiting. As the couple continued walking the path, Miller noticed a restaurant boat in the river. Miller was just reading about it in the *Moscow Times*. It was called the River Fish Restaurant. A couple of young Russian entrepreneurs got together and thought what better way to enjoy dinner than with the extra added attraction of sightseeing along the Moscow River? Miller noted that the River Fish's business was good.

The couple arrived just before 8:00 and took the elevator to the 34th floor. The 34th floor were the penthouse apartments. They found the apartment and buzzed the door. A minute later came the fumbling of a lock, and the door opened. It was a young woman in a housekeeper's uniform. She said in perfect English, "Hello, my name is Olga. Welcome and please come in. The Belevichs are expecting you."

She led them into the drawing room. It was a large room that had glass windows the full length of the walls on two sides. The view of Moscow was spectacular. There were white and grey leather sofas that made an "L" shape against the windowless walls. There was a coffee table in front of the sofas. The rest of the furniture was an art deco affair and looked expensive. The floor tile was natural Italian marble, and the room had a large granite fireplace for those cold Moscow nights. On the opposite wall was a full wet bar with stools, and two cocktail tables with two chairs each. The room also sported an oak pool table.

Olga led them to one of the cocktail tables and asked, "May I get you something to drink?"

Because it had been a long day, they both decided on coffee. Olga brought the coffee, then went back to the bar and pulled out a bottle of Tsarskaya and placed it in an ice bucket. She then filled the bucket with ice and placed it on the other table with four glasses.

Just then, Yuri and Vladlina entered the room. Yuri greeted them, "Good evening, Mr. Miller...Irena. Thank you so much for coming."

Yuri shook Miller's hand and kissed Irena. Vladlina blabbed something in Russian to Irena and kissed her hello, then moved to JT and kissed him as well.

Miller said, "Nice place you have here, Yuri. Great view."

Yuri replied, "Thank you, Mr. Miller. The apartment was a gift from the Bank of Moscow. It was an incentive for us to move to Moscow from St Petersburg."

"How do you like Moscow, as opposed to Saint Petersburg?" Miller asked.

"I have been in Moscow many times over the years. We like it, but our home is Saint Petersburg," Yuri answered.

After more small talk, Yuri had Olga move the ice bucket to the coffee table and dismissed her. The couples moved to the sofas. Yuri filled the four glasses and said, "Please toast with me. To the motherland's victory against the Nazis."

They all raised their glasses and sipped the vodka. After a moment of silence, Yuri said, "Vladlina, the fireworks are about to start. Do you mind taking Irena to the balcony patio to watch them? I want to speak with Mr. Miller."

Irena gave Miller a look, and when she and Vladlina left the room, Yuri asked, "Mr. Miller, do you like music?"

Miller answered, "Yes, Yuri, of course."

Yuri said, "On Victory Day I always play Richard Wagner's 'Ride of the Valkyries.' It was rumored to be one of Hitler's favorite compositions. I like to listen and imagine Hitler's reaction to his world falling apart around him. Just a little oddity of mine. Please indulge me, Mr. Miller."

Miller nodded, and Yuri walked over to the wet bar and opened a cabinet where a phonograph was hidden. Underneath, he fingered some record albums and pulled one out. He slipped the record from its sleeve and placed it on the turntable. Miller heard a few dust scratches before the piece began. Yuri had an excellent speaker system and was playing it loud so the rapturous music would encompass the listeners. Yuri walked over to the windows and stared out in a trance, like he was entering another dimension—a world of gleeful destruction, savoring the demise of an archnemesis. Miller listened and sipped the Tsarskaya.

When the last note was played, Yuri said, "Thank you, Mr. Miller. Now I would like to play something else for you that you may find interesting."

Miller replied, "Please."

Yuri pulled out a small remote and pushed the button. Over the speakers, Miller first heard Yuri's voice say, "You have some information for me, Mr. Miller?"

Then his own voice, "Oh, yes. You asked about vault doors and I have an answer for you. I did some checking and the vault door we are using meets the specifications you were interested in. Do you have something to write with?"

After a pause Yuri said, "Continue, Mr. Miller."

JT began again, "The vault door number is XD2-309 and the size 36" x 80." It is manufactured by Rex Technology. Let your designers take a look at it. I hope this helps."

"Yes, thank you, Mr. Miller. We will do just that. And as I said, if they decide to use your suggestion, you may receive a finder's fee. That is good, is it not?" A pause then Yuri continued, "You have been very helpful, Mr. Miller. Now that business is done…."

Yuri turned off the recording. Miller sat there with a stunned look on his face. Yuri noted this and liked it. Miller asked, "What is this? What do you want? Is this blackmail?"

Yuri replied, "Please relax, Mr. Miller. Blackmail is such an ugly word. What I wanted to point out is that if this recording came into the wrong hands, it might prove embarrassing to you. With this recording and the $5000 deposited into your account, what do you think your government would surmise? The good news is that I have it, so no one will be the wiser. All you have to do is a few favors for me from time to time."

Miller looked like he was caught in a trap. "What kind of favors?" he asked.

Yuri smiled. "Oh, nothing much of any consequence. We will talk later, Mr. Miller. Please, let's just enjoy Victory Day and celebrate Mother Russia's success."

Yuri called the girls back in, and Miller and Irena left. Yuri noted that Miller looked panicked, and so did Irena. As they got to the lift, Irena asked, "Are you okay, Slav?"

The elevator doors opened, and they stepped inside. The doors closed behind them when the Slav finally replied, "I am fine, my love." But Irena had her doubts.

☭

Irena and Miller took the river path back to Novy Arbat and back to the embassy. It was close to midnight, and Miller had to work the next morning. He would go back to his room at the man camp, and Irena would stay at her mother's. As they walked the path by the river, Irena thought about telling Miller about her involvement in all this. About Uncle Ivan. She felt bad that her Slav was visibly shaken. He did not speak much, and when she confronted him, he said he was just tired. He walked her to the alley by her mother's and kissed her good night. He continued to his room in the man camp.

☭

After Vladlina went to bed, Yuri stared out the window, looking at the lights of the city. He walked back to the phonograph and pulled out another record selection. It was Isaak Dunayevsky's "March of the Enthusiasts." Dunayevsky is considered one of the greatest Soviet composers of all time. As the music played, Yuri continued looking at the lights of the city. He thought about how easily tonight went. Even though Yuri had not done this low-level espionage work for several years, he thought his performance was superb; it was like riding a bicycle. Then Yuri said out loud to himself, "I will have this American fish eating out of my hand and then licking my fingers." He smiled and began to laugh.

☭

When Miller got to his room, he almost burst. He was smiling from ear to ear. He removed his jacket and removed a small recorder taped under his armpit. He rewound it and played it back. The sound quality was good. He called Vera and would meet with her in the morning. Miller felt proud of himself. He was able to pull off the illusion of the tortured victim or the remorseful jerk looking to save his own skin. As he stepped into the shower and the revitalizing hot water hit him, he could not help but start singing a falsetto version of "Secret Agent Man."

☭

The next day, Miller was sitting in the vault with Vera and Joe Kelly. Joe said, "Yeah, JT, just go on as before until Yuri asks for one of his favors. Act like you believe you have no choice but to do his bidding, and make Yuri believe it. We will see where this takes us."

Vera added, "Do not take any unnecessary risks, JT. We would hate to lose our project engineer."

She smiled, Miller smiled back and said, "Vera, you can rest assured my middle name is safety first. Or maybe that would be my middle two names."

☭

Bo was at the Belgrade hotel in room 1907. He was crawling around on all fours on a plastic sheet, lying on Natasha's apartment floor. He was wearing diapers and had a baby bottle nipple in his mouth. Natasha was with him, wearing black panties, high black nylons, and a garter belt with silver stiletto heels. She also sported a black rubber hooded mask that had three holes cut into it--two for the eyes, and one for the mouth. She wore nothing else. Bo was now lying on the plastic in a fetal position. As Natasha straddled Bo's head, she pulled her panties down and assumed a squatting posture. When she released the amber liquid, it splashed against the left side of Bo's face and forehead.

She announced, "Sinner, I now baptize you in the name of God the Father, His Son, and the Holy Spirit."

Just then, the apartment door opened, and Major Karlov with another man strolled in. The major said, "I hope we did not catch you at an inconvenient time, Mr. Beecher. Now please clean up and put some clothes on. I want to talk with you."

The couple's protest stopped short as Anatoli pulled from his coat a Kedr PP-91 submachine gun and aimed it at the hosts. Karlov continued, "Let's not have any more nonsense. Now hurry. Get dressed. I want to speak with Mr. Beecher."

Bo and Natasha freshened up, put on some clothes, and came back into the room. Karlov said, "Now please sit. I want to show you something."

Anatoli reached into his coat pocket and pulled out a VHS tape. He handed it to the major. Karlov slapped it into the VCR and pressed play. Bo and Natasha watched in horror as they saw their sexual exploits were well documented. Bo did not yet know what was going on and asked, "What's this about? What do you want?"

The major answered, "Mr. Beecher, what do you think Vera, your SSM, would say if she got a copy of this tape? Would she say that Bo Beecher really knows how to have a good time? Look at how he is enjoying himself? I think not. She would see a perverted little man that should not have access to US government secrets and should be brought up on sexual perversion charges.

Or what would your family and friends say, or your church members say if this tape was released?"

Now Bo realized what this was about. He thought about his orientation briefing with Vera and the Alabama CAW. He had been duped in the same way. He wondered if Natasha was part of this. "What do you want from me?" Bo asked with his head down, not making eye contact.

"Do not worry, Mr. Beecher. As long as you do what I tell you to do, you have nothing to worry about. Now get out of here, and I will contact you later."

Still looking down, Bo hurried and grabbed his belongings, then rushed out of the door like he was late for an airline flight. Karlov smiled and then focused on Natasha.

"Natasha, you are looking most lovely his evening. I am sure you will keep this little meeting of ours to yourself. It would be a shame if some unforeseen accident should befall you." Natasha nodded. Karlov buttoned up his coat and said to Anatoli, "Please allow Miss Stasevich to show you how hospitable she can be. I think you have earned it."

With that, Karlov left the apartment and closed the door behind him. Anatoli walked over and stood in front of Natasha, who was seated on the couch. Without hesitation, she reached for his belt.

Chapter Eight

CRYPTONYM – THE ANGARA CLUB

It was Father's Day, and Kurt and Nadine were walking along the Arbat. The sun was shining, and the highs were in the mid-70s. This was a very popular place to come on a nice day, and they would probably encounter others from the job site as well. As they walked, Kurt let his mind drift. He thought how long it had taken to get to this point. Kurt had been in the construction business all his life. Ever since he turned thirty, he would look at his bank balance every month. He had a figure in his head that, once reached, he would call it quits. Kurt got real close in 1987, and then the crash and bear market ensued. He panicked and sold his stocks near their lows. Man, he kicked himself for that.

Things were good now. Just a year and a half, or two, and he would be free. He and Nadine would live at their home in North Carolina and free to travel the world. He fancied Asia, she Latin America. He wanted to travel to those names that conjured up adventure and intrigue. Names like Hong Kong, Bangkok, Shanghai, and Istanbul. He wanted to visit Thailand and see the bridge on the River Kwai. He wanted to visit Hong Kong and have some suits tailor-made. Kurt had plans. Nadine, who spoke Spanish, fancied Mexico—in particular, a place called San Poncho about a thirty-minute drive from Puerto Vallarta. It was situated on the Pacific Ocean's Bahía de Banderas. Kurt and Nadine had vacationed there several times over the years.

There was a direct flight from Atlanta, which was not far from the house in North Carolina. Nadine wanted to buy or build a villa there, but Kurt didn't like the idea.

Nadine noticed Kurt's daydreaming and asked, "Whatcha thinkin' about, honey bunch?"

Kurt smiled and replied, "Our retirement, honey."

She smiled back, and at the same time saw Miller and Irena sitting at an outside café called "The Dancing Bear." She waved to them, and she and Kurt walked over.

Kurt asked, "How are you guys doing?"

Miller answered, "Just enjoying the day. How about you two?"

Kurt smiled and answered, "The same here, birthday boy."

Miller laughed and asked, "How the hell did you know?... Harry?"

Kurt replied, "Good guess, but no. From your HR file. You will be receiving a happy birthday email from the company on Monday. That's what happens if your b-day falls on a Sunday. You get the greeting a day late."

"What a gyp," Miller joked, and added, "Any money involved?"

Kurt answered, "I would not get my hopes up, JT."

Kurt and Nadine said they were going to continue to the Kremlin and take some photos. They were looking for the three Russian impersonators that worked there sometimes. One looked like Lenin, one like Stalin, and the last like Rasputin. Nadine thought it would be fun to have some photos taken with them. They charged only a few rubles. The couples said their goodbyes, and Kurt and Nadine walked off.

Irena said to Miller, "Slav, look at those two. They walk hand in hand like they are still young lovers."

Miller had noticed. Miller was having a gin and tonic and looking at the lunch menu. Irena said she was buying for Miller's birthday and he was looking at the expensive side of the menu to tease her. He found the surf-'n-'turf, 38 bucks. *A good start,* he thought. *Excellent; the black Russian caviar, 62 bucks.*

"Do you know what you want, Slav?"

"Why yes, I do, my Russian beauty. I will go with the surf-'n-'turf and the black Russian caviar. Maybe we should wash it down with a nice French

Bordeaux," Miller replied smiling, waiting for her reaction.

Irena did not disappoint and said, "What do you think, Slav, I am made out of rubles? I am good with the surf-'n-'turf, but no caviar. Who ever heard of paying 62 dollars for fish eggs? Is there something wrong with your brain? You can get onion rings instead."

Miller was laughing on the inside, knowing his order had the desired effect, but stayed stoic on the outside. "How about the French wine, my Russian princess?" he asked, waiting for the deluge.

She replied, "Do not Russian princess me. French wine....French wine? You do not even like wine. You said it gives you a headache. What is wrong with you, Slav? Sometimes you act like you have no sense."

Miller smiled and asked, "I guess that means no?"

Irena jumped back in, "Of course it means no. You are lucky I am here to protect you, for goodness' sake."

When the waiter came to the table, Miller smiled at Irena and ordered the roasted chicken with baked potato and a green salad. She realized she had been duped and changed the subject. "Were you born on Father's Day, Slav?"

JT answered, "As a matter of fact, I was. Every six to ten years or so, it falls on my birthday, and this is one of those years."

She replied, "What a nice gift for your father. How old are you now?"

Miller joked, "Twenty-five, but I don't feel a day over twenty-four."

Irena laughed and said, "You are the biggest liar. You are forty-one and an old geezer."

Miller frowned, then smiled and replied, "My dear Irena, I do not believe geezer fits the category of a man of my years. Perhaps mature is more appropriate. I believe it will be many more years before geezer is an adequate description, my love."

Radisson Ukraine Hotel building in Moscow, Russia

Harry and Sveta were finishing up their breakfast at the Ukraine Hotel. The restaurant was good and had a nice view of the Moscow River. Sveta had set up a river boat cruise, and they would be leaving shortly. The passengers were to meet in the lobby, and the people with tickets would get on the boat. Harry finished his coffee and the couple headed out. They met the others in the lobby and walked to the pier, then the boat. The boat was a typical passenger boat with a main cabin and an upper deck. It had small booths set up along the windows and tables in the center. You could order drinks but no food on this particular cruise.

Harry and Sveta chose a booth by a window. Harry slid the window open about halfway. "This is nice, Sveta. I am glad you thought of this," Harry said.

"My father took my mother and me on a boat here one summer. I thought it would be nice for us to do."

The engine chugged and the boat pulled out. After a few minutes, they floated past the Russian White House and Sveta pointed it out to Harry. Then they passed the Kievskaya Railway Station. The station had been built between 1914 and 1918 with regular service to Kiev, Belgrade, Bucharest, Budapest, and Prague. As the boat continued, they passed the Novodevichi convent, built during the reign of Ivan the Terrible.

The wind kicked up a bit and Harry closed the window. Harry really enjoyed being with Sveta and looked forward all week to their meetings. The couple decided to get off at Gorky Park. They would catch another boat back to the hotel later in the afternoon. Gorky Park first opened in 1928, and dotted throughout the park were amusements, a big roller coaster and other rides, a palace, several gardens, and a big pond which turned into a skating rink in the winter. Harry had seen the movie and had always wanted to visit.

Entrance to Gorky park 2016.

Karlov waited until after lunch before he called Yuri. He informed him that the testing on the door was almost complete, and the tainted door would be ready to install in a few weeks. The Russians had developed a highly sophisticated x-ray machine that penetrated thick construction materials far better than traditional x-ray. It used a method that bombarded materials with neutrons which penetrated deeper, with a clearer resolution. If anomalies did not show up using the neutron x-ray, it would never show up using the traditional x-ray the Americans had. This was what the Russians were counting on. It was time to push Miller to start the new door installation.

"Yes, old friend. Thank you for the information. I think our fish may pop out of the water when I ask this favor, but not to worry; I have a net to reel him back in," Yuri said.

"I am sure you do, Comrade, but do not be shy to call me to use the club if need be," the major replied.

Harry and Sveta were sitting in a seat on the Eurostar, a new roller coaster on loan from Germany for the summer. This was the Cadillac of roller coasters, and Sveta was very enthusiastic about trying it out--Harry not so much. The couple pulled down the safety bar and rested it on their laps. The coaster began its slow uphill ascent to the apex. Just as Harry thought, *So far so good*, the couple's car reached the top and began its descent. The coaster roared straight down then at tremendous speed, dipped up and to the left. Harry thought he would lose his breakfast. It made Sveta queasy as well. It roared straight for a ways, then took a hard right. Harry and Sveta held on tight. They both had their eyes closed. Finally, the roller coaster came to a halt. Thankful that it was over, the couple stood up and walked, a little wobbly, down the ramp.

When they were near the exit, Harry turned to Sveta and said, "Hey Sveta, that was fun. Let's do it again." Sveta's reply was a no comment.

Miller and Irena left the restaurant and were headed to the metro station. They stopped for a few minutes to watch the acrobats, who were a very popular attraction on the Arbat. As they continued, they stopped again to watch a dancing bear with its trainer. After each performance, the bear was rewarded with a cupful of beer. The bear looked to be pleasantly snockered and was dancing up a storm. They continued walking, made it to the metro station, and waited on the train platform. The train arrived, and just as they were entering the car a man stopped them, said something to Irena in Russian and handed her a piece of paper. The man hurried down the platform and walked away.

When the couple sat down, Irena said, looking uneasy, "A message from Yuri," and handed Miller the piece of paper. The message simply read, "Meet me at Café Pushkin at 7:00 tomorrow night. Yuri." Miller thought, *Great, he is finally making his move*. Miller kept the concerned look on his face and put the paper into his pocket.

☭

Harry and Sveta were walking through Neskuchny Garden, and she was explaining to him that the garden could be traced back to the year 1753. Back then, it had been more of a vegetable garden than the flower garden it was today. They continued to walk, when they saw some men setting up a platform. A sign read, this was to be the future site of the prototype Buran Space Shuttle OK-TVA. The OK-TVA was used for the thermal, mechanical, and acoustic testing during the design phase. Harry made a mental note to check it out at a later date. The couple continued back to the pier. They had to wait about forty minutes before they could board another boat back to the hotel.

☭

The next evening, Miller was on his way to the Café Pushkin. That morning, he informed Vera of the meeting with Yuri. She said Joe would have an operative there to watch his back. He ate beforehand at the mess hall. It was taco night. He figured he would just have a drink with Yuri. As he arrived, the same man that passed off the note was by the door. He motioned for Miller to follow him.

Yuri was sitting at a table in the back. "Hello, Mr. Miller. Thank you for coming. Please sit. May I get you anything?"

Miller had a gin and lime juice; they were out of tonic. Yuri was drinking cognac. Miller asked, "What is it you want?"

Yuri answered, "Mr. Miller, please do not be so glum. I want this to be an enjoyable experience for the both of us. Not to worry. We are just here tonight so I may ask one of my simple favors."

"And what might that be?" Miller asked. Yuri continued, "Mr. Miller, let me explain to you what is going to happen. The vault door you are planning to install on your project will be switched with another door of the same type. This door will house a listening device. Do you understand?"

Miller replied, "How in the hell do you plan on switching the doors?"

Yuri answered, "Ah, Mr. Miller, I am glad you asked that question. That will be your problem. You come up with a plan and get it done."

Miller shook his head and asked, "How am I supposed to do that without being discovered by security?"

Yuri replied, "Mr. Miller, that is precisely what you must figure out. We will meet here in one week, and you will tell me your plan. Thoroughly work out your plan like your life depends upon it, because perhaps it does. Do not disappoint me, and no excuses."

With that, Yuri drank the last of his cognac, stood up, and left. When he got to the door, the note guy followed him out. Miller stayed to finish his drink. He kind of liked the lime juice as an alternative to tonic. He thought about how he was going to pull this off. He knew he would need Vera's help.

The next morning at 9:30, Miller was in the vault room with Vera and Joe, debriefing them on the previous evening. The three of them went back and forth on how to do the door switch. Vera told them in extreme cases she could x-ray materials that were sent unsecured; as long as no anomalies showed up, the classification of the material could be changed to secure and be installed in the CAA areas. The three of them stayed in the room until they devised a plan. Now it would be up to Miller to sell it to the Russians.

The next week, Miller found himself again at the Café Pushkin. He was sitting across from Yuri, and Yuri noticed the contemptuous look Miller had in his eyes.

Yuri started, "Now Mr. Miller, like I said, I want this experience to be enjoyable for both of us, but on the other hand, if you resist or are uncooperative, it could get most unpleasant for you. I know you are American and hold your country sacred, just as we Russians do, but let me assure you, what we are doing is in no way putting your country at risk. All the information we would gather from having the compromised door in place will only provide certain information sooner than we would have normally realized. The only thing this does is give us an edge in dealing with a problem; that is all. So please, just view this as a business venture."

Miller showed no emotion and informed Yuri, "I figured out a way we may be able to get the door in."

Yuri replied, "Very good, Mr. Miller. What is your plan?"

Miller said, "The OBO PD John London has requested that TRIAD install the vault door earlier than scheduled. Evidently there are some high-level meetings scheduled in September, and John wants the door installed beforehand."

Yuri smiled, knowing this fit in with his calculations. Miller asked if the tainted door was ready, and Yuri assured him it was. Miller continued, "I will order a door from Rex Technology in a rush shipment. I will have it sent unsecured, which means the container which houses the door can be opened en route, as opposed to a secured container, which cannot. You can make the switch as it is going through customs. When it arrives on site, I will receive it. At the same time, I will notify the Site Security Manager and inform her the door was sent unsecured by mistake. Because the door is vital and scheduled for installation, I will ask her to please inspect and x-ray the door and get the classification changed. This procedure is acceptable, but SSM's are reluctant to do it because it puts the responsibility of a security breach on them. I will have to sell the idea to Vera. I will also inform John London, who could help convince her to do it, as well."

Yuri let Miller's words sink in. He thought that the simplest plan was the one that had the best chance of working. Yuri thought if it came to it, he could intervene if Vera refused. Yuri knew his team could be most persuasive.

Yuri finally asks, "And what if your SSM says no?"

Miller replied, "If she says no, the mission would still not be compromised. The door would be stored in a non-secure area of the building. I would then order another secure door from Rex and have it deposited into the SSA (Site Secure Access). This is where all the secured materials are kept before installation. I do have some ideas on how to get the tainted door into the CAA, if it comes to that."

Yuri asked, "Let's hope we will not have to use Plan B, but if we do, how could you get the tainted door into that secure area?"

Miller answered, "From the SSA there are two ways to get to the vault room. One way is through Post 2 and the CAA area that is secure, where I could not make a switch, but there is another way in. This other way goes through a portion of non-CAA or non-secure area to another secured access door called Post 3. This Post 3 leads back into the CAA area where the vault room is located. I could move the tainted door to a room in this non-secure area and make the switch en route to Post 3. To use Post 3, I will need to make a special request. I can make the claim that the Post 3 route would be easier access, which would be the truth. I would be the cleared American escorting the door, so I would have complete control of it."

Yuri thought Miller had come up with two halfway decent plans that could actually work and said, "Mr. Miller, please proceed with Plan A."

The next morning, there seemed to be some disagreement between Vera and Joe about how to proceed. Joe wanted Vera not to certify the door. He did not want the Russians thinking this was too easy and suspect something. Vera suggested they make the inspection, then quarantine the door while she claimed to be contacting Washington for guidance. This would be the game plan.

Miller went back to his office and called Rex Technology. He ordered two vault doors. One was sent secure, and the other non-secure. The non-secure door was scheduled to arrive on July 7 and the secure door on July 13. Miller informed Yuri that the vault door was on the way and was scheduled to be in country July 7, and the switch at customs could happen at that time. Miller would track the shipment and let them know the exact time the container would arrive. Yuri informed the major, and he would take care of it. The next morning, Miller received another certified check for $5000.

☭

Bo Beecher had been a basket case ever since meeting Karlov. A pending doom seemed to stay in his heart and follow him around. Either scenario was hard for him to comprehend. The first scenario was to tell the USG about the meeting. This would mean his reputation would be ruined. The second was working with Karlov and being a traitor to his country. Not a great choice. Bo mulled both in his mind and prayed to his God for guidance.

☭

In DC, Phil Mitchell, Vera's boss, was leaving his field office on Gallows Road, headed to Blair House. Phil was going to meet Colonel Ben Magsino, who had just flown in from Paris and was staying there. Ben was the head of the CIA's Russian Information Intelligence Unit. Ben was of Filipino decent. His father served with MacArthur on Corregidor Island in 1942. Ben graduated with honors from West Point in 1965 and enjoyed two tours in Viet Nam. He continued working with intelligence when he retired from the army and joined the CIA. Ben had been involved with Russian information-gathering for five years and intelligence for twenty-six. He was briefed on the espionage activities happening at the embassy in Moscow and as he read the communiqué, he thought of an opportunity he would like to pursue. He spoke to the CSA (Chief of Staff of the Army) about his idea.

The CSA concurred and told him to go ahead with the plan and said, "With everything going on with Russia like the Chechen War, the fight to launch democracy and to survive economically was a definite challenge for them. It would be worthwhile if we could push them into the right direction."

Ben outlined his plan to Phil and informed him he would be in Moscow the next week to implement it. Ben gave Phil the abridged version. He would keep the details within his own department and share only on a need-to-know basis.

☭

The vault door arrived at Sheremetyevo International Airport. It was going through customs when one of Karlov's men spotted it. Immediately a forklift swung into place, picked up the shipping container, and ushered it off to a large secure room off to the left. The major's men opened the container, pulled out the crated door, opened the crate, and replaced the door inside with the tainted one. The agent then buttoned up the crate and placed it back in the container. The forklift brought it through customs, and a customs agent stamped it through. The whole operation took about fifteen minutes. TRIAD's purchasing manager was there to receive the shipment once it cleared customs. He produced the bill of lading and received the crate. When the transport arrived at the embassy Miller was called to receive it. As planned, he called Vera and the two of them went through the motions of reclassifying the vault door. Everything was working according to plan, Miller thought, but then again, so did Karlov and Yuri.

Miller was sitting down at a table at the Angara Club. He took a sip of his drink and continued his conversation with Yuri and Karlov. "Gentlemen, the door arrived at the embassy today. I assume it was the tainted one, correct?"

Karlov replied, "Yes, we made the switch. Please go on."

Miller continued, "Vera agreed to see if she could reclassify the door. The bad news is that the door was put in quarantine until she can confirm with DC on the correct procedures to follow. She said it should take about three days if there is not a problem. If nothing comes up out of the normal with the x-rays, I would say our chances are good."

Yuri said, "Very well, Mr. Miller; let's hope we will not need our Plan B."

Karlov noticed a change in Miller. It seemed to him the contempt in his eyes was on sabbatical and replaced with a "Let's work together and not get caught" approach. He liked the change but would watch him very closely. *This one is smarter than he appears*, he thought.

Vera was at her desk when her phone rang. It was Phil Mitchell, telling her he was sending a secure fax via the US Marisat communications network. She made her way to the vault and collected the fax. On the front page it read "Code Name: Angara Club." Vera sat down at the table and began to read. When she finished the last sentence, it instructed her to shred the fax when through reading. The communiqué was basic information. The CIA would be involved in concert with the state department in the operation. Also, Colonel Ben Magsino would be in Moscow on Wednesday to brief her further. He would be accompanied by his security electronics engineer, Larry Boehlen. Country clearances were attached for the two men. After Vera read the fax, she walked to the shredder and disposed of it. She had met Ben previously. In the year she had been in Moscow, he had visited three times. On his country clearance it stated he was a liaison officer. On Larry Boehlen's it stated Embassy IT Engineer. She had never met this Mr. Boehlen.

Harry was excited. About 30% of the structural steel for the NOB was scheduled to arrive that day. Starting the structural steel would give him a big jump on the schedule. At about 10:30 a.m., the secured shipment arrived on site. Brian Cones, the CST on duty, was checking it into the SSA. As he looked over the steel, he noticed a "NO CAN DO" stamped on the side. It was in the form of letters that read "Made in Ukraine." This created quite a stir. On this project NO materials to be used in the NOB could be manufactured in Russia or on a list of satellite countries. The Ukraine was on this list. Harry was livid. The supplier knew about this and was being paid a premium to ensure the material did not come from one of these countries. This would set back project completion by a minimum of two months.

Harry called Rodney Carusso at the home office. He told him to reaffirm with the suppliers the "No Russian or satellite countries" rule. Next, he told him to airship as much structural steel as necessary to do the first floor of the NOB and not to wait for prefabrication. Harry would install, cut, and fabricate in place. He explained this would keep him going until the next shipment of prefabricated steel got there. He also requested two more welders to help with the cutting and welded connections. Rodney took it all in and wrote it down. He told Harry he would get right on it. Rodney was thankful he had a man of Harry's caliber heading up this project.

Bo just got off his cell. It was Natasha informing him that his friend the major wanted to see him at her apartment that evening. The major and Bo were to meet at 8:00. The major agreed that Anatoli would arrive at 7:00, so Natasha could show him her hospitality before the meeting.

When Bo arrived, the major was already there. Karlov focused his attention on Bo, "Please sit, Mr. Beecher. Natasha, get our friend a drink." Natasha got Bo his usual, a Jack and Coke. Bo gulped half of it down before the major started again. "Mr. Beecher, in your embassy building's SSA there is a vault door in quarantine; are you aware of this?" Bo nodded his head. The major continued, "This door will be installed in the next two weeks. The first thing I need you to do is when you are asked to inspect the door, is to accept it. Also, on the name plate is the manufacturer's name. The first 'O' in Rex Technology has a small punch mark just barely denting the steel. The second thing is that when the door is installed, I need you to verify this identification mark is in place and inform me. Do you understand my request, Mr. Beecher?" Again, Bo nodded his head. "Good. Be sure you do not disappoint me."

With that, the major and Anatoli left, and Natasha brought Bo another drink. Then another.

Ben Magisino was sitting down at the table in the vault room, getting ready to speak. He was joined by Vera, Joe Kelly, and Larry Boehlen. He started, "Vera and gentlemen, good morning and thank you for coming. We are here to go over the details of a joint operation with the CIA, state department, and MI6. The cryptonym we will be using is 'Angara Club.' I chose this name because this is where the Russians made first contact. I also thought it had a nice ring to it. Anyway, the mission's end game is to persuade Russia to make decisions that are in the best interests of the United States. Now how do we do that?

"The answer is the bug-riddled vault door. We will install this door in a studio and host mock meetings of false information in hopes of influencing the decisions the Russians will make. Larry will set up a studio in another suitable room and microphone this CPU or vault, as it is referred to, that we are sitting in now. He will set it up in such a way that the sounds in the vault are picked up in the studio with the same acoustical clarity as in the vault. This way, the mock meetings can take place here, and after the microphones are shut off, the regular meetings can proceed as usual.

"There will be two big lights installed over the entrance of this room--one red and one green. When the red light is on, the microphones are turned off, and it is safe to talk. When the green light is on, the microphones are operating, and it is not. The ambassador and his team are tasked with these mock meetings. He has agreed to this and as a matter of fact is very enthusiastic about the prospect. Nigel Crabtree from MI6 will be joining us from London, and he is tasked with writing the scripts for the meetings. The events the US government will be trying to influence will be top secret and only on a need-to-know basis. Any questions?"

Joe Kelly asked, "Ben, who will be building out the studio?"

Ben replied, "I will need two carpenters and an electrician that specializes in low voltage. I would like to find who we need on the embassy maintenance staff. Larry will install the microphones and electronics."

Vera spoke up and asked. "Ben, would you like me to speak with the maintenance chief at MEBCO to see if he has the people you need?"

Ben replied, "That will not be necessary, Vera. I have already taken care of it. The chief has recommended three individuals. I would like to interview them before I decide. If I decide these individuals are not capable, I can bring people from DC."

Joe asked, "What about TRIAD, Ben? They could lend you the people you need."

Ben responded and said, "Joe, I would like to keep the contractor in the dark on this. This is highly sensitive."

Joe kicked himself. He knew better. Joe replied, "Yes, of course, Ben. I had my head up my ass."

Ben smiled and said, "No problem, Joe. We all get our heads up there on occasion." Ben continued, "Okay, great. If there are no other questions, Larry and I will choose a suitable studio location and get started."

☭

Ben and Larry chose a room two doors down the hall from the vault. It was just the right size, and because it was to be remodeled shortly, the room was empty. It already had a solid metal door with a Simplex lock installed. Ben would have the combination changed and only he, Larry, and perhaps the Brit would know the combination. The studio would be a separate room built inside. It would be made of wood and fitted with acoustical panels on the walls and ceiling. The floor would be carpeted in the same way as the vault room. The tainted vault door would be installed on the east wall of the studio, which was the best acoustical location. Larry was torn between hard-wiring or going with wireless. Wireless would be less set-up time but not quite as reliable. He knew Ben would not want to take any chances and decided to hard-wire. He would drill one hole through the metal alloy plate of the vault room, about an inch and a quarter in diameter through the wall above the ceiling. Larry could fan out the wires for the microphones through this one hole. Larry figured out what materials and anything else he might need. Ben would take his list and have everything sent through diplomatic pouch. The items would be in Moscow in four days.

Irena was waiting for Miller at their apartment. She had made up her mind she would tell the Slav about Major Karlov. On the way to the apartment, Miller stopped at the Angara Club and picked up two pork chop dinners to take away. "Take away" was the term to use instead of "to go." For some reason, "to go" was still not in the Russian/English dictionary. When Miller walked in, Irena was sitting at the kitchen table. She was drinking a gin and tonic. He gave her a kiss, set the dinners on the stove top, and said, "Nice. Can you make me one of those, my love?"

Irena replied, "Slav, I have something to tell you."

He could see she was close to tears and asked, "What is it, Irena?"

She started, "Ivan is not my real uncle, and--"

Miller stopped her, thinking the apartment was probably bugged and replied, "Please do not say any more. I love you. I do not care about your family. Now fix me a gin and tonic before I spank your bottom."

She seemed to snap out of it and responded, "You better not, Slav, or I will crush your head like a walnut."

Miller laughed and said, "Oh, you think so, huh?"

With that, Miller grabbed her, and put her over his knee, and gave her rump a hard slap. She squirmed away and ran into the bedroom to hide under the covers. Miller followed her in and ripped the covers off of her. She hid her face in the pillow, and Miller snuggled up close to her and kissed her on the neck. She turned over and pulled his head close to hers and kissed him hard on the lips. Miller knew the pork chops would have to wait.

John London and Harry had been briefed on this espionage caper taking place on their project. Harry wasn't happy about it, but he had no choice. If this cloak-and- dagger play cost the project time and man hours, John had agreed that the contractors would be entitled to compensation. He told Miller to start keeping track of his time and any delays that occurred in the future. Miller and Harry were the only contractor personnel who knew what was going on. The others would be kept in the dark.

Bo was in the building's SSA, looking for the vault door. He asked David, the SSA superintendent, and he showed Bo where it was. He told David to uncrate the door because he had to inspect it to make sure it wasn't damaged during shipping. The light wasn't the best where the door was located, and Bo could not see the punch mark. With his fingers, he felt around the name plate and thought he found the indentation. He asked David for a flashlight, and as he looked closer, he saw the punch mark. Miller walked up and observed Bo looking for something and apparently finding it.

Miller asked, "What are you looking, for Bo?"

Bo was unaware of JT's presence and flinched. Miller noticed. "Oh, hey JT. Just checking to make sure the vault door wasn't damaged during shipping," Bo answered.

Miller replied, "I did that when it got here. I guess it doesn't hurt to check again."

Bo asked, "I thought this door was quarantined?"

Miller answered, "It was released this morning. We will start the installation in the next couple of days. We are waiting on some electrical components to finish the installation. The electrical stuff should be on site today or tomorrow."

Bo asked, "Why don't we install the door now and install the electrical later?"

Miller smiled and replied, "Good question, and here's the answer. The OBO is giving us eight hours total, to uninstall the old door and install the new. The USG does not want the vault room out of commission any longer than that. Harry wants all the materials on site and checked before we attempt it. Eight hours does not give us a lot of time, and Harry wants our ducks in a row."

Bo nodded his head in acknowledgment and Miller walked off to another area of the SSA, pretending to be looking for something, but really waiting for Bo to leave. When he did, Miller walked over to the door. He pulled out the small tactical flashlight he usually carried with him when he was in the field and looked at the name plate. At first glance, he did not notice anything amiss; then he saw what appeared to be a punch mark. He asked himself if this was what Bo had been looking for, or whether he was merely reading the name plate. He would mention it to Vera and keep an eye on Mr. Beecher.

That evening at eight o'clock, a truck carrying a secure container arrived on site. Inside was the secure vault door that Miller and Vera were waiting for. Miller pushed a dolly cart in place. Vera removed the secure lock and swung open the container door. The vault door was put in the front of the container, so it could be removed first. With the help of the driver, they used the truck cargo elevator to lower the door and place the door on a dolly cart. Vera locked the container and signaled the driver to set it down in the secure area designated for secure containers. Miller and Vera rolled the door to the SSA and exchanged it for the tainted door. For a precaution, from his coat Miller pulled out a punch set and small hammer to try to duplicate the mark. He chose a punch around the same size. He checked it in the indentation, then chose another. When he was satisfied that he had the correct punch, he lined it up and tapped it with the hammer. *Not bad*, he thought.

Then he and Vera pushed the dolly with the tainted door to Post 2. The CAG buzzed them in, and they walked down the hall two doors past the vault to the studio room. Larry Boehlen was waiting for them, to let them in. They pushed the dolly inside the room and left it with Larry. Vera had Larry sign a form, and both she and Miller left. They went back down to the secured container where the driver had left it, and Vera installed a new lock and new unbroken seal. The next morning when her team processed the materials, no one would be the wiser that the container had been tampered with.

Harry and Sveta were just sitting down at the Ukraine restaurant, one of the restaurants in the Ukraine Hotel. It was large, had a nice Gothic style to it, and served Ukrainian, Russian, and European cuisine. Sveta was trying to school Harry on the Ukrainian dishes. Harry said he was willing, so Sveta ordered for him. She ordered Ukrainian borsht, a vegetable soup made out of beets, cabbage, potatoes, tomatoes, carrots, onions, garlic, and dill. Next was the kovbasa—various kinds of smoked or boiled pork, beef, and chicken sausage. And last, Sveta's personal favorite--deruny, or potato pancakes, usually served with rich dollops of sour cream.

First came the borsht. Harry added just a touch of salt and pepper. He waited a minute for it to cool, then took his spoon and plunged it into the bowl. He tasted it and told Sveta, "This is good. What is it?"

Sveta started to tell him; then she thought she would have some fun. "Well, Harry, the red color in soup is the blood from pig's birth mixed with cow urine. It is known to cure constipation." Harry thought, *I am sure it would.* She continued, "The vegetables added have been grown in the sewage by the canal. This way they retain much higher content of vitamins than those grown in soil."

Harry could see it was hard for her to keep a straight face and decided to play along. Harry answered, "Nice, Sveta! Yes, that cow urine really brings out the flavor and the pig's blood is to die for."

Sveta could not contain herself and started to laugh hysterically and Harry along with her.

☭

Miller said good night to Vera and walked back to the man camp. He stopped by the mess hall, but it was getting ready to close. He grabbed some meatloaf, some salad, some potatoes, and for dessert, a couple bananas. He placed them in a to-go container and went up to his room. As he sat at his table eating, he wondered if Bo really had been recruited by the Russians. Both he and Harry had noticed a difference in Bo of late. He seemed moody and kept to himself the last few weeks. Miller knew this could be normal on these kinds of projects, especially for the new guys. Far from home and their families, these guys either dragged up (quit) and went back to the States or snapped out of it and got with the program. Bo was used to overseas work, so Miller did not think loneliness was the problem. Miller walked over to his CD player and looked through the CD's like he was shuffling a deck of cards. He pulled out The Band's (70's Rock Group) first album "Music from Big Pink." He punched through to the last song on side one, "The Weight." Miller turned it up, and all of a sudden, he heard Robbie Robertson play that funky little guitar intro before Levon Helm belted out the opening verse.

☭

Harry was chowing down on the potato pancakes. He would dip them in the sour cream before each bite. "Sveta, these are great. What are these, sheep droppings?" he asked.

Sveta laughed and answered, "Please stop, Harry. Deruny is one of my favorites. My grandmother would make these for me and my mother when we would visit her in the Ukraine. It is hard work, and I loved my grandmother for it."

Harry asked, "How do you make them?"

Sveta had been hoping Harry would ask. "The first thing is grate potatoes to very small pieces. This is hard part. Next you add little flour, eggs, and salt and pepper. Some people add grated onions or garlic."

Harry replied, "We will have to make these sometime. I will do the potato- grating."

The couple finished their dinner and walked back to the embassy. Harry kissed Sveta good night in front of her apartment door. When she left, he looked at his watch and hurried off to his apartment to hit the sheets.

After Miller and Vera left the studio, Larry Boehlen pulled out two plate steel/iron neodymium magnets. He placed one on each face of the tainted door. The magnets would provide a disruption of any microwave signal coming through, thus preventing the energy needed for the listening device to activate. When the Russians tried to monitor the listening device, all they would hear was silence. When the studio was set up and everything in place, Larry would remove the magnets.

When Vera left Miller, she went back to her office. She opened her desk drawer and picked out the X-rays of the tainted door. This was about the tenth time she had looked at these. For the life of her, she could not find any anomalies in the X-ray. She thought she might get Ben's take on them. After this was over, she would recommend the door be sent back to DC and taken apart to see how the Russians were able to fool the X-ray.

The First Chechnya War

The Chechen Republic is located in the North Caucasus, sitting in the southernmost part of Eastern Europe, and about 100 kilometers from the Caspian Sea. Grozny is the capitol of the republic.

With the dissolution of the Soviet Union in 1991, an independence movement called the Chechen National Congress was formed. This effort was led by an exSoviet Air Force general and the new Chechen president.

It campaigned for the recognition of Chechnya as a separate nation. This movement was opposed by the Russian Federation, which argued that Chechnya had not been an independent entity within the Soviet Union as the Baltic, Central Asian, and other Caucasian States had been, therefore was part of the Russian Soviet Federative Socialist Republic and hence did not have a right under the Soviet constitution to seek independence. The First Chechen War took place over a two year period that lasted from 1994 to 1996, when Russian forces attempted to regain control over Chechnya, which had declared independence in November 1991.

Despite overwhelming numerical superiority in men, weaponry, and air support, the Russian forces were unable to establish effective permanent control over the mountainous area due to numerous successful fullscale battles and insurgency raids by the Chechens. In three months, Russia lost more tanks (over 1,997 tanks) in Grozny than during the Battle of Berlin in 1945. The widespread demoralization of the Russian forces in the area and a successful offensive to retake Grozny by Chechen resistance forces led the Russian president to declare a cease-fire in November 1996. The US government's view was that any former satellite country taken over by Soviet Russia had a right to sovereignty after the fall of the Soviet Union, as long as they intended a democratic nation.

This view was camouflage, and the real reason was to look after the interests of the American and European oil fields in the Caspian region, and also to protect and utilize the pipeline running to Grozny. It was in the best interests of the United States for an independent state which would be easier to manipulate or deal with than Russia. Ben Magsino looked at the memo from Langley. Ben's first directive would be to persuade the Russians, to conclude it was in their best interests, to sign a peace treaty and recognize Chechnya as an independent nation. Ben would work with the Brit on the best way to accomplish this.

Lotte Hotel in Moscow 2015.

The next morning at 6:20 a.m., Ben Magsino was sitting down having his coffee, getting ready for breakfast at the Lotte Hotel on Novinskiy Boulevard. The five-star hotel was the first choice for visiting government employees of a certain pay grade assigned to Moscow. Only a five-to-ten-minute walk to the embassy, and the same to the Arbat district. A perfect location to the city center. Larry Boehlen wasn't quite as lucky. He was staying at the Belgrade. Not bad, but not as nice as the Lotte. Ben sipped his coffee. A few minutes later, in walked Nigel Aloysius Crabtree. Nigel was wearing a Gieves & Hawkes tweed plaid three-piece suit made in Scotland and was looking sharp. He was in his early forties, clean-shaven, with curly brown hair and a slightly pompous air to him.

He walked over to Ben's table and asked, "Please excuse me, sir. Colonel Magsino?"

Ben smiled and replied, "Yes, you must be Nigel. Please sit down."

Nigel said, "Good morning Colonel. Yes, thank you. Nigel Aloysius Crabtree reporting, sir."

Ben answered, "Fine. I hope you had a good flight over last night."

Nigel replied, "Not too shabby, Colonel. Only three and a half hours from London. I did not get a chance to have dinner, so I could eat a raw wildebeest this morning."

Ben smiled and said, "Well then, we need to get you fed. Let's get some food." The Lotte had a great breakfast buffet that catered to the American and British palate. They had it all. Ben went through the line and chose some scrambled eggs, ham, hash browns, rye toast, and oatmeal. Nigel filled his tray with bacon, fried eggs, sausage, crumpets, kippers, baked beans, and marmalade.

Ben asked, "Nigel, are you going to eat all that?"

Nigel responded, "You bet I will, Colonel, except maybe not all the kippers. Look a bit dodgy. Oh, bloody hell. I forgot the deviled kidneys."

Nigel went back to the line and Ben walked over and put his tray down on the table. He picked up his coffee cup to get a refill at the coffee station. As he walked over, he made a mental note to check what the hell deviled kidneys looked like.

☭

When the two finished breakfast, they strolled to the embassy, and Ben escorted Nigel to Vera's office. Nigel would have to go through the badging process and security briefing. When he was through, he would meet Ben in the studio with Larry Boehlen.

☭

Harry was in his office with Tom Scaraponi. Tom said, "Here you go, Harry. I got the new safety jackets in. These have more pockets and Velcro fasteners."

Harry looked them over and chose an extra-large. "These are nice, Tom," Harry replied and put it on. The new ones were bright yellow, while the old ones were orange. On the sixth level, two CAW's, Donny Green and Stacy Wakefield, were ripping out sheetrock. Donny and Stacy usually stuck together. One reason was because they were like two peas in a pod, and the other was that nobody else much liked them. CAW's were another breed, and being a smartass was a prerequisite. You had to be tough, or the other guys would eat you alive just for kicks.

Donny and Stacy were the worst. They would go out of their way to harass coworkers. Management wore white hard hats, and the craft people or trades wore other colors. On the whole, trade guys did not cotton too much to management guys. The CAW's felt they were the ones out working their asses off while management were in their cushy offices making the big bucks. As the pair was working, they saw a white hat on the floor below them. When a CAW said, "white hat," it was a derogatory term.

Stacy said, "Look Donny, let's fuck with this white hat."

Donny replied, "I think it's the safety engineer. See, he is wearing a shiny new safety jacket—piece of shit."

Stacy moved behind another CAW working on the floor. Without the CAW knowing it, Stacy grabbed the claw hammer out of his toolbox. Stacy then moved to the stairwell and placed the hammer on the floor by the edge of the stair landing. The stairwell was open, with only wooden guard rails around the stair landing. As the white hat approached the stairwell on the floor below, Stacy slid the hammer off the edge with his foot and it fell to the floor below, just missing Harry by a foot. Harry looked up and just caught a glimpse of Stacy moving away from the opening, trying to get out of sight.

Harry yelled, "Goddammit, Stacy, I see you. Stop where you are."

Harry hurried up the stairs to see Donny trying to get to the stair landing on the other side of the building. "Donny, stop right there or I swear I will have you back in the States by tomorrow morning. No bonus, no 330 [330 was the number of days you had to be out of the country before you got the foreign workers tax credit], no nothin'." Stacy and Donny stood still. Harry was livid. "What the hell was that?" Harry asked.

Stacy answered, "It was an accident, Harry."

Harry shouted, "Accident, my ass! You sons-of-bitches tried to bean me." Harry reached for his Motorola and said into the mic, "Tom, you have a copy? This is Harry."

There was some static; then Harry heard, "Go ahead, Harry. This is Tom."

Harry said, "Tom, we have a situation. Meet me on the 6th floor."

Tom answered, "On my way, Harry."

When Tom got there, Harry informed him, "Tom, it looks like our friends Stacy and Donny are at it again. These idiots kicked a hammer off over the side of the stairwell and tried to bean me."

Stacy replied, "We didn't try and hit you, Harry. Just wanted to give the white hat a little scare. We didn't know it was you. You had the new safety jacket on, and we thought you were the safety engineer, and--"

Donny interrupted and asked, "What's this *we* shit, Stacy? You are the one who kicked the hammer."

Harry replied sternly, "Stop it, both of you. Tom, write these guys up for unsafe work practices and whatever else you can think of. If you find these guys again breaking any safety regulations, they are gone. I don't care what it is. You bastards better grow up fast or start looking for another job. AM I CLEAR?"

The pair nodded, and Tom wrote them up. Harry was tired of their shenanigans. He thought he should make an example of the two; he hated to lose them, because they were good workers, but good workers or not, if they tried pulling anything like that again, they were gone.

When Vera was through with Nigel, she walked him down the hall to the makeshift studio. Ben and Larry were inside working. The studio was set up and ready to go, except for a few more speakers Larry was installing inside. The tainted door was installed in a corner of one of the studio walls. Larry tried to install the speakers in such a way as to completely surround the door with the sounds coming from the vault. After Larry installed the microphones in the vault, he would conduct a series of tests to ensure that the listening devices were placed in the best locations to pick up all of the sounds coming from the room. There were three desks set up outside the studio in the room. In one of them, Ben was sitting looking at Vera's X-rays of the tainted vault door. He also did not see anything out of the norm. He thought to himself, *how did the Ruskies do it?* Ben then heard a knock on the door. He fumbled with the Simplex lock to let the guests in. It was Vera depositing Nigel with the two Americans.

As Nigel walked in, he said, "Blimey, this is some set-up."

Ben replied, "Hello, Nigel. I see you have your embassy badge--good. Hi, Vera. Are you finished with him?"

Vera responded, "Yes, Ben, he's all yours."

"Great, Vera, thank you," Ben said.

Vera replied, "You're welcome, Ben. Now I am late for a meeting and have to run. I will see you later."

With that, Vera left the room and hurried down the hall. Ben said, "Nigel, this is your desk."

Ben called in to the studio, "Larry, can you come out here for a moment?"

As Larry walked in, he replied, "Sure, boss. What's up?"

Ben said, "Larry, I would like you to meet Nigel Crabtree. Nigel, this is Larry Boehlen."

Nigel put out his hand and said, "Glad to meet you, mate."

"Likewise," replied Larry.

Ben continued, "Nigel, Larry is our security electronics engineer. Larry, Nigel is our script writer and strategist. If you will excuse us Larry, I need to speak with Nigel in the vault for a few minutes. By the way, how are things going?"

Larry replied, "Not bad, Ben. I should have all the hardware installed by COB today and will start the testing tomorrow. If all goes well, I will be ready on my end by tomorrow evening."

Ben answered, "Great, Larry. You can get back to it. Nigel and I will be next door."

With that, Nigel and Ben walked back down the hall. When the pair were situated inside the vault, Ben started, "Nigel, what do you know about 'The Angara Club'?"

Nigel thought a minute and replied, "It is a propaganda assignment to provide false information to the Russians in hopes of swaying them to act in a way we fancy. Is that correct, sir?"

Ben said, "Yes, Nigel. Our first directive is to convince the Russians to sign a peace treaty with Chechnya and to agree to their right to sovereignty. My question for you, Nigel, is how do we do that?"

Nigel replied, "Well, my first reaction, sir, is that the Russians respect only the side that is strongest. In my mind, the reason the Russians fancied a cease-fire in the first place is because the Chechens were holding their own in the mountainous regions of the country and the Russians were taking on too many casualties. When the Chechens took back Grozny, that was it. The cease-fire hiatus would provide an opportunity to allow the Russians to reformulate their battle plan. Would you say that was a fair assessment, Colonel?"

Ben replied, "Yes, I do, Nigel. Please continue."

Nigel continued, "Quite right. Now if the Russians only respect strength, we must make them believe Chechnya is stronger than it actually is. How do we do that? We make the buggers believe that Britain, the United States, Germany, and France are supporting them—not only financially, but also ready to send in troops if need be. Now none of this will be made public, but the illusion of this will be apparent in the false information we supply them here."

Ben thought, *Great, the Limey and I are on the same page*. He then asked, "Nigel, how soon can you come up with a meeting script based on what you have just told me?"

Nigel answered, "Colonel, we will have to start slow at first, then speed up the progression of propaganda with each weekly meeting. I would like to get copies of the ambassador's meeting minutes for the last several weeks, so I can start altering the existing narrative to the one we are trying to convey."

Ben replied, "I will get the minutes from the ambassador. Nigel, I need the first meeting script in six days. Will that be a problem?"

Nigel squirmed in his chair a bit and answered, "Colonel, I would have preferred a fortnight, but if six days is the target, it will be ready."

☭

At 8 a.m., the CAW door installers were leaving the SSA with the vault door. They pushed the dolly down the hall to the vault room. A CST was waiting for them, and he would monitor the work until the new door was installed. The clock was ticking. They had only eight hours to uninstall the old door and install the new. They would not leave the vault room until the work was completed. Harry would send up some sandwiches at lunch time;

the CAW's would eat fast and keep working. The QC inspection was scheduled for 4 p.m.

Nigel was at his desk, pounding out the script. The first mock meeting rehearsal with the ambassador was scheduled for day after tomorrow; the script would be ready. Larry was still tweaking the sound system in the studio. He just needed to finish adjusting the volume controls for each speaker. He just about had it.

Bo looked at his watch. It was 3:30 p.m. He closed down his computer and made his way to the vault room to see if the door installation was complete, so he could do his inspection. When he got there, the door was installed, and the electricians had just finished. The CAW's were touching up the paint around the door. The first thing Bo did was look for the punch mark on the name plate. It was there. He went through the quality-control checklist and it all looked good. Joe Amato, OBO Electrical Engineer, was there, verifying that the electrical connections were correct and complete. Vera was there as well. She said she was there to fill in for her CST (Construction Surveillance Technician) while he was on break, but actually, she was there to watch Bo. Vera saw him make a point to look for the punch mark on the name plate of the door. She was sure Miller was right. Beecher was compromised.

That evening, Miller met Yuri at the Pushkin to inform him that the tainted door was installed. Yuri was happy. Once Karlov verified from Beecher the door with the punch mark was installed, he would send Miller another $5000 check.

Joe Kelly had a tail on Bo Beecher for more than a week, and so far, no unusual contacts. The Russian operative he had watching him tonight was Moshi. At 8 p.m., Bo left the camp and was on his way to the Belgrade. Moshi followed him up to the 19th floor, watched him go into apartment 1907, and waited. On the door was a sign that read "Massage Therapist - Natasha Strasavich." Moshi knocked on the door.

Natasha looked at Karlov and he said, "Anatoli, go see who's at the door."

Anatoli opened the door and Moshi said in Russian, "Hello. I would like to schedule an appointment."

Anatoli replied, "The massage therapist is busy now. Come back in an hour." Moshi nodded and left. He went down to the lobby where he could see the elevators. He would try and get a glimpse of them as they left.

☭

Karlov yawned then said sternly, "Do not waste my time, Mr. Beecher. Do you have something to report?"

Bo replied, "Yes, the vault door was installed today, and the punch mark was on the name plate. I certified the door and signed off on the installation."

The major answered, "Excellent, Mr. Beecher. I was afraid you would disappoint me, but you have not. Now get out of here. I will contact you later."

Bo protested, "You said verifying the vault door would put an end to this. Why do you need to contact me?"

The major smiled and replied, "Mr. Beecher, I say a lot of things. Sometimes I mean them; sometimes I do not. In your particular instance, I did not."

Beecher's face turned red. Without saying a word, he left the apartment. Karlov commanded, "Natasha, get in here."

Natasha hurried into the room. Karlov continued, "Anatoli, wait for me downstairs in the bar. I will be down momentarily after Natasha shows me some hospitality."

Anatoli chuckled faintly at the comment and left immediately. Natasha, as if on cue, unbuttoned her dress and let it fall. She unhooked the back clasp of her bra and set free her flawless breasts.

Karlov looked Natasha up and down and said in a buttery tone, "Come here, Natasha. If you are a good girl, Daddy has a present for you. If you are a bad girl, Daddy will have to punish you. Your choice, my dear."

☭

Anatoli took a seat at the bar. Snezhinka strolled up, and he ordered a coffee. Moshi kept up the surveillance. About thirty minutes later, Karlov came down and walked to the bar and over to Anatoli. He said something, and Anatoli stood up and the pair walked out to the street, where a waiting car whisked them away.

☭

Now that the vault door was installed and the studio ready, Larry Boehlen removed the neodymium magnets from the tainted door. Larry walked out into the hall to give Ben a call on his cell.

"Ben Magsino."

Larry said, "Ben, we are now open for business."

Ben replied, "Thank you, Larry. Good work. Enjoy your evening."

☭

Larry walked back to his desk, where Nigel was just finishing the first draft of the script. All he had to do was sweeten it up in the morning and let Ben review it before the rehearsal. He was ready for a break. Nigel said, "Larry, I'm knackered. Do you fancy going out for a wee beverage this evening?"

Larry thought about it and replied, "Why not, Nigel? What hotel are you at?"

Nigel amswered, "The Hotel Lotte."

Larry laughed and replied, "The Hotel Lotte? Well, la-di-da. Nice digs. They've got me at the Belgrade. Not bad, but no Lotte. How about after work we go to our rooms and clean up a little, then meet in the Lotte's lobby at 9:00?"

Nigel replied, "Sounds good, mate."

Chapter Nine

THE THESPIAN AMBASSADOR

A year earlier, in September 1996, Arnold Schwarzenegger was in Moscow at the grand opening promoting his new Planet Hollywood Café. It had been open almost a year and was very popular. Nigel and Larry walked through the door and were seated at a table. The place was moderately packed, but still a table was available to them.

Nigel asked, "What do you fancy, Larry?"

Larry looked at the menu and replied, "I am going to go with the mushroom and olive burger, french fries, and a Tuborg. What about you?"

Nigel said, "I will have the bistro sirloin steak. It comes with salad and chips. As for the beverage, let's see…I guess a Heineken would do."

The waiter came and took their orders. When he returned with the drinks, there were an additional two shots of vodka on his tray. As he set the drinks down, Larry informed him, "Excuse me. We did not order vodka shots."

The waiter replied, "Tonight is free vodka shot night. All people get free shot."

Larry responded, "Oh, okay, thank you."

They finished their dinner and the shots sat there. The two just wanted dinner and a few beers. They both had busy days the following morning. Finally, Nigel said, "Bloody hell." He picked up one of the shots and continued, "Here's to you, mate. Over my lips, past my gums--look out, liver, here it comes." He slammed it back and replied, "Bloody awful. This must be the bottom shelf."

Larry laughed, picked up the other shot, and said, "To the best pop group to ever come out of England...the Beatles."

Nigel held up his beer and finished the last of his Heineken as Larry drained his vodka shot for the toast. Nigel liked the Beatles, but he was more of a Stones fan. After the shots started to kick in, the pair decided to stop by the Hard Rock for a night cap. It was only a few blocks away. The first Hard Rock opened in London in the early '70s and Nigel had been a frequent visitor for years. He was curious what this one was like. The evening was cool for late July, but not too cool, so they sat outside on the patio and ordered vodka shots. As they sat there, they heard music coming from an alley up the street. After the shots, they decided to investigate on the way home. As they got closer to the music, they saw several bohemian types mulling around outside. As they walked up, they heard the band kick into the Rolling Stones' song "Sympathy for the Devil." That was it. The pair had to go in and check it out.

They paid the guy at the door two bucks each to get in. The place was a converted warehouse and converted in a low-budget way. They had a lobby that sold Baltika and Stariy Melnik Russian beer and Stolichnaya vodka shots. Past the lobby was a very large room. In the back was the stage, and the rest of the place was just open floor for dancing and mingling. The smoke was thick, and the place looked like a fire trap. The venue was packed to the rafters with inebriated bohemian and hippie types. The Russian Rock and Roll band was hot. These guys were doing covers with note-for-note precision.

Larry and Nigel decided to settle to the left of the stage against the wall. As they did, a very attractive Russian teen with green hair asked if Larry had a light. He told her he did not. She asked his name just as another equally attractive friend of hers walked up. She had blonde hair.

Larry replied, "My name is Larry, and this is my friend Nigel."

The two girls looked their new acquaintances over and the green-haired one replied in pretty good English, "My name is Zhanna, and this is my friend Katya."

Nigel entertained the ladies while Larry went and got vodka shots and

Baltika beers for the four of them. In a few minutes they would all start on the journey to inebriation. Zhanna started to snuggle up to Larry and Katya with Nigel. The band played the starting guitar notes to "All Along the Watchtower", the Jimi Hendrix version. Larry grabbed Zhanna's hand and led her to the dance floor. Nigel and Katya were right behind them. The four of them were having a great time dancing, drinking beer, doing vodka shots, and enjoying each other's company in their three sheets to the wind states. While they were waiting for the next song to start, a cigarette girl walked by and Larry bought a pack of Marlboros and a Bic lighter. Larry did not smoke, as a rule, but occasionally when he was snockered it seemed like a good idea. Zhanna borrowed the Bic. She pulled out a crumpled-looking cigarette, lit up, took a long drag, then passed it to Katya. She did the same and passed it to Nigel. Nigel looked at Larry.

"Larry said, "What the hell, Nigel. Go for it."

Nigel put the joint to his lips and inhaled deeply. He coughed like he was having a tuberculosis attack as the others laughed. Larry took his turn and the group passed it around until the joint had become a nub. They all got pleasantly ripped, and just as Larry was taking the last hit, the band started in with the Beatles classic "Back in the USSR," and the crowed went crazy.

After the last dance, the girls wanted to continue the festivities at the Hungry Duck. Nigel and Larry were not hep to the goings-on at that establishment but were happy to hang with the girls, so they agreed. They stopped a taxi, and the four drunk and stoned partygoers got inside.

Zhanna said, "Mr. Larry, when we get there, Katya and I will dance on the bar for you."

Larry answered, "Sounds good. Nigel and I will dance as well."

Zhanna replied, "I am sorry, Mr. Larry, but only women are allowed to dance on the bar--no men."

When they got there and went inside, Nigel and Larry noticed all the young girls dancing on the bar with the men staring up from their seats. They deposited themselves at a place by the bar. Larry saw a big sign in English that read, "All girls dancing on the bar must remove their panties and be wearing a dress."

Larry informed Nigel, who started having momentary heart palpitations as he readied himself for the show. Zhanna and Katya could not get their underwear off fast enough and joined the others on the bar.

☭

The next morning Nigel was at his desk finishing up the editing job on the script. It had to be complete by 10 a.m. when he would meet with Ben for the review. Nigel felt like he was in a coma from the previous night's alcohol abuse. His head felt like it was in a vise, his body ached, and his stomach felt like he drank a gallon of turpentine--besides that, he didn't feel too bad. He took another three aspirin and continued typing. Nigel heard a fumbling of the Simplex lock, and in crawled Larry. Larry looked like he just got out of a clothes dryer and was wearing dark shades.

Nigel said, "Morning, old chap."

Larry just looked straight ahead. When he moved his head, it hurt. "Yeah, morning, Nigel," he replied weakly. Then he asked, "How are you feeling this morning, Nigel?"

Nigel replied, "Bloody awful, but in a good way."

Larry laughed, and it hurt. He said, "I hear you. That was a night for the record books. Damn, that was fun, but I am paying the price now."

Nigel responded, "Quite right. What happened with you and Zhanna after the Hungry Duck?"

Larry replied, "We took a taxi to the Belgrade. I gave her the boot this morning before I came to work. What about you?"

Nigel answered, "My slapper was daft, but blimey, she had nice knockers though. I gave her the push at 4:00 this morning so I could get a few hours' sleep."

The pair heard the fumbling of the lock once again, and in walked Ben. He was clear-eyed and full of energy, in contrast to the other two. Ben greeted them, "Morning, gentlemen." Then he stopped. He looked closer at the two. Both looked frazzled, and Larry was still wearing his sunglasses. Ben asked, "What the hell happened to you guys last night?"

Nigel spoke up. "Oh, nothing much, Colonel. Just a bit of team-building."

Ben replied, "Oh…okay, fine. Larry, everything ready on your end?"

Larry answered, "Yes, sir. I finished it up last night."

Ben continued, “Great, Larry. Nigel, is the script ready for my review?”

“Right-o, Colonel, sir,” he replied, and he handed Ben the pages.

☭

At KGB headquarters, Lieutenant Maxim Sokolov was busy at his computer. He was trying to focus additional microwaves at the approximate location of the vault room at the American embassy. Maxim wanted to give the signal a boost if he could. He checked the communication between his computer and the listening device in the vault door. He was getting back a signal. That was all he needed. Any sound coming from the vault room would automatically be recorded on his computer. So far nothing had been recorded. He would provide a full transcript to Karlov after each recorded meeting the Americans might have.

☭

At 2:00 p.m., the ambassador and his staff entered the vault room. The light above the vault door was flashing red. This meant the microphones were turned off and it was safe to speak. Copies of the script were on the table in front of them. Ben, who was already at the table, started after everyone settled down, “Good afternoon. Thank you all for coming. In front of you is a copy of a dialogue script we will be going over this afternoon. We will go over this several times until we get it exactly right. Just think of this as a play we will be performing. Please ask your questions as we go. I will answer them and may make suggestions on improving your performance. Now let’s get started. Ambassador, if you please...?”

Exterior and interior of Bolshoi Theater in Moscow.

That evening, Miller was putting on his blue suit. He was looking forward to an evening out with Irena, Harry, and Sveta. Harry was able to get four tickets to the Bolshoi Ballet. Part of Russia's renewal program was to bring a more modern theme to the ballet. In 1995 the longtime director of the ballet, Yuri Grigorovich, who reigned with an iron fist for over thirty-one years, was forced out so new director, Vyacheslav Gordeev, could focus on modern ballet instead of the classics. However, there was still a desire for the classics occasionally, and this evening a special performance of *Romeo and Juliet* was scheduled at 9:00. Miller wasn't too keen on the ballet itself but was interested in the Bolshoi Theater. The original theater was opened in 1825. Its classical Greek design had eight vertical columns in front, with the chariot of Apollo on the portico completing the architectural flair. The five-tiered auditorium was renowned for its size and excellent acoustics. It had gilded stucco, murals on the ceiling, and in the center a huge tiered crystal chandelier. It could seat over 2100.

On the other side of the coin, Irena and Sveta loved the ballet. Sveta and Irena's father would take her to the Bolshoi when she was a little girl. Irena trained as a ballerina up until the age of eleven. She just hadn't progressed as her instructors would have liked and was cut from the company, but that did not stop her love of the ballet. *Romeo and Juliet* was Irena's favorite. Written and composed by Sergei Prokofiev in 1935, the ballet is based on Shakespeare's tragic love story.

Irena and Sveta were getting ready in Sveta's apartment. Harry made reservations at the Tverskaya Restaurant across the street from the theater on Petrovka Street. They would have dinner and drinks, then walk across the street to enjoy the ballet. Harry and Miller showed up at Sveta's apartment at about the same time and collected their dates. The girls were excited, and some of it was wearing off on Harry and Miller. After dinner, the two couples walked out of the restaurant and crossed the parking lot. Harry and Miller stopped to look at the theater.

Miller asked, "Harry, why do you think they went with the Greek architecture?"

Harry replied, "I don't know; maybe the Greek thing was the rage at the time."

Miller thought about it and responded, "Yeah, probably." They all walked across the street to the entrance of the theater. Harry handed the tickets to the ticket-taker, and she provided them with the stubs. As they walked in, an usher showed them to their seats. Harry got 2nd-tier seats with a great view of the stage. Harry and Miller were thunderstruck by the beauty of the place.

Miller said, "Wow. Look at this place, Harry. I have been to the Met in NYC and I thought that was impressive. This place puts the Met to shame."

Harry answered, "Yeah, look at that finish work. They didn't skimp on the materials. The guys who built this were extremely skilled craftsmen."

The couples sat in their seats and Irena grabbed the Slav's hand and asked, "Do you know *Romeo and Juliet*, Slav?"

Miller replied, "Not on a first-name basis. Just kidding, my love. I know the general gist of the story. You know, boy meets girl, boy loses girl, boy drinks poison, girl stabs herself with dagger."

Irena looked confused and asked, "Slav, what is gist?"

Miller answered, "Plot, my love."

Irena said, "Oh, I see. I think it is the most beautiful story. It is all about the love in a young boy and girl's heart."

Slav replied, "Not to mention the feuding of the Montagues and Capulets."

The orchestra started and the ballet dancers entered the stage for Act 1, Scene one. Sveta informed Harry, "This good scene, Harry. This is where the Capulet and Montague servants are fighting."

As the ballet went on, Harry and Miller were actually enjoying it. Finally came the famous balcony scene: "Romeo, oh Romeo, wherefore art thou Romeo." Then the sleeping potion scene and Romeo's death. Miller looked at Irena and saw tears welling up in her eyes. He looked at Sveta and observed a loose tear that had escaped the duct, slowly making its way down her cheek. He gazed at Harry and his eyes were closed, catching forty winks. Sveta noticed and shook Harry awake. At the end of the performance, the curtain fell and the auditorium lights went on. Harry, Sveta, Miller, and Irena followed the crowd out of the theater and onto the street.

☭

Joe Kelly and Vera were sitting at the conference room table in the vault. Joe said, "Vera, it seems you were right in your suspicions of Bo Beecher. He was meeting with Major Karlov at Natasha Stasivitch's studio at the Belgrade Hotel."

Vera listened, then asked, "Are we sure, Joe?"

Joe replied, "We are sure that they had met. We are not sure what they had discussed. I think it is time to bring Mr. Beecher in for questioning." Vera agreed.

☭

The next morning while having coffee at the Belgrade Hotel restaurant, Larry saw a familiar face. Larry looked surprised and asked, "What the hell are you doing here, Justin?"

Justin Anthony was a state department contracts guy responsible for the MI6 contract. He was in Moscow for a few days. Larry and Justin worked out of the same office in Paris.

Justin replied, "I heard you were here, Larry. I just came to meet with Ben and finalize the MI6 agent's contract. It has to be finalized before I can approve payment to the Brits."

Larry asked, "How long are you here?"

Justin answered, "I leave tomorrow morning, early. I was hoping I would have more time so you could show me around town. Maybe next time."

Larry responded, "Too bad. There are definitely some sights to see. The MI6 agent's name is Nigel. Great guy. The two of us have become buddies." As Larry said this, a mischievous plan came to his mind. He discussed with Justin.

☭

That morning, Nigel and Larry were sitting at their desks as Justin Anthony walked in. Larry spoke first, "Morning, Justin. What are you doing in Moscow?"

As rehearsed, Justin answered, "I am here to finalize Nigel's contract. Hello, Nigel. Do you have a few moments?"

Nigel replied, "Hello, old chap. Sure, what can I do for you?"

Justin asked, "Nigel, if you don't mind, could you pee in this container for me? To finalize your contract, a drug screening is one of the checklist items. Just a formality."

Larry's trick was having the desired effect. Nigel looked like he had been hit with a ton of bricks. He knew he would come up dirty after the other night. Panic started to envelop Nigel. If he failed, which had a 99% probability, and the results put on his permanent record he could kiss his career goodbye. He wondered how the hell he could get out of this.

Nigel said, trying to be nonchalant, "No worries, old boy, but is this really necessary?"

Justin assured him it was and handed him the cup. Nigel took the cup and walked slowly down the hall to the latrine. He went in and tried to pace out a solution; on the fourth pace, Larry and Justin entered the latrine laughing, having trouble containing themselves.

Justin said, "On second thought, Nigel, a drug screening will not be necessary."

Nigel finally got it and replied, "You dirty buggers."

Harry walked into Bo's office. "Hey, Bo. I just saw Vera, and she asked me to tell you she would like to see you in her office."

Harry turned to walk out of the room when Bo asked, "Harry, she wants to see me now?"

Harry replied, "That's what it sounded like. Call her on your cell to confirm."

With that, Harry walked back to his own office.

Bo called Vera. "Vera Collins," she answered.

Bo said, "Hi, Vera. This is Bo. Harry said you wanted to see me?"

She asked, "Yes, Mr. Beecher, can you come to my office a moment?"

Bo replied, "Sure, Vera. I will be right there." Bo shut down his computer and walked to Vera's office.

"Come in, Bo," she said. After he entered, she continued, "We will need to go to the vault. I have a few things to discuss with you."

Bo went into pure panic mode. *Does she know? How am I going to get out of this?* When they arrived at the vault, Joe Kelly was already inside. Bo and Vera settled in their seats and she began, "Mr. Beecher, we need to ask you a few questions. Just tell us the truth." Bo nodded and Vera continued, "Bo, were you at the Belgrade Hotel on Wednesday night?"

Bo answered, "Yes, I was seeing Natasha."

Joe asked, "Was there anyone else with you when you saw her?"

The pair saw a reaction on his face like he was mulling over an answer in his head before he replied. Vera reassured him and said, "Bo, just tell the truth and you will be fine."

Bo simply replied, "Yes."

Joe asked impatiently, "Who was there with you?"

Bo answered, "Two men."

Joe was starting to lose his cool and replied iritated, "Mr. Beecher, quit stalling and tell us your relationship with these two men."

Bo's face turned red. He knew there was no way out and informed Vera and Joe of all the facts. By the time Bo was through, he was bawling like a baby.

Vera said, "Mr. Beecher, the US Government is not concerned with what happens between consenting adults, even though it may prove embarrassing if it were made public. What the US Government is concerned with is lying and not informing us of a contact with the Russians. The rule states you must fill out a contact report if this is the case. You did not. What do you think we should do with you, Mr. Beecher?" Bo just sat there sobbing. Vera continued, "Mr. Beecher, pull yourself together. The way I see it, we have two options. The first would be to revoke your security clearance, terminate your employment, and have you on a plane back to the States by tomorrow morning." She let that sink in a moment and continued, "The second is for you to continue working for the Russians and keep us informed by giving us complete details about your meetings. Which do you prefer?"

Bo could see a light at the end of his cold, dark tunnel. He said, "Vera, I have always been a proud American and have been ashamed of myself with what had transpired. I seemed to be getting in deeper and deeper with no way out. I swear on my mother's grave, no more deceit, and what I have told you is the truth. I would prefer the second option."

With that, Vera replied, "Good answer, Mr. Beecher. You may go now." After Bo left, Joe said, "Too bad we need that SOB. If we sent him back to the States now, the Russians would know something's up."

Vera answered, "I agree with you, Joe. When this is over, we can take the appropriate action."

☭

Yuri and Karlov were having lunch at a small restaurant at the GUM when Karlov said, "Yuri, everything is in place. The signal from the door is coming in loud and clear. All sounds coming from the Americans' vault room are being recorded automatically, 24 hours a day. We will now know all of the Americans' sensitive information about our Motherland. This is a very happy day for Mother Russia and for the KGB."

After the fall in '91, the KGB had been broken up and weakened. The Russians thought it best to change its name to placate the West. The name KGB conjured up a ruthless police state persona, precisely why Karlov wanted the name to grow in stature, not diminish. There was still a small faction called the KGB, but this too was on the way out. The new names were the secret police agency, FSB, and the espionage agency, SVR. This was just camouflage, because internally it was still the KGB. Karlov believed the name change was nonsense. Karlov secretly hoped the success of this mission would give the KGB agency more significance and catapult it back to its former greatness.

Yuri replied, "Well done, Major. I knew I could count on my old friend. Be sure to send me the manuscripts of the meetings as soon as they are available. The so- called diplomatic meetings are scheduled for next month. I want to know beforehand who is going to be there. Now it is a waiting game."

The major asked, "What do we do with the Americans?"

Yuri answered, "We will need them to obtain copies of the top-secret drawings of the embassy's secure areas. This way we can fine-tune our microwave signals to those locations, but beforehand we will have our fish plant untraceable listening devices. When we are through, the Americans will not be able to fart without us knowing about it. The secure areas will not be built for several months, so we have time. For now, Comrade, do nothing with the Americans until after the summit. What is the term the Americans use? Oh yes, keep them on ice. We will later decide their fate."

Karlov responded, "Very well, Yuri. Yes, we can always pull them from the freezer and thaw them out when we need them."

The routine set in on the embassy site. The construction activities continued, and the mock meetings went on as scheduled. The Russians were recording and analyzed the disinformation they were receiving. The diplomatic meetings scheduled were now referred to as a "summit" to negotiate a peace treaty with the Chechens. It had been scheduled for early September. On August 20, the Russians surprised the international community when they succumbed to international and national pressure and announced their interest in discussing a peace treaty deal with Chechnya. This deal would include a prisoner exchange, and the Chechens wanted British, French, and German diplomats to broker the deal. The Russian side would include General Alexander Viktorovich, the Russian president's national security advisor, and Chinese foreign Minister Kwon Choa, who had been instrumental in handling China's normalization of relations with the West in the difficult period after the Tiananmen Square protests of 1989. The Russian president himself would also be in attendance.

Yuri was not a fan of the peace treaty. He was with the other hardliners who wanted to go back in to level Grozny and make the Chechens pay for their insolence, no matter how many Russian lives it might cost. The hardliners wanted to make them an example, in case other satellites had any such notions. Karlov was supplying General Viktorovich with the embassy intel. The general thought he would be privy to the West's internal meetings before the negotiations took place, like playing cards with a stacked deck—the only way the Russians wanted to play. They were right; the deck was stacked. Only thing was, it was stacked in the Americans' favor.

☭

Harry was in his office. Lately he had been playing classical music as he worked. He was listening to "The Flight of the Bumblebee" written by Nikolai Rimsky Korsakov for his opera "The Tale of Tsar Saltan" when Kurt knocked on his door and asked, "Harry, got a minute?"

Harry replied, "Sure, Kurt, come on in."

As Kurt entered Harry's office, he heard the music and said, "Goddamn, Harry. What in the hell are you listening to? Trying to get all hoity-toity on us?"

Harry answered, "Shit, no. I am starting to like this crap. Anyway, you could use a little culture yourself instead of listening to Hank Williams or the Gatlin brothers all the time."

Kurt replied, "I'll have you know I have broadened my horizons. I recently picked up some Buck Owens and George Jones."

Harry responded, "Damn, Kurt, you are one renaissance man. What can I do you for?"

Kurt asked, "Harry, Miller is overdue for his R&R. Can we go ahead and schedule his dates?"

Harry thought it over. With all the Russian stuff going on, John London wanted to keep him on site, but now nothing would happen until the summit, three weeks away. Harry said, "Let me talk with JT, and I will get back with you."

Later that day, Harry went to see Miller. Miller was in his office working on his weekly nightmare, the daily construction reports. As Harry walked in, Miller greeted him, "What's up, Harry?"

Harry sat down then asked, "JT, you know you're due for an R&R?"

Miller chuckled and answered, "Hell yes, I know. I also know the PD wanted to hold up on it because of the vault door installation."

Harry replied, "Exactly. The door is complete, and nothing should come up before the summit. I think we can let you out of here for a week. I would like you to be ready to leave Sunday. Have you thought of where you might want to go?"

Miller answered, "I was thinking of Budapest. Do you mind if I take Irena?"

Harry said, "Fine. You can take who you want, but you have to spring for her ticket."

Miller replied, "I knew that, Harry. Let me check with her, and I will get back with you."

Harry said, "Fair enough. Let Kurt know as soon as you can so he can purchase your ticket. He can actually get both tickets for you and Irena, and you can reimburse the company."

Miller replied, "Sounds good, Harry."

☭

That evening Miller was lying in bed with Irena and asked, "Irena, if you could go anywhere in the world for a week, where would it be?"

Irena looked at him, confused, and asked, "Why you ask me this, Slav?"

The Slav replied, "Just answer the question, and I will tell you."

Irena thought about it, then thought some more and finally confirmed, "Anywhere, Slav?"

He answered, "Anywhere, my love."

She said, "Well, I first thought of Paris, but there are so many wonderful places in the world to visit. Vienna, Amsterdam, Bali, Thailand, Fiji. I have a cousin that lives in Thailand at Pattaya Beach. After Perestroika, lot of Russians vacation and live there. It is quite popular. Aeroflot have direct flights to Bangkok. I always wanted to go."

Bangkok had the reputation as a Mecca for debauchery, and Miller thought he would rather visit sometime in the future in a single status capacity, but what the hell. Miller asked, "Irena, is that where you want to go?"

She replied, "Oh yes, Slav. It will be so much fun. We can lay around on the beach, ride the elephants, drink mai-tais and get massages. I will get a massage every day."

She sold Miller. He said, "Okay, it is settled. Can you be ready to leave Sunday?"

She answered, "No problem, Slav. Wait, I want to show you something I have for the trip."

She went into her drawer and pulled something out, then went into the bathroom. She came out a minute later wearing a string bikini. It was about the size of a postage stamp. She smiled as she saw Miller's reaction. He whistled, the sailor's mating call, and she ran and jumped on the bed beside him.

On Sunday, Irena and Miller were at the Sheremetyevo International Airport. They boarded Aeroflot flight 722 for Bangkok. Miller wanted to stay one night at the Nana Hotel, which was next to the Nana Plaza entertainment center. The place was made famous by American soldiers on R&R during the Vietnam war. It was full of go-go bars and nightclubs with women who would comply with the most provocative of carnal requests. The couple was standing at the taxi stand, inquiring about a ride. One hour to Bangkok 500 baht. One- and one-half hours to Pattaya Beach for 600 baht. The exchange rate was approximately 33 baht per dollar. Irena wanted to go directly to Pattaya, so that's what they did. When they got there, they checked into the Royal Plaza Hotel. Both took showers, ordered from room service, and went to bed.

At the airport, Chung Van Hoang watched the couple's taxi drive away. Chung worked for The Tong. The Tong was the General Department of Military Intelligence for the Vietnamese government. Chung was on assignment in Bangkok and had agreed to watch the couple after he received a request from his old friend Dimitry Karlov. In 1991 Chung had worked with Karlov on the assassination of Askar Akayev in northern Kyrgyzstan, who had just been elected president. After the Soviet Union's collapse, Askar secessionist forces pushed for Kyrgyzstan's independence. The Russians thought if they could stop Askar, they would stop Kygyzstan's independence attempts. The assassination was later aborted when it became clear the secessionist forces were too strong and would not stop with the assassination of one man. Chung was assigned by the Tong to work in concert with the Russian KGB. Chung had reported directly to Karlov during the operation. Chung was fluent in Russian, and he and Karlov had remained friends after the mission was terminated. Before Irena left Moscow, she informed the major of the planned trip, and Karlov thought it best to keep tabs on them, so he contacted his old friend.

☭

Miller and Irena woke early and went down to enjoy the hotel's breakfast buffet.

"Look at all the fruit, Slav. What's that fruit that looks like a porcupine?"

The Slav answered, "The hell if I know. I do know that those are lychees and those red ones are dragon fruit."

Irena picked up a lychee, picked off the peel, tried it, then commented, "I like these, Slav. Really sweet."

Miller said, "Here, try the dragon fruit."

He prepared a piece and handed it to her. She tasted it and replied, "These are good too, but I think I like the lychees better."

After breakfast, they walked along the beach. They stopped at a stand that sold straw hats. Irena got a wide brim that made her resemble a Chinese coolie, and Miller got a small-brimmed Panama. They continued walking until they got to Walking Street. This was the area that had the nightclubs, restaurants, and the like. The couple would meet Irena's cousin at 1:00 at the Sea Zone restaurant.

"Look, Slav, here is the restaurant where we will meet Oksana."

Miller looked. They were early, but it was hot, and Miller could go for a drink. The Sea Zone had a nice outside eating area with a nice view of the Gulf of Thailand. The couple sat, and a short heavyset woman with a great smile came to take their order.

Miller said, "I will take a gin and tonic with plenty of ice."

The woman answered, "So sorry. Gin, no have."

Irena replied, "Get a mai-tai. We are in Thailand."

The woman answered, "Mai-tai, have."

They ordered two, and Miller pulled out the tourist tour guide and looked it over. He finally asked, "Irena, how bad do you want to ride the elephants?"

She answered, "Oh Slav, we are in Thailand. We have to ride the elephants."

Miller said, "Well, we have to go to Chiang Mai for that. A fifteen-hour train ride."

Irena replied, "I do not care if it is twenty-five hours. We have to go."

Miller looked the guide over again and saw the train would pass over the River Kwai. *The Bridge on the River Kwai* was one of his favorite movies. *Nice,* he thought. The train would stop at the bridge so passengers could get off and walk over it. The next morning the train for Chiang Mai would leave at 10:00.

The first round of mai-tais tasted so good they ordered another. The mai-tais were served in hollowed-out pineapples and were outstanding. Just then, Irena's cousin Oksana walked up and said in Russian, "Irena, give your cousin a hug and introduce me to that handsome man with you."

Irena, also in Russian, replied, "Oh, Oksana. You look wonderful. This is my boyfriend, Slav, so hands off." Irena continued in English, "Slav, this is my cousin Oksana. Oksana, this is Slav."

Oksana said, "Nice to meet you, Slav."

Miller answered, "Nice to meet you, Oksana. Can I get you a mai-tai?"

She replied, "You bet you can. A big one."

The three chatted while sipping their mai-tais. Oksana was about the same age as Irena, with similar features. She had been in Pattaya for three years and worked for a real estate developer, selling condos. The trio looked at the menus and decided on the Sea Zone's specialty, deep-fried red snapper.

After they ordered, the woman instructed them, "Please follow." She led them to a tank that was full of fish. The woman said, "Choose fish, please."

The three pointed to the red snapper they wanted and then went back to their table to wait for the seafood delight.

The next morning, Miller and Irena were on the train heading to Chiang Mai. They were getting close to the Kwai River and Miller was getting excited to see the bridge—Irena not so much. The train stopped just before the bridge so the passengers could get out and walk across if they wanted. The train would pick them up on the other side after about thirty minutes. Miller and Irena got off the train. Miller took some photos of the bridge before they began to walk across. He had a flash of Alec Guinness and the scene where Alec is walking across the bridge and spots the wires that the bombs are connected to.

Miller pulled out the tour book and said, "Irena, this book says there were actually two bridges here, both built by prisoners of war. The first wooden bridge was completed in February 1943, then replaced a few months later by the steel bridge we see today. The curved steel bridge spans are original and were brought from Java by the Japanese. The two straightsided spans came from Japan, and replaced the other curved spans after they were destroyed by Allied bombing in 1945. In 1952 when Pierre Boulle wrote the original book, he had never been there but knew the 'death railway' ran parallel to the River Kwae (Thai spelling) for many miles, and assumed it was the Kwae it crossed just north of Kanchanaburi. He was incorrect, it actually crossed the Mae Khlung. When David Lean's film came out, this gave the Thais something of a dilemma. Thousands of tourists flocked to see the Bridge on the River Kwai, and there was none, all they had was a bridge over the Mae Khlung. With commendable foresight, the Thai authorities officially renamed the Mae Khlung the river Kwae Yai ('Big Kwae')."

Irena said, "Who cares, Slav? I want to get to Chiang Mai and ride the elephants."

Miller replied," This bridge is part of the history of WWII and the Asian campaign."

Irena answered, "Sorry, Slav, but women are not much interested in war things."

On the other side of the bridge were restaurants and shops. Miller bought two waters and he and Irena re-boarded the train.

Nigel was at his desk pounding out the weekly script. Larry had just walked in from the studio and sat down at his desk. Larry and Nigel loved talking about WWII. They were both history aficionados on the subject, Larry from the American point of view and Nigel from the British. They enjoyed sharing their views with each other.

When Nigel seemed to be at a break, Larry asked, "Nigel, if you could name the top three factors for the Allies' victory over the Nazis, what would they be?"

Nigel thought and replied, "Well, let's see. Hitler's foreign minister Ribbentrop at the Nuremberg trials said the main reasons, he believed, were the unexpected resistance of the Red Army, the American industrial machine, and the success of Allied air power. Hitler told Ribbentrop when they were in the bunker, and the Soviets were closing in, that the real military cause of defeat was the failure of the German air force or Luftwaffe. I think in the broad sense Ribbentrop was correct, but I believe the success of Allied air power would not have been possible if it had not been for the British recovery of the enigma machine and the breaking of its code. This gave the Allies a stacked deck as to what the Germans were planning and would respond accordingly."

Larry thought about that and responded, "I think another major factor that should not be overlooked as to the importance was Operation Mincemeat. If that operation had not been successful, the Allies would have lost more troops on a massive scale, and that could have been the deciding factor of the Allied victory."

Operation Mincemeat was a ploy of British Naval Intelligence in 1943 to deposit a dead body off the coast of Spain. Attached to the body's right wrist was a lock and chain device used by bank couriers at the time. Attached to the chain device was a briefcase containing several forged documents which the Allies hoped would quickly fall into the hands of the Nazis. The plan by British Naval Intelligence and MI6 was to dupe the Nazis into believing the planned Allied landings in Southern Europe would take place in Greece and Sardinia, instead of the intended island of Sicily.

Nigel replied, "You have a point there, old chap. Did you realize Ian Fleming, of James Bond fame, was on the Naval Intelligence team and was tasked with choosing the body and supplying the documents in the deception ploy?"

Larry answered, "Golly, good show, old chap. Shall we give it another go?" Larry did his best English accent and continued. "Nigel, nice try. As you know, Fleming had the original idea for the mission, but it was Montagu who was in charge of the body and identity. Literary references refer to the story as 'The Man Who Never Was.'"

Nigel was impressed and replied, "Quite right, old boy. I met Ian Fleming when I was eight or nine when me mum took me to Stanfords book shop for a book signing of his novel "From *Russia with Love"*. I think me mum fancied him for more than his literary prowess--and by the way, old boy, your attempt at an English accent was bloody awful."

Larry responded, "What do you mean, Nigel? I sounded just like you."

Nigel replied, "Hardly, old boy."

Nigel got back to work on the script, and Larry walked down the hall to the latrine.

☭

The train pulled into Chiang Mai station at 4 a.m. The sleepy-eyed couple gathered their belongings, and Miller picked up his and Irena's suitcases. The pair walked down the platform and out to the street. Outside the station, even at that hour, several taxis were waiting. One of the taxi drivers motioned them over, and the pair complied. Miller deposited their luggage in the taxi's trunk and Miller said," Le Meridian Hotel, please."

The driver set the meter and off they went. Miller picked Le Meridian because it was close to the Night Bazaar and they also offered day trips that included elephant riding. The couple was scheduled for the trip the following day and would leave the hotel at 7 a.m. and return at 7 p.m. The tour would include the elephant show, which consisted of watching trained elephants painting. Easels would be set up and the elephant would hold a brush in his trunk and paint a picture on the canvas. Next would be an hour-long bamboo rafting trip down the Mae Tang River, and finally the elephant riding in the Measa Valley.

They arrived at the hotel, and just before the couple entered the lobby, Miller spied an ATM and used his credit card to get several thousand baht. The pair checked in, and as they entered the elevator, Irena asked, "Are you tired, Slav?"

He answered, "Not really tired, just feel like I have been cooped up on a train for fifteen hours and wouldn't mind taking a walk."

She agreed, "Me too. It is close to 5:00 and will be light soon."

The couple went up to their room on the 7th floor and deposited the suitcases. They went back down to the lobby and inside was a little convenience store for guests that was open 24 hours. The pair purchased coffees to go.

When Miller was paying the cashier, he saw they had five-packs of Cohibas behind the counter, so he bought two packs.

Irena asked, "Slav, do you really have to smoke those stinky things?"

The Slav answered, "Yes, my love. Remember our bargain. As long as I smoke outside and not inside, all is well. That was the agreement."

Irena frowned and asked, "What, are you a lawyer now?"

Miller replied smiling, "No, my Russian beauty, just sticking up for my rights."

He handed her one of the coffees and they walked outside. Miller opened one of the packs and lit up.

Irena asked, "Which way, right or left?"

Miller took a minute to get his bearings and saw they were on Chang Clan road near the intersection of Loi Kroh. He pulled a ten-baht coin from his pocket and looked at it. On one side it had a picture of the Thai King and the other was a temple of some sort.

He said, "Heads we go right and tails we go left."

He flipped the coin in the air and let it fall to the sidewalk. The king's face landed up, so the couple headed right down Chang Clan road. The sun was just coming up and small shop owners and their families were getting their wares ready for the day. They walked past the Pantip Plaza and spent a few minutes sitting on the steps of the plaza to finish their coffee. They took another right down Sridorn Chai. Miller made sure he was paying attention so they would not get lost going back to the hotel. It was almost 6 a.m. and the couple found a restaurant open that had outside seating near the sidewalk. It was called Tianzi Tea House. They sat at a teak table about two meters from the sidewalk.

A few minutes later, an older woman with a nice big smile and missing a front tooth took their order. They ordered coffee and the waitress left a menu. On the menu it said they specialized in macrobiotic food. Irena asked, "What is macrobiotic food?"

Macrobiotics was a movement that gathered steam in the '70s and '80s. It was a Japanese health diet that claimed to heal all your ills. Several celebrities swore by it and still do. The Slav replied, "I just know it is a health diet of some sort based on eating whole grains."

Irena was intrigued. She looked over the menu at the dishes. Brown rice, miso soup, steamed vegetables with fish, buckwheat pancakes, rice cream (porridge). Irena said, "Let's try it. I will get the buckwheat pancakes, brown rice, and steamed vegetables. You get the miso soup and rice porridge so I can try."

Miller agreed, except he also ordered ham, potatoes, and eggs. When the food arrived, the waitress left a bottle of maple syrup and Irena smothered the pancakes and took a bite. She said, "These are good." She grabbed Miller's rice porridge and doctored it up with soymilk and honey. She responded, "This is nice too." Next she looked at the miso soup and asked, "What is this green stuff in the soup?"

Miller replied, "That's seaweed or sea vegetables."

She picked up a medium-sized piece of the seaweed and popped it into her mouth. Miller watched as her face contorted and her eyes began to water. It felt slimy in her mouth and she spit it out, trying hard not to retch. Miller sat amused and asked. "May I order you another bowl, my love?"

☭

After breakfast they continued down Sridorn Chai and passed the Imperial Mae Ping Hotel. Most of the stores were open now. They came up to a place where about five young women were sitting outside by the sidewalk.

"Masaaad. Masaaad?"

Miller surmised they were saying "massage" in Thai and the establishment the women were sitting in front of was a massage parlor. Irena said, "Oh, let's get a massage, Slav."

He replied asking, "Irena, can we wait till we get back to the hotel? I wouldn't mind having a swim beforehand."

She said, "Oh, look. There's a Buddhist temple."

The temple was Wat Chang Kong. The couple walked up the stairs. There were many Buddha statues of all kinds with offerings in front of them. There was a young girl and her mother selling sparrow baskets outside by the steps. There were four sparrows per cage or basket. The Buddhists believed if you opened the cage and freed the sparrows it would bring you good luck. Miller bought two baskets for Irena and himself. When they released the birds, Irena laughed with glee.

Major Karlov was sitting at the desk in his office. He had just received the latest information on who would be attending the summit, and other information. As he was reviewing the document, his phone rang.

"Major Karlov," he said.

The voice on the other end replied, "Hello, Dimitry. This is Chung."

Karlov greeted his old friend, "Hello, Chung. How are things in sunny Thailand?"

Chung answered, "Fine, Major. Even better now that my wife left to visit her mother. She won't be back for two weeks."

The major responded, "My congratulations, old friend. Now if I could get my wife to do the same thing, we could both enjoy a vacation. How are our friends doing?"

Chung replied, "They were in Pattaya for two days, then took the train to Chiang Mai. They got there this morning. The couple had not made any suspicious contacts and have been under constant surveillance."

Karlov responded, "Thank you, Chung. Please keep me abreast if anything changes, and please do not enjoy too many Thai women while your wife is away, my friend."

Chung chuckled then replied, "Thank you for your concern, Dimitry, but as you know, Thai women are like eating rice. In an hour, you are hungry again."

Karlov laughed, then they said their goodbyes, and Karlov got back to the document. The updated schedule included the American Secretary of State Madeleine Warren, the British Prime Minister Robert Minor, German Chancellor Helmut Gerhard, French Prime Minister Lionel Alain, and the newly elected Chechen President Movladi Aslan, all scheduled for the summit. US Ambassador Franklin Miles and his wife Nancy would host the event.

The next morning Irena was excited. She and Miller were in the hotel restaurant having coffee when she said, "I am going to ride the biggest elephant they have. Do elephants wear shoes like horses?"

Miller answered, "I don't think so. I believe their feet are tough enough on their own. I want to see the artist elephants. It said in the guidebook they can draw trees and other elephants, and they never draw the same picture twice."

Irena replied, "I don't believe it. Who ever heard of an elephant painting a picture?"

He said, "Believe it, Irena. Here is a photo of an elephant doing just that. I am sure none of them are any Van Gogh, but who knows?"

She asked, "When is our minibus leaving?"

He answered, "We need to finish our coffee and get outside. It's almost time."

The pair walked out to the hotel parking lot where their minibus awaited. They paid the driver and went on inside the van to sit down. Inside was an American sitting with his Thai wife. He appeared to be about five or six years older than Miller.

Miller greeted the couple, "Hello. How are you guys? Looking forward to the trip?"

The American answered, "May and I did this a few years ago. It's fun if you like elephants. My name is Mel Rosenblum; this is my wife May."

JT replied, "I'm JT Miller, and this is my friend Irena."

Mel asked, "What brings the two of you to Thailand?"

Miller answered, "Vacation. We fly back on Monday."

Mel asked, "Back to where?"

Miller started to explain when the driver, who was also the tour guide, entered the minibus and informed them, "We leave now. Two passengers no show up. It 7:15, we leave now." He started the van and off they went.

Miller continued to explain and afterward asked, "What about you, Mel? What brings you to Thailand?"

Mel thought a moment then replied, "Well, I was drafted in 1969. I was such a schmuck. I wanted to take one year off between high school and college; that's when they got me. I was drafted and did a tour in Viet Nam in 1970. I was there eleven months, two weeks, and five days, but who's counting. When I got out and back to the States, I had a hard time assimilating. I was home for about two years when I decided to try my hand at the import/

export business. I moved to Bangkok and started to sell Asian products via mail order. I started with classified ads in different magazines, then went on to quarter-page ads. Lucky for me I had the chutzpah and landed a Pier of Asia Imports contract. It was lucrative, I met May, got married and stayed."

Mel was 6 foot 3 inches tall and May was about 4 feet 8. They made a great pair.

☭

The minibus arrived at the elephant camp and the passengers got out. The driver/guide, whose name was Dang, led them to the elephant arena. He pointed to the wooden stands around the arena, where the passengers chose their seats. Mel said, "I think Dang wants to start his spiel."

Dang smiled at them and started, "Elephants been revered in Thailand many centuries. In Thailand they important in battle, kings rode elephants fighting the Burmese to defend Thailand on many occasions. They have intelligence, memory and pleasant nature. Thai legend says marriage like elephant. The husband is front legs, that choose direction, the wife the back legs, providing the power."

When Dang finished, almost as if on cue canned trumpets came out over the loudspeakers, and about ten elephants with their trainers on their backs entered the arena. The elephants circled the arena twice as the trumpets blared. They called this the Elephant Parade. After the parade was finished, the elephants and trainers moved to different areas of the arena. Starting from left to right, each elephant and trainer did a series of tricks.

Irena said to Miller, "Look at that one, he's rolling over like a dog, and that other one is lifting his trainer up on his back with his trunk. I love the elephants, Slav."

Miller was happy that Irena was enjoying it. Mel said to Miller, "Look at that one schlepping that log. I understand they can lift over 600 pounds with their trunks. I wonder if elephants can get hernias."

When the show was over, out came five easels, which were placed in different areas of the arena. The trainers led five elephants carrying wooden boxes that contained paint and brushes. The trainers set up the easels and added the canvas. Next, they selected a brush, dipped it into the paint and handed it to the elephant who took it using its trunk. The elephants then took brush to canvas.

Irena called out, "Watch that one, Slav." The couple watched as the elephant, whose name was Chati, drew one line until the brush was out of paint. The trainer exchanged the old brush for a new one filled with paint, and Chati continued to finish a big tree with leaves and an elephant standing underneath it. The results were astounding.

"Wow! That elephant is smarter than you, Slav," she teased.

Miller answered, "That may be, my love, but I am better looking."

Irena replied, "Oh, you think so, do you? I am sure Chati is much more handsome if you are another elephant."

Miller answered, "I cannot argue with that, my love."

With Miller gone, Harry had to take over some of his duties. He was at his desk working on the daily construction reports and cussing under his breath when John London walked into his office. John asked, "Harry, got a few minutes?"

Harry replied, "Anything for you, John. What do you need?"

John said, "I was going over the schedule and it looks as though we are sixty days behind. Would you agree with that?"

Harry answered, "Well, yes and no. When you run the Primavera program you are correct, it shows sixty days late, but the way the schedule is set up, some of the activities needed to finish a milestone are actually completed but it does not reflect that in the program. I would say we are about fourteen days late, but we can pick some of that up during the finishing work. I actually think we are in fairly good shape."

John said, "Okay, I can buy that. Let's keep a close eye on it so we can identify problems and make adjustments before the project starts going south."

Harry responded, "I could not agree with you more. We have a project controls guy coming in next month to help us with that."

John replied, "I thought Miller was doing a good job with it."

Harry answered, "He is, but he has other duties, and we need someone to focus just on the schedule."

John asked, "When does Miller get back?"

Harry replied, "He will be back to work on Tuesday."

John said, "Before he left, he said he was working on an RFI [request for information] for the west side of the building, where the atrium is. What is that about?"

Harry answered, "As you know, the whole west side, where the atrium is, has a bow in it or is curved. As far as I know, Miller said the curve information for the structural steel has an error in the calculations. I will make sure that when he gets back, he goes over the problem with you."

John responded, "Okay, Harry."

At the elephant camp, Miller and the rest were getting ready for the elephant ride. They had already done the bamboo raft trip and had lunch. When the trainer walked up with Irena and Miller's elephant, Irena asked the trainer, "What is the elephant's name?"

The trainer just looked at her, confused, and said something in Thai. May caught the conversation and said something in Thai back to the trainer. He answered and she said to Irena, "So sorry, Irena. The trainer man no speak English. He say elephant's name is Preecha. Preecha mean very wise in Thai."

Irena said, "Thank you, May. What is your elephant's name?"

May said something to her trainer and he answered. After he did, May looked a little concerned and said, "Trainer man said his name is Ram. It mean huge thunder." The trainer noticed May's concern and assured her Ram was gentle as a lamb and nothing to worry about. She thought in Thai, but the English translation was "Famous last words."

The elephants had wooden seats on their backs that would accommodate two. The Thai word for the seats was a howdah. The trainer brought Preecha to the loading platform and Miller and Irena climbed up into the seat on the elephant's back.

Irena called out, "This is high up here, Slav."

The trainer latched the safety bar in place, then sat just behind the elephant's head, and off they went. The trainer wore blue overalls and sported a straw coolie hat not unlike the one Irena had on. The overalls were worn but clean. He also carried a thin, short bamboo stick that was used to control the elephant. Preecha trekked through the lush jungle of the Maesa Valley. The couple were enjoying the ride. Mel and May rode beside them.

Lieutenant Maxim Sokolov had noticed that the Americans had stepped up their secret meetings. They were now having them two and three times a week. He thought that was to be expected because of the upcoming summit. He had informed Karlov of this fact, and Karlov had just informed Yuri at his office at the Ukraine Hotel. Yuri replied, "That is good, Major. The more information we retrieve, the better. Do we have a firm date for the summit?"

Karlov answered, "Not yet, but it looks like early September. We should have confirmation soon."

Yuri responded, "Keep me informed, Major."

Yuri walked over to his bar and removed a bottle from one of the cabinets. Karlov noticed the Blue Label and remarked, "Yuri, my friend. I see you have paid the extra rubles for, as the Americans say, the good stuff."

Yuri replied, "That is quite observant of you, Bolshevik. Now grab two glasses from that cabinet and let's enjoy this nectar of the gods."

As the elephants rounded a curve in the trail, Irena spotted three Thai boys on the side of it with a wooden box, lying on the ground. As the elephants got up to the boys, one of the boys reached down and pulled a wooden slat from the box. Five small life forms appeared and scurried across the road in front of the elephants.

The trainers started yelling hysterically, "MUSIK! MUSIK!"

The elephants took off in different directions, crashing through the jungle. The trainers grappled to keep the elephants under control. Miller and Irena were holding on for dear life as the elephants trumpeted and ran. Mel and May's elephant thundered into the jungle like a locomotive. The three boys were pointing and laughing at the commotion. When the trainers finally got the elephants under control, the boys picked up their box and ran away.

Miller asked, "Are you okay, Irena?"

She replied, "What a stupid question, Slav. Of course, I am not okay. Those stupid kids. Did you see them laughing at us?"

Miller smiled and said, "Boys will be boys."

As things settled down, Mel and May rode up next to them. Miller asked, "Hey Mel, that was some ride, huh?"

Mel said, "Oy vey! Those schmucks almost killed us."

May chimed in, "The box the boys were carrying was a musik trap. They are placed near the rice paddies to help keep them away from the rice."

Irena asked, "May, what is a musik?"

May thought and could not remember the word. She then asked, "In English what do you call a mouse that is very big?"

Miller answered, "You mean a rat?"

May showed recognition on her face. "Yes, that is it. The poor elephants do not like these rats and are very afraid."

Mel interupted, "I'm not a big fan myself, honey."

May continued, "The caught rats are usually sold to rural food vendors, who prepare them on a charcoal brazier and sell to customers. It is a Thai delicacy."

Mel thought about that a moment and supposed maybe with a little mustard they wouldn't be too bad.

Colonel Ben Magsino was back in DC and working on preparing a list of talking points for the upcoming summit. Later in the day, he would meet with the Secretary of State to compare notes. The pair would work together on a comprehensive list of clear objectives for the meetings. Ben would fly back to Moscow a week before the summit to meet with the ambassador, Chechen president, and the foreign diplomats from Britain, France, and Germany. He wanted to make sure everyone agreed to the plan going forward. They would try for a Rolls but would settle for a Ford. The Russians were showing signs of changing their minds, but Ben knew it was a ploy to better their position during the negotiations. The Russian army had been sustaining many casualties, and the Russian people wanted out. The only holdouts were the hardliners—Yuri and his bunch.

Miller and Irena were checked in at the Green Lotus Resort on Thawiwong Rd in Patong, an area around Phuket. They would be there two days before they flew back to Moscow. The resort had wood bungalows made of teak located right on the beach. The couple were on the way to the resort spa where they had scheduled Thai massages. This would be Irena's first Thai massage. She had a massage in Chiang Mai, but that was a Swedish massage, and there is a world of difference between the two. Miller went with the Thai in Chiang Mai, so he knew what to expect; Irena did not.

Thai Massage is a Buddhist therapeutic technique, dating back 2500 years. Traditional Thai Massage tones the muscles, increases the joints' range of motion, and balances the flow of energy throughout the body. To achieve the desired results takes several sessions before the muscles and joints are accustomed to the techniques and become flexible enough to comfortably endure the treatments.

Miller warned her but she said, "Slav, do not be such a baby. I do not mind a little discomfort if it will improve my health."

The Green Lotus had six massage tables set up on a long deck platform that ran along the beach. Each table had a canopy over it, which draped see-through white mesh curtains around the area of the table. The mesh drapes could either be used for sun shade or mosquito netting. The two were led to the tables, where they were instructed to disrobe and lock their belongings in small cabinets that were at each massage station. There were large towels on each table in case the clients were modest and wished to cover themselves. The masseuses were small women but very strong.

As Irena lay face up on the table, the masseuse started to apply a medium amount of pressure with both hands moving up and down the legs, then her arms. The woman had Irena turn over and did the same thing, including her back and shoulders. Irena called out, "Slav, this is not bad. I am probably in better shape than you."

Miller yelled back from the other massage table to her right, "They are just tenderizing the meat, my love. Just wait."

Next the masseuse had Irena sit on her rear with her legs and feet in front of her. The woman got behind Irena and grabbed both of her wrists and pulled straight back, gently. Then the small woman put both of her feet in the middle of Irena's back and pulled on her arms, getting leverage with her feet, at the same time increasing the pull tension. Irena could hear a series of small pops, then suddenly a big loud pop that even Miller heard. Irena yelled out, thinking she had been paralyzed.

Miller asked, "Are you okay, my Russian beauty?"

Irena replied, "Mind your own business, Slav."

The masseuse laughed nervously and said, "So sorry, lady," and continued. This was when it got uncomfortable. That little woman got Irena in many different positions, twisting, turning, and contorting her body to places she never believed possible. The woman snapped, crackled, and popped every joint Irena possessed. She bit her lip and swallowed the pain because she did not want to give the Slav the satisfaction. When the time was up, Irena was thankful. She had to be helped up off the table by the woman. The woman then sat Irena in a bamboo chair, gave her a cup of hot green tea, and said, "Drink tea, please." Irena drank and felt better. Miller enjoyed the show but kept his trap shut.

Yuri was outside on the balcony of his apartment listening to Rachmaninoff, his composer of choice when he had a problem to work out. Yuri was pacing while he thought of a way to sway public opinion in favor of continuing the Chechen war. Another terror attack on Russian soil would probably do it, he thought, but he knew the Chechens would not dare when the two sides were so close to signing a peace treaty. *Perhaps we could take matters into our own hands*, he thought, *then blame the Chechens.* Yuri thought this was possible but had to work it out so it could never be traced back to him.

Miller and Irena were in bed sleeping. They would be leaving for Moscow in the morning. At 2 a.m., Irena hobbled from bed to the suite's kitchenette for a glass of water. As she reached for the faucet, she heard a crackling of paper coming from a cabinet below where the small trash container was kept. She stopped to listen, and the noise stopped. When she reached for the faucet a second time, the crackling began again. She opened the cabinet below slowly where she thought the noise was coming from. As she looked inside, there staring back at her were two beady bloodshot eyes, as if to say, "What the hell do you want?"

Irena slammed closed the cabinet door at the same time screaming, "SLAV!....SLAV!"

Miller jumped out of bed and ran to the kitchen. "What's wrong?" he asked.

"I will show you," she replied and opened the cabinet door. Miller looked inside and saw the trash can but nothing else. "It was there, Slav," she said.

Miller asked, "What was there?"

She answered, "Bolshoi krisa...er…ah...big rat."

Miller turned on all the lights in the kitchenette and looked again. He saw in the corner of the cabinet behind the trash can a hole where apparently the rat had gnawed through. He took a pair of his socks and jammed them into the hole. He said, "It won't keep it out for long but hopefully for the rest of the night." He then moved a table in front of the cabinet door. He said, "Come on, Irena, let's go to bed."

She asked nervously, "How can I sleep with that thing here?"

Miller took her by the hand and led her back to bed. She jumped under the covers and Miller followed. In about two minutes, as Miller was lying there trying to sleep, he heard that Harley Davidson begin its road trip. He got up and gently turned Irena over on her side, then went back to sleep with one eye open.

On Tuesday morning, Miller was back at his desk drinking coffee and checking emails. He and Irena got into Moscow at about midnight and he was in bed at the camp by 2 a.m. He felt reasonably well after only four hours of sleep. After he finished, he thought he better go see the boss and walked to Harry's office. When he got there, he found Harry hanging by his ankles upside down from some kind of contraption. His face was beet red.

Miller asked, "What the hell are you doing, Harry, Batman imitations?"

Harry replied, while still hanging upside down, "Morning, JT. Glad you're back. I am stretching the vertebrae in my spine. Feels great in the morning. It also increases the blood flow."

Miller said, "Harry, you may want to think about getting out of that thing. Your head looks like it is about to pop with all the blood rushing to it."

Harry straightened up, unhooked himself from the machine, and then spoke, "It is called an inversion table. John let me use his APO box and I ordered one from the States. Want to give it a try? Your insurance is paid up, isn't it?"

Miller looked at the table and said, "Okay, I'm game. What do I do?"

Harry replied, "Simple, just put your feet on those bars and slide your ankles through those padded stirrups. Now lie straight back and swivel upside down."

As Miller followed the instructions and lay back, he got that dizzy, like he was going to fall feeling, as the blood rushed to his head. The sensation lasted only a moment and he continued until he was hanging upside down.

As Miller hung there, Harry said, "Now just relax."

Miller unclenched his muscles and let his body go limp with his arms hanging straight down. As he relaxed, he could feel the spaces between the vertebrae starting to stretch and pop. It felt good.

Miller stated, "Damn, Harry. I like this."

Just then, Kurt walked through Harry's door and observed the goings-on and remarked, "Gentlemen, I would have never suspected before this very minute that the both of you have a screw loose. By the way, JT, welcome back."

Miller switched to the upright position and said, "Kurt, you need to check this out."

Kurt smiled and replied, "Thanks but no thanks. I have lived sixty-two years without using that apparatus, and I think I can go on not using it until they write my obituary. Harry, you got a minute? I need to talk to you about the craft personnel you want to deploy this month."

Miller unhooked himself from the machine and walked to the door. He said before leaving, "See you guys later. I need to catch up on things."

Harry replied, "JT, check with John about the atrium RFI. He wanted to talk to you about it before you send it in."

Miller offered, "Okay, Harry. I will go see him before lunch. Adios, amigos." Miller walked back to his office, and Harry and Kurt got down to business.

Yuri was meeting secretly with one of his advisors, General Nikita Brezhnev. The general was known as "The Butcher of Kazan." In the early '80s, this Tatarstan city started a pro-democracy movement that was gaining momentum. Brezhnev was sent to quash it. He rounded up several members of the movement, and his men shot ten in the town square and hung their bodies upside down for the city's population to see. The other members were shot and their corpses were thrown into the Volga River. During the campaign, a sniper bullet ricocheted, caught Brezhnev in the cheek, and grazed down to the left side of his mouth. It left him with a face that appeared to be in a permanent state of grimace. The general was ruthless, and that was precisely why Yuri wanted him.

Yuri said, "Well, Nikita, you know the problems, now let me hear your solutions. How do you see the best way to proceed?" Brezhnev was a hardliner like Yuri, and they trusted each other—up to a point. The general suggested they blow up an apartment building outside the city center, and this could be blamed on the Chechens. The general said that to change public opinion, there needed to be catastrophic casualties, and blowing up an apartment building with innocent civilians should fit the bill. He suggested the deed happen after the peace treaty was signed and the prisoner exchange completed.

"This way, we save our comrades and have more time to work out a plan. Any violence by the Chechens against Russia would void the peace treaty, and the war could begin again. Yuri, I will work out the details. I am honored you have chosen me for this assignment, and I will not fail you."

Yuri replied, "Nikita, be sure you do not."

Miller was heading out to the job site. He wanted to check on the progress that had taken place while he was away. He could see some changes. The additional structural steel needed for extra support was complete on floors one and two, with level three being worked on. As Miller continued walking, he smelled a familiar aroma. As he descended the stairs, he saw Joe Amado, OBO's electrical guy, walking up smoking his signature La Stinca cigar, a Nicaraguan brand that Joe had been smoking for years.

Miller teased, "God damn, Joe, when are you gonna quit buying those cheap cigars? The aroma smells like burning rubber bands."

Joe replied, "Burning rubber bands, my ass; I'll have you know these cigars have been rolled by hand in Nicaragua by brown-haired nymphomaniac virgins using only their toes. Tell me you can say the same thing about those Cohibas."

Miller said, laughing, "See, Joe, that's where you went wrong. My Cohibas are rolled by brown-haired naked nymphomaniac virgins using only their toes, and each virgin has very large bosoms."

Joe responded, "Your mind is a very large bosom."

Miller answered, "You bet it is, my friend."

They both laughed and Joe asked, "How are you doing, JT? How was Thailand?"

Miller replied, "It was good. Have you been there?"

Joe said, "Oh, yeah. Rosa and I have been there several times. We might retire there someday."

Miller answered, "I can see the attraction. Good food, friendly people, plenty of things to do, and much cheaper than the States."

Looking at his watch Joe interjected, "I'll see you later, JT. I have a meeting with John, and I am running a little late."

JT replied, "Okay—later, Joe." And they both continued on their way.

Nigel kept cranking out the scripts, and the performances were taking place three times a week. The ploy seemed to be working and would help marinate the Russians before the peace treaty summit. Larry kept busy taking care of the equipment and monitoring the meetings. They were both sitting at their desks and Larry was checking his emails. He saw one from his sister and said to himself, "I wonder what the heck she wants."

His sister could not understand why Larry did not want a more conventional life that included staying at home, a nagging wife, kids, a mortgage, and being broke like she was. The last time he had seen her, she was still angry at him for reading her diary when he was seven years old and she fifteen. Even though she drove him nuts on occasion, she was his sister, and unlike his older brother, whom she had not spoken to in ten years, Larry was in contact. He was happy with his life and at this point had no intention of changing a thing.

As Larry was reading the email, in walked Ben Magsino. He was back in town and had just come from the airport. Ben greeted them, "Morning, gentlemen. How are things?"

Nigel answered, "Good morning, Colonel. Just plugging away, sir."

Ben said, "Keep doing what you're doing, Nigel. The brass in DC are very pleased."

Nigel responded, "Thank you, sir."

Ben asked, "How are you doing, Larry?"

Larry replied, "Everything is good on my end, Ben. No glitches. Everything has been working perfectly."

The colonel answered, "Good to know, Larry. We don't want any slip-ups during the summit. I have a meeting with the ambassador in a few minutes. I just wanted to touch base with you two. Let me know if you need anything."

With that, Ben left, leaving Nigel and Larry to get back to work.

Yuri was thinking about the general's proposal. He liked the plan, except for choosing a building outside of the city center. The more Yuri thought about it, he concluded a building within the city center would invoke the most emotional impact. He would discuss this later with the Butcher.

Chapter Ten

THE SUMMIT

Ben was waiting outside the ambassador's office. The ambassador was on the phone, so Ben had to wait. As Ben sat in a chair going over his notes, Phyllis, the ambassador's secretary, was at her desk eating a cupcake.

The intercom buzzed and she said, "Mr. Magsino, you may go in now."

When Ben entered the ambassador's office, the ambassador said, "Hello, Ben. Sorry to keep you waiting."

Ben replied, "Hello, Franklin. Nice to see you again."

Franklin continued, "Ben, I asked you here to invite you to a little get-together at Spaso House tonight. The secretary of state and the British, French, and German leaders will be arriving in Moscow this afternoon. Nancy and I have scheduled a meet and greet for tonight at 7:00. Cocktails and hors d'oeuvres will be served. I hope you can make it."

Ben responded, "Certainly, Mr. Ambassador. I will look forward to it."

Franklin replied, "Great, Ben. I was hoping you would say that. I thought it would be nice to break the ice before we start the negotiations. See you tonight."

With that, Ben walked out of the office and headed back to the Lotte Hotel. Ben was feeling a little drained after his flight and thought he would rest a bit before he met with the diplomats.

☭

That evening, Ben entered Spaso House. The cocktails and hors d'oeuvres were being served in the Chandelier Room. When Nancy, the ambassador's wife, saw Ben, she walked over, took his arm, and said, "Hello, Ben. Nice of you to make it."

Ben replied, "I would not have missed it, Mrs. Ambassador."

Nancy responded, "Ben, please call me Nancy."

Ben answered, "Certainly. Thank you, Nancy."

Nancy said, "Come with me, Ben, I want to introduce you around."

Still holding his arm, she led him to where Madeleine Warren, the Secretary of State, and Robert Minor, the British Prime Minister, were having a lively discussion about the differences in thought patterns between the liberal and conservative mind.

Nancy interrupted, "Excuse me, Madeleine, Robert. I would like to introduce you to Colonel Ben Magsino."

Madeleine said, "No need, Nancy; Ben and I are old friends. Nice to see you, Ben. How is your wife Janet?"

Ben replied, "Nice seeing you, Madeleine. Janet is fine."

Madeleine said, "Ben, I don't think you know Robert. Ben, let me introduce you to Robert Minor, the Prime Minister of Britain."

Ben responded, "It is a pleasure to meet you, sir."

Robert replied, "Ben, your reputation precedes you, old boy. I look forward in getting to know you better during the next few days."

Ben answered, "Thank you, sir. The pleasure will be mine."

Nancy said, smiling, "You ex-military men are always so proper, with the sirs and all. Madeleine, Robert, if you would excuse us a moment?"

They both nodded and she led Ben to where Helmut Gerhard, the German chancellor, and Lionel Alain, the French prime minister, were arguing good- naturedly about the attributes of French Chardonnay and German Riesling wines. As the couple walked up, Nancy said, with a grin, "Give me a good ol' French Chardonnay anytime, but when I am in the mood for a beer, I will take a German Pilsner."

The Frenchman smiled and nodded, but it was the German who

responded. "Mrs. Ambassador, I will say we Germans are known for our excellent beer, but our Riesling wines will compare with the best of French wines."

Lionel replied, "Nonsense, Helmut. The German wines still taste of the foot fungus from the peasant women crushing the grapes. There is no comparison."

Nancy interrupted, "Now boys, behave yourselves. I would like you to meet Colonel Ben Magsino."

The German said, "Oh yes, Colonel Magsino. I understand you are the man responsible for the narrative we will be following during the negotiations. Bravo, Colonel."

Lionel chimed in, "Bonjour, Colonel. If I may be so bold to ask, perhaps you could help us settle a little dispute. Helmut and I have been discussing the differences between German and French wines. Which one do you find superior?"

Nancy stopped him right there. "Now come on, Lionel, don't drag Ben into it."

Ben replied, "Good evening, gentlemen. It is nice to finally meet the both of you. As far as wines are concerned, that is a good question; the answer could follow different avenues. On reputation and variety of the wines, France is the clear winner, but the German Riesling is a unique wine, with the grapes grown only in the Rhine area of Germany, so the French have nothing to compare it to. To summarize, in my opinion, if you want your senses and palate to experience a Riesling, Germany has the best. If you wish to experience a Chardonnay, the French wines are superior."

Nancy responded, "Nice, Ben. Spoken like a true diplomat."

Just then, the President of Chechnya was announced unexpectedly and escorted by the ambassador. "Excuse me ladies and gentlemen, a slight change of plans. President Movladi Aslin will be joining us this evening. It seems he has arrived in Moscow a day earlier than previously scheduled. With that, I give you the President of Chechnya. Please welcome him to Moscow and Spaso House."

The diplomats moved in and welcomed the new President of Chechnya. Nancy took Alsin's arm and led him to one of the waiters who was carrying a tray of martinis.

"Mr. President, a martini?"

Movladi Aslin was a Muslim and did not drink alcohol; not that all Muslims do not drink alcohol, but Movladi did not. Movladi replied, "No thank you, Mrs. Ambassador, but perhaps I may have a soft drink?"

Nancy responded, "Of course, Mr. President. What would you like?"

Alsin answered, "Perhaps I might have a Coca-Cola?"

Nancy asked, "Of course. Would you like ice?"

Alsin responded, "Yes please; just a small portion, Mrs. Ambassador, thank you."

Nancy motioned to one of the waiters as her husband walked up and joined the conversation. Ben was looking at the president's face, trying to get a read. He had a nice strong face, bearded, and looked as if it was lived in. It was the eyes that held Ben's attention. His eyes had a glassy glow like a Svengali or the Russian Rasputin. Ben knew this in itself was not a concern, but it was noted. Movladi Aslin was known as the Hero of Grozny. He led the attack taking back the city from the Russians. He was educated in Britain, and the West believed he could be a valuable asset in the region. Not all Western leaders held that sentiment, however. A lot of these guys took the help of the West and swore to preserve a democratic government, but once in power, those promises seemed to fall by the wayside. During the coming days, Ben would access Aslin's personality traits and include those assessments in his report to DC. This was part of Ben's job, and he was good at it.

Nancy noticed Ben's attention to Aslin and thought he might want a closer look. She placed her hand in the president's and walked the few steps to introduce him to Magsino. She said, "Mr. President, I would like to introduce you to Colonel Benjamin Matthew Magsino."

Aslin replied, "Nice to meet you, Colonel, but please call me Movladi."

Ben said, "Thank you. It is nice meeting you as well, Movladi, and please call me Ben." He then asked," How are you feeling about the summit?"

Aslin answered, "I pray to Allah that all goes smoothly and quickly. I look forward to beginning the rebuilding and healing process of my country."

Ben said he understood and with any luck the process would go swiftly. He added, "Of course, Movladi, there is always the unexpected, and as you know, the Russians make strange bedfellows."

Aslin laughed and replied, “Quite right, Ben, quite right.”

Nancy and Aslin excused themselves, and she led the president away to chat with the German and French diplomats. Ben hoped the wine conflict had been resolved.

☭

“JT, you got a copy? This is Harry.” Harry spoke into the Motorola.

Harry heard some static and then, “Yeah Harry, this is JT, go ahead.”

Harry squeezed the mike button and spoke, “JT, I want to remind you we have to get the monthly site photos in today. The operations guys have their projects status meeting tomorrow morning, and Rodney needs the photos. I am working on the narrative.”

JT answered, “I remembered, boss. I am getting the photos now. Any particular area you want me to focus on for the corporate guys?”

Harry answered, “Yes. Get some good shots of the pile drilling and installation of the casings for the CAC and mail room buildings. This is an activity we started ahead of schedule, and at the home office; they eat that up.”

JT replied, “I hear you, Harry. Anything else?”

Harry said, “No, that’s it. Pick out the ten best photos and send them in with the narrative.”

Miller ended with, “Sounds good, Harry. See you in a few. Over and out.”

Miller signed off and started to walk to the CAC buildings. Harry continued writing the monthly narrative on the construction activities for that month—basically, a summary which would be sent in with the photos. When Miller completed the task, he went back to his office and tried to download the photos onto his computer, but it wasn’t working. He got an error message that said, “Too much data. Unable to download.” Miller tried a few things, to no avail. He picked up his desk phone and pressed the IT guy’s code. Miller listened and on the third ring a voice on the other end said, “Jon Knutsen.”

Miller said, “Hey, Jon. I need your expertise. For some reason I can’t download some photos. Can you come over and check it out?”

Jon answered, “Sure, JT. Give me a minute and I will be right over.”

Miller replied, “Nice. I’ll be here.”

Jon Knudsen entered Miller’s office and said, “Okay, JT, move over. Let me see what's going on." With lightning speed, Jon checked the usual culprits and he came up with a solution. "JT, I think I know what's happening. I need to delete the downloading program from your computer, then reinstall it. It will take about twenty minutes."

Miller responded, "Great, Jon. I'll take this opportunity to go outside and smoke a stogie. I'll see you later."

With that, Miller went outside to the designated smoking area.

☭

Ben had the screen set up in the vault. He was preparing a PowerPoint presentation for the leaders assembled. Ben looked around the conference table and seated, looking back at him, were the ambassador, secretary of state, British and French prime ministers, and the German chancellor. The Chechen president would attend only the formal talks with the Russians.

Ben began, "Madeline, gentlemen, we have several things on the agenda, so let's get started. First, I want to talk about the peace treaty conditions. Number 1 is the prisoner exchange. We know the Russians are in agreement with this. Number 2: All Russian troops will leave the country. This should be a no-brainer, but with the Russians, we need to make this clear. Number 3: Chechnya will have the right to sovereignty and govern the way it sees fit. No interference. And finally, compensation. We will demand the Russian government make restitution in the form of 100 billion dollars. This money will be used to rebuild the Chechnya infrastructure that the Russians have seen fit to destroy." Ben paused, then said, "All right, then. Any questions and or comments?"

Madeleine Warren squirmed in her chair and asked, "Ben, do we actually believe the Russians will agree to pay 100 billion in restitution? The government is almost broke."

Ben grinned and replied, "Madeleine, this is our starting point. It gives us some room when we start to negotiate. I know the Russians will try to whittle that down."

Madeleine responded, "Gotcha, Ben, of course."

Lionel Alain, the French prime minister, interjected, "Pardon, Colonel, but please tell them we do not accept rubles."

They all chuckled and Ben paused, waited then announced, "Madeleine, gentlemen, I am not sure if you are aware, but the very room we are sitting in is being bugged by the Russians. The good news is that we know about it and have the ability to turn the listening device off and on at will. I can assure you, it is presently off. The Russians know we are meeting today and are expecting to hear a meeting; therefore we must oblige them." Ben turned off the projector and reached into his briefcase. Inside were copies of a script Nigel had prepared. He passed them out and continued, "In front of you is a script we will be performing for our good friends. In it is an alternative version of the meeting that has taken place. Prime Minister Minor, I would like to thank you for MI6's participation in this project. This joint venture has proved invaluable."

Robert Minor answered, "Don't mention it, Ben. It is in both our countries' interests. Please go on."

Ben continued, "Everyone, please take a few minutes to go over your lines in the script. When you are ready, we will rehearse before we do it live for the Russians."

The German Chancellor interrupted, "This will be great fun, Colonel. Perhaps you are not aware of this, but Germany has some of the best actors in Europe. It is in our blood."

The French Prime Minister responded, "Herr Chancellor, I am afraid that we must differ again. Just like the wine, France has the best. To prove my point, I will give you two names...Charles Boyer and Brigitte Bardot."

Helmut thought about this a moment and replied, "Excuse me, Mr. Prime Minister, but I must inform you that Charles Boyer is half German, and I understand the larger half."

Ben interrupted before the Frenchman could respond, "Gentlemen, let's not get off track. Please go over the scripts and we will get started."

In Istanbul, Yusef Solak was sitting down at an alfresco café along the Bosphorus. The Bosphorus is a strait that connects the Black Sea with the Sea of Marmara. Yusef was drinking black tea and waiting for his breakfast. Mr. Solak was a bomb expert and considered top in his field. He learned his trade in the Turkish army fighting the Kurds. Yusef had no qualms over taking human life. He justified it by believing he was not the one responsible; it was on the head of the one paying for the services. After all, he was just a poor businessman trying to make a living. Yusef was a master at demolition. He knew exactly where to place the charges to do the maximum amount of damage. If you needed something blown up using components of the devices being untraceable to the authorities or devices that could point the authorities to an innocent entity, Yusef was your man. The waiter arrived and deposited a basket filled with chunks of feta cheese, black and green olives, freshly baked white bread, fruit preserves, and honey.

Just as he was about to dig in, his cell phone rang. Annoyed, he answered, "Merhaba (Hello)." The voice on the other end shouted, "Yusef, speak English if you know what's good for you. This is General Brezhnev, and I don't have all day."

Yusef answered, "If it isn't my old friend the Butcher. I am glad, Nikita, that you are still your old charming self. What can I do for you on this beautiful day in Istanbul?"

The Butcher said, "Listen, Yusef. I have a job for you. I need you in Moscow to discuss the details."

Yusef replied, "Ah, but General, it is getting cold there now. Perhaps we could meet in the south of France. I have not thawed out since my last visit to Moscow."

The general said, "Yusef, stop your insolence. The money will be wired to your account as always. I need you here by next Friday."

Yusef always got his fee up front, especially when dealing with the Russians. He would not make a move until it was deposited. He had done several little projects for the general in the past—two bridges and a train depot in Tatarstan. There was also that little thing at Smolenskya metro station in Moscow about eight or ten years ago. That was the first job he had done for the general.

Yusef said, "Nikita, as soon as the transfer is complete, I will make the arrangements and inform you when my plane arrives."

After the conversation was finished, Yusef started on his breakfast. Brezhnev leaned back in his chair. He was satisfied. He knew the little Turk was the best.

At the Kremlin, Russian president Georgy Chernenko was meeting with his national security advisor, General Alexander Viktorovich, and Chinese foreign Minister Kwon Choa. Later they would travel to the US Embassy for the first round of peace treaty talks. They would arrive at the south gate and be met by the American Ambassador and Secretary of State at the main entrance. Because of the ongoing construction, TRIAD had been instructed to build a covered walkway from the main entrance to the Spode building. From there, the world leaders would walk through Spode, then enter the CAA space through Post 2 and make their way down the hall to the conference room. All construction activities would halt while the summit was taking place. John had assured Harry the site would be closed down for no more than three days for the event. Vera's team of CAG's and CST's would act as ushers, being stationed along the route, showing the leaders the way.

When the hour had arrived and the police motorcade was assembled at the Kremlin, the Russian leaders and the Chinese foreign minister walked to the ZIL4104 limo and got inside. As a precaution, two other identical ZIL4104 limos would occupy other places in line throughout the motorcade. An assassin would have to play "Eeny, meeny, miny, moe" to guess which of the limos the leaders were riding in. The motorcade arrived at the south gate of the embassy. The three limos entered the sally port at the CAC building. Two CAG's came out and checked each car. With an inspection mirror they checked underneath each vehicle, searching for bombs and anything else someone might try to smuggle in. They also looked under the hood and did a quick look inside the vehicle. When they were satisfied, the CAG motioned inside the building for the anti-ram gate to be opened. The Russian limos entered and were ushered to the diplomatic parking lot. The Russian president and his negotiators stepped out of their vehicle where their bodyguards were waiting.

A four-piece marine ceremonial guard waited, standing at attention on the edge of the parking lot as the leaders were ushered behind them. The center two marines carried flags. One carried the Stars and Stripes and the other the state flag of Russia. The leaders followed the marines the short march to the main entrance of the embassy. There waiting for them was the RNO (Russian National Orchestra), the ambassador and his wife Nancy, and Madeline Warren, Secretary of State. As the ceremonial guard led the procession, the RNO played an old Russian march called "Eagle," a lively selection that happened to be one of the Russian president's favorites.

The parade came to a halt in front of the entrance of the embassy where the diplomats were standing in wait. Madeline approached the Russian president with the ambassador and his wife close behind. She reached out her hand and said, "Nice to see you again, President Chernenko."

The Russian smiled and replied, "Thank you, Madam Secretary."

He gazed at the ambassador and his wife and said, "Hello Ambassador, Mrs. Ambassador. So nice of you to welcome us. Let me introduce you to General Viktorovich, and I believe you know Chinese foreign minister, Kwon Choa?"

Madeline replied, "General, Minister, welcome." They nodded and she continued, "Mr. President, before we go down to the conference room and get to work, the orchestra would like to play a few selections."

She nodded to the orchestra leader and they began to play the National Anthem of the Russian Federation. The general removed his hat and they all stood straight, almost at attention, in reverence, as the notes floated through the air. When the Russian selection was complete the RNO played "The Star-Spangled Banner," during which they all continued the pose. When it was over, they walked through and under the covered walkway to the conference room.

Lieutenant Maxim Sokolov was at his computer, making sure everything was working properly. If anything went wrong while recording the talks, he could find himself in Siberia—or worse, the gulag. Sokolov was on loan from the Seventh Directorate, the agency responsible for carrying out the surveillance activities. Karlov had the lieutenant set up an intercom through the phone lines to Yuri's office at his apartment at the Ukraine hotel. There he and Yuri would listen to the talks. Yuri and the major were sitting in his office, each sipping a shot of Tsarskaya and waiting.

The major said, "Yuri, it should begin any moment now, my friend."

Yuri answered, "We shall see how the peasant Chernenko and the others handle themselves." Just then, something started coming over the intercom.

During the conference, Ben Magsino would stay in the studio and listen. It was up to Madeline and the ambassador to control the meeting and bring home the bacon. She would confer with Ben during the breaks. The first diplomat to enter the conference room was the ambassador, followed by the Russians and Chinese. Bringing up the rear was Madeline. The Chechen president and the French and German leaders were in the room, waiting. When the introductions and pleasantries were over, both sides put on their game faces and were ready to rumble. General Viktorovich stared at Movladi Aslin, trying to intimidate him. Movladi stared back with those glowing eyes. On the table were glass pitchers filled with ice water, and off to the side on another table were coffee, tea, and assorted pastries. In front of each place at the table was a copy of the agenda.

The group sat down, and Madeline went for the water. She filled her glass and drank half of it before she began to speak. "Gentlemen, please let's get started. First, I want to thank you all for coming. With any luck, I am optimistic we will get through this relatively quickly. The first item on the agenda is the prisoner exchange. I think we are in agreement with this point. Russia will return all Chechen prisoners, and Chechnya will return all Russian prisoners. I think this could actually begin immediately as we work out the other details."

General Viktorovich spoke up first. "That is unacceptable. We have twice as many Chechen prisoners as you have Russians. Chechnya will release all Russian prisoners, and Russia will release 50 percent of the Chechens."

Movlodi could hardly contain himself and replied, "And, General, what do you propose to do with the prisoners you wish to retain? Keep them in concentration camps?"

The general responded, "They will be well treated."

Movladi fired back, "Nonsense. There is no such thing as a Russian prison where the inhabitants are well treated. No, this is a must. We surrender all

Russian prisoners, and Russia releases all Chechens. It is that simple."

The general responded, "Russia could consider surrendering 70 percent of the Chechens. That is, of course, if you could offer some other form of compensation."

The Russian president sat listening. He wanted the peace treaty signed, but he had to show strength and perhaps receive some concessions in the process. Madeline spoke up, speaking directly to President Chernenko.

"Mr. President, the war has been bleeding your resources since 1994. It makes no sense to hold Chechen prisoners once the treaty is signed. The cost to house and feed the prisoners will continue to eat away at your country's coffers. I propose this: You release 90 percent of the Chechens now and the remaining 10 percent when the treaty is signed."

Movladi nodded in agreement. The general began to speak, but Chernenko stopped him and said, "Madam Secretary, Russia may consider 80 percent now and the release of the others when the treaty is worked out. This is just insurance to give the Chechens the incentive to complete the peace treaty process. The Russian government also expects the West to provide 20 million dollars in compensation to help feed and house those prisoners during that process."

Madeline looked at Movladi, then at the French and German leaders, then back to Movladi and asked, "President Aslin. What is your answer?"

Movladi looked around the table and said to the Russian, "Agreed except for one small detail. As you have said, President Chernenko, as insurance Chechnya will retain the same percentage of Russians. If this is acceptable, we can move on."

The general's face went red as he jumped up in protest. When the general got excited, he had an uncontrollable twitch, mostly around his left eye. This sudden convulsive movement was fluttering like a butterfly.

Chernenko again intervened and motioned the general to sit down and said, "Excuse us a moment." The three spoke a few minutes in Russian with one another. At first the general was keyed up, then settled down when Chernenko and Kwon Choa reminded him they were prepared to accept an even exchange and now they would also receive 20 million for the trouble. The Chinese minister thought they should take it and move on to more important matters. Madam Secretary and the others watched as Chernenko turned to face them. He simply replied, "Agreed."

Yuri was livid. He thought President Chernenko acted weak. He should have been more aggressive, he thought. Then something occurred to him. The gas canister filled with the 3-methylfentanyl was in the vault door. All he had to do was instruct Lieutenant Maxim Sokolov to activate the remote-controlled device inside the canister and everything would be solved. Yuri might even be catapulted to president of the motherland. He knew he had the support of the hardliners, but whom could he blame for the assassination? The Americans would find out the truth. There was no denying it, once they examined the vault door. He could blame Chernenko himself, and with the help of planted evidence, it might work. He could make Chernenko out as a martyr for the betterment of Russia, but it was a big risk. He would have to kill his old friend Dimitry; he couldn't take any chances. He knew Karlov was strong but once they put his head into the metal vise and applied the pressure, you were done for. After the excruciating pain, your brain felt like it was coming out of your ears and you would say anything to please them to stop the pain. Yuri would give it some more thought.

He picked up the vodka bottle and asked, "Another Tsarskaya, Dimitry my old friend?"

"Do not mind if I do, Yuri. You are always the good host."

"Thank you, Major. Now let us hope our peasant president will show more of his bear persona and less of his rabbit. We shall see."

The diplomats took a break. Madeline walked to the studio to confer with Ben. Ben thought the first round went well. He also had a new respect for Movladi. He had shown he was tough and also employed good arguments for his points of view. *So far, so good,* he thought. The meetings would continue and last long into the night. If they could not agree on all points, they would meet the following morning and hash something out, come hell or high water. That was the plan, but the Russians could throw a monkey wrench into it at any time. Ben did not think this would be the case. He felt certain Chernenko was caught between a rock and a hard place. The Russian people wanted out. It was only the hardliners who wanted the war to continue.

☭

In the last weeks, Bo had been behaving himself. He had not spoken to Natasha since his last meeting with Major Karlov. He focused on his job during the day and his faith at night. He prayed to his god and continued to ask for forgiveness. Natasha was busy with her massage practice and also busy with Anatoli and Major Karlov when they came over for some special attention. On occasion, Anatoli would bring over one of his KGB buddies. Sometimes Natasha would think of Bo. She liked his weirdness during sex and missed it. He could turn from a spineless confused small boy to a dominant sexual beast. She liked that in him. Bo, on the other hand, had been on the straight and narrow. For a time, Bo believed he could control his impulses, but once in a while they would rear their ugly head. When the monsters did show up, he prayed. When they started to win, the purging got more severe. At this point, Bo was feeling righteous, but he did not know how long the feeling would last before the fiend that lived within would return.

☭

Miller and Irena were sitting down in Sveta's living room, waiting for dinner to be ready. Harry was there as well, along with Alexei. Sveta was in the kitchen. Alexei was excited because he would be trying out for the Russian Boys Hockey Academy the next morning.

Irena was teasing him and said, "Alexei wants to be just like his hero Alexei Kovalev, who plays for America's New York Rangers."

Miller responded, "I know him. He's a good player. Fast and smart."

Alexei said, "He used to play in the Moscow league until he went to America in 1992 season. It was after the 1992 Olympics where the American scouts saw him play. They recruited him soon after."

"What position do you play, Alexei?" Miller asked.

Alexei answered, "I play forward, Slav, just like Alexei."

Miller said, "Nice. Are you ready to show them your stuff tomorrow?"

Alexei replied, "I am ready. I have been ready."

Miller liked Alexei's self-confidence. Harry drifted into the kitchen to grate potatoes for potato pancakes. Harry loved the damn things, but Sveta laid down the law. If Harry wanted potato pancakes, it was he who would do the grating. Harry thought that was a fair compromise. Irena yawned as she walked into the kitchen and went up to her mother and kissed her on the cheek.

She asked, "Is there anything I can help with, Mamochka?"

"Yes, my little Dochenka. Could you set the table?" Sveta answered with a wink.

Irena moved to the linen closet and selected a new tablecloth hidden under the others. It was a surprise for Alexei. In red, white and blue, printed in large letters was "New York Rangers 1996" with a photo of the whole team, including Alexei's hero. She fitted it over the table, then called out, "Alexei, help me set the table."

Alexei shrugged and got up from the sofa. He walked to the small dining room and was drawn to the tablecloth. He stood there mesmerized, admiring it. He said, "Oh, thank you, Mama. Look, there is Alexei and in front is Wayne Gretzky. He is my second-favorite player. Mama, I am afraid I will spill borsht on Alexei. May I take it and hang it on the wall of my room?"

Sveta replied, "Of course. But hurry, because dinner is almost ready."

Sveta and Irena were pleased that Alexei liked it. He took the Rangers from the table and ran to his room. Irena went back into the linen closet and chose another tablecloth. She set the table, and soon dinner was served. After dinner, Harry looked around the table and felt warm inside. This had been a family gathering where Harry hadn't felt like the odd man out. He felt as if he was actually home and a part of this family.

After three days of meetings, a peace treaty agreement was hashed out. It had not been easy. The essence of the peace treaty document was simple. It was just a document about ceasing military operations. Neither side would surrender and the treaty did not proclaim a winner. The prisoner exchange had been agreed to after the first meeting. There would be no compensation on either side, but both sides agreed to denounce the war and maintain a peace. The governing relations between Russia and Chechnya would be worked out later. Neither side had an advantage in the current document, but at least they had an agreement. Movladi was ready to start rebuilding his country. France, Britain, and Germany had agreed to loans up to 10 billion dollars for rebuilding Chechnya's infrastructure. Ben was satisfied that Madeline and the ambassador had done their best. That was all he could expect from them. Perhaps the agreement was not everything he had hoped for, but now Chechnya and the US had a way forward.

☭

Yuri reached up into the top shelf above the bar in his apartment. He grabbed the bottle with the Blue Label and pulled out two glasses. Yuri filled them and said, "Dimitry, a toast to our peasant president, who later showed more bear than rabbit at the summit."

Yuri actually now had a small amount of respect for Chernenko. He decided he would keep him around for a while. If he was caught with being involved in the building bombing, he would say it was Chernenko who had ordered it.

Major Karlov said, "Yes he did, didn't he, Yuri? Perhaps Chernenko is smarter than he looks."

Yuri smiled and replied, "Perhaps, Major. Perhaps."

Yuri held his glass up and said, "Za zdaróvye (For health), Bolshevik."

Karlov followed and with his glass up replied, "And to you, Comrade, and to Mother Russia."

☭

Ben and Nigel were having breakfast at the Lotte before they walked to the embassy. As they were sipping their coffee, they noticed a small man with dark Mediterranean features scoping out the buffet. He was short, wore a thick dark beard, and looked fit in a skinny sort of way. He chose scrambled eggs and white bread with butter and jam. As he moved to a corner table Nigel thought there was something familiar about him. He churned it over in his mind until it came to him.

He asked Ben, "Sir, did you notice that small bloke with the dark features who just sat down?"

Ben answered, "Yes, Nigel. Something unusual about him?"

Nigel responded, "Sir, his name is Yusef Solak. He is a Turkish bomb expert. He sells his services to the highest bidder. He was employed by the Russians during the Chechnya war. They used him, as far as MI6 was able to confirm, on three bridges going into Grozny. He was responsible for over 300 Chechen lives and has been on the radar for about a year."

Ben asked, "Any idea what may have brought him to Moscow?"

Nigel said, "Not a clue, sir, but I think it is safe to say he is not here because he fancies the weather."

Ben excused himself and walked to the lobby. He pulled out his cell phone, making sure he was not in earshot, and called Joe Kelly.

"Joe, this is Ben. How soon can you get to the Lotte restaurant?"

Ben caught Joe just as he was entering the embassy. Joe was just outside the south gate as he responded, "Morning, Ben. I can be there in five minutes."

Ben replied, "Make it three, Joe. Hurry."

Joe slipped his phone into his jacket pocket and started a fast jog to the Lotte. Ben waited in the lobby, and about four minutes later he saw Joe out on the sidewalk. Joe walked into the lobby and Ben intercepted him before he walked into the restaurant.

"Joe, thanks for getting here so fast."

Joe answered, "No problem. What's up?"

Ben said, "I need a tail on a guy. I will show you. He's having breakfast in the restaurant."

The pair walked into the restaurant and sat with Nigel. Yusef was still there, having a second cup of tea. Ben continues, "Joe, the small man with the beard at that corner table is Yusef Solak. We need to know why he is in Moscow. Keep a 24-hour tail on him. Is that clear, Joe? I will give you more details later at the embassy."

Joe replied, "Okay, Ben, I got it."

With that, Nigel and Ben got up and left. Joe stayed behind to watch Yusef until he could get his operatives in place.

☭

When Yusef was finished with breakfast, he went back up to his room. Joe waited in the lobby for his operative. When his operative arrived, he was briefed and took up Joe's position in the lobby. The only exit from the hotel was through the lobby, except for the fire doors located by the kitchen. There were two. As a precaution, Joe would watch these doors on the outside of the hotel from a small park located across the street until Yusef showed his face. Joe had to wait about thirty minutes before Yusef showed up in the lobby. As he left, the operative followed him out but not to close. After Joe saw them leave, he went back to the embassy to get intel on this Yusef Solak.

Main entrance to the Moscow Zoo 2015.

☭

After Yusef exited the lobby, he descended the hotel stairs and turned right down Novinskiy Boulevard. It was a sunny day in Moscow, and Yusef was enjoying the walk, wearing just a light jacket. He had no idea he was being followed. He continued down Novinskiy until he got to Barrikadnaya and veered left toward Krasnopresnenskaya metro station. As he got close to the station, he saw the familiar stone facade of the Moscow zoo, looking like a storybook castle. On either side of the entrance, it had two steeples. To the right of the entrance, one steeple had a large clock at the top, and on the left was a higher steeple with stained-glass windows. The 53-acre or 21.5hectare zoo was founded in 1864 and nationalized in 1919 with the city of Moscow taking charge of its operations.

Yusef paid the admission and entered the zoo. As he entered, he saw a big pond with hundreds of different species of ducks and other waterfowl enjoying the day quacking and fluttering around. Soon, many would be flying south for the winter. Yusef followed the road and crossed the foot bridge to the left. He passed the monkey cages. He paused and watched their antics for a few moments. He continued past the large bats, the zebras and elephants. Yusef stopped at the underground aquarium and descended the stairs. He smiled at the thought of what a delightful mess it would create if he were ever employed to blow up a target at the aquarium. He looked at his watch and continued; he would have time to see the sharks. Yusef liked the sharks.

He walked to the shark tank and gazed through the glass at a great white swimming past. Yusef thought of how misunderstood the shark was by the general population or the masses. Allah had seen fit to place the shark at the top of the underwater food chain for the simple task of controlling the populations below. Without the sharks to intervene, the fish populations become unbalanced. Research has shown that massive depletion of sharks had cascading effects throughout the ocean's ecosystems. But to the masses, the shark was to be hunted and feared. *How silly the masses are*, he thought. *So easy to manipulate*. Yusef considered himself to be like the shark. His business did help mitigate the population of the masses, thus contributing to the health of the world's ecosystem.

Yusef stayed a few more moments, then looked at his watch again. He bid adieu to the great whites and ascended the stairs to the sidewalk above. He followed the path to the large mammal exhibits. He passed the white bears or polar bears, then the white tiger, and finally the Amur leopard (Panthera pardus orientalis). This leopard is a beautiful creature with black spots on a white and brown background. The Amur leopard is a subspecies native to the Primorye region of southeastern Russia and the Jilin Province of northeast China. It is the rarest leopard in the world, with less than thirty estimated to have survived. Over the years they had been poached nearly to extinction for their beautiful fur for women's coats. The Amur can run to speeds of up to 37 miles per hour and can leap 10 feet vertically and 19 feet horizontally.

Sitting on a bench in front of the exhibit was a man. He was wearing a dark turtleneck sweater and appeared to be in his mid-fifties. The man was also wearing a sneer that would not wash off. It was the Butcher of Kazan, more formally known as General Nikita Brezhnev.

As Yusef walked up, the general turned to face him and said, "You are late, Turk."

Yusef replied, "Günaydn (good morning), Nikita. It is so nice to see you are so free with your pleasantries this morning. You never seem to disappoint."

The general looked at him with his permanent sneer and said, "Solak, let's get down to business. I do not have much time." Yusef nodded, and Brezhnev continued, "We have a top-secret operation we need you to be a part of. The mission is simple. We will blow up an apartment building in Moscow and blame it on the Chechens."

Yusef reached in his pocket, pulled out a packet of Murad cigarettes, chose one, and lit up. He took a long drag and let the smoke drift out through his mouth and nostrils. The Turk looked straight at the general and asked, "Is there a target in the building, Nikita?"

The general answered, "No, Yusef. We want to destroy the whole building and blame it on the Chechens. We want as many of the inhabitants killed as possible."

Yusef mulled this over and asked, "General, you plan on killing innocent Russians?"

The Butcher answered, "Yes, they will have to make the ultimate sacrifice for the betterment of Mother Russia."

Yusef asked, "When do you want this to take place?"

The general replied, "In three weeks' time. I have chosen three possible sites for this to take place. I want you to look these buildings over and choose the one that would be easiest for you to destroy. Look over the structural construction and make a choice. I have arranged for you a Russian operative to take you to these locations disguised as workers for the People's Gas Company, reading the usage meters. The meters are located in the basements, which will give you free rein to examine the structural aspects of the buildings. Once you have chosen, this same operative will assist you with the demolition."

Yusef had a habit of pulling on his beard when he was thinking. He did this and asked, "Does this operative have experience?"

The general answered, "Yes, as a matter of fact. When you speak with her, you will see. She goes by the code name Tanya."

Yusef looked appalled and replied, "General, a woman is out of the question. This is a man's game. A man is better suited for the hard work and nerves of steel required to perform this task."

The sneer on the general's face seemed to get more intense. He thought, *This insolent little Turk dares to question me?* He stared straight into Yusef's dark eyes and said, "She is the best we have and will be working with you on this. She has been chosen carefully. You will not be disappointed."

Yusef answered, "We shall see. When do I meet this Tanya?"

Nikita replied, "She will meet you at the Lotte lounge tonight at 8:00 for dinner. This will give you a chance to get acquainted."

Yusef still did not like it, but he nodded; he was willing to give it a try.

Between 1992 and 1996, great advances in camera technology appeared. A new photographic system called APS, or "Advanced Photo System," had been introduced. With improvements in optical lenses and film-loading technology, cameras were getting smaller and the zoom lens capabilities more powerful. The man at the white tiger exhibit was taking a photo of his girlfriend with his new Canon EOS Kiss.

He said, "Tatyana, move more to your left. Nyet, to far, go back right. Good. Hold it there."

Tatyana stood there looking bored. The man took several photos, but his focus was on the two men behind the girl. He had been following the short dark man since he left his hotel. Moshi had been assigned by Joe Kelly to keep tabs on this man and to photograph any persons he might meet. When he got the call, he was snug in his bed with Tatyana, and he thought it would be a good idea to bring her along as camouflage so he would not be detected.

Tatyana pouted and said, "Moshi, I want go back to the Belgrade. I am tired and these animals scare me."

Moshi replied, "A little longer, just until the small dark man goes back to his hotel."

She asked, "How long will that be?"

Moshi was getting tired of her lip and said, "You will go back when I tell you. Do not make me beat you. Clients do not like a puffy face and bruised body."

Tatyana shuddered, then seemed to wake up and got back in line, doing what she was told. Moshi liked it that way. Tatyana was just one of several girls who worked for him, and occasionally Moshi had to beat one to keep the others in line. Moshi did not enjoy this as other men in his profession did. He did it out of necessity for order, and not for pleasure.

Later that evening, Moshi was back at his apartment at the Belgrade. He pulled the film from his camera and placed it in a manila envelope. He took the elevator downstairs to the lounge to find Nikolai. Moshi saw him and motioned him over. When Nikolai reached him, he said, "Nikolai, take this to Medusa at the Irish bar. She is waiting." Nikolai nodded and received the package. He slipped it into the pocket of his coat and walked out of the lounge to the street.

Yusef was sitting at a table in the Lounge Bar on the first floor of the Lotte Hotel. He was waiting for his drink order. He took his packet of Murad cigarettes and placed them on the table. He chose one and lit the end with a Bic lighter. Within moments, the waiter was there with his drinks and a small side of feta cheese. He ordered a double shot of Yeni Raki in a tall glass, a bottle of flat mineral water, and a small bucket of ice. The clear shots transformed into a white liquid once water was added. This was due to the aniseed flavoring, which promoted the reaction. Sometimes raki was called aslan sütü, or lion's milk, by the Turks. He filled the tall glass of raki three-quarters high with water, then added ice until the glass was full. He took two small sips, then nibbled on the feta. Any Turk over the age of twelve knew always to sip the raki and never gulp. Raki had a habit of sneaking up on you when you least expected it.

The waiter walked up followed by a Russian woman. She had an attractive face and framed around it was long, curly blonde hair. Even though this woman was wearing a dress, her bulging muscles could not be disguised. They protruded through and she looked like an ad for The Goddess of Body Building. She had muscles on top of muscles.

She offered Yusef her hand and said, "Hello, Yusef. I am Tanya. The general said we will be working together."

Yusef could not believe it. This woman was half beauty and half beast. He finally answered, "Yes, that is what I understand. Please sit. Something to drink, perhaps?"

She looked at his drink and asked, "What is it you are drinking?"

Yusef answered, "This is raki. It is the national drink of my country. They call it lion's milk. I would be honored if you would try one."

She replied, "How can I refuse?"

Yusef instructed the waiter, and off he went.

☭

Joe Kelly was still at his office and had just finished developing the film Moshi had sent him. Earlier, he completed Yusef's background check and confirmed Nigel's information. Yes, Yusef was a dangerous man. As he looked at the photos, he recognized General Brezhnev, The Butcher of Kazan. There was no mistaking his scarred face. If Yusef was meeting with the general, this was not good. He picked up his phone and dialed. Ben Magsino needed to be informed immediately.

☭

The waiter returned with the raki, and Yusef showed Tanya how to prepare it. When it was all mixed to perfection, she took a drink. "This is nice, not too strong, and tastes like licorice," she said. Then she took another drink and the milky fluid began to work its magic. She could feel it warming her extremities.

Yusef said, "Here, eat some feta cheese. It goes well with raki." Tanya broke off a chunk and gobbled it up in one bite, then washed it down with more raki. Yusef continued, "Tanya, let me give you a fair warning. The raki should be sipped slowly. It is stronger than the taste would suggest." Yusef could tell she was already feeling the effects.

She replied, "Thank you, but no need to warn me. Yes, I am a woman, but I am also Russian. In my village when my mother was giving birth, there was no medicines, so my mother drank vodka for the pain when out I came."

Yusef was not sure how to respond to that information, so he took a sip of his drink and a bite of feta. Tanya watched him as he did. She thought he was not bad- looking for a Turk. He was small, and Tanya knew she could beat him in a fist fight and could make mincemeat out of him, if it came to that.

Finally, Yusef asked, "Tanya, would you like to order something to eat?"

She replied, "No, but I will have another lion's milk."

Yusef said, "I would not advise it. We still have much to discuss tonight."

Tanya answered, irritated, "Yusef, please stop warning me. There is no concern. I will have another lion's milk." Yusef ordered another for her and himself.

☭

At the bar, Moshi ordered a tap beer, trying to blend in, keeping tabs on the couple and staying out of sight. He had the buttonhole camera with him and would have to get a photo of the Russian. He would have to wait for his opportunity a little later when more people came in for dinner. At 10:00, another operative would take over. Moshi hoped to have the photo by then.

☭

After the third lion's milk, both Yusef and Tanya were looking a little sloppy. Feeling no pain, Tanya smiled and asked, "What is it, Yusef, that Turkish men find so attractive about Russian women?"

Yusef pulled on his beard as he thought, then laughed to himself, knowing most Turkish men were satisfied with anything wearing a dress. He laughed and replied, "I would say number one is the way they can hold their raki."

She laughed and asked, "Do you find me attractive, Turk?"

Yusef smiled and replied, "Yes, of course, Tanya, in a muscular sort of way."

She answered with an annoyed tone, "What is wrong, Turk? You do not like a muscular woman? Do you think I am too strong for you? That I could break you in two?" She laughed.

Yusef responded, "To be quite honest, I have not given it much thought."

She said, "You lie. I saw you looking at my breasts. Let me see what kind of man you are. Put your arm on the table."

Amused, Yusef complied. She took his hand and rested her elbow on the table, and Yusef followed suit. She asked, "Have you ever arm-wrestled, Turk?"

Yusef was getting tired of Tanya's sass, so he took the gloves off and said, "Do not make me laugh, Russian. I was arm-wrestling when you were playing with dolls. I will tell you what. Yes, I will arm-wrestle you if you agree to the terms."

She asked coolly, "And what are these terms?"

"If I win, you take your clothes off and stand on this table until the waiter throws you out. If you win, I will let you come up to my room for a night cap and have your way with me," he replied with a grin.

Tanya thought about it and said, "Not so fast, Turk. If I win, you take your clothes off and stand on the table until the waiter throws you out. But first order us more lion's milk, and be quick about it."

Moshi looked at his watch. It was almost 10:00. He got up from the bar and began positioning himself closer to the table. Moshi waited for the waiter to bring the couple's drinks, then intercepted him as he turned away. This was directly behind Yusef. He asked the waiter directions to the toilet, at the same time taking several photos of Tanya and one of the two sitting together. He made a pit stop at the toilet, then went back to his roost at the bar where he would await his replacement. A few minutes later, a man in a gray suit took a seat at the end of the bar. Without saying a word, Moshi paid his bill and walked out of the Lotte.

☭

Tanya had a determined look on her face. She took another gulp of raki and let the milky fluid float uninterrupted to her digestive tract. She belched before she spoke. "Are you ready, Turk?" She laughed and continued, "Be prepared to show this bar your naked skinny little Turkish body."

Yusef laughed. "Do not be so sure, Russian."

With that, he took Tanya's hand and they both got into the arm-wrestling position. Yusef instructed, "On three. One . . . two . . . three!"

Instantly their arms clenched. Tanya was surprised at the little Turk's strength. Their muscles and joints endured the strain. It went back and forth. At times it seemed Yusef had the advantage, and at times the girl. Yusef thought his elbow joint would dislocate, but he was not giving in. Just then, he forced Tanya's arm almost to the table, but she fought her way back. With her other hand, she grabbed her glass of raki and drained it, smiling at Yusef, taunting him. He picked up his own and drained it. The tussle lasted a few more minutes when Tanya lifted her elbow from the table to get more leverage against the Turk. This was against the rules, but it worked. She was able to pin Yusef's arm to the table.

Tanya laughed and said, "Now, Turk, strip for me."

Yusef replied, "You broke the rules, Russian. You forfeit the match."

She did what Russians do when caught in a lawless act or lie: she denied it. She was taught that it did not matter how you won, as long as you did. She asked, "You are crazy, Turk? It is my word against yours. That is, of course, unless you have a witness."

He looked around and no one was close enough who would have seen. This was precisely why Yusef always got his money up front with the Russians. He casually reached for his Murad cigarette box. He thought as he tapped the box to pack the tobacco. He opened the box and chose one of the sticks, lit up, and took a puff.

He said, "Okay, Russian, we will compromise and call it a draw on one condition."

Tanya looked at him closely. She was getting tired of Yusef's terms and conditions and asked, "And what is this condition?"

Yusef replied, "Very simple, Ruskie. You come up to my room for a night cap."

Tanya smiled and asked, "And why would I agree to such a condition? To see your skinny Turkish body? I do not think so." She thought a moment then responded, "I know what we will do. We will both take our clothes off and stand on the table--that is, if you are not afraid, Turk."

Yusef pulled on his beard and replied, "Agreed, but we shall have one more lion's milk before we do the deed."

Tanya laughed and asked, "Need some courage?"

Yusef answered, "Yes, you are correct--not to get on the table, but to cope with the shock of what's under that dress you are wearing."

Tanya said, laughing, "Poor skinny Turk is frightened by a woman that is as strong as a man!"

Yusef shrugged as he caught the waiter and ordered two more double-shot rakis.

☭

The man in the gray suit was still sitting at the bar. It was a few minutes before midnight and he was nursing his beer, keeping an eye on his targets. It would not be long until he switched to coffee. As he sat there, in walked two Russian hookers on the prowl for inebriated older foreign gentlemen. Russian men were out. Too many times after the services were rendered, they refused to pay. The older foreign gentlemen not only paid, but if the girls did their job efficiently and to the client's satisfaction, they would normally receive a tip. Olga and Raisa were in their late thirties and were no beauty queens. The two were average lookers, but with enough makeup and with dim lighting, they looked quite attractive. Not many nights went by when they did not catch their prey. The two had regular jobs during the day but were not paid enough rubles to make ends meet.

Olga eyed the men sitting at the bar and motioned to Raisa, and the pair found two empty stools. Olga sat down next to the man in the gray suit. She took a handful of peanuts from a dish at the bar and ordered two tap beers for her and Raisa. Olga tried to make eye contact, but the man in the gray suit seemed preoccupied. Finally, Olga tapped him on his shoulder and asked for a light.

The man replied, "Sorry, I do not smoke. Please excuse me." The man got up and walked through the bar to the water closet.

☭

Yusef had just drained the last of his raki. Yusef said, "Finish your drink, Russian, and let's do this."

Tanya complied and asked, "Ready, Turk?"

Yusef nodded and stood up; so did Tanya. Yusef took off his shirt, then his shoes, then his pants. He was standing there in his boxer shorts and socks. Tanya unzipped her dress and stepped out of it. She was still wearing her high black boots, panties, and bra. Yusef was mesmerized, enjoying the view. He was starting to like her muscular body much more after she was almost naked. All of this took place in less than ten seconds.

Tanya commanded, "Okay, Turk, take it all off."

She removed her bra and panties, revealing an almost perfect female body- builder body. Yusef could also make the determination that she was a natural blonde. Yusef removed his boxer shorts, and he could tell Tanya was impressed. The two held hands, stepped up on to their chairs, then to the table. It wasn't long before the whole bar noticed. As they stood there, some people cheered, some threw food, and others also got into the act, including Olga and Raisa. Soon, many couples were taking off their clothes and standing naked on the tables. Yusef thought, *Only in Russia.*

Tanya yelled, "Waiter, bring me more raki, you swine!"

The man in the gray suit was returning from the toilet when he witnessed the commotion. He saw other people in the bar taking photos, so it would not seem odd if he took some as well. From his pocket he pulled out his Canon Sure Shot and got a few shots of the couple. Almost as quickly as the rebellion started, the waiters employed the help of the hotel's bouncers and got everyone under control and down from the tables. After Yusef and Tanya stepped down from the table, he signed his bill and wrote his room number on it. Casually, Yusef and Tanya picked up their clothes, holding them in a ball, and walked naked through the bar to the elevators. On the way out, Tanya eyed Olga and motioned for her to come along with them. Olga was only too happy to comply and told Raisa she would be back. The three revelers got into the elevator en route to the night cap in the Turk's room.

☭

The next morning Joe Kelly, Ben Magsino, and Nigel Crabtree were looking at the photos from the night before. Ben asked, "Joe, have we identified this woman operative with Solak?"

Joe replied, "Yes, her name is Anna Ivanov. Her code name is Tanya. She is twenty-eight years old, a body builder, and was in the Russian army demolition unit under General Nikita Brezhnev for six years. She learned her trade from Russia's top bomb expert, Borya Bortnik. Tanya and Bortnik were briefly lovers until his untimely death last year when he was shot by a Chechen soldier when trying to retreat from Grozny as the Chechens were taking back the city. Tanya narrowly escaped."

Ben frowned and asked, "Anything to add, Nigel?"

"No, sir. That is basically what MI6 has on her."

Ben said, "Okay, gentlemen, we can rest assured they are here to blow something up, but what and why? We need to answer those two questions. Any ideas?"

Joe responded, "We will have to maintain surveillance and make sure our cover is not blown. I think we should know shortly of the 'what,' and perhaps the 'why' will be answered as well."

Ben answered, "Joe, you are in charge. I don't have to tell you that something big is brewing and to have your best men on this."

Joe replied, "I am using my best Russian operatives. It is best if we use Russians instead of Americans. Less chance of our targets getting wise."

Ben nodded then said, "Agreed, but if you need anything, be sure to let me know. Nigel, you have any ideas?"

Nigel answered, "Well, sir, if I may be so bold, I think it might have something to do with discrediting the Chechens. Just a hunch. Why else would General Brezhnev want to blow something up on Russian soil?"

Ben replied, "You have a point, Nigel. There are many hardliners in the State Duma that would like to continue the war, but they could also be planning an assassination of a rival or opposition leader. Joe is right. We watch them and see what they do."

It was Wednesday at 10:00 a.m., and that meant the OBO Coordination Meeting. This was a construction management meeting where the USG was informed of the project progress and other construction-related activities. This was also a showcase for some OBO personnel that you would think were running for Congress. They liked to show how smart they could be and liked to play the game "Gotcha." The rules for "Gotcha" were simple. Look for anything wrong the contractor may or may not be doing, regardless of how slight, then carry on like the sky was falling. Miller reasoned that if they nitpicked on the small things, it would keep the contractor on their toes for the larger issues.

The OBO had their side of the table, and TRIAD had theirs. On the contractor's side were Harry, Miller, Bo, Charlie, Kurt, and Tom Scaraponi, the safety guy. Harry usually led the meeting. On the OBO side were John London, the PD; Lou Bost, the construction manager; Vera Collins, the site security manager; Vera's team leader Arsenio Wells, in charge of the CST's and CAG's; Joe Amato, OBO's electrical engineer; Hameed Hussain, OBO's civil engineer; and last but not least, Andre Petrov, the mechanical engineer. Copies of the previous week's meeting minutes were provided. Included in the minutes under different categories was a list of issues with the status of when these items would be resolved.

Harry started, "Good morning, everybody. As usual, let's get started with safety. Tom, would you walk us through it?"

Tom began, "Sure, Harry. Last week we had no recordable accidents that resulted in loss of time worked. As of today, we have had 112 consecutive days without a loss of time work incident. Our toolbox meeting for this week is ladder safety. Yesterday Lou and I did our weekly site walk to identify any safety concerns and addressed the items. Would you like to add anything, Lou?"

Lou nodded then answered, "Yes, Tom. Some of the leading-edge handrails on the third level were knocked down with the crane cable while bringing up materials. We need to fix this right away. Also, it appears the crane operator has not been using his horn when he is flying materials overhead. The USG safety regulations stated in EM385 clearly state that when flying a load overhead, the horn must be sounded to warn workers."

Tom replied annoyed, "Lou, I go through great pains monitoring the crane operator, and he is using his horn. I am not sure where you got your information."

Lou said, "Well...er... I didn't think I heard it."

Tom responded heatedly, "Then you were not listening."

Harry intervened to keep the peace and said, "Lou, we will do our best with the crane horn. Charlie, get someone up on the third level and repair those guard rails. If there is not anything more on safety, we will move on to submittals."

Miller liked when Lou used the word "appears" when he wasn't sure about something and wanted to nitpick. Rules were rules; the contractors were either following them or not following them, not it "appears" they were not following them. Miller thought, *Just another day in paradise*, when his stomach growled. He looked at his watch. Still another hour and forty-five minutes until lunch time.

☭

Yusef and Tanya were driving to the first apartment site. All three were within a five-mile radius and in or near the city center. The first site was a few blocks from the British embassy. The bleary-eyed pair were disguised as meter readers and dressed in blue uniforms wearing black caps on their heads. They carried flashlights along with them.

Tanya said, "Follow me, Turk. The entrance to the basement is around the back."

The pair walked around and entered the basement entrance. Yusef, with his flashlight, studied the beam and column configurations. He reasoned this was one of those buildings built in the early 1960s and designed to last only about twenty-five years. He was checking whether the owners had added extra support beams over the years. This was usually the case but not always. When they did install additional supports, it was usually at a minimum. He pulled out a note pad and tried to figure out how many charges he would need to do the job. When he finished, he was satisfied this building was a good choice. He motioned to Tanya they were finished, and the couple left to go to the next building location.

Moshi and his driver Serkon were parked out on the street, sitting in a dark- blue Lada sedan. Serkon was provided to Moshi and had been vetted by Joe Kelly for the assignment. Moshi and Serkon had tailed the two from the Lotte. It did not take a genius to see what they were up to. Moshi could not believe General Brezhnev actually wanted to blow up an apartment building, killing many Russians. Why?

Harry was just finishing up the meeting and said, "Okay, I guess that does it. Anyone have anything else?"

He looked around the room, and no one spoke up. Harry continued, "Meeting adjourned."

As Harry was gathering up his notes, John London and Lou came up and John asked, "Harry, can you and JT stick around a few minutes? Lou and I want to go over something with you."

Harry looked around the room. JT was just walking out the door. Harry said loudly, "JT." Miller turned around and Harry said, "JT, John and Lou want to go over something with us."

Miller answered, "Sure, Harry."

He walked over to a seat by Harry, and John and Lou took a seat as well.

Harry asked, "What can we do for you, John?"

John said, "Well, Harry, we are not there yet, but soon we will be installing the secure galvanized steel window and door embeds. We need you to submit how you plan to reinforce around the embeds before placing concrete. There will be a lot of weight and pressure twisting on the embeds, and I just want to make sure you give this some thought. The last thing we want is for the embeds to get damaged during the process."

Harry smiled and replied, "John, I am glad you asked that question. JT, would you like to explain?"

Miller said, "Sure, Harry. John, Lou, this is a major concern to TRIAD as well. If we damage an embed and have to replace it, we would have to wait at least three months, sea shipping it to Moscow. The less preferred method for us is air shipping because it is so damn expensive. To try to mitigate possible problems, I have created a Power Point presentation on the correct installation procedures of the embeds, including the bracing. During the preconstruction activity meeting before the installation starts, I will present this information to the superintendents and workers involved in doing this work."

Lou asked, "JT, can you email this to us for our review?"

Miller replied, "Lou, this is an internal document--but sure, I will email you and John a draft."

John said, "Thank you, gentlemen. Glad to see we are on the same page with this."

Harry responded, "Absolutely, John. Adequate bracing before concrete is a must." Harry and Miller left the OBO conference room grateful that this week's coordination meeting was over.

Chapter Eleven

THE TURKS

Bo was having lunch alone in the mess hall when his cell phone rang. He looked to see who was calling; it was Natasha. He had not been in contact with her for two months. He knew what this was probably about. Bo answered, "Hello."

Natasha said, "Mr. Bo, the major just rung me up. He wants us to meet him tonight at 7:00 at an office a few blocks from the Belgrade. If you come here first, we can walk together." Bo agreed. After he finished his lunch, Bo walked to Vera's office to inform her. He was not taking any chances.

Yusef and Tanya had just finished surveying all three buildings. As far as Yusef was concerned, all three had substandard structural support and would collapse like a house of cards. It would be up to Brezhnev to choose which one.

As the two were driving, Tanya giggled and asked, "Did you have fun last night, Turk?"

Yusef answered, "Just one of my usual nights, Russian."

Tanya laughed. "You lie, Turk. I bet you have not had sex for two years except with your hand."

Yusef replied, "Nonsense, Russian. Now hurry, we must get back to the general and report. He needs to choose so I can make the preparations."

Bo arrived at Natasha's apartment at 6:30. She opened the door and already had on her coat. She greeted him, "Hello, Mr. Bo," and held out her hand.

Bo did not take it and said, "Let's go, Natasha, and get this over with. I wonder what the son-of-a-bitch wants now."

Bo felt more confident now that Vera and Joe Kelly were in on it. Still, he feared the Russians releasing his indiscretions to his family and his church could still complicate matters. The couple walked to the elevators in silence. They got down to the street and walked east toward the Arbat. When they arrived at the second intersection, Natasha pulled out a piece of paper with scribbled directions and studied it. They walked one more block and turned left. About halfway down the street on the left was an office building. There were no markings on the outside, but when they walked in, it resembled a police station. Natasha and Bo made their way to the receptionist's desk.

The woman gave them a hard look and asked in Russian with a look of contempt, "What do you two want?"

Natasha answered, "We have a meeting with Major Karlov."

Looking annoyed, she said, "Stay here. I will check." A few minutes later, she came back and commanded, "This way." The two followed her down the hall to a small office where Karlov was waiting. The woman said, "Here they are, Major. Anything else?"

Dimitry replied, "Please inform Lieutenant Belsky we will be paying him a visit. Thank you, Nadia."

The woman left and the major focused on his guests. "Hello, Mr. Beecher, Natasha; so glad you could come." Karlov loved toying with them. He knew they had no choice. He continued, "Please follow me. I want to stop by one of the interrogation rooms before we have our discussion."

They walked to the corridor, then down the hall to the stairwell. The major opened the door, and the three walked down the stairs to another stairwell door. On the other side was a guard post, and without an authorized pass, nobody could go further. When the guards saw the major, they stood at attention and motioned the three passed. The three walked down the hall to interrogation room "F." The major knocked on the door and Lieutenant Belsky opened it. Inside were two men and a woman. They were strapped to tables face up with their feet dangling over the end. Grey duct tape covered their mouths.

The major said, in a pleasant tone, to the couple, "Let me introduce you to my friends. These three were arrested for crimes against the State. They have refused to confess. We are here tonight to see if we may not persuade them. Lieutenant Belsky, if you please."

Belsky walked to the wall; hanging upon it were several different persuaders used in interrogation techniques, each one invented to supply excruciating pain to a distinct part of the body. Belsky first chose a police baton, then changed his mind and picked up a cat o' nine tails or lash. He walked over to the first man then looked at the major.

The major said, "Mr. Beecher, the technique the lieutenant will be using tonight is called flagellation. You may be more familiar with the term flogging. This particular form of flogging is called bastinado. It involves striking the bottom of the victim's bare feet. Lieutenant, please proceed."

Belsky stood back about eight feet. With the swing of his arm the lash flashed and snapped through the air. He continued this movement three more times for practice, then focused on his target. The lieutenant swung the lash around and hit squarely the bottom of the first man's feet. The man screamed, but the sound was muffled through the duct tape. Natasha and Bo winced. The lieutenant smiled and kept up with the lashing until he reached a total of ten. The man passed out at eight, so there was no need to go further. Bo was sick to his stomach and felt like he had to vomit. Natasha felt faint. No matter how hard she struggled, she began to lose consciousness. As she fell, Karlov caught her and set her down on the floor.

When she came to, Karlov informed her, "No need to worry, Natasha. It is not you on the table tonight, and if you are a good girl, you never will be. That goes for you, Mr. Beecher, as well."

Major Karlov helped Natasha to her feet and addressed Belsky, "Lieutenant, proceed at your leisure and put the signed confessions on my desk by tomorrow morning."

Karlov led the pair down the hall back to his office. He motioned for them to have a seat. He buzzed Nadia on the intercom, and within 30 seconds she was at his door. He asked, "Nadia, would you be so kind as to bring our guests a cup of tea?"

She nodded, and a few minutes later she returned with the tea on a tray with milk, sugar, and spoons. She set the tray down on a side table and left. The major got up and slowly walked to the table.

"Mr. Beecher, how do you like your tea? Milk and sugar? Medium sweet?"

Beecher nodded, and Karlov added a splash of milk and two cubes of sugar. He stirred it and handed Beecher the cup with the spoon inside. He prepared Natasha's the same way. He let them drink a bit of the tea to settle them down and finally said, "I must apologize if this experience has made you feel uncomfortable. It was not my intention." He lied. It was exactly the response he was looking for. He reached into his shirt pocket and pulled out a very ordinary-looking ballpoint pen. He handed it to Bo and asked, "Mr. Beecher, do you know what this is?"

Bo looked at the pen and replied, "A ballpoint pen."

The major chuckled and said, "You are partly correct, Mr. Beecher. It is really much more. What you have in your hand is a pen camera. With it you will take photos of the top-secret drawings showing where all the secret secure areas will be located in your new embassy building. A very simple task for a smart man like yourself."

Bo asked in a neutral tone, "And if I refuse?"

The major smiled and replied, "I assure you, Mr. Beecher, you do not want to know. But I will tell you this; it would be most unpleasant for you and Natasha if you did refuse. I think we understand each other."

He chose a button on the intercom and pressed it. A few minutes later, Lieutenant Belsky walked into the office.

Karlov said, "Lieutenant, show these two out. But before you do, take Mr. Beecher to your office and show him how to operate this camera. Mr. Beecher, you have one week to retrieve the information I have asked for."

With that, Belsky showed the couple out of the major's office, and they walked down the hall to his own.

☭

At the Ukraine Hotel, General Brezhnev was sitting down with Yuri in Yuri's office apartment, running his finger over the rim of his empty glass. Yuri noticed and asked, "Nikita, may I freshen your drink? A little more ice, perhaps?"

Nikita replied, "Yes, thank you, Yuri. I could use another."

Yuri fixed his drink and inquired, "How is everything going with the mission? Is that Turk of yours behaving himself?"

The general responded, "No problem there. I put Tanya with him....Oh, excuse me, Yuri, I believe you know her as Anna Ivanov."

Yuri laughed. "Ah yes, Nikita. Good choice. She will take care of the Turk."

Yuri had met Tanya at the Angara Club about eight years earlier when she was nineteen or twenty. She had gotten into an altercation with two young Russian men at the bar when a fight ensued. She laid both of them out flat, then calmly went back to her table to finish her drink. Yuri was impressed, so he had recruited her and introduced her to the general. Ever since, the general had taken her under his wing. Yuri had not seen her in years, but he understood she had become quite competent at demolition under the tutelage of Borya Bortnik until Borya's untimely death.

The general said, "Yuri, I have been informed the Turk has finished his reconnaissance of the three targets."

Yuri's tone changed as he replied impatiently, "And?"

The general continued, "Yusef said all three targets have substandard structural support, so any of the three targets will work in our favor. As soon as you choose which target you prefer, Yusef will start the preparations."

Yuri responded, "General, I want to look over the target locations once more on the map before I make that decision. I will inform you no later than tomorrow afternoon."

The general said, "Very well, Yuri. Thank you. I will look forward to hearing from you."

Yuri replied, "Good night, Nikita."

☭

Ben Magsino, Joe Kelly, and Nigel had been in the vault conference room for the last hour trying to grasp what "The Butcher" might be up to. Joe asked, "Ben, do you want me to get the names of the occupants of the apartment buildings?"

Ben replied, "Yes, we need to check that. Just run the names through the database to see if any of the occupants have political ties. My gut feeling is we will not, but I do not wish to speculate; let's just go with the facts. Joe, keep up the surveillance and inform us of anything we need to act on quickly, just as you have been doing. Nigel, how is your misinformation program going? You and Larry have everything under control?"

Nigel answered, "I think so, sir. I receive the talking points from MI6 and create a script based on those talking points. When I finish the script, I send it to military intelligence via secure fax for review. Once it is approved, I submit to the ambassador for immediate communication to the Russians. Larry ensures all communication systems are up and running. We make a jolly good team."

Ben said, "Thank you, Nigel. You and Larry keep it up. Gentlemen, we all know what we must do, so let's go do it."

With that, Ben left the vault with Joe and Nigel in tow.

☭

The next morning, Nigel walked down the hall to the studio and sat down at his desk. He noticed an official communique from the Paris office. He wondered what it might be. Nigel opened it and read its contents. Nigel was not quite sure whether he liked what he had just read.

Just then, Larry walked in from tinkering with something in the studio control room and said, "Morning, Nigel, old chap. Did you hear the news?"

Nigel asked, "No, what news?"

Larry replied, "You and I, old friend, are going to be in Moscow for the next two years. You know what that means, old boy?"

Nigel answered, "Yes, I did know," as he held up the communique, "and not a clue, but let me guess--I need to get me mum to send me thermal underwear?"

Larry replied, "No, we have two glorious years of dating Russian women. It is an endless smorgasbord out there."

Nigel thought about a large negative and said, "Yes, and two years of freezing our willies off and seeing the sun only two months a year."

Larry answered, "Don't exaggerate. I have a date with Zhanna tonight. Do you want to call Katya and tag along?"

Nigel replied, "Sorry, old sport. I will be here late tonight."

Larry said, "Suit yourself, Nigel. Oh, by the way, I picked up some Russian sweet rolls this morning. They are in the other room. There might be some danish left."

Nigel responed, "Thank you, old sport. One of those would hit the spot this morning." Nigel was grateful and hoped there may be some chocolate topped custard bismarks in the mix, as he headed off for the pre-diabetes delights.

☭

That night, Miller and Irena were sitting at their usual table at the Angara Club. The waiter was setting down an order of beef ribs in front of Irena and pork chops in front of Miller. He took his knife and fork, cut a piece of the pork chop, placed it into his mouth, and savored each chew. After he swallowed, he licked his lips and said, "Done to perfection. How are your beef ribs, my one and only?"

Irena replied, "For goodness' sake, give me a minute to try, Slav." She picked up one of the ribs, took a bite, and said, "Yes, these are nice."

Miller also got a side order of potato pancakes. Harry got him hooked on the damn things. Miller noticed the waiter forgot the sour cream. He looked for him, but he was nowhere in sight. He said, "Irena, I need to go and find some sour cream. I will be right back."

She replied with a smile, "Hurry, or I might have to eat one of your pork chops."

Miller said, "You do, and I will spank you."

Irena looked confused and asked, "What is this 'spank' word?"

Miller replied, "It means hitting or slapping your bottom."

Irena said, "Oh, you think so, do you? I will slap *your* bottom!"

Miller laughed and walked to the waiter station. His waiter was there, and he asked for the sour cream. The waiter apologized and told Miller he would bring it to the table. Miller agreed, and as he was walking back, he saw someone he recognized from the embassy but did not know.

Miller nodded and asked, "Hi, how are you doing?"

The man responded, "Great. Do we know each other? You look familiar."

Miller said, "We have passed each other occasionally at the embassy. My name is JT Miller. I am the project engineer working on the new building. What are you here for?"

The man replied, "Nice to meet you, JT. I am Larry Boehlen. I am a communications engineer, better known as the IT guy. I came to Moscow to help out for a while. When do you expect to be finished with the building?"

Miller said, "The schedule indicates June 2000. I suppose we'll make it."

Miller noticed the attractive young pink-haired Russian girl with Larry. Larry said, "This is my friend Zhanna. We came here for a little booze, dancing, and rock'n'roll."

Miller replied, "Hello, Zhanna." She nodded and he continued, "It sounds like you and Zhanna have a good plan. I am here for the pork chops."

Larry asked, "Nice. Are they good?"

Miller answered, "Damn good. Also try the potato pancakes and smother them with sour cream. Good, and good for you."

Miller looked over at his table and Irena was watching him. He said, "Gotta go, Larry. My friend is waiting. Nice meeting you both."

Larry replied, "Same here."

Miller walked back to his table. Irena asked, "Who were those people?"

Miller said, "Some guy from the embassy and his girlfriend."

Irena informed him, "His girlfriend looks like a slut."

Miller laughed and said, "Some men like that in a woman."

Irena asked, "Do you like that in a woman? Would you like me to be a slut?"

Miller laughed again. "No, I think you have just the right amount of slut already," he teased.

Irena asked irritated, "Oh, so I am a slut now?"

As Miller got back to his dinner, he saw half of one of his pork chops gone. Irena was sitting there looking at him, smiling. She informed him, "I told you, Slav."

Miller jumped up and grabbed Irena, put her over his knee, and spanked her hard three times very quickly. He returned the favor and informed her, "I told you!"

☭

Larry and Zhanna got their drinks and found a table near the dance floor. Her favorite Moscow band was playing there tonight. The band's name was E-Sex-T, an alternative metal band. The name was short for Elephant Sex Troubles. Larry noticed the audience was on the younger side and many wore punk or gothic garb. Zhanna, with her pink hair, looked right at home. Larry wasn't a big fan of metal music, but he was a big fan of Zhanna, so he was good.

The band was getting ready. They entered the stage and started tuning up. After a few minutes, the band kicked off into a hard, driving beat. Zhanna grabbed Larry's hand and they went to the dance floor. It was kind of like a free-for-all out there—all these kids jumping around and bumping into each other, not really dancing in the conventional sense. One Russian guy with spiked hair started to crowd surf. Crowd surfing, also known as body surfing, is the process in which a person is passed overhead from person to person. As he was being passed in Larry and Zhanna's direction, they put up their hands and supported his weight to pass the surfer on to the next group. Zhanna thought this was great fun. Larry, not so much.

Zhanna and Larry were drinking vodka shots with a draft beer chaser. The music was loud and chaotic. Larry noticed the more he drank, the better it sounded, so he upped the alcohol consumption, and Zhanna was happy to do likewise. The more the pair drank, their inhibitions became less, and the more they experimented with dirty dancing techniques—not consciously, but more because of the vodka-fueled frenzy they were experiencing. They pumped, grinded, and made quite a pair. After a while, a tall woman with dark hair noticed the couple and walked over. As the band played another pounding beat, the woman got behind Larry and started rubbing up and grinding his backside in time with the music. Larry just went with it.

When the song was over, the woman said to Zhanna with an erotically provocative voice, "How is my little cherry tonight? Do you need to be nibbled on until you pop, baby girl?"

Zhanna went up to the tall woman and gave her a long, passionate French kiss. She pulled away and replied, "You bet I do." The tall woman whispered something in her ear, smiled at Larry, then walked away as mysteriously as she came.

Larry watched her walk through the crowd and asked, "Who was that?"

Zhanna laughed and replied, "Nobody, Mr. Larry," then snuggled up to him and said, "Let's go to your house, Mr. Larry."

How could Mr. Larry say no? The inebriated couple walked an erratic line the few short blocks to the Belgrade Hotel. They entered the lobby then walked through to the elevator. Larry reached for the 16th-floor button, but Zhanna deflected his hand away and hit 19.

Larry asked, holding Zhanna tight and kissing her neck, "Where are we going, honey?"

Zhanna replied, "A surprise, Mr Larry."

They got out at the 19th floor and walked down the hall to room 1907. Zhanna knocked on the door, and a few moments later the same tall woman that Larry had met earlier opened the door wearing just a pair of black panties. Her beautiful breasts looked like works of art hanging down in front of her. Without saying a word, Zhanna took Larry's hand, stepped up to the tall woman, and kissed her hard on the mouth. She then kissed Larry in the same fashion. The tall woman closed the door, put her arms around the both of them, and led them the rest of the way into the apartment.

As they walked inside, she whispered to Zhanna, "Are you ready, my little cherry?"

Zhanna laughed and replied, "I am if you are, you old slut."

Natasha laughed, then focused on her new playmate. She kissed Larry as Zhanna undid his belt and let his trousers fall to the floor. At that moment, all three shared the sexual excitement for what was about to come. Larry took a moment to thank the universe for his good fortune.

☭

The next morning, Moshi and Serkon were observing Yusef and Tanya at one of the buildings they had visited previously. Yusef was doing a more accurate survey of how many charges he would need and where to place them. He would be using C-4 plastic explosives. He would need twelve charges and twelve electrical detonators. The electrical detonator employed a brief charge to set off a small amount of explosive material that caused a chemical reaction that triggered the C-4 to explode. Yusef would hard-wire these detonators in place to each charge, then terminate the wires to the main remote-control box that would be left inside the building. Once complete, Yusef could set off the explosion with a hand-held remote-control device that would fit easily inside his pocket. This remote-control device had a range of 300 meters. The couple stayed inside the building for 45 minutes, then emerged and drove back to the Lotte. Moshi and Serkon continued the surveillance.

Bo Beecher had discussed with Vera and Joe Kelly what Major Karlov had asked him to do. Vera contacted her section chief Phil Mitchell and asked for guidance. Phil discussed it with the higher-ups, and they came up with a plan. DC would revise the particular top-secret drawings showing where the secure work areas were located. The revisions would show bogus locations in areas where only low-level administration work was taking place, and not top-secret activities. These drawings would be produced to fool the Russians, and nothing else. Bo handed his badge to the CAG on duty and checked into the secure drawing room located in the ACF (Access Control Facility). Vera had left a roll of three drawings with a note attached to it that read "For Bo Beecher Only," signed Vera Collins. Bo unrolled the drawings on the table. He pressed and bent the first drawing flat on the table. He removed the pen camera from his pocket and took several photos of the drawing. He continued this process with the other two drawings as well. When finished, he slipped the camera back into his pocket, checked out of the room, and left. When he got back to his office, he phoned Natasha to set up a meeting with Karlov.

Yusef had made the arrangements to buy the C-4, detonators, and electrical components from Turkey. This particular supplier, Necdet Hafeez, supplied the same materials to the Chechens, along with Skorpion submachine guns and Czech-made grenade launchers, during the war. If the bomb components were identified, Yusef wanted them traced back to him. The materials would be slipped into Russia by boat. It would be Necdet's boat. This way, Necdet collected on the freight charges as well, and he always traveled with his shipments. All of his deliveries were COD, and Necdet would be there to collect at the end of the transaction. This was how he did business.

The route was simple. He would leave Trabzon in northeast Turkey, then cross the Black Sea to Sochi. From there, the materials would be flown to Moscow on Russian military aircraft. Necdet would deal face-to-face only with the person responsible for paying him—in this case, Yusef. Necdet never dealt with the Russians directly. Yusef had done business with Necdet in the past, and he seemed reliable, as arms dealers go.

Yusef punched the buttons on his cell phone and waited. A few moments later, he heard, "Necdet Hafeez."

Yusef said, "Hello, Necdet-bey [Mr.]. This is Yusef Solak, my friend. Is my package ready for delivery?"

Necdet replied, "Yes Yusef-obi [my brother]. My boat should be in Sochi tomorrow evening sometime between 7 and 9 p.m., Inshallah. Please be waiting me at pier six."

Yusef answered, "Good, Necdet. I will be waiting you."

☭

Bo Beecher was at the Arbat MacDonald's. He had just ordered two cheeseburgers and a Coke. He waited for his order, then took a seat at a corner table. A few minutes later, in walked Lieutenant Belsky. He saw Bo in the corner and calmly made his way to the table. He sat down and said, "Good evening, Americanski. Do you have something for the major?"

Bo slid the pen across the table to Belsky. The lieutenant slid the pen into his top shirt pocket and said, "Thank you. The major will be pleased. He will contact you later through the girl. Do you have any questions?"

Bo shook his head and the lieutenant continued, "Good. I must go now. Dasvidaniya."

With that, the lieutenant got up and walked out of the restaurant. Bo felt relieved for the moment. He looked down at his tray and picked up the remaining cheeseburger, removed the paper wrapper, and took a bite.

Yusef was alone waiting at pier 6. Tanya was not on this trip because Necdet refused to deal with women. He believed women should be left at home, and no exceptions. Yusuf lit a Murad cigarette and continued pacing up and down the pier. He had been at it since before 7:00 p.m., and it was now 8:30. He gazed across the water and thought he made out boat lights in the distance, but then they faded away. A few minutes later, he went through the same exercise, but this time the lights held steady. Necdet was at the helm of his Sanmar pilot boat. He had bought the boat in 1982 when he was briefly in the small-cargo shipping business. After his first wife died, Necdet frequented the waterfront bars along the Bosporus, drinking much raki, when he fell in with an arms dealer named Ahmet. They became partners and worked together until Ahmet was killed in a knife fight in Istanbul a few years later. After the incident, Necdet went out on his own and had been quite successful.

As Yusef watched the lights of the boat getting closer, he had one of the general's men back the army transport vehicle into place. As the boat got closer, he could make out Necdet at the helm. Yusef waved as the pilot boat approached the pier.

Necdet waved back and yelled, "Yusef, my old friend. Sorry I am a little late. Had to dodge a Turkish patrol boat."

"No problem," Yusef called back. "It is good to see you, Necdet, my brother. I see you are still running *The Elif*."

The Elif was the name of his boat. He had named her after his first wife. In Turkish the meaning of "Elif" is "the girl who spreads light."

Necdet replied, "She's a good boat, Yusef. Best pilot boat on the Black Sea."

Necdet's sons Ismail and Selim jumped off on to the pier then tied the bow and stern lines to the dock cleats. Both boys carried Akdal Ghost 9mm handguns strapped to their sides. When the boat was secure, Yusef sent the men assigned him to retrieve the merchandise. The materials were in two sealed wooden crates. One crate carried the C-4, the other the detonators and other electrical components. Yusef had the men open the crates so he could check the contents inside. This was customary. Yusef went over the materials and was satisfied. He had his men close the crates and carry the merchandise to the truck for transport.

Yusef said, "Everything is acceptable, Necdet."

He motioned to another man, who brought a cloth bag filled with cash. Necdet did not accept checks. With his sons covering him, Necdet took the bag to his boat and counted it. He returned a few minutes later.

Yusef asked, "Are we good, Necdet?"

Necdet answered, "Yes, Yusef-bey. Nice doing business with you."

Yusef pulled an envelope from his pocket and said, "Here is a little something extra, my friend, for your troubles."

Necdet responded, "Thank you, Yusef. May Allah bless you."

With that, the pair shook hands and said their goodbyes. Necdet took his place at the helm and started the engine as his boys released the stern and bow lines, then jumped back onto the boat. *The Elif* slowly pulled away from the dock, then gradually picked up speed, leaving foam in its wake.

Earlier, Moshi and Serkon had followed Yusef to the Kremlin. Once inside, Yusef was free from surveillance—or at least from the American operatives. The Russians were watching; they were always watching. Yusef was flown by helicopter, with the general, to the military airport. The general had a plane waiting with four soldiers to be commanded by Yusef for the pickup. The flight to Sochi was only two hours, and Yusef hoped to be back in Moscow with the goods just after midnight. The man in the grey suit was sitting in his car watching the main gate at the Kremlin. He got out to stretch his legs and lit a cigarette. He looked at his watch; a little after 1:00 a.m. He took a puff, then heard the engines somewhere in the sky above. He looked but could not see where the engine sounds were coming from. Then finally he saw the helicopter coming down in the Kremlin compound before he lost sight of it behind the tall brick Kremlin walls. He got back into his car and waited. About ten minutes later, Yusef exited the main gate. He was being driven by a man wearing a soldier's cap, driving a military-green Lada. The man in the grey suit followed them to the Lotte.

The man in the grey suit was a good operative, and Joe Kelly liked him. His name was Alek Sokoloff. He was 33 years old and originally from Russia, he had been living in Berlin for the past fifteen years and the last four of those years worked as a detective for Berliner Polizei (Berlin Police). He migrated in 1981 with his mother and stepfather. His mother's name was Mischa. She had met Lev Sokoloff in Moscow in 1979. Lev was a writer who worked with the Russian International News Agency. His job was to report news to the international community that would spin a positive light on Mother Russia. Mischa was one of the copy editors who would review the stories before they went out over the wire. She thought Lev was one of the most brilliant men she had ever met, and likewise Lev was attracted to Mischa from the start. He started dating her, and they soon were married. Alek had been fifteen at the time, and he and Lev had become great pals. They quickly formed a close-knit family. In Lev's free time, he had written a book called *Corruption, Lies, and Murder in the Soviet Union.* He kept this book secret, for obvious reasons.

When the International News Organization sent a group to Moscow, Lev was able to sneak a manuscript to a journalist from Germany. At the time, it was one of only a handful of accounts of what really went on inside the country. When the journalist returned to Germany, he passed it on to a publisher friend of his who liked the work. To publish his book, Lev would have to come to Germany. The journalist and publisher worked out a plan. The International News Organization had scheduled a journalist award ceremony to be taking place in Berlin in a few months. They had talked with the president of the INO, and he had agreed, after reading the manuscript, that Lev could be added to the list of recipients. The Russian government sometimes would permit a citizen to leave the country to receive a prestigious award. The INO would send the request directly to the Russian government, inviting Lev

Sokoloff and his family to attend the ceremony in Berlin.

The Russians agreed, and while in Berlin, Lev and his family defected to the West. Lev's book was published and was very successful. Lev published it using a pseudonym, but he was not sure if that would keep him safe. It did not. Seven years after the book was published in 1989, the Russians retaliated. Mischa had received word from her brother that he would be in Berlin for business. She assumed it had something to do with petroleum, because that was his field. Dimitry received an eight-hour pass and would cross through the "Iron Curtain" from East Berlin into the West, do his business, then cross back within that eight-hour time period. He would have time for lunch and had invited Mischa and her family to join him.

Mischa was excited to see her brother Dimitry, and she and her family met him at the Henne restaurant situated at the very edge of the Kreuzberg district, five meters from the Berlin Wall. Dimitry had been charming during dinner, and Mischa enjoyed the news from home. Lev and Alek had known Dimitry in Moscow and had got on quite well. They dined on chicken, potato salad, and freshly baked bread; all had a wonderful time. That evening, Lev felt like he was coming down with a cold and went to bed early. The next morning, he was dead.

The doctor's report read "heart attack." Mischa's maiden name had been Karlov, and her brother was Major Karlov. Dimitry had kept his affiliation with the KGB a secret to all except those within the agency. Even though the death seemed to be from natural causes, Alek knew it was his uncle who had killed his stepfather. Mischa would not let herself believe it. At the time, Alek had been at the police academy and not a member of the force. He had petitioned the Berlin police for a more thorough investigation but was refused for lack of credible evidence to proceed further. Sometimes Alek felt responsible for not recognizing the ploy against his stepfather beforehand. After he graduated the academy, Alek stayed with the Berlin police for seven years. Three as a cop and four as a detective until he resigned to take the Moscow post working with the Americans. He thought perhaps someday he would give his kind regards to his uncle.

☭

Yuri and Karlov were going over the Bo-provided photos of the top-secret drawings for the secure areas. Yuri noticed the rooms were located on the 4th and 5th floors in the middle of the building, instead of the top floors as was usual.

Yuri asked, "Dimitry, can we be certain these are the true locations? Could Mr. Beecher be, as the Americans say, trying to pull a fast one?"

The major replied, "Possibly, Yuri. I did take Beecher and his girlfriend to an interrogation room to witness what happens if you choose to be dishonest to the state. His girlfriend fainted, and the Americanski wet his trousers."

Yuri laughed and said, "Good, Major. A very sensible deterrent to show them those things. It could be the Americans simply changed the secure rooms to the middle area of the building to confuse us. We will proceed as if this is the case. More Blue Label, my friend?"

Karlov responded, "Yes, thank you, Yuri. I have missed this exquisite carnival of the senses since my last visit. You know, my friend, the British capitalistic do-gooders do not have a clue about most things, but they do know how to make a superb double- malt scotch."

Yuri poured more of the brown liquid into their glasses and set the bottle on the table. He then replied, "Quite right, Major, and please help yourself when you feel the need." Yuri sipped his scotch and continued, "Dimitry, I believe it is time to pull our other fish from the freezer. I want Miller to plant our new Cosmos-3 listening devices in the concrete floor slabs for the secure rooms, just in case Beecher is compromised. Get the girl to find out if this is the case."

Karlov replied, "Yuri, Beecher and the girl are not getting along at present, but I will persuade her to get back into Beecher's good graces. It may take a little time."

Yuri answered, "Major, do what you think is best with the girl. I will take care of this Miller."

Yuri held up his glass and the major followed. They drained their glasses of the last of the malted goodness. At that moment Yuri's housekeeper entered and announced that General Brezhnev had arrived. Yuri told her to have the general wait in the study.

Yuri said, "If you will excuse me, Dimitry, I have a matter to discuss with the general. We will talk later, old friend."

Karlov replied, "Of course, Yuri."

With that, Yuri escorted the major to the door, then walked to the study to attend to his other guest.

It was lunch time and Miller picked up a small green backpack, then walked to the mess hall. He decided on something quick and grabbed an apple and banana to go. He ate the fruit on the way to the embassy gym. He walked through the south entrance, past the embassy cafeteria and commissary. He descended the stairs and passed through the double glass doors to the gym check in desk. At the desk was a young Russian woman checking membership cards and handing out towels. Miller handed her his card. She put it in a drawer and handed him a towel. Miller took the towel and found an open locker he could use. He pulled his gym clothes from the backpack, changed his clothes, and to get his blood moving, he started on the treadmill. He did a mile just to loosen up, then did his rounds through the various machines.

Miller liked the gym. It was well equipped with a swimming pool, full basketball, squash and handball courts with a generous assortment of free weights and machines. He always ended his workouts shooting hoops at the basketball court. He checked out a ball and as he entered the court, he noticed half of it was partitioned off for a Jazzercise class. Jazzercise combined dance, strength, and resistance training with popular music for a fullbody workout. Kirsten Knudsen was conducting the class. She was Jon Knudsen's sister, TRIAD's IT guy. Jon had told her about a job opening as fitness director at the embassy. Kirsten liked the idea and applied. To her surprise, she got the job. Miller had met her a few times when she was with Jon. Miller waved, and she smiled as he took his ball to the unused portion of the court.

He watched the class for a few minutes and thought it was quite entertaining. The class was attended mostly by out-of-shape diplomat and embassy workers' wives. Nancy, the ambassador's wife, was there working up a sweat with a few of her chubby friends. Every class Kirsten tried to mix up the music and would feature different artists. Today she was featuring Elvis.

The music was sounding good as Miller finished up his basket-shooting. He took a shower, dressed, and looked at his watch. 12:50 p.m. He had ten minutes to get back to work. He dropped off the used towel with the Russian girl. She opened the drawer and gave him his card back. Attached to it was a paper clip holding a folded piece of paper. He took the paper and realized it was a note. The note read, "Meet tonight at 7:30. My apartment. Yuri."

Miller asked the girl, "Who gave you this note?"

She answered, "I do not know. It was left here with your name on it." Miller thanked her, put the note into his pocket, and headed back to work.

When Miller got back to the office, he informed Vera about the note. She contacted MEBCO security, and they checked the footage on the gym desk surveillance camera to see if the person who left the note could be identified. They looked at the footage from noon to 1:00 p.m. There were several people who came to the desk during that time, and any one of them could have left the note. They did see the Russian girl finding the note after it was left at 12:40 p.m. She then opened the drawer and attached it with a paper clip to Miller's card. The camera footage was a dead end.

In 1994, a joint venture of Moscow City Telephone Network, T-Mobile, and Siemens offered Russia's first mobile phone service for the public in Moscow. In 1996, cell phones in Russia were still very expensive, especially for the common Russian. To have one was a sign of status and was reserved mostly for the Russian elite. Because the technology was reasonably new in Russia, the KGB could not easily monitor conversations. This changed in 1998 when the 1G analog cellular networks were replaced by the 2G digital cellular networks. The Americans, except for the CIA and their operatives, had been briefed, when speaking into a cell phone, to assume the Kremlin was listening. The CIA used a closed-system network through the Marisat communication satellites which could not be hacked as long as they stayed within the network. As far as US intelligence agencies were concerned, they believed the network at present was secure.

☭

Miller arrived at Yuri's just before 7:30. Olga the housekeeper showed him to the drawing room. She asked, "May I get you anything, Mr. Miller?"

He answered, "No, I'm good. Thank you."

Olga smiled and left the room. Miller stood looking out the picture window at the lights of the city. Vera had briefed him on the faux revisions of the top-secret drawings. She kept Bo's name out of it, because she was not quite ready to disclose to Miller that Bo was a part of this Russian ploy and vice-versa.

A few minutes later, Yuri entered. "Good evening, Mr. Miller. I see you are punctual, as usual."

Miller had that disgusted look on his face and asked, "What do you want, Yuri?"

Yuri smiled and replied, "Ah, Mr. Miller—also as usual, you wish to get to the point. Cannot fault you for that. Please sit."

Yuri motioned to a chair at the table by the kitchenette and bar area. Miller sat in the chair, and Yuri reached for the bottle with the Blue Label from the top shelf and set it on the table. He asked, "Mr. Miller, will you join me?"

Miller was going to abstain from alcohol that evening, but he had never tried the Blue Label scotch. He had heard the Blue Label was the smoothest of the smooth. He said coolly, keeping the disgusted look on his face, "Yes, thank you, Yuri. Just a little ice."

Yuri fixed the drinks and handed one to Miller. He then walked to another table, pulled open a drawer, and reached in for Bo's photos. He placed them in front of Miller and asked, "What do you think of these, Mr. Miller?"

Miller looked at the photos and put a surprised look on his face. He replied excitedly, "Where did you get these? The photos are the top-secret drawings for the embassy building!"

Yuri chuckled and said, "I know that, Mr. Miller. Do you think they are genuine?"

Miller responded, "Hell yes, they're genuine. Where did you get these?"

Yuri believed that Miller had confirmed what he thought—the drawings were real. The excited anxiety that Miller expressed convinced him. He said, "Now Mr. Miller, you know I cannot make you privy to how we obtained these photos. But rest assured they are only for illustration purposes."

He took the photos, pointed to three highlighted areas, and said, "Mr. Miller, I need to know when you will be installing the concrete floor slabs in these areas. Do you have a scheduled date?"

Miller looked confused and angry. With disgust in his voice he said, "What do you want to know that for?"

Yuri got hard. "Please remember, Mr. Miller, you are already in deep. You will answer my questions and obey my requests, or you may find your throat slit—or better still, we may just let your government know you have been spying for us. If you do not cooperate, you are no good to us, Mr. Miller, and anything that is no good to us, we discard into the trash. Make your choice. Either cooperate or face the consequences."

Miller put shock on his face and nodded. Yuri continued, "Good, Mr. Miller. I am glad you are seeing it my way. Like I said, I want this to be an enjoyable and profitable experience for the both of us. Now, when will those floor slabs be installed?"

Miller answered, "I don't know exactly. I will have to get back with you on that. I know it should be in the next few weeks."

Yuri replied, "See, Mr. Miller, that was not so difficult, was it? As soon as you have a date, let me know immediately."

Yuri walked over to the drawer where the photos were kept. He pulled out a small box and handed it to Miller. Yuri said, "From now on, use this cell phone to contact me. My digits are stored under the name Sasha. Use it to contact me and no one else. Do you understand?" Miller nodded and looked visibly shaken. Yuri continued, "Good. When you know the scheduled date, I want you to inform me in person. Now go."

Miller got up and picked up the cell phone box; at the same time, Olga entered the room to show JT out. After Miller left, Yuri sat back and thought the meeting went well. Yuri sensed Miller was shaking in his boots. This was where Yuri was wrong.

☭

As Miller walked back to camp, he was pleased with his performance. He wondered how he had developed his acting skills. He thought it was probably the hundreds of construction coordination meetings he had run or attended over the years. As a contractor, you are always going to try and snow or at least, slant the truth a bit to the client in one thing or another. In meetings and everywhere else, the contractor wants the client to believe everything is coming up roses when in fact there may be a dandelion or two. Miller had worked hard at being good at the game, and now it was bearing additional fruit.

☭

Harry was in Sveta's kitchen as he swore and looked at his knuckles. He had been grating potatoes with a potato grater when he nicked his hand. Sveta smiled, because Harry did this about every time he used the grater. She thought how lucky she was to have met him. The last few months, Harry had attended the weekly ritual of going to church with Sveta and her son, then to McDonald's after the service. Harry was not much of a churchgoer, but it seemed to make Sveta happy, so he went. He just liked being with her and Alexei. The three had formed a bond, and Sveta was grateful.

Harry called into the other room, "Sveta, I can't find the pepper."

She got up from the couch, walked to the kitchen, and pulled it from the cabinet, it was usually kept in. Harry noticed and muttered, "Damn, I looked in there."

Harry was preparing the meal that evening. He was preparing fried salmon, asparagus, potato pancakes, and a beet, cucumber, and onion salad with olive oil and white vinegar. Harry wasn't a bad cook, but he always left the kitchen looking like a cyclone went through. Harry was happy as a clam with this activity. He was grating, dicing, seasoning, and frying. About every three minutes between tasks he was sipping a glass of white wine. Harry knew only cretins drank red wine with fish, and Harry considered himself no cretin. He wanted everything perfect tonight.

Harry called out, "Sveta, just a few more minutes on the salmon, and dinner is ready."

Sveta had already set the table and lit the candles that Harry had brought. They provided a nice glow for the intimate meal the two of them were about to share. Harry brought out the food on platters and set them on the table. They each helped themselves. Harry had tried something different with the pancakes and had added sliced olives. He watched Sveta take a bite and saw from the look on her face that she knew this pancake tasted a little different. Harry smiled. He knew she was determined to figure it out.

Finally, she said, "You put olives in the pancakes, Harry. I think tastes good."

Harry answered, "Yeah, not bad. More wine, my sweet?" Harry filled her glass, then his own. They chatted during dinner on a variety of subjects. Harry had noticed Sveta's English was getting better with each passing week. He loved to hear her talk with her Natasha Fatale accent. As a matter of fact, Harry seemed to love everything about her. Sveta had noticed Harry had seemed a little anxious all evening. She wondered what that was about.

After dinner, Harry asked, "Shall we sit on the sofa, darling?"

Sveta smiled and Harry took her hand, then led her to the couch. She sat, and Harry walked back to the table for the wine and glasses. He filled them and handed one to Sveta.

He smiled and said, "A toast, my sweet—to us."

Sveta returned the smile as they clinked glasses and sipped. Harry reached into his pocket and pulled out a small black box. He opened it and Sveta saw the glitter of a beautiful diamond engagement ring.

Harry started to speak. "Sveta, I know...ah...I am older than you...and... you...ah... are so beautiful and wonderful, and me an old goat and all...and... ah...well, all I know is I am happy when I am with you, and I want you to be with me always. I want to take care of you and Alexei. Will you marry me?"

At first, Sveta's eyes began to water; then tears started flowing down her cheeks. Her body began to shake. Harry asked, confused, "Are you alright, my darling? I did not mean to--"

Sveta stopped him as she moved over into his arms. She snuggled her head into his chest and sobbed. She could not control herself. Every cell of her being was happy. When she stopped crying, she said, her voice cracking, "Da. Da, I will marry you, Mr. Harry Clark. I love you and will make you the best wife in the world."

Harry took her hand, and she could see Harry had tears in his eyes as well. She kissed him, and at that moment, all was well in the couple's universe. Harry took the ring out of the box and slipped it on her finger. It fit perfectly. Vera had helped him pick it out. It had a split shank frame in 14 K two-tone gold encrusted with diamonds. It was beautiful, and Harry had spent a few bucks. Sveta hugged him and said, "It is so beautiful, Harry."

Harry replied, "Everything looks beautiful on you, darling."

Sveta got up off the sofa and took Harry's hand. She led him to her bedroom in that Viking style of hers, and the two consummated the engagement. After the lovemaking, the couple lay in bed together, exhausted and happy. As she rested her head on Harry's chest, she held her hand up, admiring the ring. She loved it.

As she lay there, a thought came to her and she asked, "Harry, what is a goat?"

Harry said, "It is an animal that provides milk and has a reputation for being stubborn and not too good-looking."

Sveta snuggled closer to Harry and whispered into his ear, "To me you are the most beautiful man in the world with the most beautiful heart, and I love you."

Harry responded, "And I you, my darling."

They laid there together thinking of the future, not talking as both were alone with their beautiful thoughts.

☭

Yuri was sitting down with General Brezhnev. He asked, "Nikita, is the Turk ready for the assignment?"

The general replied, "Yes, Yuri. We just need to know when you wish to proceed."

Yuri answered, "In a few days. I need to complete a small task at the American embassy with one of the Americans. I am afraid a bombing of this magnitude might upset the apple cart. I will let you know. Perhaps by the end of the week."

The general responded, "Yuri, we will be ready when you believe the time is right."

Yuri said, "Fine, Nikita. I will inform you."

With that, Brezhnev nodded and clicked his heels. He turned and walked briskly out of the room.

☭

Miller had discussed with Vera and Joe about the listening devices Yuri wanted him to plant in the phony secure areas. After discussing with the higher ups in DC, Miller had the go-ahead to plant the devices. DC figured only routine office duties were going on in those areas, so the Russians could listen all they wanted. Besides, DC wanted to inspect the Russian listening devices, and Vera and Joe didn't want Miller's cover blown. It was a win-win. The concrete topping slabs were scheduled to be placed on Thursday. It was now Tuesday and Miller had to inform Yuri. Miller pulled out the cell phone Yuri had given him. He went to the speed dial and pressed Sasha.

Yuri answered on the third ring. "Hello, Mr. Miller. Do you have something for me?"

JT answered, "Yes, the topping slabs are scheduled to be installed on Thursday."

Yuri said, "Excellent, Mr. Miller. Come to my apartment tomorrow night at 7:30. We will discuss what you must do. Please do not be late."

☭

Larry Boehlen had just hung up the phone in his room at the Belgrade Hotel. He had just talked with his sister, and he always felt a little depressed after talking to her. This particular call had been stranger than usual because of the second-to-two-second time delay between the words he spoke and her hearing them, and vice-versa. The conversation seemed fragmented, and they were continually talking over each other because of the delay. She had been on her soapbox again about Larry settling down and starting a family.

Larry walked over to the window and opened it. Zhanna had left an almost empty pack of Marlboros in his room with about three smokes left.

Larry did not usually smoke, except occasionally when he was drinking, but he felt like he could use one now. He slid one of the cigarettes from the pack and lit the end. He inhaled and blew the smoke out the open window. He began to wonder why he didn't feel the urge to settle down. To him, it felt normal to live the life he was living; to her, it wasn't normal. When Larry was about thirteen, his sister had her first child. He remembered visiting her at her apartment and noted the place was always a mess, with baby toys askew and the whole place smelling like a diaper pail. Then again, when his brother had his kid, the same thing, and his siblings were both chained to their homes, taking care of them. Even at that young age, Larry knew he didn't want any part of that scenario for a long time to come.

Not long after his sister's second child, her husband left her, leaving her alone to raise them. She was devastated and depressed. She moved back home to her parents' house and just moped around. Larry was in high school then and felt sorry for her and his little niece and nephew. To make matters worse, their mother liked to rub her nose in it about her bad choice of boyfriends and husbands—good-for-nothing bums, she would say. Larry left right after high school to go to school in Colorado. He was glad to leave the drama. He would come back every year or so, and gradually things got better for his sister as the kids got older. His parents loved his niece and nephew, and what started as something negative turned into something wonderful for all of them. During this time, Larry was mostly away living his life, but when he did come back to visit, he enjoyed the experience. Larry thought someday he would get the urge to settle down, but not just yet. As far as women were concerned, he enjoyed living the overseas life, where American men had the pick of the litter. As for now, he felt he still had new horizons to discover. Larry took the last drag from his cigarette, looked to make sure no one was down below, and flicked the butt out the window.

Miller was sitting across the table from Yuri in Yuri's apartment at the Ukraine Hotel. Yuri slid a small box in front of Miller and said, "Mr. Miller. Please open the box in front of you."

JT picked up the small box and lifted up the cover. Inside he found two small devices. They were approximately the diameter of a pencil, about an inch to an inch and a quarter long. They were made of wood like a pencil, but felt hollow and extremely light. There was a small metal band—or what appeared to be metal—about 3mm wide in the middle of each device. Also, inside the box were four small plastic tie fasteners with quick locks on the ends.

Miller asked, "What do I do with these?"

Yuri replied, "It is quite simple, Mr. Miller. In the secure locations that we have discussed, you simply tie the devices to the floor slab steel mesh mat before the concrete is installed. You make sure the steel bands on the devices are touching the steel mat. The steel bands on the devices are magnetized. Simply place the devices on the steel mesh, then tie on with the plastic ties. The ties are just insurance the devices will not fall off during the placing of the concrete. We will know if you do not install these devices correctly and they are not functioning. If that is the case, you will not like the consequences."

Miller nodded and Yuri continued, "Do you have any questions?"

Miller asked, "How am I going to install these without being detected?"

Yuri laughed and replied, "Mr. Miller, you are a smart fellow; we have confidence you will find a way."

Miller nodded and put the devices and plastic ties back into the box. He slipped the box into his pocket and got up to leave. Yuri informed him, "Do not disappoint me, or as you Americans say, there will be hell to pay."

☭

After Miller left, he went directly to the embassy to meet with Vera and Joe Kelly inside the vault. He handed over the devices and explained how he had been instructed to install them.

Joe said, "JT, come back tomorrow morning and retrieve the devices. We will have plenty of time beforehand to analyze these and get the information back to DC."

After JT left, Vera asked, "What do you think, Joe? How do these work?"

Joe replied, "The way JT explained it, I would surmise that the steel mesh mat will act like a giant antenna and receive radio signals to supply power to the devices. It would be my guess that the listening capability will be quite powerful."

After that, Joe took several photos of the devices from many different angles, then accompanied Vera to the X-ray machine, where they repeated the process.

☭

The next morning, Miller went to see Joe Kelly and retrieved the devices. Next, he headed to the fake secure areas for the installation. As Miller arrived at the slab placement location, the workers were just finishing using an air compressor to blow the area clean before the concrete was placed. The workers would be none the wiser, but the CST on duty would be.

As Miller approached the area, he saw Willie Morehead, the CST. He asked, "How you doing, Willie? Haven't seen you in a while. You been on vacation?"

Willie was a big, heavyset black guy from Virginia. He was good-natured, and JT liked him. Willie amswered, laughing, "Sheet, I wish, JT. Vera has had me on the night shift, 8:00 to 5:00. I am not crazy about it, but we all rotate. It's not too bad, I guess. No one here to mess with you."

JT replied, "Yeah, I hear you, Willie. Some days I wish I could work the night shift, but unfortunately I need to be here during the day."

Willie said under his breath, "JT, I have been briefed. Just do what you need to, and if I can help, let me know." Miller thought, *great Vera was thinking ahead.*

Miller replied, "Thanks, Willie. I'll let you know."

The concrete pour would be done using a concrete bucket they would pass through an open window. The workers would use a chute, then rake into place. The OBO was not crazy about this method, but it was only about a 7 cubic meter pour. Miller thought he would take Willie up on his offer to help. There were too many workers around, and they might get suspicious about what he was doing.

Miller yelled over to Willie, and he sauntered over. Miller said, "Willie, just stand in front of me while I do this."

Willie replied, "No problem."

JT knelt down and installed the first one. The whole process took about a minute and a half. They then moved to the next location and installed the remaining one. Having Willie there with Miller, no one was the wiser. Miller thanked Willie and JT moved off to the side to wait for the concrete. He would monitor the device areas and make sure the concrete vibrator workers did not get close enough to damage the devices.

☭

The next day, Lieutenant Maxim Sokolov was at his computer trying to locate the newly installed listening devices. He focused the microwaves to the location where he believed the devices were installed. He was wearing headphones, and so far, he was hearing only static. He moved the dial that would direct the radio signals where he wanted them. He directed them 3 more degrees northeast, but still nothing. He increased the frequency and moved an additional 2 degrees in the same direction, but still nothing. He looked at the plan of the embassy again and realized he might be too far east, so he went back 10 degrees to the west. The static seemed to lessen. Two more degrees west, and the static stopped completely. One and a half degrees, more and voilà, Lieutenant Sokolov heard voices. The devices had been installed and seemed to be working perfectly. He fixed the frequency and began recording.

He picked up the telephone and dialed. On the third ring he heard, "Major Karlov."

He answered, "Major Karlov, this is Lieutenant Sokolov. I have located the new listening devices installed in the US embassy. They seem to be transmitting perfectly."

The major replied, "Well done, Lieutenant. Have you fixed the frequency and begun recording?"

The lieutenant answered, "Yes, Major. Is there anything else you would like me to do?"

The major said, "No, Lieutenant, that will be all."

"Yes, sir."

The major hung up the phone, then picked it up again and dialed. On the second ring he heard, "Yuri Belevich."

The major said, "Ah, Yuri, old friend. I just want to inform you our American fish has done what you have demanded from him. The new Cosmos 3's have been installed and are working perfectly."

Yuri replied, “That is good news, Dimitry. May I offer you an invitation to come to my apartment for a little celebration? I have just obtained another bottle of the Blue Label and some fresh Beluga caviar. Please come and join me.”

Karlov answered, “Yuri, you are a prince among men. How could I refuse such a kind offer? I will be over within the hour.”

CHAPTER TWELVE

THE MAN IN THE GREY SUIT

General Brezhnev and Yusef were meeting at the Pushkin Café. At another table, the man in the grey suit, Alek Sokoloff, was sipping his coffee. Alek had trailed Yusef from the Lotte Hotel. Yusef would rather walk to where he was going instead of going by car or metro if at all possible. Alek wondered what they were discussing. Could this be it, the general giving Yusef the go-ahead? This had been the closest Alek had been to the general. Up close, the general's permanent sneer looked much more menacing. He could not hear the conversation, but the general looked animated as he spoke.

Brezhnev said, "Yusef, I have been given authorization to proceed with the operation. We want the explosives to go off at 2:00 on Sunday morning. Most people will be home in bed at that time, and it should accomplish the desired effect."

Yusef asked, "You mean, to kill as many Russian citizens as possible?"

Nikita replied, "Okay, Turk, if you wish to look at it that way—but it is for the greater good."

Yusef smiled, thinking that is how demagogues usually thought. Everything else was inconsequential—not for the greater good of the people, although they would portray it that way, but for the greater good of the demagogue.

Yusef responded, "I am not here to judge, General. I am here to get paid.

The act is on your head. The plan will be carried out as requested."

The general said, "Fine, Yusef. I will leave it in your hands. Do not fail me."

Yusef replied and asked, "Have I ever, General?"

The general smiled and said, "I will be in touch."

He got up, straightened his uniform, and left. Yusef ordered more coffee. He had some thinking to do. The plan was that Yusef would detonate the explosives just outside the Lotte, which was in range for the remote-control device. When he had finished the operation, he would walk the short distance to the Angara Club, where Major Karlov would be waiting for him in a car outside to whisk him to the Kremlin heliport. There would be people milling around outside the club at that time of night, and the pair would not be noticed. From there, he would fly to Sochi, where a military transport would fly him to Turkey.

Yusef knew the chances were good he would never arrive in Turkey. With a mission as provocative as this one, the higher-ups would not want to take a chance of witnesses. What tipped him off was that Major Karlov was to meet him and not the general. Yusef did some checking, and he found Karlov was a trained assassin who worked for the KGB. He would be employed from time to time for special assignments. Yusef did not take chances and came up with a Plan B.

Necdet Hafeez was sitting at his kitchen table in Istanbul. He was looking at navigation charts. *Yes, it will work*, he thought to himself. From the Black Sea he could take an inlet and get to the Sea of Acov. From there, he would take the Don River past Volgograd to the Volga River. From there, it was easy. He would continue up the Volga until he got close to Nizhniy Novgorod, where the Moscow River came in. He would continue in his boat, *The Elif*, up the Moscow River until he got to the Ukraine Hotel boat dock. There he would meet Yusef and they would travel back the same way to Turkey. For this, Necdet would be paid $100,000 before Yusef even set foot on the boat. Any Russian patrol boats he had to bribe to get through, Yusef would take care of. He thought he would be safe once he got past Volgograd.

He would arrive at the Ukraine Hotel boat dock one day before and wait. Necdet would take his son Selim. His other son Ismail would stay in Istanbul and mind the store until they got back. The only thing that worried Necdet was timing. It was now mid-October. Parts of the Volga were frozen solid from mid to late November and would stay that way until spring breakup. If the operation was held up again past early November, they would have to come up with a Plan C.

Yusef finished his coffee and decided to walk from the Pushkin back to the Lotte. He left money on the table for the coffee, got up, and walked out of the café. Alek Sokoloff took his time and followed him out. Yusef walked quickly. Fifteen minutes later, he climbed up the stairs to the hotel and took the elevator to the lounge. He chose a table near the fireplace. A waiter walked over to take his order. Yusef ordered raki. When it came, he did not mix with water; he just added ice. Yusef downed the whole drink in one gulp. *Ah, that tasted good,* he thought. He caught the waiter's eye and ordered another. This one he took his time with; he added water and sipped. He pulled out his cell phone and punched some digits. A few moments later, Yusef listened to the ring in his ear.

After several rings, he heard, "Necdet Hafeez."

Yusef answered, "Necdet-bey. It is on for Sunday morning at 2:00. I will meet you about fifteen minutes later."

Necdet said, "That does not give me much time, Yusef-obi, but I will be there. Be sure to have the funds."

Yusef replied, "Agreed. I will meet you at the pier."

Yusef hung up, and Necdet began to make the final preparations. Next, Yusef phoned Tanya. They would meet at the Kremlin on Saturday night at 8:00. They would be dressed in the blue uniforms, as before. It would take two hours to set the charges and detonators. Yusef wanted to be finished by midnight or 1:00 a.m. at the latest. He would check out of the Lotte just before 2:00 a.m., after he collected a few personal items. The rest he would discard. On the way to the boat dock at the Ukraine Hotel he would set off the charges. He would be at Necdet's boat fifteen minutes later.

☭

Charlie Manes was looking at a column that had just been poured with concrete into an existing column. He thought the concrete looked good. The general foreman saw Charlie and walked over. His name was Lennie Roesner. He was called Rosie. When Lennie was a kid, he got tagged with the nickname in grade school; it stuck, and Lennie had used it ever since. All of the men or women who worked for Rosie liked him. He was a straight shooter and would stick up for his people if he believed they were in the right. As long as you did not cross him, he treated you fairly. Rosie was fifty-six years old and four years previously had married a Filipino girl named Imee. She was twenty-three years old, and Rosie loved her with all his heart.

Charlie said, "Rosie, we need to start the column wraps on these columns. Harry was asking about them today."

Rosie answered, "Yeah, Charlie, the guys are fabricating them now. We will start the installation after lunch."

Charlie replied, "Sounds good. I will let Harry know."

Column wraps were steel brackets that would get bolted from the existing column to the newly poured column. It was structural insurance, and after installation would be inspected and signed off by a structural engineer. A torque test of the bolts would be performed, and any bolts that did not pass muster would be replaced and tested again. Rosie lived in a one-bedroom apartment in the man camp, which he shared with Imee. She was pregnant with their first child. That afternoon, Imee had gone to the commissary to purchase some special food items because she was going to make a Tagalog dish for Rosie. Tagalog means a member of a people native to the Philippines inhabiting central Luzon, around and including Manila. Rosie had met Imee when he was working on an administration building at the US naval base in Subic Bay. When the US pulled out in 1992, Rosie married her and took her back to the States.

After work, Rosie felt tired as he entered their apartment. He called out, "Hi honey, whatcha cookin? Sure smells good."

As usual, Imee stopped what she was doing and ran to meet Rosie at the door. Rosie was a big guy, and Imee was tiny. She always jumped up on him and hung on like she was climbing a tree.

He kissed her and she answered, "A special Filipino dish, Rosie. I hope you like."

Rosie replied, "I am sure I will, honey. I want to go and lie down for a while. Let me know when it is ready."

"Okay, Rosie. Do you want me give you massage?"

Rosie answered, "No, honey, just want to rest a little before dinner."

She replied, "Okay. Me wake you when ready."

Rosie went into the bedroom and Imee continued with her cooking. Like most Filipinos, Imee loved music and loved singing. Rosie had met her in a karaoke bar. When he entered the bar, he heard some girl singing "Somewhere Over the Rainbow." When he looked, he saw this tiny little thing belting out the song like she was Mighty Mouse. For Rosie, that was it. He fell for her immediately.

After work, Miller took a shower, put on clean clothes, and got ready to walk over to the Angara Club. Harry and Sveta had invited him and Irena for dinner. Irena would meet him there. He wanted to go a little early to have a few gin and tonics, because it had been a rough day. When he arrived, he walked up the stairs, passed through the metal detector and the Russian goons, then went to the bar and got a drink. He walked over to the restaurant area and sat down at one of their usual tables.

A few minutes later, Irena showed up. She saw that he already had a drink and asked, "What is this, Slav? How many drinks have you had? Are you turning into a drunkard?"

Miller answered, "Far from it, my suspicious, accusing Russian beauty. I just got here, and I was thirsty."

She replied, "Sure. I just saw Tatyana leaving when I came in. Were you with her, Slav?"

Miller responded, "You behave, or I will slap your bottom."

She replied, "You think so, do you? I will slap *your* bottom."

They both started laughing and Irena moved over to hug and kiss Miller. She said in a cuddly tone, "I love you, Slav. I missed you. I have not seen you since Wednesday."

Miller replied, "It is only Friday, my love."

She said, "It seems longer."

Miller looked across the room and saw Harry and Sveta walking toward them. When they got to the table, Irena stood up and kissed Harry on the cheek. Then she kissed her mother. Miller got up also and kissed Sveta. He moved to Harry and said, "Sorry, Harry; I'm not kissing your ugly mug."

Harry answered, "Oh, and I was so looking forward to it."

They both laughed and Miller asked, "How are you guys?"

Harry replied, "Quite well."

He pulled the chair out for Sveta, and she sat down. A few moments later, the waiter showed up with a bottle of the Soviet champagne and four glasses.

Miller said jokingly, "Don't let Irena open it," and he pretended to duck and cover. They all laughed, and Irena kicked Miller under the table.

Miller asked, "Harry, what put the hole in your change purse, my friend?"

Harry replied, "Sveta and I have an announcement to make."

Irena asked, "Oh, Mamochka, you are not pregnant again?"

Sveta shook her head then looked at Harry and asked, "Harry?"

Harry replied, "Just one minute. Everyone needs to have a glass of champagne."

He picked up the bottle and started filling the glasses. He passed them around, then held up his own. He began, "Sveta has decided to make me the happiest man in the world and has agreed to be my wife. A toast to us and our upcoming marriage."

They all sipped, and Miller responded, "Congratulations, you two. I am not surprised. You make a wonderful couple."

Then Irena said with tears in her eyes, "I am so happy for you, Mamochka. I think Harry is a wonderful man and you will be very happy."

Sveta answered, "Yes, I am very happy, and I will make Harry the best wife in the world."

Harry responded, "And I will make Sveta the best husband."

In Moscow, the American tobacco companies were trying to make inroads into the recently opened market. There was an area in Moscow where there were several kiosks that sold nothing but cigarettes—mostly American cigarettes, but even the Russian brand was produced by an American company. They were sold at a dirt- cheap price. An advertising campaign ensued to convince as many Russians as possible that smoking was cool, and the campaign succeeded. In the city center there were several billboards that displayed the Marlboro Man—rugged, good-looking, smiling, and wearing a cowboy hat with a bandana tied around his neck. The Russian girls loved this guy and mostly all smoked Marlboro cigarettes because of him. Earlier in the evening, Donnie from "almost beaning Harry" fame had just come back from his R&R when his buddy Larry pounded on his door.

"Open up, Donnie. Did you get them? Open up."

Donnie opened the door, smiling. "Come in. Let me show you."

He opened up one of his suitcases, and inside were two Stetson hats in cardboard hat boxes, one brown and one black. They considered themselves outlaws, so white was out of the question. Also, there were two sets of leather chaps and two sets of spurs. He opened his other suitcase and inside it were two sets of snakeskin cowboy boots, one tan and the other set a greyish white. Also, in the case were two pearl-button cowboy shirts and two black leather vests.

Larry replied, "Shit, Donnie, you did good. The Russian girls are gonna love us."

Donnie asked, "Did you set it up with the band?"

Larry said, "Sure did. It cost me a hundred bucks. You owe me fifty. As soon as they see us walk in, they will stop whatever song they are playing and kick in with the theme to *Rawhide*."

Donnie asked, "I thought you were going to get them to do the *Bonanza* song?"

Larry replied, "I tried, but a couple of them already knew *Rawhide* from the Blues Brothers movie. I heard 'em do it. They do it good. It is set for around 11:00."

Larry thought about it and said, "Yeah, *Rawhide* is probably better anyhow."

☭

After about thirty minutes, the Tagalog dish for Rosie was ready. Imee tasted it again and added just a little salt and pepper. She called, "Rosie, it is ready. Time to eat." She placed the platters on the table. She called out again, "Come on, Rosie, it will get cold." She walked into the bedroom to wake him. She shook him and said, "Get up, Rosie." Rosie did not respond. She turned on the light and Rosie's face had a blue tint to it. She cried, "Rosie...Rosie, get up." Rosie did not move a muscle. Suddenly fear overtook her. "Rosie... Rosie."

Imee knew something was wrong. She ran out of the apartment and down the hall to Tom and Terry Scaraponi's apartment and banged on the door. She yelled, "Help! Help! There is something wrong with my Rosie. There is something wrong with my Rosie."

Terry opened the door and asked, "What is it, Imee?"

She said, "There is something wrong with my Rosie. I shake him, but he no get up."

Excitedly Terry yelled to Tom, "Tom, call Dr. Brinkman, the embassy doctor. Tell him we have an emergency. Then bring the defibrillator to Rosie's apartment."

Terry and Imee ran to the other apartment. The first thing she did was feel Rosie's pulse. *Good,* she thought, *there is one, but faint.* His face seemed a little blue and felt cold and clammy. She took the pillow out from under his head. She needed to get him flat. She opened his mouth and checked for any foreign objects in his mouth. She then put her hands on his chest and began CPR. She gave thirty chest compressions, then two rescue breaths, and repeated the process. She pressed down about two inches with each chest compression.

Imee kept yelling, "Save my Rosie. Save my Rosie."

Tom appeared with the defibrillator and without saying a word opened it up and took out the paddles. He reached in his pocket for his knife and opened it. Terry moved out of the way, and Tom cut open Rosie's shirt to expose his bare chest. He stuck one paddle on the upper chest and one on the lower, then turned the machine on. It immediately began to analyze Rosie's condition. In a digital display, it read "No shock needed. Continue CPR." Tom removed the paddles and Terry continued the CPR. They could see Rosie was responding. His face lost the blue color and had a healthier look. His pulse was stronger as well. Terry continued with the CPR until Dr. Brinkman showed up with paramedics and an ambulance to take him to the clinic.

As the paramedics lifted him off the bed and put him on the stretcher, Rosie opened his eyes. He didn't say anything, but his face had a puzzled look as if he were thinking, *What the hell is all this?*

Dr. Brinkman said, "Mr. Roesner, don't say anything. I am going to put a cherry-flavored aspirin in your mouth. Just let it dissolve there."

Imee was visibly shaking as she followed the paramedics out. Terry said, "Tom, I will go with them. Can you inform Harry what has happened?"

With that, Terry caught up with Imee and placed her hand in her own as they followed the paramedics out.

Harry and the rest of his party had finished dinner, drank more champagne, and were just enjoying the night. They liked the band and were dancing up a storm. Kurt and Nadine were there as well, and all were having a great time. The band was doing a Bob Marley tune, and many were on the dance floor. As they were getting into the groove, all of a sudden, the music stopped. Miller and Harry looked up and saw these two guys that looked like they were from Central Casting for a Gene Autry movie, complete with chaps and spurs.

Harry said, "Look at those two knuckleheads." With that, the band kicked in with the *Rawhide* theme. As the cowboys walked across the front of the stage, several Russian girls were screaming and several more were pawing at the two cowboys. Then one really beautiful girl took Donnie's hat, to try it on. When she did, Harry and Miller realized the knuckleheads were none other than Donnie and Larry.

Harry moved over to Miller and said, "When God was giving out brains, those two got the pinhead portions."

Miller answered, "Or no portion at all."

Harry turned to go back to his table when he saw Tom Scaraponi making his way through the crowd, coming toward him. Harry's heart stopped, because he knew by instinct that Tom was carrying bad news.

Tom said, "Harry, I have been looking all over for you. It appears Rosie might have had a heart attack. Not sure yet, but Dr. Brinkman is checking him out at the clinic."

Harry asked, "Is he okay?" Harry really liked and respected Rosie. He was genuinely shaken by the news.

Tom replied, "I don't know for sure."

Harry said, "Okay, Tom. Thanks for informing me. You can go home. I will stop at the clinic and see how he's doing."

Harry informed Miller and Kurt and asked them if they could take Sveta home. They both said hell no; they were going with him. When they informed the girls, they understood and said they would walk with Sveta to her apartment to wait for them. Sveta had invited both Irena and Nadine over for coffee.

Harry said as he moved toward the exit door, "Great, we will see you over there in about an hour."

Sveta called after him, "Okay, Harry. See you then."

☭

When Harry, Kurt, and Miller arrived at Rosie's room, he was sitting up in bed with an IV connected to his arm from a bag hanging from a hook on a cart. Dr. Brinkman was there, along with Imee and Terry.

Rosie said, "I don't know what all the fuss is about. I feel fine, Doc. Just a little indigestion."

Dr. Brinkman replied, "Mr. Roesner, you have had an event where your pulse was almost nonexistent, and you were barely breathing. Terry had to revive you with CPR. We will not be sure what kind of event it was until more tests are run. The equipment needed for the tests is not here in Russia, so you will have to go back to the States once you are stable."

Rosie responded, "Nonsense, Doc. I really do feel fine."

Just then, Rosie saw Harry and called out, "Tell him, Harry. I'm fine. I need to get the 5th-floor deck poured. Without me, the guys will screw it up."

Harry smiled and replied, "Granted, Rosie, I agree that you are probably too mean to die, but we need to follow the sawbones's advice. Not that there is anything wrong with your cantankerous ass, but for insurance reasons. Dr. Brinkman, would it be possible to find a good hospital and doctor in Germany who could do the tests? A shorter flight, and I would like to get Rosie checked out as soon as possible."

Dr. Brinkman thought for a moment and said, "As a matter of fact, one of the best hospitals in the world for Rosie's condition is located in Frankfort. I believe Frankfort is only a three-hour flight."

Harry replied, "Great, let's go that route. Okay with you, Rosie?"

Rosie said, "There is nothing wrong with me, Harry."

Harry responded, "That's good, Rosie, but let the doctors in Germany make that decision. As soon as they release you to come back to work, you fly back here. Deal?"

Rosie thought about it and said, "Okay, deal, Harry. But tell Tom he owes me fifty bucks for cutting up my favorite shirt. It was my only Columbia."

Harry laughed and replied, "Don't worry, you old horse thief; I will get you two Columbias once you get your ass back here. I will be money ahead because no one knows concrete like you. Now get the wax out of your ears and listen. Obey what the doctor tells you to do and don't make a fuss. As soon as we can get you checked out, the sooner we can get you back here. Imee, can you make sure Rosie behaves?"

Imee nodded, then with tears in her eyes, gave Harry a hug.

Necdet Hafeez was at the helm of the *Elif.* He was just approaching the Volograd Reservoir. He reached into his coat and pulled out a cigar case. Necdet smoked Black Label Partaga Prontos. He chose one from the case and lit it with his Turkish floral-patterned Zippo. The lighter was a gift from his first wife Elif. He thought that it brought him good luck and always had it with him. As he lit the cigar, he saw a cockroach trying to stow away, running across the deck in front of him and disappeared through a small crack where the bilge pump was located.

Necdet hoped to be at the Ukraine hotel pier sometime after midnight. He would spend the rest of the next day with his son, fishing and just enjoying himself. They would also eat at the Ukraine restaurant, at which he hoped he and Selim would appear as just another father son having an outing. The next early morning he would meet Yusef and be $100,000 richer. As Necdet moved through the river, it was cold and dark. Very little moonlight was showing through the clouds. His son Selim was wearing his Russian parka as he came up from below to bring his father a cup of hot coffee. Necdet thanked his son as he took the coffee and took a sip, then another. *That tastes good*, he thought. He took a puff of his Partaga, then another sip. Necdet thought how merciful Allah had been to have invented the simple pleasures of coffee and tobacco. They went together like feta and olives, or honey and bread.

He remembered a story his father once told him. When Necdet was a boy, his father would take him camping in the foothills of Mount Ararat. Necdet's job was to prepare the coffee for his father. One evening as Necdet was preparing the coffee a thought occurred to him, so he asked his father, "Papa, where does coffee come from?"

His father smiled and replied, "Necdet, you are a very smart boy for asking such a question, and I will tell you. In a land very far away on the continent of Africa there is a country. This country is on the east side of the continent. It has many rugged mountains just like in Turkey. This country is called Ethiopia. Now it is a very poor country, but many years ago it was very rich. At that time, Ethiopia had been called Sheba and included other lands as well. The Queen of Sheba was the most beautiful woman in all the land. Some scholars have said her name was Makeda. Do you remember your uncle Mustafa?"

Necdet replied, "Yes, Father. He is a shepherd who lives alone with his flock in the mountains."

His father said, "You are such a smart boy. I am so proud of you. Well, there was another shepherd in Ethiopia or Sheba, not unlike your uncle Mustafa, and his name was Abdula. Abdula also lived alone with his flock, but he dreamed one day he would marry Makeda and she would be in love with him, as well. He prayed to Allah every day to make this happen. Abdula prayed and prayed, and then one night in a dream he saw his sheep very happy, running around, rubbing heads, just having a great time. This confused Abdula and he wondered why God had forsaken him. Was God telling him to just be happy with his lot in life and forget about his love for Makeda?

"The next day as Abdula was tending his sheep, the oldest ram in the herd was having a hard time climbing the mountain to get to the area that had the sweet green grass. Abdula thought he might have to carry the beast. The old ram went to rest under what Abdula thought was a grape or berry bush. The ram started to nibble on clumps of the fruit. After a while Abdula observed the old ram standing up as he kept eating the berries. Soon the old ram was dancing around the bush and finally ran up the mountain where the other sheep and sweet grass were waiting. He even mounted one of the ewes in the herd on his way up.

"Abdula could not believe it. He walked over to the bush and collected some of these berries the ram had just eaten. When he tried one, he realized they were not berries or grapes at all, but some kind of bean. They tasted bitter and not at all pleasing. Abdula thought that maybe if he dried and roasted the beans, he could make a tea and consume the beans in that way."

Necdet asked, "What happened then, Father? Did Abdula marry the queen?"

His father laughed and replied, "Do not be so impatient, my son. The story will unfold to you in the appropriate order. Now, where was I? Oh, yes. Abdula dried and roasted the beans. As he did this, the beans gave off the most pleasant aroma. He crushed the beans into a powder and added some to his cup. He then boiled some water and added it to the cup as well. Abdula loved the aroma as he smelled his cup. He took a sip and thought it was good. He added a little sugar and some sheep's milk and drank it down. Abdula thought how wonderful it tasted. He then drank another cup, and Abdula felt the great energy just like the old ram. Now it all made sense. God had not forsaken him but provided him a gift fit for a king—but in this case, it would be for a queen.

"Twice a year, the Queen of Sheba invited those of her kingdom to present her with special gifts. If she was pleased, they would be rewarded, usually with gold or silver, but Abdula reasoned she would be so happy with his gift that she would marry him on the spot. Abdula was very excited. The next time this event would take place would be in two months, and Abdula had to prepare. He visited his brother Sokar and asked if he would look after his flock while he went on his quest. Sokar agreed. Next he went to the town to visit Akbar the tailor. Abdula would have the best suit of clothes he could afford. Now for the most important part of the quest. He went back to the stand of bushes where he had found the beans. He chose only the very best beans and the ripest. As he was gathering the beans, a nomad happened by. His name was Ezeikial.

"Abdula called out, 'Good morning, nomad. How are you this fine morning?'

"Ezeikial answered, 'Fine, my fellow traveler. I see you are gathering the beans from my favorite bush.'

"Abdula asked, 'Oh, you know of this bush?'

"Ezeikial replied, 'Yes, I do, shepherd. My people have enjoyed the kaffa or coffee bush for many years. This area in the Mankira Forest is called the Kaffa region where the coffee beans grow. We gather the coffee beans before we travel a long distance. When we get tired, we chew them for their great rejuvenating power.'

"Abdula asked, 'You call it a coffee bush?'

"Ezeikial answered, 'Yes, my friend. In my native tongue coffee means thunder. The wise ones named it such. Some dialects in the north call it bunna, but my people prefer to use the name coffee as the wise ones.'

"With that, Ezekial gathered some beans and placed them in a sack. He bid Abdula farewell and continued on his journey. After the nomad left, Abdula experimented with the beans. He noticed the ripe beans had the best flavor, but the less ripe greener beans seemed to give more energy. He decided on a 50/50 blend of ripe to green beans. *This is it*, he thought. *The queen will love my brew, which I will call coffee*. Abdula gathered several sacks of the ripe and green beans and secured the sacks to his father's burro, which he had borrowed for his quest. He was now ready and had to be on his way because the queen's castle was several days journey. He collected his suit of clothes from Akbar and said goodbye to his family.

"After many days, Abdula arrived at the queen's castle. Outside the castle a long line of people waited for an audience with the queen. As he looked at the people, he saw the great gifts they carried. Some had lions with unusual colors to their coats and monkeys who could do strange tricks. Some had leopards from the Far East and elephants from India. Abdula was not disheartened. He knew he had the brew that would please the queen and make her his wife. He waited in line for three days, then finally it was his turn. The guards escorted him into the palace courtyard where the queen was waiting sitting upon her throne. There were guards on each side of her and ladies-in-waiting sat at her feet. When Abdula saw the queen, he was awed by her beauty.

"The queen called out, 'And you there, what is your name and what gift do you have for me?'

"He answered, 'My name is Abdula, from the high plateau country. I have discovered this wonderful rejuvenating beverage. It is called coffee. If you will allow me, I will prepare it for you.'

"The queen replied, 'Please proceed, Abdula.'

"From the burro he took a small brazier and set it on the ground. He added the charcoal and lit a fire on top. The queen requested one of the ladies-in-waiting to sing a song while they watched with anticipation as Abdula finished his preparations. When the coals were ready, he laid a skillet over the top and also a pot of water. He removed a bag of the mixed beans from the burro and poured some into the skillet. When he did, a wondrous aroma filled the air and traveled through the queen's court. Nobody had ever smelled such an aroma. When the beans were roasted, he ground them, then added them to a cup. He added hot water with a little sugar and sheep's milk, then handed the cup to one of the guards. The guard tasted it to be sure it was fit for the queen to drink. When the guard was satisfied he handed the queen the cup. When the queen tasted it, she loved it and drank the whole cup and asked for another. She could feel the brew giving her energy, and she loved the flavor.

"The queen said, 'I love this gift, Abdula.'

With that, Abdula took the other five bags of mixed beans off the burro and presented them to her. The guards carried the bags away. The queen asked, 'And what reward may I give you for such a wonderful gift, Abdula? Gold, silver?'

"Abdula replied, 'No, my queen. I wish only for your hand in marriage.'

"The queen looked stunned; then she smiled, then she started laughing, and everyone in the court started to laugh as well. Abdula felt humiliated, and his heart began to break. With his head held low, he started to lead his burro out of the court.

"The queen called out, 'Wait. Come here.'

"Abdula obeyed, and when the laughter died down, she continued, 'Abdula, although your gift is very special, I am sorry I cannot grant the request you have asked, for I am betrothed to King Solomon. Please, Abdula, choose one of my ladies- in-waiting. Any one of them would make a wonderful wife.'

"Abdula thought about this. How foolish he was to think a queen would be willing to marry a poor shepherd like him. He chose one of the ladies, whose name was Israk, and she bore him many sons. Now, Necdet, do you know the moral of the story?"

Necdet thought and thought then finally said, "Never fall in love with a queen."

His father replied, "Well, not exactly, my son. Remember, all things are possible and perhaps someday you might very well marry a queen. No, my son, the moral of the story is when one door closes on you, another one opens."

Necdet missed his father and all his stories. He thought his father was right. He had married a queen, and her name was Elif. Just as Necdet was deep with emotion, he was shaken out of it when all of a sudden two Russian river patrol boats were upon them from out of nowhere. He yelled, "Selim, quick, full steam. We will outrun those beet-eaters."

Selim threw more coal into the hopper and the *Elif* started to pull away. The patrol boats saw this and began to fire. Both Necdet and his son got down low. A few of the rounds ricocheted off the bow with no serious damage. The *Elif* was fast, but it was a moonless night and hard to navigate. If Necdet hit something at the speed they were traveling, the pair were done for. Necdet preferred the risk, for he thought it was better than spending the rest of his days in a Russian gulag; or worse, they could be river pirates disguised as Russians. If this was the case, the chances were good they would be tortured and killed. Either way, Necdet felt he was better off taking his chances.

☭

Ben Magsino had been in Moscow for the last four days, keeping track of what Yusef Solak and Tanya were up to. In the vault were Ben and Joe Kelly. Joe called Alek on his cell phone.

"Alek, what is Yusef up to?"

Alek said, "Yusef is in his room. Tanya just showed up and went up there. She was carrying a bottle of some sort. Perhaps she and Yusef plan to share a night cap."

Joe thought about that. He knew it was tradition for the members of the Russian bomb squads to share a bottle of vodka the night before a mission. Joe replied, "Okay, Alek. Stay with them until Moshi gets there. Tell him to call me when he does."

Alek answered, "Yes, sir. I will inform him." Joe communicated to Ben his theory. Ben had the same thought about the tradition. Whatever they were up to, both men thought it would happen the next day or night.

☭

Tanya was in front of Yusef's hotel room door. She knocked. A few moments later, Yusef opened the door and asked looking annoyed, "What are you doing here, Russian? I was hoping I would not see you until tomorrow night."

Tanya replied, "Listen, you skinny Turk. It is tradition we share this bottle of vodka the night before the mission. It is for good luck."

Yusef said, "It did not do your friend Borya any good. I have my own tradition of going to bed early and getting plenty of sleep--so be gone, Russian."

Tanya answered, "Do not be so Turkish. Get two glasses."

Yusef shrugged and walked over to where the mini bar was and retrieved two wine glasses. Tanya came in and closed the door behind her. She filled the glasses and handed one to Yusef. She lifted her own and said, "To a successful mission, Turk."

Yusef responded, "And to you, Russian."

They both drained their glasses and she filled them once again. She lifted up her glass a second time and said, "To our mothers."

Yusef looked at her strangely and asked, "To our mothers? We are going to bomb an apartment building, killing many innocent Russians, and you want to toast our mothers?"

Tanya looked at him like she was sniffing something disagreeable and said, "Do not be so dramatic, Turk. What is your mother's name? We always toast the mothers. Now what is her name?"

Yusef looks at her, smiled, and replied, "I am not telling you, Russian. What are you going to do about it? Kill me? I don't think so."

Tanya answered, "No, but I can make every movement you make very uncomfortable."

Now the Turk looked at her like he was smelling something disagreeable and said, "I don't think so, Russ--"

In mid-sentence, surprising Yusef, she head-butted him, which disoriented him. She then punched him in the stomach, knocking out the wind. Yusef stood there grasping for breath. She threw him to the floor and with one hand pulling on his hair and her forearm pushing down on his throat, she asked him one more time, "What is your mother's name?"

Yusef complied and said in a guttural fashion as people do when they have someone pressing down on their throat, "Buket. Her name was Buket."

She lifted him up and said, "That's better. Now raise your glass and let's drink to Buket."

As she raised her glass, which left her exposed, Yusef punched her hard in the stomach, returning the favor she had just offered him. As she buckled, he kicked her legs out from under her, and she hit the floor. He then got on top of her and grabbed her throat, saying, "Do not ever do that again or I will not be so kind." He then kissed her hard on the lips and pulled up her dress.

She angrily called out, "Get your skinny Turk body off of me."

Yusef didn't listen. He started to rub her through her panties until he felt Tanya's moistness. She pretended to struggle, then reversed course and pulled Yusef closer to her. Her body trembled as Yusef removed his trousers and revealed his hardness. As he positioned his body back on top of Tanya, she took her hand and guided Yusef inside of her.

Necdet had turned off his running lights as Selim pushed the *Elif* as fast as she could go. Necdet was at the helm and was trying to navigate in the dark at high speed. The Russian patrol boats were falling behind and soon gave up the pursuit but not before discharging several more rounds, which did more damage to the *Elif*. Necdet figured they probably radioed ahead so he would be wary. He had Selim slow the *Elif* down, but they would continue with the running lights turned off until they reached the Moscow River.

☭

It was Friday night, and Harry gave Miller the next day off. After they visited Rosie at the clinic, Miller, Harry, and Kurt met the women at Sveta's apartment. Miller and Irena stayed for one cup of coffee before they took the metro to their own apartment. They were lying in bed when Irena asked, "Is it not wonderful, Slav, about my mother and Harry?"

Miller replied, "Yeah, they both seemed so happy, like they were floating in the clouds."

Irena asked, "Do you love me, Slav?"

Miller answered, "Of course, my love."

Irena said, "I bet I love you more than you love me."

Miller replied, "Let's not make this a contest. I know I am very happy when I am with you." Irena moved closer and rested her head on the Slav's shoulder. Miller began to think about it. He did love her, but was she the one? Was he really ready to settle down? He just wasn't sure, but the more he thought about it, he thought maybe she was the one.

Irena asked, "Slav, how many childs you want?"

Miller corrected her. "My love, it is how many children do you want?"

Irena replied, "I think two would be nice. One boy and one girl close to the same age. What do you think?"

Miller tried making light of it. He said, "I think eleven childs would be nice. One after another."

Irena responded, "Are you crazy? Eleven childs? Do not be so foolish, and it is eleven children, not childs."

Miller laughed and said, "You are quite right, my love. Thank you for correcting me. And when I come home from work and there are toys all over the house and dinner isn't ready, do I have your permission to beat you?"

Irena asked, "How could you ask such a thing? I will beat you...you svenina."

They both laughed. Miller kissed her and said, "I do love you, my little Russian cabbage."

Irena jumped on top of Miller, pinned him down, and said, "So now I am a cabbage, am I? Are these the breasts of a cabbage?" She rubbed them against the Slav's face. "Is this the bottom of a cabbage?" She put his hands on her backside. "Are these the lips of a cabbage?" She kissed Miller's lips, then slowly moved down to the Slav's more private parts.

☭

The next morning, Irena and Miller slept in until 10:00. They went to the Starlite Diner for breakfast. Miller asked, "And what are you having this morning, my Russian beauty?"

Irena said, "I think I will get the spinach and mushroom omelet with bacon and rye toast, with a cup of hot chocolate. That sounds good, does it not? What will you have?"

Miller replied, "I am feeling like a little south of the border this morning, so I will consume the huevos rancheros smothered with green chili and hash browns. Maybe some tortillas on the side."

The couple planned to just enjoy the day. They had not done that in a long time. Even though the weather was cold, they were dressed for it. After breakfast they would take the metro to the Arbat and just walk around watching the acrobats and the other performers on the street. As they walked, Miller thought how he enjoyed these little outings with Irena. She was funny and a good companion, and most of all she laughed at his jokes, most of the time. He thought to himself that he really did love her, and he knew she loved him.

☭

Necdet and Selim had reached the Ukraine Hotel just after midnight. They slept on the *Elif* and now were just finishing breakfast at the hotel restaurant. Necdet ordered more coffee, and soon he and his son would try their luck fishing from the pier. After the little episode with the Russian patrol boats, no other problems arose. Necdet and his son would enjoy the day, and in a few hours, he would be $100,000 richer.

☭

Joe Kelly was in his office when his cell phone rang, and he answered. It was Moshi reporting in. Yusef and Tanya had spent the night in his room, and she had just left. He stayed at the hotel, keeping an eye on Yusef and waiting for Alek to relieve him. Serkon, his driver, had followed the girl to her apartment near the Kremlin.

Joe replied, "Good, Moshi. As soon as Alek gets there, go home and get some sleep. It is going to be a long night."

After Joe finished the conversation, Ben walked into his office and said, "Joe, I want to go over the possible targets. Even though we have surveillance on our suspects, I want an agent at each one of the possible target locations just in case."

Joe and Ben walked down to the vault to discuss. After they had finished, Ben went to see the ambassador to keep him informed. Ben had a sixth sense about these things, and every indicator was telling him it would be tonight.

☭

General Brezhnev was in his office when his phone rang. It was Yuri. "Is everything ready, General?" Yuri asked.

The Butcher replied, "Yes, Yuri. Everything is set."

Yuri asked, "And we are taking precautions?"

"Yes, Yuri. Just leave it to me."

Yuri said, "General, do not fail. Be sure there will be no evidence leaving a trail back to us. Call me when the deed is done. I will be at my dacha outside Sochi."

The general answered, "Yes, Yuri, I will inform you."

Yuri put down the phone, thought a minute, then dialed again. "Major Karlov."

Yuri said, "Hello, Dimitry. I was just calling to make sure everything is ready for tonight."

Karlov answered, "Yes, of course, Yuri. I will be waiting in my car in front of the Angara Club just before 2:00 a.m. Anatoli will be driving, and I will be sitting in back. The front seat will be reserved for Yusef. We will drive to the Kremlin and once through the gates, Yusef will relax. I will then pull out my garotte and strangle Yusef from behind. So much cleaner than using an ice pick or gun—right, my friend?" Yuri chuckled and the major continued, "Anatoli will pull over and I will get out. Anatoli will then drive outside of Moscow to the Yakut Forest where he will deposit the body. The wolves will have devoured the Turk before the sunrise. What about the girl?"

Yuri replied, "The following morning at training General Brezhnev will have an unfortunate accident befall her. Something to do with a malfunctioning machine gun."

The major asked, "And the Butcher was good with that? After all, she has been his protégée for the last ten years."

Yuri started to chuckle and answered, "It seems the general's protégée has been soiled in the general's eyes after he became aware of her indiscretions with the Turk."

Karlov started to chuckle as well and said, "Excellent, Yuri. That seems to have worked out quite well for us. So much easier, with the general on board with our plan. Is there anything else, my friend?"

Yuri answered, "Yes, Dimitry. We will need to trail the Turk after the charges are set. He may have smelled a rat and made alternative arrangements to get out of the country. This he must never do."

Karlov replied, "Agreed, Yuri. I will take care of it."

After the conversation, Yuri sat back in his chair and picked up his glass from the table. He called into the other room, "Vladlina, are you ready yet? We have to get to the airport." She answered back she was almost ready. Yuri looked at his watch, shook his head, and took another drink from his glass.

Miller and Irena had a wonderful day. They wandered the Arbat, watched the performers, had ice cream, and were back at their apartment by late afternoon. The plan was to take a nap and get ready to go to the Angara Club for pork chops. Harry and Sveta would be spending the night at the Ukraine Hotel. They hadn't been there for a while and were both looking forward to it. Alexi was at a friend's until Irena would collect him at about 10 p.m. after she and Miller had dinner, danced a bit, and had a few drinks. Later at the Angara Club, Miller watched as Irena was devouring one of her pork chops. As usual, she had sauce all over her chin and chewing like she had not eaten in a week. He noted it was one of those crazy things he loved about her. Her love of pork chops was like her love of life.

She noticed him watching her and asked, "What are you looking at, Slav?"

Miller answered, smiling, "Nothing, my love. I was just thinking what a beautiful woman you are, even with all that sauce on your chin and eating those chops like you are a savage beast."

She replied, "That is right. I am like a wolf, so you better watch out."

When they finished, Miller wet the cloth napkin and cleaned Irena's face and fingers, then his own. He ordered two more gin and tonics and sat close to her, holding her hand. Miller had a feeling at that moment, everything was right with the world.

☭

At 8:30 p.m., Yusef left the Lotte heading to the Kremlin. Alek followed him out of the hotel on foot, and Serkon stayed behind Alek in the car. After Yusef was behind the Kremlin gate, Alek and Serkon waited outside the wall in the car. He called Joe Kelly and informed him.

Joe said, "Alek, we think it will happen tonight. Keep your eyes on the lookout for the gas truck Yusef and Tanya used before. They probably will use the same ploy to install the explosives."

Alek and Serkon waited, and about thirty minutes later, they saw the gas truck. Alek said, "Serkon, follow the truck."

Serkon replied, "Which one?"

Sure enough, there were four gas trucks in a row leaving the Kremlin, each going in a different direction. The windows were dark so they could not make out which one Yusef and Tanya were in. Alek informed Joe. Joe in turn called his operatives set up at the possible targets to be on the lookout for the gas trucks and if they spotted Yusef and Tanya. Serkon just chose one and followed it. Ben was with Joe in the vault. All they could do now was wait until one of the operatives spotted them.

☭

Miller walked Irena to her mother's apartment. She would pick up Alexei at his friend's on the floor above. At the apartment door, Miller swept Irena up in his arms and said, "I love you, my Russian princess." And he kissed her like he really meant it.

She was taken aback, and with tears starting to come to her eyes, said, "And I you, my Slav." She buried her head in his embrace, trying to hide her emotion. Miller kissed her again, said goodbye, and walked down the stairs heading back to the man camp. Irena went inside the apartment, trying to compose herself. She wiped the tears from her eyes, then went up to retrieve Alexei.

☭

Yusef and Tanya parked at the back of the apartment building. They carried the explosives and detonators in duffel bags to the basement. Yusef started on one side and Tanya on the other. It was 11:30 p.m., and with any luck, Yusef thought they would be finished by 1:00 a.m. First, they had to set the explosives to the support columns close to the 1st-floor beams. They had to use ladders to accomplish this. Then they would go back and set the detonators and connect the remote-control box with the detonator wires. It was dark, and even with flashlights, Yusef had to be careful to connect the wires correctly. If he did not, some of the explosives may not detonate. If that was the case, it might not bring down the building, and the mission would be a failure.

☭

Joe Kelly contacted each of his operators, and no one had seen the gas trucks or anybody resembling Yusef or Tanya going in or out of the suspected target buildings. Alek and Serkon were the only ones, and they were still following their gas truck, which was now on the outskirts of Moscow. Ben was with Joe, and they both had a sneaking suspicion they had been duped. Both men's brains were churning for answers. Moshi was staked out at the Lotte in case Yusef showed.

☭

Harry and Sveta had finished a late dinner and were drinking wine and talking as they sat listening to the restaurant's piano player. They lost track of the time. As they got up to leave, Sveta suggested a walk down by the hotel's pier to view the river. Harry looked at his watch and it was little after 1:00 a.m., way past Harry's bedtime. Harry thought, *What the hell*, and he and Sveta left through the exit door. As the couple walked, they enjoyed the star-filled night. There were some dinner boats out floating on the river. One was tied to the pier and was closing up for the night. Another smaller boat that looked out of place was at the end of the pier. As they walked up, they saw two men on the deck. They appeared to be fishing. In cursive on the back of the boat was written *The Elif.* On the pier was a bench where the couple sat down.

Sveta asked, "Isn't it a beautiful night, Harry?"

Harry answered, "Yes, darling. The stars are so big and bright. You can even see the Milky Way."

Sveta looked confused and asked, "The Milky Way?"

Harry replied, "See all the stars that kind of look like a long cloud of stars?"

Sveta said, "I think so."

Harry continued, "Well, that is referred to as the Milky Way because in the broad sense it resembles spilt milk."

Sveta responded, "Okay, Harry, I think I see it now."

Harry asked, "See that constellation there low in the sky with the three bright stars?"

Sveta replied, "I know, that is Orion the Hunter."

Harry said, "Oh well, I was trying to impress you with my star knowledge."

Sveta moved closer to Harry and said, "Everything you do, my Harry, impresses me. I do not know how I ever lived without you. You bring me such joy." Sveta had a way of making Harry feel like he was the most important man in the universe, and he loved her for that."

Yusef and Tanya finished at 1:10 a.m. Everything was set and ready to go. All Yusef had to do now was push the little red button on the remote, and boom, assignment completed.

Yusef said, "Tanya, you go back to the Kremlin. I will walk back to the hotel from here. I will have just enough time to take a shower and then meet Major Karlov in front of the Angara Club."

Tanya replied, "Okay, Turk. Kiss me before I go."

Yusef responded, "Not now, Tanya, I have to go."

She informed him, "Listen, Turk. You are going to miss me."

Yusef answered, "Maybe, but not now. Until we meet again, Russian."

With that, Tanya got into the truck and drove away. Yusef walked fast up the alley, then up the street to the Lotte.

Moshi saw a familiar figure walking toward him. He moved back into the shadows and waited. It was Yusef. Moshi thought, *Where the hell have you been, Turkish swine*? He waited for him to get inside the hotel, then called Joe Kelly. Joe answered, and Moshi informed him, "I have located the Turk. He has just come back to the Lotte."

Joe replied, "Keep an eye on him. Follow him if he leaves. I will send Alek and Serkon as your back-up. *Do not lose him.* Maybe he has not yet set the charges and we still have time to stop him." Joe then contacted Alek, and soon he and Serkon were on the way back to the city center and the Lotte Hotel.

Miller was lying in bed at the man camp and couldn't fall asleep. He kept trying to imagine Irena with him in Tucson—trying to imagine what daily life would be like with her. She was a Muscovite and used to living in the city. Miller lived outside of town on three acres, with mountain views and a fifteen-minute drive into Tucson. He knew he would have to teach her to drive. In Moscow she was accustomed to the metro and neither she nor her mother owned a car. Then he began to think about all the other guys that married foreign women. Some worked out, and some cost them dearly, financially. There was no doubt about it; marriage was a gamble, just like investing in the stock market or playing dice. You could not calculate the outcome.

Earlier, Irena had tucked her brother Alexei into bed. He told her, "Someday, Irena, I will be a professional hockey player. I will show you."

Irena smiled, and asked, "Can you get me box seats to your games?"

Alexei replied, "Yes, you will see. You and Mamma can come watch me play."

Irena said, "Sweet dreams, Alexei. I love you." She kissed him on the cheek.

Alexei answered, "I love you, Irena."

When Irena went to bed all she could do was think of the Slav. *I think he loves me, but he may not know it yet. Yes, we will have two children—one boy and one girl.* Irena had always liked the name Thomas for a boy and Isabel for a girl. She thought of the Slav with his eleven childs. How ridiculous. She laughed at herself for thinking childs instead of children. She thought she would like to live in San Francisco, but she might like this Tucson place the Slav talked about. Maybe she could get a cowboy hat. She laughed again, thinking of herself as a cowgirl riding a big white horse. She continued with the wonderful thoughts until she got sleepy and the sandman came to possess her.

At about 1:50 a.m., Yusef emerged from the Lotte. He started walking toward the Novy Arbat. This had always been the plan; after the detonation, he would veer back to the old Arbat then the Angara Club to meet Karlov. Yusef looked at his watch. Five more minutes. He walked passed the Irish bar and continued walking. Every step he took in this direction was one step closer to the boat pier and Necdet. Yusef decided the time was now. He took out the device and hit the red button. Yusef heard the explosion and started to run to the Ukraine Hotel. Moshi momentarily was taken off guard but after a few moments was back on his tail. He was starting to wish he kept himself in better condition and had quit the smokes, but Moshi liked his vodka and cigarettes. Even so, Moshi was keeping up. He noticed a man running on the other side of the street, keeping up with the both of them. This bothered him, but he focused on his objective to catch Yusef at any cost.

Miller heard the explosion. He looked out his apartment window, which faced the street, and he could see smoke and fire. He got dressed, grabbed a Cohiba, and walked outside. The smoke and fire looked like they were in the direction of Sveta's building. He walked, but then he began to run. It was Sveta's building. The six-floor apartment building was devastated. People were outside who lived nearby. Some were trying to help and others just watching in shock. As Miller got closer, he could hear the agonizing cries for help. The building went down like a house of cards. On the side where Sveta's apartment had been there were whole pieces of the building lying in the street. He looked through the rubble. The shock had not hit him yet. He just moved on instinct, looking for survivors and hoping two of them would be Irena and Alexei. He walked past dead bodies mostly cut to pieces. He was numb to the screams and the moans of agony. He helped a small boy from out under a heavy timber. He kept going, just searching through the rubble. He removed debris that covered another woman, then helped her up. No serious injuries, and she was able to walk away. He was hoping for the same scenario with Irena and Alexei.

More friends and family members began to show up, looking for survivors. Miller kept going. He tried to figure out where Sveta's apartment could have landed after the blast. He searched in several areas—then when he pulled up a piece of drywall, he saw her. Irena's eyes were closed, and she had a small amount of blood on her forehead. When he removed the rest of the drywall covering her, he saw it: a portion of timber had splintered and was sticking out the left side of her stomach between her navel and rib cage. It did not look good.

Miller patted her face to get her to come to. She opened her eyes and saw Miller standing over her. He half smiled and asked, "How are you, my Russian princess?"

She replied faintly, "Where are we, Slav?"

Miller said, "Don't talk, Irena. I will go get some help."

She screamed, "Do not go, Slav. Stay here with me. Why am I so cold? What happened?"

Miller was with her, kneeling down, trying to put pressure on her wound to stop the bleeding. She continued, "I do not feel so good, Slav."

Miller replied, "Nonsense, my Russian beauty. You are fine." Then he yelled, "GET A DOCTOR OVER HERE, NOW!"

Irena asked, "Who is the doctor for? Did someone get hurt?"

Miller responded, "My love, there was an explosion. Your apartment building was destroyed."

Irena asked excitedly, "Where's Alexei?"

Miller answered, "I don't know, Irena."

She cried, "Find him, Slav. Find him."

Miller said, "He will be fine, my love, and so will you. We still have to travel to Paris to see the Eiffel Tower and hike the Great Wall of China."

She replied, "You just want to go there for the Chinese girls, Slav. Do not lie to me."

Miller was glad she was somewhat her old self. He said, "Nonsense, my love. I want you to be with me always. I want to have our eleven childs."

She coughed before she spoke. Miller thought maybe some of the blood had seeped into her lungs. She said, "No eleven childs, Slav. We will have one boy and one girl. The boy will be called Thomas and the girl will be called Isabel." After she coughed again, Miller knew that Irena did not have much longer. A doctor now was futile.

Tears started welling up in his eyes and he said softly, "Irena, it is children, not childs, my love. You have chosen the two most beautiful names for our children. Thomas and Isabel. I will take Thomas to his baseball and hockey games. You will take Isabel to piano and her ballet classes. We will take her to see *Romeo and Juliet* and she will fall in love with the ballet, just like her mother. We will be so proud of them, Irena."

Irena was starting to lose consciousness. Once again Miller tapped her cheek. She awoke and whispered faintly, "Such beautiful thoughts. I love you, Slav, with all my heart. Thank you for taking me to see the ele--" She trailed off and lost consciousness again.

Miller finished her thought. "Elephants, my love. Yes, that was wonderful, my Russian princess...Irena...Irena."

He shook her and kept calling her name. She did not respond.

☭

Joe Kelly spoke into his cell phone. "Alek, you and Serkon wait outside the Angara Club out on the street. Moshi is in pursuit of Yusef, and he may double back and come your way."

Alek and Serkon ran down from the Lotte, where they had just arrived. They made it to the Angara Club in about three minutes. They kept their eyes open, looking for anyone who could be Yusef or Tanya. Alek noticed a blue Lada parked in front. It looked like a Russian government vehicle. As he moved over for a closer look, the door opened, and a woman got out. It was Tanya, still in her blue gas man outfit. As she opened the door, he got a glimpse of the man she was talking with sitting in the back seat. The man was Major Karlov. Alek thought, *Good old Uncle Dimitry*. He motioned to Serkon to follow Tanya, which he did. Alek thought this was his chance to pay his regards to his favorite uncle. The driver, Anatoli, was not there. Karlov had sent him away while he was speaking with Tanya.

Alek decided to make his move. He flung the door open that Tanya had just left by. As Alek opened the door he said in a friendly voice, "Hello, Uncle. It is your loving nephew, Alek."

At first the major did not recognize him and looked puzzled. Then he realized, and the danger signals ran through him like a dam had just been opened. He reached for his pistol, but Alek was fast. Alek took his knife and slashed Karlov's throat. Karlov looked stunned as a severed vein spurted blood onto his shirt. Karlov opened the door and tried to get away. After a few steps, he collapsed out in the street. Alek closed the Lada's door and walked into the street to where his uncle had fallen. He pulled his body to the curb. Karlov's eyes showed a small flicker of life.

Alek looked down at the pathetic man and said, "Give my regards to Czar Nickolas, Uncle." Then Alek spit in his face and walked away.

☭

Yusef was in the home stretch to the pier. He had gained a lead on Moshi and knew he could make it, if Necdet was ready to shove off. He rounded the hotel and was at the beginning of the pier. Necdet already had the motors running. Necdet saw Yusef coming and ordered his son to untie the lines. Yusef was running full speed down the pier to the boat. Moshi had not reached the pier yet. Yusef thought he was home free when the shot rang out. Yusef flinched but kept running. Then the second shot rang out, and Yusef fell. He was dead before he hit the ground. Necdet could see the assassin by some trees left of the pier. As Moshi got to the pier, the assassin ran deep into the trees. Necdet took the calculated risk. He ran from the boat to Yusef. He felt over his body for a bulge of something then found it tucked under his shirt.

Yusef removed the package and said, "A deal is a deal, Yusef-obi. May you reach the gates of paradise, inshallah'."

Necdet then jumped back into the boat and the Elif was gone before Moshi arrived. Moshi was breathing hard when he leaned over Yusef to look for vitals. There were none. When Sveta recognized Moshi, she and Harry came out from under the bench they were hiding under. The couple witnessed the whole affair.

Sveta asked, "Who is he?"

Moshi replied, "He is suspected in the apartment building bombing."

Harry asked, "There was a bombing?"

Moshi answered, "Yes, an apartment building near the American Embassy, about thirty minutes ago. That is all I know. The man lying here is Yusef Solak. He is a Turkish bomb expert whom we believe is responsible."

Sveta called her apartment to check on Irena and Alexei, but there was no answer. Harry and Sveta hurried back to the hotel, and in the parking lot there was one taxi in the front that hadn't gone home yet.

Miller felt like he had been kicked in the stomach. The emotional pain was strong as he hunched over and vomited. A few hours earlier he had been one of the happiest men alive; now the unbelievable pain of loss--of love, of life, of direction--overtook him. He was on his knees with his face to the ground, rocking back and forth, when Sveta and Harry arrived. They saw Miller and ran to where he and Irena were.

When Sveta saw Irena, tears came to her eyes. She cried, "Oh my little Lapooshka. What have they done to you?" She leaned over and took Irena's hand. She began to recite an old nursery rhyme in Russian that was Irena's favorite when she was a little girl. Miller was still on the ground rocking back and forth, mumbling something.

Harry went over and said, "Hey, JT. Come on, get up. There is nothing else you can do. Come on, JT."

An ambulance came to take Irena and others away to the morgue. When the technicians tried to touch Irena's body to put her on a stretcher, Miller and Sveta stopped them. Sveta took out her handkerchief, wetted it with saliva, and cleaned Irena's forehead and face. She brushed her hair and put on lipstick. When Sveta was satisfied, Miller picked her up into his arms one last time and placed her on the stretcher.

He said, with that pain still in the pit of his stomach, "Sleep well, my love."

Miller, Harry, and Sveta were the first to leave St. Andrew's Church. They had just attended a Russian Orthodox service for Irena and now would be in the procession to the cemetery for the burial. Alexei had been found alive. He was badly bruised and had some broken bones and lacerations, but he was alive. He would be in the hospital for another three weeks. The ride to the cemetery was slow and long. The three rode in silence. When they arrived, they were escorted to the gravesite. The hearse carrying Irena, backed up to the pulley system that was set up to lower the casket into the grave. Soon, Irena hung over her final resting place. Most of the embassy and TRIAD staff were in attendance. Kurt and Nadine, Charlie and Kathy, Tom and Terry, Bo, Joe Kelly, Vera, Ben, the ambassador and his wife Nancy, the OBO staff and Nigel and Larry Boehlen were there as well. They had a short service, and then as the priest prayed, the casket was lowered into the ground. Miller carried the portrait that he and Irena had done on the Arbat. It was still in the artist's brother's frame as Miller set it on top of the casket.

Harry asked, "What is that, JT?"

Miller answered, "Just something I want her to have."

After the casket was set down into the ground, Miller took a shovel and filled it with soil. He dropped it on top of the casket and handed the shovel to Harry, saying, "Harry, I'll just walk back. See you later."

With that, Miller just walked away, heading to the street. Harry was worried about him. When Harry finished with his shovelful, he handed it to Sveta. With tears in her eyes, she plunged the shovel into the soil and finished the ritual.

☭

As Miller walked, he felt lost and he felt numb. Numb to the pain and numb to reality. He had a dazed, confused look on his face. He stopped into a bar on the way and ordered a shot of Tsarskaya, then another. He stayed there until he could barely walk. He took a taxi back to his room at the man camp and passed out on his bunk. This was what he had been hoping for—to be oblivious to all things for a few hours. The next morning, he awoke to a sound of knocking at his door. He got up slowly to answer it. His head and body ached.

It was Harry. "Morning, JT. Just thought I would check in on you. Is there anything I can get you?"

Miller replied, "No, Harry. I'm good. I will probably head down to the mess hall in a bit."

Harry said, "Listen, JT. I want you to take a couple of weeks off. Go home and sort this all out. When you are ready, come back, and we'll finish building this embassy."

Miller didn't know how to take the offer. He answered, "Let me think about it, Harry. I will let you know tomorrow."

Harry said, "Okay, JT. Let me know later if you want some company in the mess hall."

When Harry left, Miller started to figure out his next move. He knew the short- term solution he had succumbed to the previous night for the pain, was not a viable option long-term. He thought maybe going home for a few weeks was a good idea. He knew he had to keep busy and not just sit around and mope. He had a small house he had owned for years on three acres. It was outside of Tucson by Picture Rocks. Over the years, he added an L-shaped redwood deck and an office off the deck. It had great views of the Tucson Mountains and was next to the Saguaro National Forest. It was a lush area with paloverde, ironwood, and mesquite trees, with many different species of cactus as well. This had always been the place Miller retreated to after each project or after a crisis of some sort. He always felt better here. He needed to find a method for the pain to go away.

He remembered a counseling facility not far from his house called the Desert Sunrise Retreat. It was situated on twenty acres in the Saguaro National Forest, and the place and grounds kind of reminded Miller of a desert Shangri-la. About five years previously, Miller had done a boundary survey of the property, and while he was there, got a tour of the facilities. It was a place people went to who had had a traumatic life event happen to them, and the counselors were trained to help them get through it. Miller had never gone in for these types of facilities; all he knew was that he wanted the pain to stop and was willing to try anything.

He decided to take Harry up on his offer, and a few days later he was checking into the Tucson facility. He signed up for the seven-day intensive counseling program. The Desert Sunrise Retreat had small bungalows set all over the twenty acres, where the guests stayed. They were connected to each other and the main facilities by a narrow pathway. Inside, the bungalows were made of wood and resembled a combination of a Japanese tea house and a cowboy bunk house. Miller put his bags down and flopped onto the bed.

A few minutes later, an Asian-American woman appeared at his door. Her name was Chee. She said, "Come on, Mr. Miller; you are wanted in the main meditation lounge."

Miller got out of the bed reluctantly and followed Chee outside as she explained meditation was the first best thing for his recovery. She said, "As you relax your mind, the goal is to not think of anything. You focus on your breath, not your thoughts. At first it will be difficult; then it will become easier. You train your mind to control your thoughts."

Chee showed him how to get started, and she stayed and meditated with him. Just like she said, at first, he had trouble not thinking of anything; then it became less difficult. After two days, the pain would stop when he would meditate. Now it was time for the next session, which was designed to give him more confidence and make him believe he could conquer any adversity. The first part was exercise. They put together a routine for Miller, which he followed, but added weight training. As he felt stronger, he felt better. Next there were mind exercises designed to train his mind to focus on the positive aspects and limit the negative. It was working. Miller had come to accept what had happened to him and realized it did not have to affect the rest of his life. Irena was at peace, but he was still living and had to make the most of it.

After the sessions were completed, Miller went back to his house. On his own, he would follow the techniques he had been taught for several more months until he began to feel whole. With the time Miller had left in Tucson, he trimmed trees on his property, painted the sheds, went hiking, and just enjoyed being home. After the R&R (rest and relaxation) was over, Miller knew he had made the right decision. He now felt he could go back and continue his life in Moscow.

CHAPTER THIRTEEN

DASVIDANIYA

The day after the explosion, Joe Kelly and Ben Magsino were in the vault. Joe was briefing Ben on the latest. Joe said, "Yes, the explosion was well orchestrated. Three hundred Russians dead—half of those were women and children—and 150 injured. The Russian state television is blaming it on Chechen rebels. Of course, they have no proof. It is the hardliners spreading this story, and it seems they have elected our old friend Yuri Belevich to be in charge of the investigation. I would guess that soon the treaty with Chechnya will be revoked and the Russians will go back to war. What we got from Tanya is that after the explosion, Yusef was to meet Major Karlov in front of the Angara Club. It seems Yusef had other plans. Interestingly, they found Major Karlov's body lying in the street in front of the club. There are either no witnesses or no one is talking. The major received a slash wound to the throat which severed a carotid artery. He was dead within minutes of the attack."

Ben asked, "Joe, do we have any idea who could have taken him out?"

Joe replied, "At this point, no. But I would also say whoever it was probably did us a favor."

Ben asked, "So there was a boat named the *Elif*, which appeared to be waiting for Yusef at the Ukraine Hotel pier?"

"Yes, Harry Clark, TRIAD's project manager, was there with his fiancée and they both saw the boat's name. It seems after Yusef fell, one of the boatmen ran over and removed a package from Yusef's shirt, then jumped back on to the boat, and was gone."

Ben said, "It was probably the boatman's payment for smuggling Yusef out of Russia."

Joe replied, "The state TV is calling Yusef's death a robbery. I guess if they are trying to sell the Chechen rebel theory, that makes better sense."

Ben asked, "Do we know who shot Yusef?"

Joe answered, "Again, not as yet. The speculation is that the Russians took care of Mr. Solak so he could not talk. If it was the Russian hardliners who orchestrated the bombing, they could not risk a witness."

Ben offered, "Yes, that makes sense. Where is Tanya now?"

Joe said, "She is waiting in a safe house until we can get her out of the country. She is cooperating because she knows she's a dead woman if she stays in Russia."

Ben asked," Do we know how the Russians were able to deceive us as to which building, they would be bombing?"

Joe answered," It seems they had another demolition crew scouting an alternative site. General Breshnev did not want to take a chance that Yusef or Tanya had been detected, so he changed the location at the last minute. Yusef had to calculate a new bomb configuration for the building once he arrived at the target location, according to Tanya." Ben nodded.

☭

When Miller got back to Moscow, he went through the motions—did his job during the day and went back to his room in the evenings. He went out occasionally to dinner with Harry and Sveta, but for the most part he laid low. When his two-year contract was up, he decided not to re-up and thought he would go back to the States. The day before he was to leave, Vera summoned him to the vault. As he walked in, Vera was there along with Joe Kelly and Ben Magsino.

Joe Kelly began, "Well, JT, I understand you are leaving us. What will you do now?"

Miller answered, "I thought I would take some time off until spring, then go back to work. Harry has asked me to come to his next project. Now that he will have a wife to support, he is thinking about doing one more. I have not decided."

Ben said, "JT, you did a great job as one of our operatives. For someone who had never been trained, you were outstanding. How would you like to come to Langley in the spring for training? We would like you to attend the academy."

This particular scenario had not occurred to Miller. He replied, "Thank you, but right now I just want to go home for a while."

Ben said, "I understand, JT. If you decide later you would like to explore this opportunity, contact Joe or myself and we will set you up in the program."

Miller thanked them, and as he got to the door of the vault, Vera came up to him and took his hand. She said, "JT, all the best to you, and if there is anything I can do, please let me know."

JT nodded. She then gave him a hug and kissed him on the cheek. Miller turned and walked through the door and slowly down the hall.

Yuri was at the Kremlin attending a ceremony. He had petitioned for his old friend Major Karlov to receive one of the highest honors Russia could bestow: The Hero of the Russian Federation medal, awarded to those committing actions or deeds that involve conspicuous bravery while in the service of the state. The major's wife was there to receive the award.

After the ceremony, Yuri was stopped by state reporters and asked about Major Karlov. Yuri responded, "The major and I started out together more than twenty years ago in the service of the state. We were on several missions together, and he was a man of impeccable talent and bravery. Dimitry was the brother I never had. I loved him. I will also say that I will not rest until the assassin or assassins who ended his life prematurely are caught, tried, and brought to justice. That is my pledge to you."

Another reporter asked, "Mr. Belevich, what is the latest on the apartment- building bombing?"

Yuri continued, "We have arrested three Chechens whom we believe were responsible for the bombing. We are still interrogating them to get answers.

Of course, the Chechnya government is denying any involvement; this is absurd. Gentlemen, if you please, no more questions. I am leaving to take Major Karlov's wife to a reception in his honor, and we are late. Thank you very much."

With that, Yuri walked past the reporters and exited the room. Yuri's bombing suspects were in the hospital, badly beaten, with their tongues cut out. The day after the bombing, the three alleged suspects were chosen at random from the jail, where they had been serving five-year sentences. They had Chechen blood and they would do as the bombing scapegoats. Yuri would soon be parading them about on state television trying to instill hatred for the three Chechens with the Russian masses.

☭

Harry was in his office when the phone rang. It was Tom Scaraponi. He said, "Harry, I have some bad news."

Harry replied, "Go ahead, Tom; spit it out."

Tom said, "Rosie didn't make it."

Harry was shocked by the news and asked, "What do you mean, he didn't make it? He was doing fine."

Tom answered, "I know, but he died in his sleep at the German hospital. He was off the heart monitors and was scheduled to fly back here in a few days. While the night nurse was doing her rounds, she found him."

Harry said, "Goddamn it all. Tom, call Rodney Caruso at the home office. He usually takes care of these things. No; scratch that. I will call Rodney. Thanks for informing me."

Tom replied, "Sure. I'm sorry to be the bearer of bad news."

Harry asked, "Does Imee have family in the States?"

Tom responded, "Yes, her mother and sister have been living in Rosie's house in Phoenix."

"Okay, thanks. I'll take care of it."

Harry hung up, but before calling Rodney, he went into the break room and poured himself a cup of coffee.

☭

Miller was boarding his plane at gate 27 at Sheremetyevo International Airport. The stewardess smiled at him as he walked past her down the aisle. He stopped at row 17 and looked for seat E. It was a window seat located at the bulkhead where the emergency exit row was located. Miller always requested a bulkhead seat because it gave him more leg room. He stowed his carry-on in the overhead compartment, but before he did, he pulled out Daniel Defoe's *Robinson Crusoe*. He sat back in his seat, buckled up, and began to read. The plane left the terminal and taxied down the runway to get in line for take-off. As the plane lifted off the ground, Miller looked out the window as the plane gained altitude and watched the sights of Moscow getting further and further away. The plane seemed to follow the Moscow River until the sights of the city disappeared and were replaced by the green and white frozen forests below.

☭

Harry and Sveta had decided on a spring wedding. They would be married in Paris at the Basilica of the Sacred Heart, commonly known as Sacre-Coeur Basilica. The basilica had a small chapel dedicated to couples that were intent on tying the knot. Harry had secured the 10 a.m. April 23rd time slot. Miller would fly in and would share the best man duties with Alexei. In the meantime, Harry had rented an Arbat flat close to the embassy, where the three of them would live until Harry's job was completed.

☭

Miller arrived in Tucson at 5:20 p.m. He rented a car at the airport and took I-10 West toward the center of town. He decided to take the scenic route to his property and just enjoy the sights and smells of Tucson. As he drove, he noticed a few new restaurants, a gas station, and a new supermarket that had opened up in his absence. He also noticed the vegetation was a dark green and surmised there had been adequate to above-average rainfall that year, which was not always the case. He drove with the window down and breathed the cool desert air into his lungs. He loved the smell of it.

When Miller got to Ina Road, he turned left, continued for a mile or so, then veered left again onto Wade, which turned into Picture Rocks Road. As he drove through the Saguaro National Monument, the sun was setting behind the Tucson Mountains as he passed Wasson and Panther Peak a few miles from Picture Rocks and his home. It was a classic Tucson sunset with orange, yellow, and blue painting the sky above, with the huge long-armed saguaro cactuses looking like lost souls silhouetted against the darkening sky.

Miller pulled up to the cattle gate he had installed years before. He searched in his backpack, found the key, and opened the Master lock with the chain attached. He looked around and said to himself, "Damn, it's nice to be home." He got back into the rented car, drove down the driveway, and parked next to his old four-wheel drive Ford truck waiting in the carport. He pulled his suitcases from the trunk and deposited them on to the redwood deck. He found the key to the house, unlocked the lock, and slid open the patio door. As he did, the security alarm sounded, and he moved quickly to shut it off. Miller looked around the house and everything looked just as he had left it. *Nice!* he thought to himself.

He went into the kitchen and fixed himself a Tanqueray and tonic with plenty of ice. He then opened his office, where he stored the outdoor furniture, and pulled out his white wicker rocking chair and wicker end table that he had touched up with white acrylic the last time he was home. Miller set them up in his favorite spot on the redwood deck. It was now dark outside with no moon, as he looked up at the sky and gazed at the galaxy of stars. He deposited the gin and tonic on the table and headed back inside the house. He went to his stereo and looked through the CDs on the shelf. He first chose The Flying Burrito Brothers' (1970s Country Rock Band) blue album, then changed his mind and went with the Band's *Last Waltz*, popped it in, and flicked the button to the outside deck speakers. Before he went back out, he stopped by a wall in the kitchen where his old Stetson cowboy hat hung waiting and put it on. He then walked back outside and sat in the rocking chair. Miller reached in his top shirt pocket and grabbed the Cohiba he had been able to sneak past customs. He lit the cigar, then took a sip of his drink as Rick Danko sang "It Makes No Difference" in the background. Miller was home.

In Moscow, Harry and John London were in the courtyard where the embassy flagpole would be installed. It was tradition to drop American coins in the embassy flagpole foundation before the concrete was placed. This was for good luck.

Harry asked John, "Do you have any quarters?"

John replied, "No, Harry, what do we need?"

Harry said, "We usually drop in two of each coin. I have a couple of dimes, three nickels, and a shitload of pennies."

John replied, "Wait, Harry, I'll be right back."

John went inside the embassy to Uncle Sam's, an after-hours sandwich place and bar/nightclub in the evenings. John walked up to the cashier and he was in luck; not only did they have quarters; they had some half dollars and three Susan B. Anthony dollar coins. He retrieved the coins and walked back to Harry, who had been waiting in the courtyard. John handed Harry the coins and Harry dropped them in the flagpole excavation. He picked up his Motorola, pressed the button, and said, "Charlie, this is Harry. You got a copy?"

Charlie replied, "Go ahead, Harry; this is Charlie."

"Yeah, Charlie, are you guys ready with the concrete to place the flagpole foundation?"

Charlie answered, "Yeah, Harry. The concrete truck is at the gate now. We're ready if you are."

Harry said, "It's ready, Charlie. John and I just dropped the coins in. Make sure the concrete crew doesn't try and fish them out."

Charlie replied, "Got it, Harry. I will send the concrete guys over there now."

Harry said, "Thanks, Charlie. Ten-four, over and out."

With that, Harry and John started walking back to the office. John asked en route, "Harry, do you have time to go over the manpower reports? Our count is not quite the same as yours. We need to straighten it out."

Harry answered, “Sure, John. Let me pick up the reports and I’ll meet you at your office.”

John replied, “Okay, Harry. I’ll meet you there.”

John and Harry continued their walk back to the office. In early 2000, TRIAD was granted substantial completion of the Moscow embassy by the US government. This meant all the technical security systems were in place and the only things left to do for final completion were the punch list items—things like touch-up painting, adjusting door swings, polishing the floors, and the like; everything that would be required for the embassy staff to occupy the building. For the next six months, TRIAD worked on completing these items; then in July of 2000, the US embassy in Moscow was open for business.

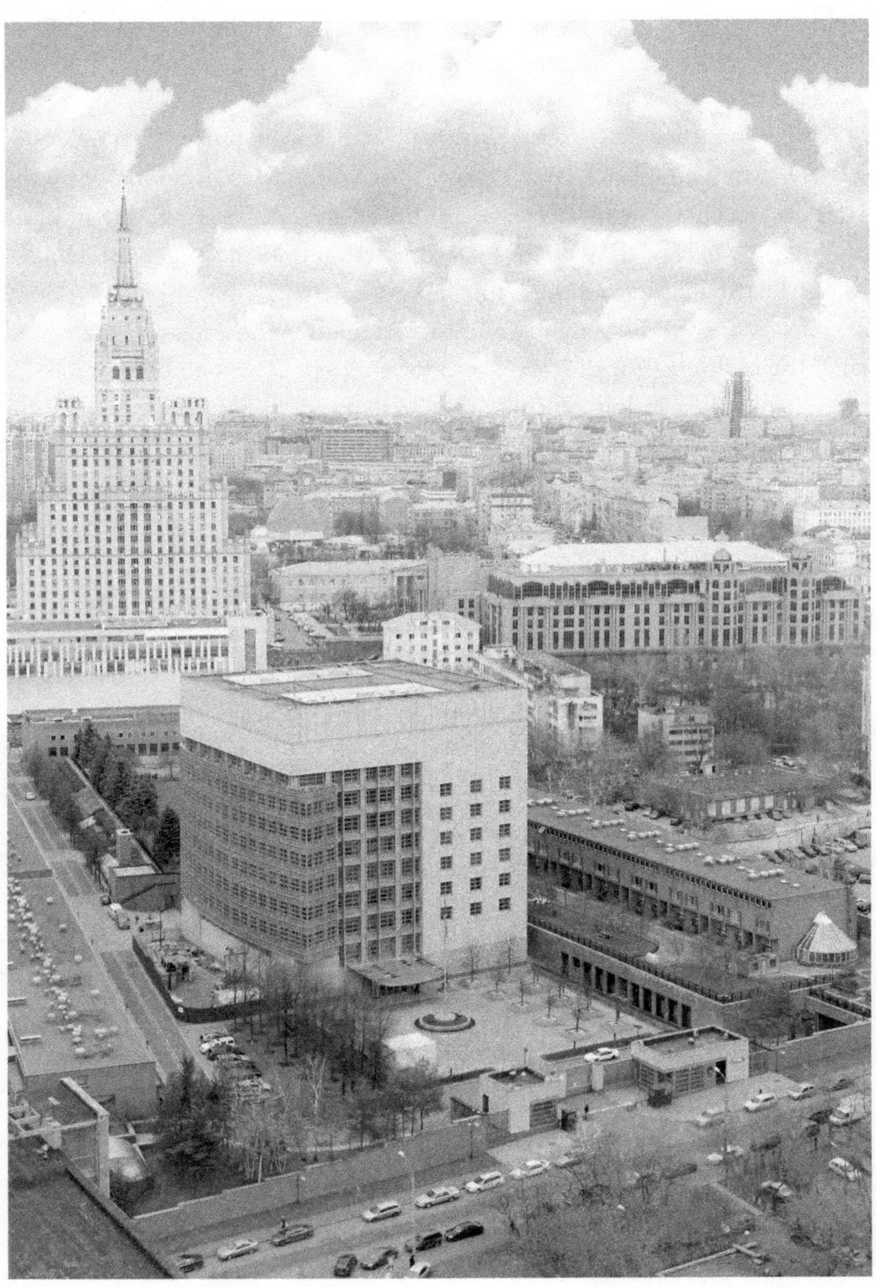

Yuri had been successful in blaming the Chechens for the Moscow apartment building bombing. As a result, the treaty between the two countries was broken, and in October of 1999, Russian troops entered Chechnya for the second time. Yuri became more powerful within the Russian government and was popular with the Russian people. At the beginning of 1999, President Georgy Chernenko dismissed his prime minister and promoted Yuri to that position. In late 1999 Chernenko resigned, appointing Yuri president. In 2004, Yuri Belevich was re-elected President of the Russian Federation. Years later, he would be successful but also implicated in the interference of a US presidential election using an internet propaganda campaign. The one thing Yuri had not been successful in was finding Major Karlov's killer.

ZPS

Zachry-Parsons-Sundt, A Joint Venture

May 22, 1997

Mr. Thomas J. Mitchell
Moscow, Russia

Subject: **Moscow SCF Project - Favorable Acceptability Review**

Dear Thomas:

I am pleased to advise that the United States Department of State, **Bureau of Diplomatic Security has granted a favorable "Acceptability Review" for your employment here in Moscow.** For your information, in addition to requiring a TOP SECRET clearance for this project, all project personnel who are designated to work in Moscow on a long-term basis, must also undergo an "Acceptability Review" conducted by the Department of State, Bureau of Diplomatic Security. The purpose of the "Acceptability Review" is to determine an individual's long-term suitability for assignment in Moscow. Those personnel not receiving a favorable "Acceptability Review" will not be permitted to work on the project in Moscow. In some cases, personnel have been deployed to Moscow prior to the completion of the "Acceptability Review" process. In those cases where deployment has occurred and an unfavorable "Acceptability Review" is rendered, such personnel must be repatriated to the United States.

Very truly yours,

W C Chancellor

Wade C. Chancellor, P.E.
ZPS Project Director
Moscow, Russia

JK/jk

EMBASSY OF THE
UNITED STATES OF AMERICA
MOSCOW

OFFICE OF THE AMBASSADOR

June 19, 2015

Thomas Mitchell
OBO LT TDY

Dear Thomas:

Mariella and I send our best wishes to you this month as you celebrate your birthday. I hope you take some time to celebrate with your friends and family.

I hope the upcoming year for you is filled with much success, and I thank you for all of your contributions to our Embassy's work.

Sincerely,

John F. Tefft
Ambassador

CPSIA information can be obtained
at www.ICGtesting.com
Printed in the USA
LVHW091943050520
653768LV00004B/6

9 781977 214935